A Question of Sincerity

Sabrina Blaum

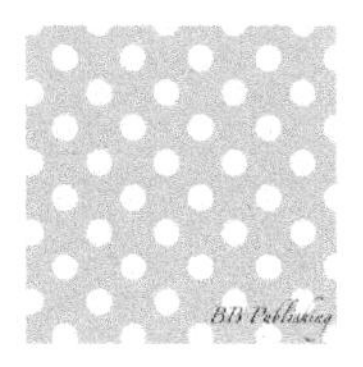

Babette B. Publishing

contents

Book Cover by getcovers.com

ISBN Ebook: 978-1-961771-00-0

ISBN Paperback: 978-1-961771-01-7

Library of Congress Control Number: 2023911814

For my late father, Leo. Because you were with me when I wrote most of this.

Foreword

A sentence in *The Truce* mentioning Elizabeth and Claudia started as a funny throwaway line, until I realized I wanted to know their story and see their journey to a happy ending. So, I wrote it. As it turned out, their travels to this distant shore were more complicated than I anticipated, as this is the first book I've had to rewrite. Thankfully, I got it done faster than expected, perhaps in part because the story suddenly clicked.

I hope you enjoy this spinoff of *The Truce.* As always, you don't have to have read *The Truce* or any other novel in the *Constellation* series to follow along each installment.

the same old changes

Claudia Khoury hadn't expected her last week at *Little Feet* daycare to end with a flood. She'd usually still be at work, but they'd had to close yesterday for a busted pipe that had swamped the bathrooms and hallways, even getting as far as into one of their classrooms.

The repair and cleanup crews were supposed to be at work through the weekend, so by early next week, things should go back to normal. Yet, not for Claudia. She'd start a new job on Monday as a legal expert at *Helping Hands*, a charity aiding people, mostly women, in getting back on their feet after divorces or after coming out of an abusive living situation.

Claudia had gone to law school once she'd completed her bachelor in criminal justice. After failing her first bar exam eighteen months ago, she took a break. During that time, she did odd jobs here and there, but nothing stuck. Then, on a whim, she had applied to work at a daycare, and she'd been with *Little Feet* ever since. Well, until she quit two weeks ago after receiving word that *Helping Hands* had hired her for their legal expert position.

Claudia didn't know what had stopped her from trying for the bar exam again. She had four more tries in Texas, and some states permitted unlimited attempts, which remained useless as she had no desire to move. While her parents had immigrated to the United States from Lebanon before she was born, Dallas had been their home ever since, and she liked it here.

Yet, when it had come to returning to school, to once more settle in and study, she'd balked. At first, she'd attributed it to burnout. She'd gone to law school right after finishing college at twenty-two, and since then, all she'd done was study. It had made sense to take a break. She'd finally felt as if she could breathe again.

And working with kids proved to be a lot of fun, especially with the added benefit of being off once she got home. No homework, no research, nothing. She'd gotten used to life without studying. But she missed law, or better, she missed her dream of helping people—that was why she'd wanted to become a lawyer in the first place, until law school and the bar exam had disabused her of that notion. She wondered if that disillusionment had also caused her to seek shelter in a vastly different position.

When Sammy, her best friend, had emailed her the job ad for *Helping Hands*, she'd applied right away. She hadn't known they'd been searching for someone in the legal field. The position had sounded perfect—she'd be helping people for real—and she didn't even need to be a 'finished' lawyer. In fact, the job description stipulated that they'd prefer applicants with legal experience over practicing lawyers. Claudia's work during law school in a pro bono clinic providing legal advice to victims of domestic violence was the perfect fit. Better yet, her interview had been a success, and they'd sent her an offer a few days later. When she had told her family, they had been over the moon, especially her mother and grandmother.

On Sunday, Claudia arrived at her parents' home in a quaint Dallas suburb right before one p.m. for their regular Sunday lunch, which, most of the time, also included her grandmother. Her family could be a lot, but she loved them dearly and enjoyed their close-knit togetherness.

"You're late. Are you all right?" her mother, Mona, asked as she hugged Claudia, who suppressed a fond eye roll even behind Mona's back as her mother would be able to tell. She worried at the drop of a hat, and Claudia loathed to add to her plate.

"Yes. All's good. I just slept badly last night."

Mona released her and touched her cheek and forehead. "Are you getting sick?"

"No, no."

Mona narrowed her eyes. "Are you sure? I can make you a cup of sage tea."

"That's OK. I'm really fine." Claudia withdrew. She hated the mere smell of sage, yet it had always been one of her mother's go-to remedies when Claudia had a cold or a stomachache. Drinking something that made you nauseous didn't improve things.

Mona hummed. "Come on in. We're all ready, just waiting for you. After lunch, you can tell us about your new job tomorrow." Mona marched ahead into the dining room, seemingly assured Claudia would be right behind.

"I already told you all about my new job." She knew she would have to go over it again, as her mother could hardly contain her happiness over Claudia's return to her true profession. Her parents always supported her, but they still had clear preferences, and studying law and then working in a daycare was not what they'd had in mind.

"Hi, *hayete*," her father, Kareem, said as she entered the room.

"Hi everyone," Claudia said, kissing her father's cheek.

Kareem patted her shoulder.

"Come, sit next to me." Her grandma, Salma, gestured at the chair next to her.

"Of course, *teta*." She settled into the designated seat.

"Did you lose weight, *habibte*? You're too tall to go on a diet. Men don't like stick women."

Claudia stifled a grimace. Who cared what men wanted her to look like? Besides, so far, none of her partners had had any issues with her on that front. But no, she wouldn't get lost in memories of her ex, Mandy, who'd tried to control every aspect of her life, including her friendships. When Mandy had demanded she end all contact with Sammy, because of course every woman Claudia interacted with would want to fuck her, she'd reached the point of no return. While Sammy was a lesbian, and their friendship had always been super close, they'd had no inclination to go there. And they'd had plenty of opportunities to do so. But none of that had mattered to Mandy, and so Claudia had ended things.

So much for not getting lost in ponderings about Mandy. That break-up still stung, and she sort of attributed her still ongoing fling with Tom to this. She knew they had no future either, and while she wasn't heartbroken about that, she still felt drawn to him. He was fun. And hot. They'd met three months ago at a meet-and-greet alumni event at her old law school. She'd attended in part for nostalgic reasons and to spread her feelers tentatively about finding her way back into her field of study.

Lost in thought, Claudia suddenly realized that her grandma was frowning at her. "I'm fine, *teta*."

Salma turned to Mona. "She needs to eat more. Haven't you noticed that? How could you allow her to look like this. She's just skin and bones."

"She's fine, *oumi*," Mona replied.

Claudia's grandmother had moved to the States after her husband's passing two years ago, and she split most of her time between Claudia's parents' place and her Aunt Sonia's, who lived in Waco. As always, she pointed out where her daughter could do better—much to Mona's exasperation, yet did that stop her from doing the same to Claudia? Of course not.

"Have you heard Johnny's back home?" Mona asked.

"Really?" Claudia poked at her food on the plate. She wasn't all that hungry, and she hoped her grandma would be fooled by the strategic maneuvering of her food around the plate and not get into another lecture about food and her figure.

"Yes, and you won't believe what happened!?"

"Must we gossip at the table?" Kareem asked.

"It's not gossip, but the truth. Janey told me herself. Johnny has returned home like a good son to be there for his mother, and he brought a wife."

"Oh," Claudia exhaled, relief flooding her that this wouldn't turn into a round of, "What about him, isn't he nice? He'd make a great husband." Her mother felt Claudia needed to settle down, and much as with her job, she had... preferences. But Johnny? Never in a million years. She and Johnny's little brother, Theo, had played in the sandbox together. Theo was like a brother, and while Johnny was insanely handsome, it would still feel like incest to her. She shuddered.

"That's good. About time," Salma grumbled. "Eat, *habibte.*"

"Yes, *teta*." Claudia put a fork of *kibbeh* into her mouth since her grandmother would not be fooled.

"No, no. He eloped, came back with this wife no one has ever met before or even heard of! Janey's besides herself," Mona said.

Claudia frowned. That didn't sound like Johnny. Besides, Claudia had always thought he was gay. Last she spoke to Theo, there'd been talk about this wealthy old guy Johnny was messing with. Then again, he could be bi like herself. Not like he had to inform Claudia about it.

"He did *what*? What's wrong with the wife?" Salma asked in a sharp tone.

"Why would there be anything wrong with her? Wouldn't he then just have avoided his family meeting her all together?"

Both her mom and *teta's* gaze snapped to her, but they didn't have to say a word for Claudia to duck her head.

"Just saying. Besides, why would he marry someone if there's something wrong with them?" she mumbled.

Mona sighed. She stroked Claudia's cheek. "Infatuation can make you blind, *hayete.*"

Claudia nodded. Her mother had a point.

That evening, Claudia set several alarms to ensure she'd not be late for her first day at work. She had volunteered as a babysitter for the charity several times over the last eighteen months after first hearing about *Helping Hands* when her favorite tennis player, Andrea Krieger, touted the organization in a post-tournament interview. She'd been curious and had checked them out since Andrea had also mentioned that they were located in Dallas. Claudia had liked their mission and had signed up for volunteer services.

The job interview for her new position had been with Elizabeth Lancaster, the head and founder of the charity. Claudia had been surprised by this at first, but she figured that given the woman had started this charity and turned it into a success, it made sense she'd be quite involved with most aspects.

Elizabeth had seemed friendly but closed off—the definition of professional with her long, brown hair coiled in a tight bun, dressed in a navy-blue skirt suit with a white blouse and black pumps. Her make-up had been flawless and her smile, while genuine, had held a hint of distance. Still, Claudia had had to ward off a flush, as Elizabeth Lancaster had turned out to be the type of woman that left Claudia breathless. Her subtle British accent didn't help matters either.

Claudia had little experience with bosses. Klara, who ran *Little Feet*, was a moody woman. Fair, but if you caught her on the wrong day, all bets were off. Still, miles lay between the two women, not to mention, Claudia's gaze had never lingered on Klara's graceful neck, her soft looking skin, or her delicate features. She needed to keep an eye on that. The last thing she needed was a crush on her boss. At least, they'd not be in the habit of working together.

Even though the interview had gone well, she took nothing for granted, and so the fear of her alarms failing and oversleeping had kept her up most of the night, and at the first beeping noise blaring from her phone, she'd jumped out of bed and stumbled into the bathroom.

Though Claudia preferred dressing casually, and at the daycare that had been fine, her new job demanded a different outfit. She dressed in a black suit with a silvery blouse, and while she felt confined and out of place in her attire, she was keen on doing her best at her new job.

At nine a.m. sharp, Tilda Swan, Elizabeth's chief administrative officer, an imperious woman in her mid-sixties with an austere, no-nonsense demeanor, led Claudia to her office and gave her the rundown of a general workday, giving her access to the computer, and instructing her to check her calendar for her appointments today. She had the morning to familiarize herself with everything, and then at one, her first meeting would start.

Claudia felt her palms grow damp as she acted like the put-together adult she was supposed to be, but never felt she was. She could do this. She knew she could. Claudia had spent the last two weeks familiarizing herself with the materials *Helping Hands* had sent her, and she knew the law enough to handle what they would throw at her. Yet, self-doubt wasn't particularly rational, and by the time Tilda left her office, Claudia wondered if she should have stayed at *Little Feet.*

the pettiest of motivations

Elizabeth Lancaster awoke Saturday morning to breakfast in bed—a tray filled with toast, strawberry jam, eggs, a pot of tea, and a bushel of freshly picked daisies. She smiled and turned to face her husband, Tom, who sat next to her on the bed, grinning sheepishly.

"What's the occasion?"

"I missed you?"

"Is that a question?"

He scratched his head. "No. It's a fact. I… I know I've been insanely busy at work. You've just gotten back from your trip to San Antonio last week, and now I'm heading out this coming weekend to Odessa. It seems like we barely see each other anymore."

Elizabeth drank a sip of her tea, repressing a grimace. She didn't add sugar to her black tea. "Hmm, yes, but every marriage has times like that, when careers have to take priority."

"Isn't that bad, though?"

"If it lasts, yes, but if it's a phase, I see no harm."

"Your charity is hardly a phase."

She frowned. "Neither is your job. You just made partner, and if I recall correctly, you worked long and hard hours for that. Not to mention the money that—"

"Yes. And you know how much I appreciated your help."

Elizabeth tilted her head. "We're married."

"Exactly. And I feel like we should try to be more... present. Have you thought some more about what we discussed last month?"

Elizabeth narrowed her eyes. "You mean me not being so controlling and obsessed with *Helping Hands* and spending more time at home?"

"That's not what I said."

"Not in these words, no, but I can read between the lines. You knew when you married me that *Helping Hands* is my priority."

"Yes, but the charity is a success, and—"

"It was a success five years ago, too."

"My job is busy and demanding. It's different work than you do."

"More important?"

"I didn't say that either."

She held his gaze.

He sighed. "I meant that it's easier for you to delegate things at work. It makes sense you'd do that so we can spend more time together."

"What time? You're gone at least as often as I am. Let's say I'd delegate work—mind you, I'd have to hire new people since Tilda couldn't pick up all the slack—and then I sit at home and twirl my thumbs while you're... in court or at the office talking to your clients?"

"Again, I won't be as busy in the future now that I've made partner. I've proved my worth."

"I doubt they're OK with you slacking off now."

He pursed his lips. "It sometimes seems like you don't want to spend more time together."

Elizabeth reached out and grasped his hand. "I do want to see you more. I've missed you, too. But I won't take a different approach to *Helping Hands*. I love my work, and I'm good at it. I don't want to delegate tasks I enjoy doing or that are important to me. Things will ease again. We could cut or reduce other things. For example, you could take shorter trips with Sebastian. Your monthly outings don't have to be full weekends in the wilderness."

His brows furrowed. "What about your card games?"

"Those are one Friday night a month. You can't compare that to an entire weekend away."

"You never said you minded these trips before."

"I don't. But when we're talking about spending more time together, wouldn't *that* be something we should look at first before we encroach on our work commitments?"

"We'll see. I'll talk to Sebastian. Perhaps we can only head out every other month."

"You do that."

They still managed to enjoy the rest of the weekend together, heading to a local book fair before eating at a new Italian restaurant Elizabeth had been meaning to try.

After some contemplations, Elizabeth had to admit that Tom had a point. Over the last three months, they had let their relationship slide with both consumed by work. She would consider some concessions at *Helping Hands* if she saw a similar commitment from Tom. She doubted his weekends with his old school buddy Sebastian would see a reduction. In all honesty, Elizabeth had actually enjoyed some of these weekends alone, or she booked her own travels to coincide with these weekends so they wouldn't lose more time.

Elizabeth hadn't had many romantic relationships in her life, and before Tom, she'd only lived together with one of her long-term partners, Logan. They'd been together four years in her late twenties and split when... She couldn't even remember. Nothing had torn them apart. They'd just fizzled out. That had been the story of most of her relationships and life. A lack of enthusiasm and passion. Until Tom had entered her life. He added a certain unpredictability, like when he ended up delaying her arrival at the office Monday morning, as he had a rare morning off and had convinced Elizabeth to spend it together.

Right past eleven, Tilda greeted Elizabeth with a frown when she strolled in, unused to her boss showing up late, and too familiar with Elizabeth to hide her displeasure at this shortage of discipline. Elizabeth appreciated Tilda's commitment to *Helping Hands*, though she wished she'd be more circumspect in her disapproval. To be fair, Tilda was the only one who ever dared to look at Elizabeth in this manner.

They'd hired a new legal advisor after their old one had retired—a position close to Elizabeth's heart. Many of their patrons needed legal advice or support. She'd interviewed several candidates that were all unsuited, too severe, too rigid, too... full of themselves. There was even one who seemed to believe that their patrons caused their own predicaments. Elizabeth had felt a migraine jutting at her temples during that quick conversation.

She'd settled on Claudia Khoury, an earnest young woman who brimmed with idealism and enthusiasm that the world hadn't yet choked out of her. It would surprise people to learn how much cynicism ran through Elizabeth's veins, given her profession. She preferred to call her attitude realistic instead, however others—mostly her best friend Kat—argued the former. She'd never confess this to anyone, but she'd started *Helping Hands* because she knew her mother would hate nothing more.

Elizabeth had left England and moved to the United States after her grandmother had died and left her with a hefty inheritance. Elizabeth's family, aside from her grandmother, were stifling, and their ambitions for Elizabeth's future had never matched her own. So, once her one true ally had passed and she'd had the means to leave, she did just that, much to the vocal displeasure of her mother.

Mary Lancaster ran her home and business affairs with an iron fist. She had little patience for incompetence and failure, something Elizabeth, to her chagrin, seemed to have inherited. They differed in one key aspect, though. Mary believed there were the right and the wrong kind of people, the ones deserving of help, fortune, and happiness, and then the... peasants. She equated wealth with virtue, and that notion had never sat right with Elizabeth, nor with her grandmother.

Still, as much as Elizabeth was her grandmother's grandchild, she also was her mother's daughter, and so she'd housed and nurtured ambition, she'd striven for success and control, but unlike her mother, she wanted all these things to be... not bad. She didn't want to hurt and dismiss others, although she sometimes struggled to show that.

Oh, she excelled at schmoozing with sponsors and convincing them to support *Helping Hands*. It was more the personal interactions that left her confused at times. Her mother's teachings ran contrary to those of her grandmother, and so she'd often been stuck in the middle, ingesting both their lessons, and trying, often failing, to resolve the tension, the contradictions between them.

So, when she'd reached the United States twenty-three years ago at the tender age of twenty-two, she'd set out to fulfill her grandmother's legacy—helping people society had forgotten and neglected—all the while establishing a legacy her mother would long to burn to the ground.

After setting up in her office, Elizabeth sought out their new hire, Claudia, to welcome her on her first day. A rumbled "Come in," rang out a brief moment after Elizabeth's knock.

"Hello, Claudia. How are you settling in? I'm sure Tilda helped you adjust." She strode inside, taking in a somewhat ruffled looking Claudia. Strands of her long black hair had come loose from her bun. She seemed tense, uncertain, with her wide brown eyes and the tight grip with which she'd seized a folder as her gaze darted around the room.

"Ms. Lancaster, hello. Yes, she did. Ms. Swan has been very thorough. It's just... It's going to take me a moment to get used to this. It's quite different from my previous employment." Claudia rose and stepped around her desk toward Elizabeth, who'd nodded but remained silent. "Is there something you need?"

Elizabeth's gaze traveled up Claudia's lanky form, dressed in a severe looking black pantsuit. It stood at odds with the bubbly, almost gregarious woman she'd met during their interview. In fact, for a second there, she'd reminded Elizabeth of a puppy. She supposed first day jitters could do that to a person.

"No, no. I merely meant to ensure you're all set. This is an important position, and I need you at your best. Our patrons depend on our advice, given that by the time they reach us, their legal situation is often precarious."

"I understand. I've studied the information you'd sent. I'm ready. You won't need to worry." Claudia straightened, and with that, her attitude once again matched the woman Elizabeth had hired.

"That's good to know." Perhaps the boss checking in on you before you got to do anything wasn't an encouraging sign to employees. Then again, Claudia would do well to get used to Elizabeth's tendency to micromanage and be involved in all aspects of her charity. "I'll leave you to it, then. Tilda will answer any of your questions, although you may also seek my advice if you deem it applicable."

Claudia nodded. "Of course. I just wanted to say, I'm really excited to be working here. Helping people."

And there was the puppy. Elizabeth was a cat person through and through, so she startled upon realizing that the smile wanting to form on her lips was almost fond. She suppressed it, but held Claudia's open gaze. "You're in the right business, then."

Elizabeth arrived home to Raji, her beloved eight-year-old cat. Tom was once more working late, which she'd expected. Their talk this weekend, or more accurately, Tom's request for her working fewer hours, had been an ongoing issue over the last year. Again, she'd reconsider if he'd reciprocate in kind, yet there had never been any attempt to do so. Aside from this one issue of contention, they usually got along well, and her mother's doomsday prognosis of their relationship seemed far away.

When Elizabeth had introduced Tom to her family, her mother's first response, later, when they'd been alone, had been a sniff, followed by the words, "You're fooling yourself, Lizzie. He'll leave you for a younger woman. He's too handsome, and too young. Marrying a man ten years younger! What were you thinking?"

"He's nine years younger, Mother."

Mary had waved her off, and Elizabeth had dropped the topic, leaving the room in search of Tom. He'd been sweet, warm, and attentive, and little had changed since then. Sure, they'd gotten busier, especially when he'd worked to buy into the firm and she'd travelled to rope more people into becoming sponsors for *Helping Hands*. But again, such phases existed in every relationship.

Her phone ringing startled her and when she gazed down, expecting a call from Tom to apologize for likely once more working past ten, she smiled at Kat's name popping up instead.

"Hi, stranger," Elizabeth answered the call.

"Hi, Liz. How are you? Sorry I've been absent a bit. Work has been insane. I wish they'd reduce the number of episodes per season." She sighed.

Kat, or better, Kathryn Johnson, starred as the lead actress in a science fiction show called *Fixing Time*, where a group of agents attempted to solve historical mysteries for paying clients by traveling through time. It wasn't a blockbuster, but it had its dedicated following, and Elizabeth had enjoyed the first season before time constraints and a strange headspace took her out of it.

"I suppose that's wishful thinking?"

Kat groaned. "Don't I know it. But enough about that. I don't want to talk about work. Tell me what's been going on with you. And no shop talk either. Someone's birthday is coming up. Got any big plans?"

"Don't remind me. No. I shall just ignore leaving my mid-forties."

"Oh, please. It's not that bad."

"Wait until it's your turn."

"You're in a mood today," Kat said. "Everything OK at work? Tom?"

"I thought there'd be no 'shop talk'?"

"Well, there won't be any from me, but if there's something that's bothering you. Go ahead."

"Everything's fine at work. I just hired a puppy as the new legal advisor after Martin retired."

"Wait what? A dog? I know Martin had his issues, but replacing him with a dog? And as a cat person, aren't you supposed to be the enemy of dogs?"

"You know full well that I'm not talking about a real animal, and for the record, a cat person doesn't have to hate dogs. I'm... indifferent toward them. I find their energy and commitment exhausting."

Kat laughed. "Yet you hired a human who reminds you of a dog. Do they pee on the carpet? Is that your way of pushing Tilda into retirement?"

"You're ridiculous. No, Claudia is just very young and believes in the good in people, in helping people. She seems very... cheerful at times, though she also has an earnestness to her that appealed to me during her interview. She'll be a good fit. Besides, I'd never do that! I need Tilda."

"You know, given that you've started a charity called *Helping Hands* that is in the business of, well, helping people, shouldn't you find such qualities in a new employee on point?"

"Yes, and I'm not complaining."

"Then what are you?"

"That's the question, isn't it?" She had no answer for Kat. She should be happy, or at least content. But something was nagging at her, and she couldn't quite place her finger on it.

a truth that bites

Claudia's first day at work had been a whirlwind of anxiety and exhilaration. She'd worked herself into a stitch—one of the low points: her awkward run-in with Elizabeth. She supposed you couldn't call it a *run-in* when your boss checked up on you in your office, though that had to be better than being called to appear there, much like the dreaded call to the principal's office. Not that this had ever happened to Claudia, as she'd been too well-behaved in school.

Dealing with patrons—ones that could talk in coherent sentences, who didn't have trails of snot running down their noses or threw tantrums because they were tired but refused to take a nap—had been surreal, but exciting. Claudia hadn't realized how much she missed working in the legal field until she returned to it. On her first day, she'd helped one woman with her custody paperwork, and another asked about applying for a restraining order. Her final patron had ended up staying longer and chatted with Claudia about law school, as she considered applying herself.

Her first month at *Helping Hands* passed much the same, and with time, Claudia's confidence grew. She'd only seen Tom sporadically over the last four weeks, both busy with work, but then he'd texted her early in the week, asking her to come by Wednesday after work. He had an upcoming business trip the coming weekend, and suggested they'd meet before. Claudia had received that message right after both Tilda and Elizabeth had expressed how pleased they were with how Claudia fit in at work. In this exuberant mood, she'd agreed right away before calling her mother, who wanted an update on work.

By the time she left *Helping Hands* on Wednesday, Claudia realized how happy and content she felt in her new position. Yes, it had only been one month, but she had a good feeling about it all. For the most part, she'd only seen Elizabeth in passing, but their interactions had been friendly, and so Claudia had also put that worry to rest, especially after the compliment early in the week. Tilda still sometimes intimidated her—a lot—but fortunately she had needed little assistance and seemed to have won even her over.

Her patrons' issues seemed mostly straightforward, and so far, she'd not encountered anything she couldn't handle. Claudia hoped this trend would continue.

She arrived at Tom's apartment shortly after five and, once inside, he greeted her with more enthusiasm than she'd expected.

"Someone's in a chipper mood," Claudia said.

"Yes, well, things are going fantastic at work, and I get to see you again." His handsome face broke out into the charming grin that had first piqued Claudia's interest when they'd met.

She chuckled. "Work seems to go great for both of us."

Tom stepped closer. "Let's not talk about work. It's been too long, and we won't see each other for a while after this."

"What did you have in mind?"

Tom pulled her closer.

"No dinner?"

"Later."

That 'later' never happened as Claudia fell asleep first, and when she came to an hour later, she heard Tom talk on the phone. At first, she thought he was about to order takeout—her stomach grumbled angrily—but the cadence of his voice, soft and affectionate, made her still and listen.

"I'll be home soon. Love you, baby. Yes, I'm sure we can revisit breakfast in bed again. Bye."

Claudia froze, her heart hammering in her chest. *Back home. Love you, baby*. He surely wasn't talking to his *mother*. No. That had to be... Another woman? She blanched. Claudia didn't cheat—she'd never betrayed a single soul in her life. In fact, she'd never date anyone who was in a relationship, but this might have changed now, thanks to Tom Pittin. She didn't know what to do. She could confront him, of course, but she'd hate the subsequent conversation. They weren't serious. Just a bit of fun. He was her rebound guy, really, but he still wasn't supposed to be in a relationship. *Oh, God, what if he's married*?

She recalled how, for the longest time, they only met at her place or at hotels, even though he lived in Dallas, too. Tom had said something about repairs or renovations. She didn't remember, as they'd been busy. Claudia gritted her teeth. She couldn't believe this. How dare he involve her in this? She knew she wouldn't get any answers unless she confronted him, but she dreaded that almost as much as the unknowns.

Claudia faked sleeping for five more minutes, during which her mind raced on a rollercoaster, but finally, she decided to get out of his apartment and call Sammy—she truly should have known better. What lawyer lived in such a small apartment? Then again, he'd told her he was between houses and planned to buy a home soon. Those were probably lies as well.

Claudia stretched and acted as if she was just waking up.

The mattress dipped as Tom joined her once more, still naked, as if he didn't just finish a phone call with his *other* girlfriend or worse, his wife. God, she could strangle him, or hit her head against the wall. She had never wanted to be the other woman. The mere thought filled her with a mixture of dread and nausea.

"I'm heading out." She rose to get dressed.

"What? Already? We haven't eaten yet, and I thought we could spend the night in bed."

I bet you did, you bastard. "Another time. I forgot something that I need to take care of." She had always sucked at lying, and coming up with excuses on the spot? How?

"But it'll be at least two weeks until we'll see each other again!" Tom scooted closer, trying to catch her hand, but Claudia pulled back, fully dressed now.

"We can text and call."

He raised his eyebrows. "Video chat?"

Claudia barely smoothened her grimace. "Sure. I'll call you." And with that, she darted out of the apartment. Yes, he likely knew something was up, but there'd been no other options, for if she'd stayed, she'd have caused a shouting scene. Or murdered him. And then what? Then *she'd* need legal advice. She scoffed. How did things go from awesome to shit in two seconds?

She sped home, almost running a red light, but right after that, she forced herself to do some calming exercises. It wouldn't do to get into an accident, especially before she'd dealt with Tom.

Back home, she immediately called Sammy, who, after some quick research, figured out that Tom Pittin was, in fact, married. Sammy cursed him out before giving Claudia his wife's cell phone number. After all, she knew her well enough, and indeed, during the drive home, Claudia had been plagued with the urge to confess, to let Tom's partner know what was going on. Now she had the chance to do just that.

"Thanks. I will. Bye, Sammy." She hung up and slammed her phone down, glaring at it in disdain as if it were responsible for what she'd done. Claudia sagged onto her computer chair and contemplated her next steps. She needed to think about this and decide if and when she'd call this Elizabeth. She should likely text her first because cold calling a stranger to tell her you've been having an affair with her husband didn't sound like a stellar idea.

The rest of the work week went by in a blur that at the same time felt like a piece of chewing gum, dragging, hanging between the sticky fingers of a preschooler. Claudia had been distracted all day, jumpy and nervous. She'd likely scared her patrons or made them see her as an incompetent fool, but she struggled to concentrate on anything other than what she'd say to this Elizabeth woman.

She'd also wondered who she was, and what she looked like. Then she chastised herself for such thoughts. What did it matter, and besides, she'd only tell her what happened, and then she'd be out of her life again. A quick in and out—raining devastation on another in a hot second. Then again, none of this was her fault, and Elizabeth deserved the truth. Claudia would want to know.

Come Friday after work, Claudia first stepped under a flesh-melting, steaming shower—at least all her lovers had called her showers that when they refused to join her. Cold or lukewarm showers were the devil. If the lever could still move farther toward red, the water wasn't hot enough.

She'd finished and eaten dinner a few minutes past six, and so she settled on the couch and stared at the sheet of paper on which she'd scribbled Sammy's information about Elizabeth.

But first things first. She needed to end things with Tom, even if it meant he would figure out what had happened. She doubted he'd confess to his wife, and if he did, that would be good, too, right?

Claudia snatched her phone to call him when pettiness rose and she typed out the text: 'We're done,' and sent it instead. Because what else was there to say? She owed him nothing. Not a *single damn thing*, aside from a swift kick in the—

Her phone sounded.

What? Why? What's going on? Call me!

Claudia closed her eyes. She didn't know what to say. *I don't date married people?* In the end, it would be the confrontation she'd avoided earlier in the week when she'd rushed out of his apartment. And no matter what he'd say, she'd contact Elizabeth regardless, not only because Claudia suffered from the 'apologizes too often' disease, but she still felt the woman should know. That way, she could make an informed decision on whether she wanted to stay with her cheating bastard of a husband.

Her phone rang. Tom.

Claudia hung up.

Just let it go. I'm done.

But why? We had such a good time
the other night before
you rushed off.
What happened? Did I say something?

She scoffed. "Good time until your wife called," she muttered into the empty room and blocked his number. There. That was that.

Claudia spent the next several minutes staring at Elizabeth's number, then heaved a sigh.

"Like a band-aid," she mumbled and composed her message.

Hi. You don't know me but there's
something important I need to tell you.
Do you have a moment?

She pressed send before picking up her tablet to watch something. Her phone chirped right after the intro of her favorite true crime series, "See No Evil."

Claudia paused the program and reached for her phone on the coffee table. Her eyebrows rose when she read Elizabeth's reply.

Wrong number.

Fair, but not helpful.

I'm speaking with Elizabeth Pittin?

Who is this and what do you want?

Claudia sighed.

My name is Claudia
and I want to talk to you.

I'm not a man,
so you won't fish me with
whatever scam you're running.

This isn't a scam, and I obviously
know you're not a man. And 'fish you'?

That's what they call it, right?
Catfishing?

Oh. But that's not what this is.
I don't know why they call it that.

Indeed. And there's even a fish by that name.

Claudia snorted.

It has whiskers.

What does?

The catfish.

Oh. I suppose. But cats eat fish,
so that's still weird.
Claudia cocked her head.

I can see that.

It's like naming a cat dogcat.
I don't think cats would appreciate that.
Claudia chuckled.

I'm not sure cats can read,
so their offense would be limited.
Also, dogs don't eat cats.

Why were they discussing animals?
Not for lack of trying.
And don't underestimate cats.

Duly noted. I feel there's a story there.
Got a dog that wanted to eat a cat?

The other way around.

A cat that wanted to eat a dog?

Raji would never!
He's a perfect angel,
unlike my neighbors' demon dog.
Claudia shook her head. What was happening here?

I'm sure your cat is completely innocent.

There was no way she'd say otherwise to a cat-crazy person. She'd once gotten into a fight with Sammy over her cat. Lesson learned, never again. People who loved cats were intense.

Of course he is.

An image loaded, and yes, Elizabeth *was* a cat-crazy person because she'd sent the 'scamming stranger' a picture of her cat—a cute gray feline sleeping curled up in a ray of sunshine.

He's cute.

He's gorgeous. But back to business.
What do you wish to tell me?

Claudia's smile froze, and she sat up straighter, wiping her hands on her sweatpants.

You're married to Tom Pittin?

Why do you ask
when you already know the answer?

Claudia worried her lower lip. This would get ugly, and she hated the idea. Such news was always terrible, but somehow... Band-aid.

I didn't know he was married.
I've just ended things with him,
but for the last four months,
Tom and I were seeing each other.

Nothing.

Claudia stared at her phone, but there was nothing.

Elizabeth? I'm truly sorry.
I just thought you should know.

Five minutes passed, and eventually, Claudia gave up and threw her phone next to her on the couch, once more glowering at it. With a heavy sigh, she picked up her tablet. Right after pressing play, her phone beeped. Claudia almost dropped the tablet in her hurry to reach it. She stared at the five words and blinked.

Why should I believe you?

Now what?

a wrecking ball

Elizabeth had had a good week, at least until everything came crashing down Friday evening. She supposed life worked like that, which was why you shouldn't be too elated when things seemed to go smoothly. *Helping Hands* was running efficiently, and she even had a few new promising potential sponsors on the line. Their new legal advisor seemed to be the great pick Elizabeth thought she would be, and overall, things had been going well.

While Tom had continued to work long hours since their discussion a month prior, he'd also been trying to be more present. Meanwhile, Elizabeth had spent her time alone continuing her *Inspector Gamache* novels and lounging with Raji on the couch. At least she had been until a text message threatened to upend her world. She'd first thought she'd been the target of a scam, but this Claudia seemed earnest enough.

She'd been nursing an off feeling, but she never connected it with Tom, or the notion that something could be wrong with their relationship. Yes, they'd been going through more of a rough patch recently, but that happened in all marriages and rarely spelled the end of things. Consequently, she now wondered if she'd been blind.

Or perhaps this would be a scam after all. But for what? What would this woman gain if Elizabeth divorced her husband? Unless she'd lied and it wasn't over and instead, she wanted her to end things with Tom so she could have him.

Good riddance, then. Oh, Elizabeth wasn't about to dump her husband on a text message exchange with a stranger, but she also refused to stay with a cheater, no matter how well they got along. She wondered what she'd missed. There'd been no real strife between them. Tom had said his long hours would decrease once the Weston case concluded. Had he lied and instead, he'd been seeing this Claudia all along?

She now questioned his trips and even his outings with Sebastian. Perhaps instead of going hiking together, these were convenient excuses for extramarital affairs, and maybe this had been going on for their entire marriage. Should she confront him? Elizabeth despised scenes and drama, and she also hated that her mother had been right. Potentially. Oh, she wished Claudia had never contacted her. Was it living a lie if you didn't know?

She also decided that she had to be in shock because she didn't feel heartbroken or devastated—just numb, and she still worried that this was some kind of elaborate prank. Elizabeth supposed there was one way to find out.

She picked up her phone and asked Claudia why she should believe her. The answer came immediately.

Because I'm telling the truth.

Any con artist would say that.

Is a con artist better or
worse than a scammer?

Elizabeth smiled. Whether a con artist, scammer, or mistress, this Claudia person (if that was even her real name) was fun to talk to.

I'd say they're the same.

Bummer. But I'm serious.
I'm not lying. For what even?

Because you want Tom for yourself?

A pause. Dots appearing, then disappearing.

We had a good time,
but I hate liars and cheaters.
So no. I've actually blocked his number.

Elizabeth's eyebrows rose.

That still doesn't change my dilemma.

I could send you pictures or text messages.
If you need proof, I mean.

Elizabeth frowned. Text messages could be doctored. Again, scammers could be clever, though this didn't seem like a con. And pictures? Did she *want* to see pictures of her husband with another woman? A younger woman, probably prettier than her. God, what a mess.

Let me think about this some more.

Of course. You have my number,
if you have any more questions.

Thank you.

And that was that.

Relief flooded through Elizabeth when she realized Tom wouldn't come home any moment, as he usually did on Friday nights, having left this morning for a business meeting in Amarillo. She'd driven him to the airport. All of that had fled her mind once Claudia had confessed their affair. Again, if it *was* the truth. She still grappled with that. Weren't there usually signs? She'd always assumed she'd know, but more so that there were serious issues in the relationship if one partner cheated. But perhaps she had been blind to them.

Elizabeth rose to feed Raji. He meowed and followed her with his tail up in the air as she brought the bowl to his spot. She petted his head while he chomped down noisily, ignoring her gesture. "Your life is so easy." Elizabeth sighed. She needed to sleep on this, though eight p.m. was too early to retire. With another sigh, she went into her exercise room and flipped on the TV, selecting a calming yoga routine that would hopefully help her sleep tonight.

The barking of the neighbor's dog jolted Elizabeth awake a little after eight o'clock. Disoriented and tangled in the sheets, she reached out for Tom, only to pat air and cool sheets instead. Amarillo, right. She shook her head when memories of her conversation with Claudia flooded her mind. God. She'd forgotten, and how bittersweet a moment to wake up unaware of the cloud hovering above her head and pouring rain on top of her.

She wanted to talk to Kat, but since she lived in California, she'd likely still be asleep now. Elizabeth got out of bed and padded into the bathroom to get ready for her day.

She checked her phone during breakfast and almost choked on her cereal when she read Tom's text message from last night.

Hey baby. You must be sleeping already. Rough day? Did your migraines flare up again? Everything's all right here. Boring. I think we'll get that account. I hope you're feeling OK. Miss you.

Elizabeth stroked her thumb over the message and her vision blurred. Surely this wasn't the message of a cheater. Although she had heard about people who cheated but had no intention of leaving their spouse—they just couldn't resist the other person or wanted to spice things up in bed. She'd admit that things had gotten a bit perfunctory there, which wasn't truly a surprise given her complicated relationship with sex.

Elizabeth decided to distract herself by continuing the preparations for the next charity dinner before she could call Kat without getting cursed out for waking her. Then again, Kat could already be on set, which meant she'd gotten up at four in the morning, but in that case Elizabeth wouldn't reach her either way. Ugh. This was not working. She needed... *something*.

Her phone sounded. Elizabeth's shoulders drooped when she saw a new message from Tom. This one only asked if she was up already. She didn't want to talk to him, at least not before she'd spoken to Kat. She replied that she'd call later.

Elizabeth managed to spend the next two hours getting some work done before she grabbed her phone and called Kat.

"Hi, Liz! Good to hear from you. I was thinking of calling you this weekend. How are you?"

Elizabeth smiled at hearing her friend's raspy voice and heartfelt greeting. "Hey. Anything newsworthy going on?"

Kat scoffed. "You could say that, but that's not why you called. Are you OK? You sound off."

Elizabeth swallowed a sigh. At times, she hated how in-tune Kat seemed to be with her moods. "Do you even have time? This might take a bit."

"For you, always."

Elizabeth smiled. "It's about Tom. He..." She had no idea how to phrase this.

"He isn't injured?"

"He might be cheating on me."

"That bastard!"

A rueful smile spread over her face. Kat's support had always been absolute, and Elizabeth had often accused her of being biased, but now it felt good to have someone completely on her side.

"How do you know? With whom? Some young twenty-year-old floozy with big—"

"Kat!"

"What? So many men here do this. It's disgusting—replacing their wives with a newer, perkier model."

"I don't know how old she is. She seems to know quite a bit about catfish."

"Wait, what? Liz, are you all right? What... How did we get to catfish?"

Elizabeth pinched the bridge of her nose. "I'm fine. It's complicated, and I don't know what to do."

"All right, tell me everything."

"OK, so last night I got a text message from this woman, and..." Elizabeth proceeded to tell Kat the entire miserable tale, including her questions, fears, and doubts. She shared how things had been between her and Tom recently, and how she never would have guessed he was cheating on her. After releasing a torrent of words that resembled a flood ready to drown her friend, Kat offered Elizabeth one piece of advice: "Meet with the woman and let her tell you the entire story."

Could things really be that easy? Though easy might not be the right word, given that Elizabeth remained unsure she could handle whatever Claudia would reveal.

an unexpected clash

Claudia didn't expect Elizabeth to contact her again, figuring the entire episode closed. She'd done her part, ended things with Tom and told his wife about the affair, so the woman could decide how to move forward. To be honest, Claudia assumed Elizabeth would let it go and stay with her husband. So many women made that choice, and while Claudia would never be among them nor could she understand such a decision, she respected it was their lives.

She'd sat down for breakfast when her phone beeped: Elizabeth, asking to meet that afternoon at *Dark Embers*, a newish (hipster, or so Claudia had heard) coffee house downtown. Claudia hesitated, but ultimately agreed to meet Elizabeth at three p.m., given she'd told the woman to contact her if she had questions.

Claudia reviewed the photo album on her phone before leaving, wanting to ensure Elizabeth wouldn't stumble over any inappropriate images—not that she had many—and while tempted to remove the one showing her and Tom kissing, she left it alone, figuring that *was* kind of the point of this entire meeting. Still, she cringed hard when looking at the picture.

Before she entered the café, she drew back. Her heart pelted against her ribcage as she hid behind a column, hoping it would block her from view while she peered into the room through the window like a damn creeper. But...

Elizabeth had told her she'd sit in a corner next to a bamboo palm (because Claudia knew the difference between that and a regular palm) with a cup of coffee—how distinctive in a coffee shop—and that she had long dark, curly hair and would wear dark slacks with a crème-colored blouse. And the woman who fit said description and sat in such a spot was none other than her boss, Elizabeth Lancaster.

Claudia fled and dashed back to her car. She was fucked.

Once she reached home, she panicked because she had basically stood up Elizabeth. Her boss. Claudia fished out her phone and composed a text message. Her hands trembled as she typed a lie—an emergency had arisen—and apologized profusely before dropping onto the floor, palpitations running wild in her chest.

A moment later, her phone beeped.

OK.

That was it? What did she expect, though? If she put herself in Elizabeth's shoes, she'd assume she'd been scammed for real at this point. Good God. What was she going to do?

I'm truly sorry.
I promise I'll make it up to you.

Claudia couldn't just leave it at that.

So you say.

She sighed and threw her phone on the couch before pacing her apartment. This wouldn't do. Elizabeth would think she was lying and that likely would make her stay with Tom for sure. Claudia didn't care if Elizabeth truly chose to do that *after* knowing all the facts, but now she didn't, and so what else was she to do but chalk this up as a crazy woman pranking her for kicks and giggles.

After hedging and hawing for ten minutes, Claudia video-called Sammy.

"How did it go?" Sammy offered instead of a hello.

Claudia groaned.

"That bad? I mean, you look kinda frazzled."

"I stood her up."

"What? Why would you do that?"

"Because Elizabeth Pittin is actually Elizabeth Lancaster."

"Huh? I gave you the right number. I don't understand. And wait... Isn't that your new boss?"

"Yes!"

"How? I don't—"

"You gave me her married name, but her maiden name, and the name she uses for all things charity related, seems to be Lancaster. At least that's my assumption. I suppose it could also be a pseudonym. I don't know. That doesn't matter in the end. She *is* Elizabeth Lancaster, my boss, and I'm screwed."

"Why? She doesn't know it's you. There are a million Claudias in the world, so how is any of this your problem?"

"Spoken like a true politician," Claudia grumbled.

"Hey! I'm just saying. No harm, no foul."

"No harm? There's been plenty of harm. I stood her up, and—"

"As Claudia the scammer, not Claudia the legal advisor!"

"What difference does that make?"

"Employment vs. unemployment?"

"Stop being a smartass and help me, Sam!"

Sammy sighed. "What do you want?"

"A solution."

"All right, then what are your priorities here? Because that'll decide what you'll have to do."

"Priorities. Let's see." Claudia settled on the couch. "I want Elizabeth to know the truth, and to believe me. I don't want her to think this was a scam."

Sammy groaned.

"What?"

"I was afraid of that."

"Why? What's wrong with it?"

"You and your damned honesty. Shades of gray exist, you know? Never mind that. You should be looking out for what's best for you—and right now, what's best for Elizabeth and what's best for you aren't compatible."

Claudia frowned. "How so?"

"She's your boss. You're a newly hired employee, so there's no loyalty or commitment there yet from the firm, if such a thing ever exists, given we're all just cogs in the machine."

"Not that again." Claudia suppressed a groan.

"That you don't like it doesn't make it false."

"Go on."

"Look, Elizabeth Lancaster has no affinity for you. She doesn't know you. You're her employee and that's it. Claudia-the-scammer is an asshole in her mind. Someone who played tricks on her for her own amusement and lied because who knows? People *are* assholes."

Claudia sighed.

"If you reveal that Claudia-the-employee and Claudia-the-scammer *are* the same, she'll fire you."

"Why would she? First, I wasn't scamming her, and—"

"No. You were just fucking her husband."

Claudia bit her lower lip. "I didn't know he was married," she pressed out.

"Do you really think that will matter? Do you think Elizabeth will want to see you at work every day once she knows you're the woman who destroyed her marriage?"

"I didn't do that! It was Tom's responsibility not to cheat!"

"Of course, but emotions aren't rational. You're a pretty young thing, and she's bound to feel insecure and betrayed. You'll be the easiest target. It's just human nature." Sammy shrugged.

Claudia narrowed her eyes. "Fine. I'll find another job then."

"You love this job! Why would you do that to yourself? All you have to do is shut up and act like this never happened."

"That's not who I am. Besides, I'd feel terrible, and it would distort our relationship."

"What relationship? She's your boss. You said you don't even see her that often."

"Still, it would always stand between us, in my mind at least. It would make everything awkward. Never mind that *Helping Hands* has my phone number on file, so she could find out that the so-called scammer-Claudia really is me, and that would make everything so much worse."

"That's true. You could change your phone number?"

"Oh, Sammy, come on now!"

"Fine."

"So I'll tell her."

"I guess so."

"Don't look so glum. Maybe she won't fire me."

Sammy snorted. "Right. You can have your honesty and optimism, but the world doesn't work like that. So please be prepared, OK? This could get ugly."

"I know. But it'll be worth it. She'll know, and then I can let it go."

Sammy sighed. "Why is this so important to you? She is no one. She's not your friend or family."

"That doesn't make it all right to let her believe she was scammed or pranked, or worse, that her husband isn't a cheating bastard. Besides, she was fun."

Sammy's brows furrowed.

"When we texted. It was fun. I liked her."

Sammy covered her eyes with one hand. "You like everyone."

"That's not true!"

By Monday, Claudia had come up with a plan. No thanks to Sammy who had told her—once more—that this would blow up in her face. Though as a consolation, she'd offered that Claudia may come crying to her when it was all over and that she'd refrain from telling her, "I told you so." With friends like these...

She'd given up on texting Elizabeth as she figured the other woman wouldn't believe a word she said. While Claudia enjoyed her job and didn't want to lose it, she still felt the need to tell Elizabeth. She hoped Sammy was wrong, and she'd be able to keep her job.

She'd been distracted throughout the workday again, but not enough that her patrons noticed (much). Claudia realized, though, that this trend wouldn't help with keeping her employed, should Elizabeth seek feedback from the people Claudia had worked with.

After finishing up with her last patron, Claudia lingered in her office. She'd noticed the week before that Elizabeth stayed late quite often, and she hoped this would be the case again today.

Sometimes fortune did favor the foolish, for when Claudia swung her purse over her shoulder and stepped out of her office, the lights in Elizabeth's office were still aglow. Steeling herself, she treaded closer and took a deep breath before knocking.

A pause.

"Come in," Elizabeth's clear voice rang out.

Claudia opened the door and her gaze fell on Elizabeth sitting at her desk, head bowed, working on a document. Her profile resembled one of the winged statues she had seen in the garden of the Belvedere Palace in Vienna, half woman, half lioness, with straight features, full lips pressed tightly together, and a downcast gaze. She wore glasses, and her pale skin contrasted with her hair and frames.

Claudia felt trapped in place when Elizabeth looked up.

"How can I help you?"

The problem with Claudia's plan? She had fretted over *when*, without giving much thought to *how* she'd talk to Elizabeth.

Elizabeth placed her pen down. "Is everything all right?"

Claudia nodded. "Well, I'm not sure."

"Did you run into a problem with one of our patrons?"

"No, it's not... It doesn't relate to *Helping Hands*."

"Oh?"

The band-aid. "I'm sorry. I never meant to stand you up on Saturday, but when I got there and saw it was you, that Elizabeth Pittin *is* you... I panicked." There. She'd said it.

Elizabeth's eyes widened and her face turned ashen. She opened her mouth, only to close it.

"I didn't know—"

Elizabeth held up one hand, and Claudia fell silent. "*You're* the scammer-Claudia?"

Claudia gritted her teeth. "I'm Claudia, but I'm not a scammer. Or catfisher."

Elizabeth shook her head. She leaned back in her chair and sent a hard glare in Claudia's direction. "What do you want?"

"Like I told you, I want to tell you the truth, so you can decide—"

Elizabeth rose. The force of her movement made her chair slam backward, metal scraping against wood. She pressed her hands on the polished tabletop and leaned forward. "So *I* can decide?"

"Yes."

"Nothing about this," she waved between them, "has been *my* choice."

"I know, but—"

"You know *nothing*." Elizabeth straightened and stalked around the desk toward Claudia.

She had a good four inches in height on Elizabeth, so why did Claudia suddenly feel like the other woman was towering over her? She resisted the urge to draw back. "I'm sorry."

"You keep saying that, but you seem to make the wrong decision at every turn."

Claudia bristled. "I had no idea he was married."

"The ring didn't give it away?"

"He obviously wasn't wearing one when I met him or any other time I saw him."

"How did you find out then?"

"He called you."

"While you were there? Why would he do that? Tom's not stupid."

Claudia ducked her head. "He thought I was sleeping," she mumbled.

"Excuse me?"

She raised her head and caught Elizabeth's flinty gaze—her gray eyes once more freezing Claudia in place. "He must have thought I was sleeping."

"I see." Elizabeth's gaze traveled up and down Claudia's frame.

She tried not to squirm. Elizabeth had the right to be angry. This was a lot.

"So you had sex with my husband for four months, then when you learned of my existence, you decided to play the hero and tell me about it. Again, what do you want?"

Claudia sighed. "Nothing. I just wanted you to know so you can choose—"

"Have you *ever* considered that I might not *want* to know?"

Claudia's eyes widened.

Elizabeth scoffed. "You forced this knowledge upon me, and now I have no choice *but* to know."

Claudia had no idea what to say. This scenario had never occurred to her. "But... Why wouldn't you want to know?"

"I hate liars and cheaters, too." She raised one perfectly manicured eyebrow. "As such, I can hardly do nothing, but if I'd not known..." She shrugged.

"Why would you want to live a lie?"

Elizabeth laughed, but it wasn't a happy or a warm sound. It wasn't scathing, but it still burned Claudia. "Perhaps I'm not fond of the idea of spending the rest of my life alone. Tom and I mostly get along. Any issues we may have had, I could deal with, live with. This, however," she made a sweeping hand gesture in Claudia's direction, "I can't live with that."

"I know you said I keep saying this, but it's true. I'm so sorry. I never wished to cause you any trouble or pain."

"You're either incredibly stupid or supremely naïve if you harbored the delusion that telling me you've fucked my husband for the last four months wouldn't cause me any trouble or pain."

She had a point.

"And I know you're not stupid."

"I just thought knowing would be better."

"Yes, if I was in your shoes and in my early twenties, knowing might be better."

Claudia frowned. "I'm twenty-eight."

"Same difference. I've still got eighteen years on you, and my life and prospects look much different as I'm racing way past midlife."

Claudia startled.

"You may not be the blonde bombshell I'd imagined you to be, but what you *are* is actually worse."

"What I *am*?"

"Don't get me wrong, you're pretty, but you're not the type of woman I could've dismissed. You're too tall and lanky, and your... chest isn't that impressive."

Claudia's mouth fell open, and she closed it again without saying a word.

"I'm talking about what generally draws the gaze of a man, and I'm not—"

"So according to you, that's big tits and birthing hips? Mind you, Tom didn't need to look elsewhere for *that.* Do you also have a height limit of 5'3 or 5'4? Or is that too tall already?" Claudia crossed her arms.

Elizabeth released a dry chuckle. "I didn't have a number in mind, but..." She shrugged. "You can't deny that men are often attracted to such physiques."

"No doubt, but aside from what you said being insulting, it also doesn't mean that a woman who'd look like that would be an airhead or boring."

Elizabeth frowned. "When did I say that? And I didn't mean to insult you, but these are the facts."

Claudia exhaled harshly. "It was heavily implied, as in, cheating is more acceptable if done with a blonde bimbo with big boobs and all that jazz. Also, intentions don't always translate into actions."

"That is correct. The point is, if you were to fit this stereotype, I could more easily dismiss it. That he was drawn to you because of your... assets."

"And now you think it's my sparkling personality that roped him in?"

"No. Now you're a beautiful young woman who seems smart, kind, and lively. Engaging. You seem quite lovely, really, and that... I can't compete."

"Why would you *wish* to compete? For someone who doesn't respect you enough to honor his commitment, and who doesn't appreciate what he has. You're beautiful, and all you said about me seems true for you, too."

Elizabeth smiled. "That is kind of you to say, but—"

"I'm not kind. I have *eyes*."

Elizabeth fell silent, holding Claudia's intense dark gaze. "I'm much older than you, and while I stay fit, I don't have the body of a twenty-eight-year-old, nor the fresh face and enthusiasm."

"There's nothing wrong with your face or your body, and the last thing I'd call you is boring."

Elizabeth's eyebrows rose. "You don't know me."

"No. I didn't mean..." Claudia rushed out. "Tom's an idiot, and look, it's not my place to tell you what to do or anything, but there are plenty of people out there who'd jump at the chance to be with you. Also, what competition? I'm out and I'd never..." She sighed.

"Then why did you leave? Why couldn't you come clean in the café when I sat there waiting for you, eventually concluding that all of this had been a distasteful prank?"

"I was too shocked, and I got scared. So I ran."

"Yet you insisted on sharing this with me, still, or again. Even though this makes our work situation impossible."

Claudia's shoulders sank. Sammy had been right. "Like I said, I thought you should know."

"One day, Ms. Khoury, you might learn that your own vision, your own truth, isn't universal, and it'll behoove you to be more circumspect in doling out whatever *you* deem best."

Claudia could only nod. By now, her heart had invaded her throat.

"You're fired, effective immediately." Elizabeth turned and strode back to her desk.

Claudia's throat burned and her vision blurred. She'd been foolish to hope for a different outcome. And what on earth had she been thinking? *Calling your boss beautiful after you tell her you had an affair with her husband?*

"This means that you leave now, Ms. Khoury. Leave your ID on your desk."

Claudia nodded. "Goodbye," she said before hurrying out of the room. God, what a mess.

a furious desolation

FIRST, THERE'D BEEN A sense of relief when Elizabeth had concluded this Claudia person had been a liar after all. While she'd been annoyed at having been stood up, her emotions had soon turned to respite because it meant that Tom wasn't cheating on her. The apology message had meant little. That woman wouldn't string Elizabeth along, as she'd decided to ignore any further incoming messages from that horrible person.

Tom would be back Tuesday night, and she'd actually looked forward to his return. Elizabeth had even felt a bit of remorse for believing such awful accusations so easily and had plans to make it up to him.

Monday at work had gone well, too, although she'd lost track of time. She had no real desire to return home early, since Tom's absence stood out more keenly after this drama. Then all hell broke loose once again. There truly had to be a moment when she'd learn and be prepared.

When the scammer had introduced herself as Claudia, Elizabeth had not once thought of her newly hired legal advisor. After all, Claudia wasn't a terribly uncommon name. Not even when the woman had knocked on her door did she suspect she was about to upend her world. It had felt good to fire her, but on her way home, Elizabeth's conscience had raised its ugly head. But how would she ever be able to work with Claudia knowing her connection to Tom, a link leading to the ruin of her marriage?

So, Elizabeth had spent her Monday evening moping, then taken off Tuesday to clear her head. That didn't go all that well. Instead of exercising, she spent hours pacing. She liked to listen to music while wandering, sorting out her confusion and frustration. While she'd never seen the images Claudia had offered to show her, she no longer doubted the veracity of Claudia's claim, as even the puppy wouldn't take such a risk for the sake of a prank or a scam.

Tom had cheated on her for four months.

Elizabeth still couldn't decide how she felt because her emotions were all over the place. She felt betrayed, and when she allowed herself to meander down that road, fury vibrated through her, and she stomped through her house, the little vein in her neck pulsing to where her heartbeat resonated in her ears.

Moments of sadness weren't any better. She'd slow down, suppress tears welling in her eyes because she refused to cry over a man who... who had broken all his promises, and who saw nothing wrong with that—their short phone call that morning almost mundanely normal—and who intended to carry on with their lives as if nothing had happened.

Yes, she'd told Claudia she wished she'd never divulged this secret. And while a part of her did long for that, if she was being honest, that option would have been awful, too. The truth generally prevailed over time, and learning of this in ten or fifteen years would have been even worse.

She didn't want to live with a cheater. But she hated the truth, and she wished none of this had ever happened.

God, she dreaded having to tell her mother. She still visited her family in England every so often, especially with her parents getting on in age, yet she wasn't looking forward to her next trip. Not only without Tom, but she'd have to listen to her mother's comments about getting divorced.

Elizabeth had tossed and turned Monday night, vacillating between staying and leaving (Could there be a viable compromise?), weighing both alternatives, but in the end, it came down to one pivotal point: she couldn't trust Tom anymore. And a relationship without trust wasn't worth having. That she still loved him and likely could find a way to forgive him couldn't overcome this issue.

Elizabeth hoped she'd be all right in the long run. She still had her charity and several events lined up, besides searching for new guest speakers. That would leave her busy enough to keep thoughts of her failed marriage at bay. She almost wondered if this bothered her more than the loss of Tom—she'd failed. And did that upset her inherently, or because it meant her mother had been right? She should try to figure that out if she planned to move on. How funny, as if people *chose* whether or when to move on.

On Tuesday evening, she picked up Tom from the airport, and on the ride home, she let him chatter on, acting as if everything was normal while she mentally edited and revised what she wanted to say to him. A part of her that was pettier than she'd ever let on had considered not picking him up, changing the locks—it was *her* house, after all—and hiring a moving company to gather all his things and send them to his work. The visual entertained her and may even have caused her a small amount of pleasure, but no. She'd not do that.

Back home, Tom still went on and on, talking about weekend plans, a new restaurant he wanted to take her to, how they should reinstate date nights—she wondered if that idea hailed from Claudia dumping him—while she just stood there staring at him.

"Are you all right?" he asked, finally picking up on the shift in atmosphere. He fiddled with his belt before opening it and pulling it out of his pants. "I'm going to take a quick shower."

"No," Elizabeth said. The first thing she uttered since saying "Hi" at the airport.

Tom froze with the black leather belt still in his hands, now hanging in the air. "Excuse me?"

"I want a divorce."

His eyebrows shot up while the hand holding the belt dropped to the side. "What? Why?"

"Because you cheated on me." Elizabeth's calm and even tone belied the jackhammer throbbing in her chest and the nausea whirling through her stomach.

"I'm sorry," he said, his gaze finding the floor.

Elizabeth tilted her head. "You're not denying it."

"No. I cheated on you, but it's over, and I never... I was never serious about her. I'm assuming she told you?"

"Why did you do it then?"

He shrugged. "I don't know. We were out in a bar, and she just... She was fun, and I had a few beers too many."

Elizabeth's hands found her hips and her posture straightened. "Are you blaming the alcohol or the woman?"

Tom only stared at her.

She wouldn't reveal any details of how she knew Claudia as it was immaterial, and while she'd chewed out the younger woman at the office and rage still simmered when thinking of her, she now felt almost protective of her in the face of Tom's refusal to take ownership of his mistake.

Tom sighed, sitting on the foot end of the bed. He wiped his hand over his face. "The alcohol and Cl... the woman didn't help, no. You've been so busy recently, and—"

"So have you. Are you blaming *me* for fucking another woman for months?"

"I don't know! Why does someone have to carry the blame? It was a mistake, and she meant nothing. I want to be with you!"

Elizabeth clenched her teeth, trying to squash the ire sloshing through her. "You should have thought of that *before* you cheated."

He hung his head, but remained quiet.

"And let me tell you something, that woman, the alcohol? None of that mattered. *You* had a wife, *you* made a promise, and it was *your* responsibility to stay faithful! Cheating isn't a mistake. It's a conscious decision to break your vows, to have sex with someone other than your spouse. There are *always* so many moments where you could put a stop to it, but you didn't. For *months* you went back to her. Do mistakes last that long?"

"Liz—"

"I'm not finished! It wasn't just one night of drunken, exuberant fun, which *still* would've been wrong, but it might've been something we could've overcome. But that's not what happened, is it?"

Tom shook his head.

"You returned to her again and again, Tom. You kept having sex with her, then coming home to *me*. To *our* bed. You had sex with *me* after you've been with *her*." She closed her eyes. "Did you at least use protection?"

"Of course! Always!" He paused. "What about counseling? We could see a counselor and talk about what's wrong with our relationship."

"What's wrong is that you screwed another woman behind my back for months. There, money and time saved. There's no fixing that." She knew. She'd played through potential 'solutions,' in her mind while nearly pacing a hole in her carpet.

"With time you—"

"What? You can earn my trust back with years of what? Suspicion? Worry? Mistrust? I don't want to live like that. I refuse to be with someone I don't trust, and I don't trust you anymore."

"You don't even want to try? You're ready to throw it all away? I love you!" His voice cracked.

"No, Tom. *You* threw it all away the moment you kept letting that woman ride your prick. I hope she was worth it. Go stay with Sebastian or get a hotel room. I don't want you here."

"Lizzie, come on! I just got back from Amarillo, and I gotta go to work tomorrow. We have an important meeting, and—"

"I don't see how any of that is my concern." She stepped closer to him. "And don't call me that. You know I hate it."

His jaw clenched. "Can I please sleep in the guest room tonight? I promise I'll be out early tomorrow."

"And your belongings?"

His eyes widened. "You expected me to pack all my things now and leave?"

"I don't know, Tom. This isn't a situation I have a lot of experience with. I just know I don't want to be around you right now."

"All right, look. I'll stay in the guest room. I'll even shower in the guest bathroom, and then I'll be out of your sight."

"I'll still know you're here," Elizabeth said, crossing her arms.

"Please. I'm so exhausted, and I just need a break."

She held his dark gaze and wavered. "One night."

"Thank you," he said, rising and pressing his hand on his chest. "I'll be gone early tomorrow and... Maybe you can think about this some more? I don't know when you've learned of this, but probably not that long ago.

So, can you make sure this is what you want? My offer to see a counselor stands."

Elizabeth chuckled wryly. "No, Tom, this isn't what *I* want, but you gave me no choice." Much like Claudia hadn't, but she wasn't married to Claudia. She spun around and left their bedroom, heading for her office as pressure settled behind her temples. God, the last thing she needed was a migraine.

Later that night, miraculously spared from a migraine attack, she lay in bed after sending a few messages back and forth with an exhausted Kat—her work schedule was insane. Raji chose that moment to jump on her bed and meowed. She petted his head while he made biscuits of her blanket before curling up against her.

"At least I have you," Elizabeth whispered, smiling at Raji's loud purring. Just being in the same space and listening to him purr helped ease the pressure in her chest.

God, she'd spend the rest of her life alone.

Gloomy, yes, but in that moment, it truly felt like that. She struggled to form deep connections with people, and she'd thought Tom would be it. He'd been her friend and her husband, and she'd seen no one else in her future. She'd *wanted* no one else.

Yet she'd rather be alone than spend years resenting him with no guarantee she'd be able to get over this hollow emptiness that filled her, and if anything did rattle in that cage, it was nothing but blinding fury.

disasters of your own creation

After her confrontation with Elizabeth—after getting fired *one month* into her new job—Claudia had sprinted to her car and driven four hours straight to San Antonio to spend a few days with Sammy. She'd texted her of the incoming visit and a need for toiletries when she'd stopped at the gas station down the street from *Helping Hands*. Sammy had asked no questions, undoubtedly aware of the cluster fuck Claudia had created, given she only sent her a thumbs up, followed by a heart, and a hug emoji. She must have known Claudia hadn't been in the mood to talk.

By the time she made it to Sammy's, thanks to several annoying traffic issues, the clock struck close to midnight.

Sammy welcomed her with a long and tight hug, and engulfed in her friend's embrace, Claudia allowed a few tears to run free.

"Come on in. I made you some tea. Are you hungry?"

"Thanks." Claudia's voice sounded rough. She cleared her throat. "No, just tea. Herbal, right?"

"Yes, Claud. I'm not about to spike you with caffeine, despite your fondness for Earl Grey." Sammy led her into the kitchen where they settled at the breakfast table with two steaming mugs in front of them.

Claudia added a dollop of honey and sighed. "You were right."

"I'm sorry."

Claudia nodded. "I'd hoped she'd..." She couldn't even make herself finish the sentence. In part because she wasn't sure *what* she'd hoped. Not getting fired, of course, but maybe also that Elizabeth would see things her way. Had she been blind?

"How did she react, aside from firing you?"

"She was angry because I took away her choice of not knowing."

Sammy's eyebrows rose. "Not knowing who you are?"

"Not knowing about Tom."

"So she had her suspicions and now she's angry at you for speaking the truth about her bastard of a husband?"

Sammy's visceral support, while a tad biased, still brought a faint smile to Claudia's lips. "I don't know if she had any suspicions, but it didn't sound like it. She said I made assumptions based on my preference. Like I'd want someone to tell me, and so I expected she'd be like that, too. And now she has to take action, you know?"

"Huh. I suppose."

"She also said it's easier to start anew when you're younger. As if she's old." Claudia scoffed.

"Isn't she in her late forties? That's different from your twenties."

Claudia waved her off. "She's forty-six, and obviously the forties are a different stage in life than the twenties, but that doesn't make her old or incapable of finding someone better. Someone who appreciates what he has!"

Sammy chuckled. "And to you, Tom didn't do that?"

"Duh! He cheated on her."

Sammy shrugged. "Perhaps she's a dragon."

Claudia slammed her mug down, tea sloshing over the rim. "Really? That's kinda... well, no. It's *all* kinds of an awful thing to say."

"How so?"

"First, you assume that if *he* cheated, Elizabeth must be terrible to live with."

"I didn't say that."

"You kinda did. It makes it sound like cheating is OK if your partner is awful. If you're unhappy in your relationship, end it. If you fall for someone else and prefer them over your partner, end your relationship.

How hard is that? No. Tom is to blame, and honestly, how can Elizabeth be a terrible person if she started something like *Helping Hands*?"

Sammy smiled fondly at Claudia, who longed to wipe that indulgent expression off her face.

"What?" she grumbled.

"You're such an innocent, sweet summer child sometimes."

Claudia narrowed her eyes. "I'm not."

"Look, not all charities or charitable contributions are done out of the goodness of people's hearts. Often, hard and logical calculations fit into such decisions. People like to be seen as the hero, the person who helps and saves others. It's fantastic for your image."

"We're not talking politics."

"No, we're not, but it's the same in the real world."

Claudia clenched her jaw. "What clout does Elizabeth get for heading this charity for the last twenty years? She used her own money to get it started, which was quite the risk, especially back then."

Sammy snorted. "You shouldn't word it like that around her because you make her sound positively ancient. 'Back then.'"

Claudia flushed. "I doubt I'll see her again, and that's not what I meant."

"How do you know all that? About Elizabeth and her charity?"

"I researched her after I'd applied for the job."

Sammy nodded. "To get back to what you were asking earlier: Some people enjoy the praise and appreciation they receive when helping others. It doesn't have to be a monetary gain. I also doubt Elizabeth would invest her money to where she'd end up broke. Again, calculated risk."

"You don't know that."

"No, and neither do you. But I'm a better judge of character, and—"

"You always assume the worst of people."

"I don't. I assume people operate on self-interest, and there's nothing inherently wrong with that. It doesn't make them bad people," Sammy said.

"It makes them selfish."

"If their self-interest injures others, yes, otherwise, it makes them smart."

Claudia groaned. "I'm too tired for that discussion."

"All right. I set up your room and left toiletries in the guest bathroom. You know your way around. If you need to talk..."

Claudia squeezed Sammy's hand. "Thank you. For everything."

"Goodnight. You'll figure something out." Sammy stepped closer and kissed Claudia's temple before leaving the kitchen.

Claudia spent the next three days holed up at Sammy's, feeling sorry for herself and refusing to contemplate her next steps. She needed to first digest what had happened and overcome the unfairness of it all. She sometimes had the urge to seek out Tom and shout at him. Claudia would never do this for many reasons, but the image, picturing such a scenario, felt mostly satisfying.

She hoped Elizabeth tore into him. Though she still felt somewhat miffed by Elizabeth's reaction, too. Claudia never meant to hurt her and wasn't the truth just that? She couldn't change any of that. The business with Tom was done, but it happened.

She couldn't understand why Elizabeth would have preferred ignorance, and this notion kept rattling in her skull. She couldn't tell if it stemmed from her need to understand or from feeling hurt by Elizabeth's parting words. She had made her feel like a child. Claudia knew people saw the world differently, and she didn't assume everyone shared her view on things. Yet shouldn't the desire for a relationship built on honesty and mutual understanding be one of the few universal hopes that united people?

How could a relationship, a marriage, even work without these two ingredients, and how unfair would it be if you falsely believed you had them, while your partner ran around having sex with others?

At the same time, she knew Elizabeth had been sincere in what she'd said. And this disconnect refused to leave Claudia alone. It just kept playing in her head like a damn movie she never wanted to see in the first place. Worst of all, her mind refused to contemplate much else.

Back home, she spent the weekend much the same, though she avoided telling her family over lunch on Sunday what had happened. Her mother could tell something was off, but for now, she seemed to have decided to let Claudia stew for a little. Miracles happened sometimes.

She resisted the urge to contact Elizabeth and apologize again. Could apologies turn into harassment? She didn't want to find out. Claudia went running every day, using the exercise to try to get her mind to shut up.

Jobwise, she likely would have to beg Klara for her position back at *Little Feet*, and then see what else was out there in the legal field. She had a bit of breathing room because of her savings. It wasn't a lot, and it only worked because her apartment was rent controlled, but it was something. It also meant she didn't have to jump back in yesterday. She could allow herself to catch her bearings and see what her next steps should be. Claudia hated having lost her job at *Helping Hands*. It had been so perfect. Damn Tom for ruining that, too.

Monday evening, her phone rang. Claudia expected Sammy as no one else had a habit of calling her out of the blue, and so she answered her cell without glancing at the caller.

"Hey. I thought you'd tired of me after last week."

Silence.

"Ms. Khoury? I doubt I'm the person you were just talking to."

Claudia's eyes widened and her face turned scarlet at hearing Elizabeth's voice. To be fair, she was the *last* person she'd expected to hear from. What now? Was she going to sue her?

"Oh. No. I'm sorry. I thought you were Sammy. My best friend, she's the only one who..." She rolled her lips. "Never mind. How may I help you?"

"I'd like to talk to you, but not over the phone or via text messages."

"Talk to me about what?" Claudia asked.

"Your job, and what happened the previous Monday."

Claudia didn't know what to make of this, and for a moment, she even wondered if this was a cruel joke. "Are you serious?"

"Of course. I'm not one for pranks or wasting time."

Claudia nodded, then when she realized Elizabeth couldn't see her, she hurried to add, "Right."

"Will you come to the office tomorrow evening? I should be done with my day by five, so you could arrive by then, if you're amenable."

"I'll be there."

"Great."

They said their goodbyes and hung up. Claudia stared at the phone in her hand as if she'd never seen one before. What had just happened? She never expected to hear from Elizabeth or *Helping Hands* again. In fact, she assumed they'd also strike her off their volunteer list.

Elizabeth would hardly call her in just to shout at her. She couldn't even fire her again. And you didn't meet with people to tell them you put out a restraining order on them. Ugh, Claudia dropped on her couch, hiding her face in a pillow. This would be on her mind until she saw Elizabeth again. And here she'd thought she was done with all of that.

no pasture for you

After kicking Tom out, in a much less dramatic fashion than she'd envisioned in her more furious moments, Elizabeth buried herself in work, chatting with several new sponsors and trying to charm them into participating in their Christmas Dinner event. This focus allowed her mind to remain steadfast and ignore all things Tom. And Claudia.

She didn't understand why the latter still took up so much of her mental space. *Because you were incredibly harsh and unfair.* You'd think her own mind would be on her side, but apparently not. When she'd texted with Kat, her friend had pointed out that she might have overreacted and cost herself a great employee, though she also acknowledged that it wouldn't be easy to see Claudia most days given their connection. Kat's solution to that? Rehire her and stay professional. Remain above it all and set some serious ground rules. Elizabeth didn't hate the idea.

Then, her mother called Wednesday early afternoon. Elizabeth wanted to ignore the call, but that would only worsen the situation. Her mother was a bloodhound.

"Hi, Mother," she said in greeting, hoping to sound cheerful enough.

"Hello, darling. How are you?"

"All right. How about you?" Elizabeth didn't want to talk about Tom. She was not at all prepared for *that* discussion. Her feelings were still all over the place, and depending on the time of day, fury or sorrow reigned, and adding her mother's commentary to the mix didn't seem appealing.

"Aside from searing back pain that won't go away and that my doctor says comes with age, I'm doing well."

Elizabeth rolled her eyes, aware of the next few words before her mother had uttered them.

"But you'll see. I used to think your dear grandmother exaggerated with her aches and pains, and with her forewarnings of the troubles of old age. She was right, though, and you will see, too."

"I hope it'll get better soon." Because what else could she say? And no, she'd been close to her father's mother. Her maternal grandmother had been more... challenging and quite mean-spirited.

Mary sniffed. "How's Tom? Is he still so busy at work? You must be more available to him. Men need their wife present at home."

"He's fine, Mother."

"If you don't heed my advice, you might have to learn the hard way."

Elizabeth clenched her jaw. She doubted Tom had cheated on her because she worked too much. She didn't. In fact, she worked less than he did, and he still had had time for an extramarital affair. Elizabeth had made time for her marriage, and for the longest she'd thought so had Tom. "Wait, what did you say?"

Mary sighed theatrically. "I asked whether you're done with that *Helping Hands* nonsense by now? Aren't those freeloaders taken care of after all these years? All the time and money you have poured into these... *people*."

Elizabeth pinched the bridge of her nose. "Oh, Mother, Tom's coming home. Let's chat another time, all right? Hope you feel better. Bye." Without waiting for an answer, she hung up. She knew if this conversation continued, it would only revolve more around her 'wasteful' work, her 'late-in-life' marriage that meant she'd never have children, and every other topic that drove Elizabeth up the wall—given her current mood, she couldn't. Yes, she may have started *Helping Hands* because her mother would hate it, but the charity and the work they did had grown on her. It was less soul sucking than anything her mother had had in mind for her.

She suddenly wondered if Claudia had heard the same chorus from her parents. Did they urge her to get married? Would they have liked and approved of Tom as a future son-in-law? What about children? Tom had told her he had no interest whatsoever in being a father, and at the point they'd gotten serious, Elizabeth had already resigned herself to a child-free life, so that had mattered little to her.

God, why was she thinking about Claudia and Tom in that way? While she didn't really know Claudia, Elizabeth excelled at reading people, and Claudia had been both honest and sincere. There was no way she'd give Tom another chance. And what she did with the rest of her life, well, that wasn't any of Elizabeth's business.

Friday was game day. No, not football. Cards. Canasta. Today, they'd play at Catherine Summers' place. They'd met around six years ago through a mutual acquaintance who felt Catherine, who along with her husband, Robert, headed *Silsum Tech,* would be interested in becoming a sponsor for *Helping Hands*. Catherine had been excited about the prospect, and since that day, she and their tech company had become major sponsors. They also became friendly, and for the last three years, they played cards one Friday a month, rotating who hosted the game among the four of them.

They always played in alternating teams. Tonight, she'd play with Catherine. She preferred playing with her over Lauren and Sandra. The latter remained preferable over Lauren, who, while not a bad player, had a mean streak running through her that made Elizabeth uncomfortable. She knew the type, and she usually avoided them, but Catherine and Lauren were old friends, so that proved to be moot.

While she'd had no plan on sharing what happened with Tom, after a glass of wine and winning the first round—basically thrashing Lauren and Sandra—it just spilled out.

"Tom and I are getting a divorce."

All gazes snapped to her, and Elizabeth regretted saying anything.

"Are you all right?" Catherine found her voice first, the card game forgotten for now.

"I'm... hanging in there."

"Why did he leave you?" Lauren asked.

Elizabeth gritted her teeth.

"Why would you assume he left her?" Sandra asked.

Lauren shrugged.

"I filed for divorce," Elizabeth said, refraining from raising her chin.

"I'm sorry, dear." Catherine reached out and squeezed Elizabeth's hand.

"Thank you."

"You hadn't been married all that long, correct?" Lauren asked.

"Five years," Elizabeth replied.

"Hmm, at least that. It's better to nip these things in the bud. My daughters' marriages are fairly new, too, especially Gretchen's, but they've both chosen well, and I have high hopes they won't become another statistic." Lauren picked up her tumbler and sipped her whiskey.

"There's no shame in divorce," Catherine said. "Sometimes people don't fit. Why torture yourself by staying with someone who makes you miserable? You'll find your feet again. You're still young."

"Not that young, and men marry younger."

"Stop being mean, Lauren," Sandra said.

"I'm not mean. Just realistic. She needs to know what's out there."

"Elizabeth isn't a newborn foal in need of protection," Sandra pointed out.

"Exactly. She's close to being sent out on the pasture where we're already grazing."

"Speak for yourself," Catherine said. "I still have plenty of life in me. Don't they say forty is the new thirty? That makes us—"

Lauren snorted. "Not forty."

Elizabeth sighed. The wine must have infused her with the delusion that blurting out her situation with Tom during game night *with Lauren* present was a good idea, because for the life of her, she should have known better. "Either way, I just wanted you ladies to know about this change in my living situation. It's for the best, in the end."

"Of course it is." This time, Catherine patted her hand. "Why else would you've done it?"

Why else indeed? She wished she had someone who would truly understand her and what she was going through. While she was friendly with her game night companions, she should talk more to Kat about all of this. Yet, her friend's schedule made that difficult, and Elizabeth abhorred being a bother.

When she was in her mid-thirties, Elizabeth had suffered from burnout and seen a therapist about it. He'd helped her a lot, and together, they worked on changing her point of view on work-life balance, and since then, she'd been better and no longer neared these wastelands. An increase in her migraines meant she needed to tread lighter, which she did whenever that occurred again.

On her drive home, she wondered if she should search for a new therapist and talk this through. Yet, the idea didn't sit right with her. Elizabeth wanted a friendly conversation about it all with someone who cared about her, and who'd understand, not pat her hand, or insinuate she'd be put out on the pasture. To be fair, Lauren never insinuated, she merely outright insulted you. In the end, Elizabeth didn't know what had stung more, Catherine's placating comfort or Lauren's bitter future prognosis.

Elizabeth couldn't seem to shake what had happened at her office last Monday night. She kept going over the confrontation again and again, and each time, both her conscience and Kat's words rang in her ear. She had fired an employee who'd been praised by both Tilda and a variety of their patrons, someone who had volunteered multiple times before being hired, all because Elizabeth couldn't bear the sight of the woman her husband had slept with.

Talk about unprofessional.

Her head pounded, and she knew she was due another migraine, and that in combination with Tom and the Claudia situation had soured her mood considerably. She knew the right thing would be to apologize to Claudia and to rehire her if she was still interested in the position.

The thing was, first, Elizabeth loathed to apologize. She wasn't incapable of it, but she'd always done so begrudgingly and with some sense of resentment. She supposed another trait she shared with her mother, yet she also didn't want to be one of those people who blamed all their issues and flaws on their mother.

Second, and this weighed even heavier, although she was wrong with how she'd treated Claudia—and if the woman hadn't still been within her probationary period, she'd have had the right to sue Elizabeth for wrongful termination—she didn't know if she could handle being around Claudia at work. Kat's suggestion of being professional and keeping her distance had merit, but she felt uneasy about that, too.

Even if Elizabeth tried, Claudia seemed the type who wandered over boundaries in her youthful assurance of doing the 'right thing.' That assumed she'd even be interested in coming back. After all, she had every right to hold a grudge. Then again, that didn't seem to be her nature as far as she could tell. So, despite knowing that this would end in disaster, she'd called Claudia Monday night, also after Tilda's pointed look and acerbic comment of: "If you continue to fire talented and promising personnel, you will end up with a permanent vacancy, and how will that serve our patrons?"

Elizabeth had only glared at Tilda, who had shrugged unfazed and then continued her work. Although she hated to admit it, she'd been impressed that Claudia had left a mark on people after only a month's work, not to mention that she had won over Tilda, of all people. So, come Monday evening, she'd called Claudia, and after an awkward first greeting, they managed to set-up an appointment for the next day. She could only hope she wouldn't live to regret this.

Formicidae and coffee

Claudia felt almost like she did the summer she was nine years old, playing in the yard and not realizing she had been sitting right next to an anthill until tiny feet crawled under her shirt and up her pants leg. She had jumped wildly in the yard—raising her arms into the air before swatting at her body, hopping from leg to leg as if lost in some spiritual peyote trance—at least she supposed it had looked like that to an onlooker. She wasn't dancing like that now, at least not on the outside. But she struggled to stay still, and the nervous energy flitting through her resembled those pesky, fascinating, freakishly strong crawlers.

She ate little all day, too nervous to even notice hunger, though she emptied one water bottle after the other to where she contemplated for a second if she needed to get checked for diabetes. Finally, the clock struck four and she could justify getting ready to head to the office. She arrived in the parking lot close to five and stayed in the car, her fingers drumming on the steering wheel as her mind conjured up potential scenarios of what would await her in Elizabeth's office.

Ten minutes later, she exited her car and marched toward the building. When she arrived in front of Elizabeth's door—the security officer had waved her through, either because he'd remembered her or because Elizabeth had informed him about an after-hours guest—she hesitated, and the memory of the last time she stood there like this along with its painful consequences flooded her mind. She shook them off and knocked.

"Come in."

Claudia opened the door, struck by an immediate sense of déjà vu from seeing Elizabeth sitting behind her desk, once more working on something. Though this time, her long, brown hair framed her shoulders in soft curls. Instead of a suit, she wore a light button-down V-neck blouse with a stand collar, complemented by black slacks. It exasperated Claudia that Elizabeth still appealed to her so much. Talk about unprofessional.

Elizabeth raised her head, her expression inscrutable, but once again she thought of ants. Not that Elizabeth resembled an ant, but Claudia might as well have been one, given the icy stare that hardened Elizabeth's soft features.

"You wished to see me." Claudia found her voice.

"Yes, thank you for meeting me."

She merely held Elizabeth's gaze.

A moment of silence stretched between them before Elizabeth asked Claudia to sit, which she did.

Elizabeth leaned back in her chair, her fingers toying with the deep blue fountain pen in her hand. "I may have acted rashly the last time we talked."

Claudia remained silent. Pointing out that 'may have' sounded like a nice euphemism wouldn't improve her already shaky standing.

Elizabeth's gaze dropped to her hands. "This isn't easy, but whatever may have happened in our personal lives shouldn't influence the work we do here, especially when such work has been exemplary and shows great promise."

Claudia wondered if Elizabeth could hear the frantic beating of her heart. "What does that mean?"

It almost looked as if it cost Elizabeth to continue speaking. "It means you are an asset to *Helping Hands*, and that is much more important than... the rest."

Disbelief rushed through Claudia. "Do I have my job back?"

"If you wish. Tilda, apparently, *forgot* to send your termination papers to HR, so you theoretically never lost your job."

"Oh, that's... good."

"Yes." Elizabeth looked like she was fighting off a small smile. "How very fortunate that something slipped Tilda's mind."

Claudia, on the other hand, couldn't suppress a grin.

Elizabeth sighed.

"So will we forget about last Monday and never talk about... all of that," Claudia waved between them, "or do you wish to clear the air and, I don't know? Do you want to talk about anything else? We did plan to meet for coffee."

Elizabeth raised one eyebrow. "The meeting you stood me up for?"

Claudia ducked her head. "Yes."

"And you feel there should be a raincheck for that?"

"Why not? We wouldn't even have to leave the office. There's a machine in the kitchen. I could get us some coffee and we can sit down and... talk?" Claudia hated how hopeful her voice sounded. She couldn't tell why this was so important to her. She realized she likely should have just shut up, thanked Elizabeth for *unfiring* her and then followed her lead regarding all things Tom. But that also would have driven her to distraction. She wanted things to be OK between them, or as all right as they could be, given all that had happened.

Elizabeth released a rough chuckle, the sound hitting Claudia like a punch. "I suppose we could have the coffee meeting we've missed before, and once we've cleared the air, everything relating to Tom and your history with him will be a non-topic in the future. When we interact after today, it will be about *Helping Hands* and the business at hand *only*."

Claudia deflated a little, but realizing that this remained an incredible offer, she hastily agreed. "Of course."

"Good. I'll admit, though, I'm not particularly fond of the... *coffee* that machine produces. Thankfully, I have my own over here." Elizabeth pointed toward a sideboard standing in the corner that housed a miniature starship—all sleek and silver—masquerading as a coffee machine.

"Uh, I'm not sure I've ever used one of those." The last thing Claudia needed was to break Elizabeth's fancy coffee machine accidentally.

Elizabeth rose and strode toward the machine. "It's not rocket science. Someone who can succeed in law school should be able to use a mere coffee machine."

Claudia's eyebrows rose. There was nothing 'mere' about this futuristic gadget. If the Decepticons used the AllSpark on this thing, it would give Megatron a run for his money.

Elizabeth turned the machine on, set a mug under its spout, and pressed a series of buttons.

Claudia struggled to pay attention to which buttons she pressed as Elizabeth's long, slender—ringless—fingers distracted her.

"And that's it. All you have left to do is press start and it'll grind your selection of beans. Do you prefer a light, medium, or dark roast?"

"Huh?" Claudia's gaze shot back to Elizabeth's face, and her serious expression reminded Claudia that this wasn't a fun chat between friends. This was still business. Personal business, but business, nevertheless. "Oh, right. A dark roast." She needed the least amount of caffeine possible, and given the hour and the company, she'd have actually preferred an herbal tea.

Elizabeth hummed and prepared her own coffee, black, a drop of cream but no sweetener, before she once more turned to Claudia. "Your preference?" She pressed another selection of buttons, and the machine once more jumped to life.

"Uh, cream and one sugar, or honey. But no artificial sweetener."

Once the coffee finished brewing, Elizabeth added a shot of cream and a spoonful of honey, then pushed the cup toward Claudia. "There you go."

"Thank you."

Elizabeth headed for the couch that stood at the back of her office next to a large window and a series of plants Claudia couldn't identify, though one seemed to be a palm tree.

Claudia joined her, settling on the other end, sipping her coffee. "Oh, wow." She licked her lips. "This is delicious."

"I know." Elizabeth drank from her own cup.

Claudia suppressed a smile.

"Why did you first decide to contact me?" Elizabeth began, then raised her hand when Claudia opened her mouth. "No, wait. You didn't know who I was then, or better, that this Elizabeth Pittin, as you called me, and your new boss were the same person."

"That's right."

"Would you still have texted me if you'd known?"

Claudia's gaze grew vacant as she contemplated the question. "I don't know. I still would've wanted to tell you, and I'm sure I'd have come up with some way to do that. Likely the wrong or most clumsy one, but I'd have still wanted you to know."

"But what's the benefit for you? What did you hope to gain?" Elizabeth asked.

"Nothing. I told you before, I didn't contact you because I want something. I just... I really hate liars and cheaters, and I'm pissed Tom involved me in this. He may have made me an accessory to infidelity, but I refuse to be turned into a liar." She raised her chin.

"The self-righteousness of youth."

Claudia frowned. "I don't see how this relates to age, as I've hated liars in kindergarten when Jenny accused me of having ripped off her Barbie's head on purpose. I doubt this trait will change with time."

Elizabeth frowned. "How do you decapitate a doll on *accident*?"

Claudia folded her arms, exasperated at how defensive she still felt over that old tale. "I was walking and brushing the Barbie's hair when I stumbled, well, I ran into something and fell. In the tussle," Claudia shrugged, "it came off."

Elizabeth's lips tightened, but it seemed obvious she was trying to hide a smile. "Are you still in the habit of running into things, or did you grow out of that?"

Claudia flushed. She wished Elizabeth wasn't so damn attractive and that her eyes were less startling, less vibrantly blue. But professionalism. She needed to remind herself of that. This coffee meeting was a blip, a onetime occurrence to lay this issue between them to rest. "Let's say it's no rare for my legs and arms to be bruised, and I often don't know how that happened."

Elizabeth's brows knitted together. "Because you bump into things a lot?"

Claudia sighed. "Obviously."

"Good."

"That I'm clumsy?"

"That no one else is the cause of such injuries."

"Oh. Right. Yes. I'd not let that happen."

A shadow fell over Elizabeth's face. "I'm not sure it's that easy."

"I didn't mean to insinuate that women in abusive relationships are weak or are allowing themselves to be abused."

"I'd hope not because that would be awful and quite unfitting of your position here."

Claudia sunk back against the cushion. "Of course. I just... My parents always preached that I should marry a good man, and that a good man doesn't hurt his wife. And I hope I'd see such red flags early, but yes, you never know."

"And you listen to your parents?"

Claudia grinned. "When I agree with them."

"Well, it *is* good advice."

"Yes, though I'd amend it to partner to be more inclusive. You can get abused in a relationship with a woman, too, and enough men are victims of domestic abuse as well."

"Very true." Elizabeth's fingers drummed against her cup. "Let's get to the pictures, shall we?"

Claudia frowned. Pictures? "Oh." She swallowed hard. "OK." Her eyelids fluttered. Elizabeth had surprised her, and their conversation and the current mood between them felt both disorienting and invigorating. Claudia neither knew what to think nor do about it, and she wished this wouldn't be a onetime 'all cards on the table' thing.

She opened the gallery on her phone. Claudia hoped that would be enough and Elizabeth wouldn't want to look at their text thread. She didn't know why, but the notion of Elizabeth reading their messages filled her with unease, and more than a little mortification. She didn't want Elizabeth to see her like that, especially since she'd never have the opportunity to get to know Claudia to form her own unbiased opinion.

a lingering sadness

Elizabeth had startled when, upon looking up, her gaze landed on a fresh-faced Claudia, her long black hair tied up in a loose bun, clad in skinny jeans and a loose maroon long-sleeve shirt. Not a lick of make-up on her tan, pretty face. Her brown eyes glowed brightly, but Elizabeth had noted fissures of nerves in the way Claudia had clenched her hands and in her too straight posture. She'd expected nerves, but what she'd not anticipated was how much it stung to see her, the reminder of the gulf that separated them, and that *this* was the face that had attracted Tom enough to cheat on her. There truly was no way for her to compete. Not that she'd intended to do so.

She also hadn't seen this moment coming, sitting with Claudia on her couch, drinking coffee after a not so unpleasant exchange. In another world, this could have been a meeting between friends, but now she needed boundaries and rules once this business with Tom was done, and they'd go back to a professional relationship.

Elizabeth braced herself, smoothing her expression to remain impassive, at least outwardly, while her heart pumped her blood so fast, she felt almost dizzy as soon as she held Claudia's phone. "Thank you," Elizabeth rasped.

"Keep sliding to the left. This is the first picture."

Elizabeth nodded as if in a trance, her gaze glued to the image before her—Claudia smiling with a fruity-looking drink in her hand, her arm slung around Tom. With a beer bottle in his hand, he pressed his cheek to Claudia's, while his arm was wrapped around her. He looked happy. She swiped to see the next picture, this time the two of them without drinks, but still entwined.

If you didn't know any better, you'd think those were beautiful images of a couple in love. They looked good together, better than she and Tom ever had. She froze at the next image as it showed them kissing deeply. Her stomach dropped and her heart, against expectations, slowed down.

Elizabeth zoomed in on the picture, trying to discern any signs of editing. To be fair, Claudia had seemed terribly earnest from the moment she'd interviewed her, and she knew this wasn't anything other than the truth, yet there was a part of her that still wished she could wake up from this nightmare and have her old life back.

The next pictures were more innocent but still showed a quiet, content togetherness. She returned the phone to Claudia. "I've seen enough."

"I'm truly sorry," Claudia said, her eyes full of sorrow, and the expression—not pity, but something that stung—infuriated Elizabeth. Never mind, how often did she plan to apologize?

"For fucking my husband?" Elizabeth blurted out, both exasperated with Claudia and herself.

Claudia's eyes widened, and she lowered her gaze. "Yes. Again, I'd have never even *looked* at him if he'd worn his ring."

"So you keep saying."

"Because it bears repeating."

Elizabeth canted her head. "Does it relieve your guilty conscience?"

Claudia released a harsh breath. "No. I still feel terrible."

Elizabeth wondered why that didn't make her feel any better.

Claudia's phone rang. She started but checked the display. "I'm so sorry, but I gotta take this. It's my mom and... Never mind."

Elizabeth nodded and leaned back, curious about what she'd learn from that conversation.

"Hi, Mom. *Chou*? No, *akid* I'll be there on Sunday. Wait, *teta* said that? Are you sure it wasn't just a—" Claudia sighed. "No, of course not. *Eh, baarif.*" She nodded and gave Elizabeth a rueful little smile. "Yes, will do. OK. *OK. Yallah* bye." She hung up, placing her phone screen down on the coffee table.

"Is everything all right?"

"Hmm? Oh, yes. Usual family drama. I have lunch at my parents' place every Sunday, and let's just say it's usually an adventure."

"What language was that?"

"Arabic. I'm from Lebanon. Well, my parents are. They moved here before they had me."

"You're fluent in both languages?"

"Yes, well, English, Arabic, and Spanish. My parents are big on education and figured speaking more languages would benefit me."

"They are correct." Elizabeth felt impressed despite herself.

"Yeah. I'll be able to take on patrons speaking those languages, too."

"I'll have to tell Tilda to add that to your file. In fact, you should put that on your resume."

Claudia nodded.

"You worked at a daycare before, right? That's an odd choice for someone with your degree." Why was she prolonging their conversation? Besides, they were supposed to discuss ground rules and work.

"It is. I just needed a break and kinda fell into *Little Feet*. The daycare I worked at."

"You must love children."

"I suppose. I like them enough, but I'm great with them. And it's always something new. They keep things interesting."

"That I believe."

"You're not a fan of children?" Claudia asked.

"No, no. I like them. They're adorable." She could tell Claudia wrestled with her next question, so she decided to spare her. "I don't have any children of my own. The timing never worked out."

Claudia nodded. "So, rules?" she asked after stillness had once more spread between them.

"Yes, rules." She needed to follow Kat's advice because she had to find a way to work with Claudia and to keep seeing her without thinking of Tom and their affair. Lord, she should have been the one to bring this up again. Why was she so distracted? "No more talking about Tom, about your affair, about my marriage. We are *not* friends. I'm your boss, and you're an employee of *Helping Hands*. All our future interactions will relate to business. No more coffee get-togethers or anything else." She'd never been friends with an employee and considered such behavior risky. Besides, a friendship with Claudia would never work.

"OK."

"Good. With that rule and some distance, I hope the memory of what got us here will fade."

"All right. Is there anything you need me to do or not do, or not say or whatever? What do you need from *me*?"

Elizabeth startled. What a strange question from this odd woman who seemed so open it almost pained Elizabeth to see. How could you live your life like that? "Your job. I need you to do your job." She didn't like how Claudia's face fell, but she recovered quickly and raised her head, nodding.

"I can do that."

"Excellent." Elizabeth handed Claudia her ID back before rising and striding back to her computer, effectively dismissing Claudia.

Claudia lingered for a moment, then nodded again and left.

She recalled Kat's insistence on professionalism, "Listen Liz, sometimes we don't like the people we have to work with, and that's OK. You can't force that. At times, you don't get along with someone, and they've done nothing to you. Here, you're in an extreme situation, and no one would blame you for getting rid of her. It would be human, really. But I know this goes against your affinity for fairness, so you'll just have to be professional and do your work."

Kat had her own struggle with a new co-star, but at least that woman hadn't destroyed her marriage.

Whenever Elizabeth thought that, she felt fury rise, not at Tom, but at herself. She shouldn't blame Claudia, yet her instinctual reaction still wanted to go there—blaming the one with whom she had no connection, no ties, no marriage vows. It would be so much easier. But she couldn't. Otherwise, she would also work things out with Tom. She didn't want to take the easy way out because she knew down the road, she'd hate herself for it, and Tom, too. But still, she'd not be alone if she could place the sole blame on Claudia.

Instead, Elizabeth would now have to be professional and avoid allowing the past to intrude on the present. At least she wouldn't have to work with her directly. She had hated that wounded puppy expression, and she'd been grateful Claudia had smoothed it quickly, because Elizabeth feared it would eventually make her cave.

Back home in her lonely, empty house—it truly was way too big for just her and Raji—she took a shower and warmed up a microwave dinner since she didn't feel like cooking or ordering take-out. She put on some music and curled up on the couch. She lay there, too tired to read, but happy when Raji jumped up and fell asleep pressed up against her chest. This was her life now. Work and Raji.

God, she was being melodramatic. But she was sad. Seeing those pictures today had hurt more than she'd realized at first. She knew Claudia had spoken the truth and Tom had admitted as much, but no, she'd *had* to go there and see it with her own eyes. Morbid curiosity be damned.

When she closed her eyes, she saw their smiles again and again. They'd looked happy. Tom had looked so joyful. She thought they'd been happy or content. They had a good life, and she'd seen no end. Then it had fallen at her feet, against her will, and there was nothing she could do to change it. At least nothing she could live with. Tears stung. She might as well sit on Mars right now and be just as far away from where she wanted to be as she found herself on her couch in her silent home.

She petted Raji, and for a moment, she hated them both. Claudia might not be at fault, but she'd still hurt Elizabeth, and it didn't sting any less because Claudia hadn't known.

how to get better at recognizing underlying power structures and still ignore them

THOUGH CLAUDIA HAD THE urge to call Sammy right after she got home from her visit with Elizabeth, she felt mostly incoherent and decided to sleep on it first. Perhaps it had all been a dream, and tomorrow, when she showed up at the office, they'd laugh and turn her away? Then again, her ID seemed unchanged. While Claudia had hoped for a positive outcome once Elizabeth had requested meeting her, she still had tried to temper down her tendency of lofty, hopeful flight. The crash always hurt so much, and she still seemed to be mostly suspended in mid-air.

When she stepped foot into *Helping Hands* the next morning, she swatted at a few remaining tendrils of fear that all of this had been some kind of joke. And once she passed Tilda, who gave her what almost counted as a smile and a nod, Claudia straightened, and her pace increased until she disappeared in her office, ready for another day at the job she had thought lost.

One woman she saw today had been on her appointment book for last week, and her first words after greeting Claudia were: "I hope you're feeling better. My uncle also caught the flu recently, and it was gnarly."

Claudia's eyebrows rose, but she covered her surprise. "Yes, thank you. I'm much better." She wondered if she should fake a cough, but also didn't want to make the woman fear she was still infectious. Not that she had been sick, but the woman didn't know what. On that note, who'd told her she'd been sick? Before her mental speed-race off the cliff could continue, Ms. Tinnes peppered her with a million questions about various legal issues at hand. And so Claudia went to work.

By the time her workday concluded, she'd only seen Elizabeth once in passing in the hallway. They'd greeted each other with a smile. Well, Claudia had grinned like an idiot and waved at Elizabeth who nodded at her agreeably. At least Claudia chose to interpret her small, polite smile as such.

On her way home, she stopped by her parents' house and ate dinner with them, much to *teta's* delight. They chatted about Claudia's job, how Johnny's new wife seemed nice (Her mother offered a play-by-play of their run-in the other day.), and *teta's* next visit to Sonia's, while her father asked Claudia for an animal with six feet where the last letter of seven was a D. He loved crossword puzzles, unlike Claudia, who only stared at him blankly until he grumbled and refocused on his booklet.

Back home, she finally video called Sammy.

"You won't believe what happened!" Claudia greeted her friend.

Sammy chuckled. "Hello to you, too."

"Yes, yes. Guess what?"

"What?"

"I'm back at *Helping Hands*, and Elizabeth isn't mad at me anymore. Well, she might still be, but she wants to separate the personal and the professional and also, we had coffee and cleared the air. So now we can go back to how things were, being professional and all."

"Wait, what? OK, tell me from the beginning."

And so Claudia did.

"Oh, wow. That's... unexpected," Sammy said once Claudia had completed her tale.

"I know."

"Why is it you seem both excited and sad?"

Claudia sighed. "Because I am?"

"Are you having any regrets? You don't have to work there if it's too hard for you. It's asking a lot of both of you, really."

"No, no. I love this job. It's perfect, and exactly what I've always dreamed of doing."

"But?"

"That moment with Elizabeth when we sat together and had coffee... I kinda liked it."

"OK. That's good, right? It means you'll be able to get over what happened, so your job shouldn't be a problem."

"Yeah, of course. It's not that. I meant what I said last time. She was a lot of fun. When we'd texted and before I knew who she was, before she saw me as just her employee."

"You *are* just her employee."

Claudia grumbled.

"I take it that's the problem?"

"There were some moments during our talk when I saw more of her, not just the professional façade, and I... I suppose I wish we could explore that."

"You want to be friends with your boss? The one who is getting divorced because her husband couldn't resist you and broke his marriage vows? That one?"

"Why do you have to put it like that?"

"Because that's how it is. Look, I adore you, and I think you're awesome. I'm lucky to be your friend, and ordinarily, I'd say Elizabeth would be lucky to have you as her friend, too."

"Aww."

Sammy narrowed her eyes. "Shut it. My point is, the rift between you is impossible to bridge, more so, you shouldn't even try."

"Why? Are we bound by a past we didn't even choose? How's that fair?"

Sammy did a face palm and muttered something into her hand that Claudia didn't fully catch, but that sounded suspiciously like, "Lord, give me strength."

Claudia pouted. Sammy wasn't even religious.

"To start with a platitude, life isn't fair. But look, first, you'd have to assume that Elizabeth found you just as interesting, and that is doubtful."

"Hey! I'm likable."

"Yes, yes, but as the mistress of her husband, you're a tough sell."

Claudia had no reply, though that didn't mean she liked it.

"Second, there's this power structure between you. She is your boss, and it's never a good idea to become close with your boss, or for your boss to get friendly with an employee."

"You know all about that, huh?"

Sammy ignored her and instead went on, "It's a lot, and the risk-benefit ratio isn't worth it. Even if you could be the best of friends, there's not merely a gigantic ravine between you, but the next hill is also steep as fuck. Why would either of you risk that?"

Why indeed? Claudia sighed. Sammy had a point, even if she hated it. It was a pity they hadn't met under different circumstances. She truly would have loved to get to know Elizabeth. Now, she would have to try her hardest to fulfill the other woman's request of being strictly professional. It would be hard, but she'd have to do it. It was the least Claudia owed Elizabeth.

Claudia worked late on Thursday, feeling like she had to prove herself to Elizabeth, not just that she could be professional, but that the confusion and turmoil they'd gone through were worth it because Claudia would remain an asset to *Helping Hands*. When she left her office, she noticed a stream of light pouring out from under Elizabeth's office door. She halted, resisting the temptation to go there and check on her. Likely not what an employee would do, but also professionalism and all communication needed to be about work. Those had been Elizabeth's words, and Claudia needed to adhere to them. So, she went home.

Friday, she encountered an issue with work, and when she asked Tilda for advice, she sent her to Elizabeth. Claudia hesitated at first, but since this was about work, it should be fine. Not to mention, Tilda said so, and Claudia assumed following her directions was a good way to live by.

She knocked on Elizabeth's door close to four in the afternoon.

"Hey. I have a question. I already asked Tilda, and she said I should seek you out, so... here I am." Claudia tried not to fidget.

"Of course." Elizabeth finished typing, then raised her head and pointed at the chair in front of her desk.

Claudia sat down. "So one of our patrons has an ex-boyfriend who has been harassing her. They also have a little boy together. He's three-years-old, and her income isn't enough to take care of them. The ex had been paying child support, but he's become volatile recently. He's been leaving her threatening voice messages, and when she went to the police, they told her they can't do anything as long as he's only talk."

"We do have a legal representation service for such cases. She wouldn't have to pay for her own lawyer. We could file a restraining order and move her into one of our housing units. But you know all that, so what's really the problem?" Elizabeth asked.

Claudia looked down, reluctant to voice her fears. "I'm scared of what he'll do if we do that. So often, these cases escalate at this point. Women are in the greatest danger when they decide to leave, and she's done that, but he... He's been following her. Showing up at her work. He says nothing, lingers around and later curses her out on the phone."

Elizabeth sighed. "He's already escalating, especially if he started to stalk her. Since the law doesn't intervene until something actually happens, we need to take action. You need to file that restraining order immediately, and she needs to inform her family and friends of the situation so that they won't share her whereabouts. Then she will have to relocate."

"What about her work? And that's not even the biggest problem. He found out she'd gone to the police, and threatened to kill himself if she doesn't stop ruining his life."

Elizabeth groaned. "I'm assuming she doesn't want to file the restraining order anymore."

"Exactly. I don't know how to handle this. How much are we allowed to do? Should I send her to a counselor? She said she's made up her mind, though. While she refuses to go back to him, she also doesn't want to pursue further legal action."

"I see."

"So, what are our options in this situation?" Claudia asked, looking expectantly at Elizabeth.

"We can't force her hand, but making her an appointment with a counseling partner seems like a sensible idea. You could also talk to her some more if you wish. Sometimes talking to a friendly face can help."

Claudia nodded, swallowing the question of "You think I have a friendly face?"

"Keep me updated. This is a hard one, and while it seems like we know what she should do, our options are limited."

"Yeah. It's difficult. I wish I could do more."

"That's understandable, but you're doing all you can here."

"All right. Thank you." Claudia rose. "I'll leave you to it."

Elizabeth nodded, turning back to her computer screen, once more dismissing Claudia without a word.

Later, Claudia had gone to the corner store across the street from the office to buy a pastry and a coffee—she was feeling snackish, and while this wasn't a substitute for dinner, after working three more hours on her cases, she needed a break. She supposed she could have headed home, too, but she wanted to tie up a few more loose ends before the weekend.

Since she'd seen the light on in Elizabeth's office on her way out, she decided on a whim to purchase her a cup of coffee, too. Claudia didn't think this was infringing on any boundaries. She was merely being considerate.

Once she returned to their floor, Elizabeth stepped out of her office.

Claudia strode toward her and held up the cup for her to take.

"What's that?" Elizabeth asked.

"Coffee, cream, no sugar. I was heading out for a snack, and I saw your light on." She shrugged. "I thought you might need some fuel too if you're also 'burning the midnight oil.'"

"Seven thirty is hardly midnight."

"Yes, but it's two and a half hours after the end of the workday."

Elizabeth canted her head. "And yet you're still working."

"I just want to close something out. Less to do on Monday, so I can leave early." She once more held out the cup for Elizabeth to take.

"I thought we didn't do coffee."

"We don't do coffee meetings in your office. Or sit down in a café. This is... a drive by coffee. Completely professional."

"Is that so?"

"Yes. Consider it penance if you wish."

"I don't. But thank you." She finally accepted the cup, nodded and walked away.

Claudia's gaze followed Elizabeth's retreating figure, then the woman stopped and turned.

"Don't work too late. It's a bad habit."

"I won't. Good night." She suppressed waving at Elizabeth and instead also turned and headed for her office. God, she was ridiculous.

stuck in a never-ending loop

While Elizabeth had followed Kat's advice before, this seemed... more challenging than expected. Perhaps because Claudia appeared to struggle with the concept of 'professionalism,' much like Elizabeth had feared. Not that Claudia was unprofessional at work—her attitude there remained exemplary. Again, it wasn't easy to win Tilda's approval.

However, from the moment Claudia had given her that 'drive by' coffee (prepared exactly how she liked it), there'd been other acts of... kindness and consideration that, in Elizabeth's mind, wouldn't fit into a 'strictly business kind of professionalism.' Though perhaps that had merely been her experience and there were other ways of doing this.

In her second week back, Claudia had left a salad she'd bought at the café across the streets on Elizabeth's PA's desk, before texting her that she had a delivery. When Elizabeth discovered the salad, Claudia had already left, and so she could only send her a quick 'thank you' message via text. She almost added that it hadn't been necessary, and while true, it would also have been disingenuous since Elizabeth had been starving and almost inhaled the salad before returning to work.

Elizabeth had also been pleased to see Claudia finding a solution with a patron who dealt with a stalking ex-boyfriend. She couldn't say she was particularly surprised that the woman didn't stand a chance against the whirlwind called Claudia Khoury, who convinced her to file for a restraining order and even to relocate with her son.

What was it about Claudia that had this effect on people? And shouldn't Elizabeth be immune given their own challenging history? She'd refrained from bringing this up with Kat because first, she didn't know *how* to even explain what she felt, and second... She thought Kat might be biased given her own drama with her new co-star.

Besides, Elizabeth had never failed at staying professional, at keeping her distance, or even at freezing someone out if warranted. Perhaps all this came down to the almost crestfallen expression that had washed over Claudia's face when Elizabeth had dismissed her after re-hiring her. But then again, why should that affect Elizabeth? She should dislike Claudia, yet she didn't.

So, Wednesday of the week after the salad incident, Elizabeth noted that Claudia once more worked late. She wondered if she'd been doing that so often because she feared Elizabeth would let her go if she didn't work hard, and she vowed to rectify that. Elizabeth stayed long because she hated coming home to an empty house (Raji would take offense at such a description.), but she'd never expected her employees to work overtime, most definitely not regularly.

Elizabeth had meant to go to her car and head home, but then her gaze fell upon the café where Claudia had purchased the salad. Since she once more didn't feel like cooking—which also annoyed her as she ordinarily loved to cook, but preparing food for just herself seemed... useless—she entered the establishment and perused their selection.

She settled on a pasta salad and picked up the same tartlet she'd seen Claudia carry the other day. Elizabeth couldn't say what made her grab the pastry at the last moment, but she did. Then she frowned at it, as if the innocuous construct of flour, eggs, butter, and cherries was at fault for Elizabeth acting out of character.

Instead of heading for her car, she left the café and strode toward their office, and much like Claudia had done the previous week, she placed the pastry on her PA's desk and wrote Claudia a text after she'd reached her car. She groaned when upon coming home, Claudia had replied with several emojis: one with heart-eyes, one who had its eyes closed and licked its lips, and a set of folded hands. She'd read somewhere that this symbol referenced a high five, but she'd stick with a 'thank you' for this current purpose.

Before she could overthink it, she sent Claudia a quick 'you're welcome' note and headed inside. Raji stormed at her and meowed pitifully. Her poor baby. She'd been neglecting him with being gone all day. But these walls still haunted her, especially their bedroom. *Her* bedroom—much like it had been before Tom had moved in. Still, Elizabeth had sought refuge in one of her guest bedrooms while she waited to get over the suffocating feeling that befell her when she entered the main bedroom.

Elizabeth's mind often vacillated with what worry should preoccupy her, and currently, either Tom or, much to her consternation, Claudia were chosen for the lead role of this unwanted calling. She refused to think about Tom at all, so she shoved that to the side, and while thinking about Claudia had its own challenges, it still seemed preferable.

She kept returning to their last conversations, and sometimes, she'd recall Claudia's warm gaze, her deep brown eyes that, depending on the lighting almost seemed black, and so often shone with sincerity. Elizabeth wondered when she'd last been around someone so genuine, and a part of her felt drawn to this earnest quality, yet that seemed like a terrible idea. She supposed she had the tendency to assume that the outward persona people presented never denoted a genuine reflection of their personality.

Then again, perhaps that notion came from having to persuade people of wealth and influence to join or help her charity in some ways. She always played a role there, and so did everyone else she'd interacted with in that regard. These few moments with Claudia so far had been different, and Elizabeth found herself confounded by them, and by how much they remained in her head.

There were moments in her daily routine, especially when she came home to her big, empty house, when she felt an ache in her chest. She missed the life Tom and she had built together, and the quiet togetherness they had enjoyed. But she had also started to wonder if she'd been more attached to their lives than Tom had been. For how else could he have stomached taking such a risk? He must have known she'd leave him if she were to find out. Perhaps he'd counted on that never happening.

She also realized that the divorce and her entire current predicament could have been worse, and for the first time Elizabeth felt grateful for not having any children with Tom, as otherwise, this would have turned into a veritable nightmare. Not that divorces with children were uncommon, but it wasn't... Elizabeth hated the very idea of it.

Last night, she had the odd thought that perhaps she also felt drawn to Claudia because the other woman could relate to Elizabeth and this entire drama in a way no one else did. Their interactions, despite everything, had an unexpected ease to them, one she'd almost had to force herself to shut down. There was even a small part of Elizabeth that wanted them back, that wanted to see where this would go. Then she'd reprimand herself, wondering what shape of insanity kept drawing her back to Claudia.

Elizabeth could charm anyone at any point, but she rarely ever was charmed *herself*, yet she had been by Claudia, by her easy-going, straightforward, and open demeanor, by the lack of affectation and the seeming purity of her motives. She hadn't seemed to want anything from Elizabeth, outside of her job back, and she supposed that might lure her toward Claudia more than anything else.

This week, she'd rejected several calls from Tom and had walked away when he'd shown up at her office. The nerve of him! At least he knew better than to come to her house. He'd hired a moving company who'd stopped by to pick up the boxes of his belongings Elizabeth had packed, as she hadn't wanted him back inside her house.

Tom had also sent her two handwritten letters, begging her to reconsider the divorce, to try counseling, and to not give up on them—again, who'd given up on whom here? He swore he loved her. She believed him. Elizabeth had no doubt Tom loved her and wanted to be with her, but he also wanted (and had taken) the freedom to carry on an affair on the side.

Some people were fine with such an arrangement. She supposed an open relationship would have taken care of this, too, but while that might work for some, it held no appeal for her. Elizabeth didn't share. They'd made a commitment to only be with each other. She'd been prepared to honor that, and he hadn't. In the end, his love meant nothing, at least nothing relating to a shared future.

There had been a moment of weakness when she'd read Tom's letters. Her heart had ached, and her chest had filled with longing—not so much for Tom, but for what they'd shared. A tiny part of her had been tempted to meet with a counselor and see if they could salvage their relationship. She'd worried she had given up too quickly and wondered if there could have been some type of compromise. So, when this feeling had risen, she'd sat down and envisioned it.

Elizabeth pictured how this would play out—weekly sessions with 'homework' assignments to rebuild trust, making lists of grievances to address, promises to do better, to listen more, to be more present. Then they would sit together at home and try to continue their routines, while every time she looked at him she'd think about what he had done and wondered whether he would do it again if given the opportunity.

With every solo trip for work or with friends, every meeting with friends or colleagues, every phone call and text message, she would grow worried or suspicious. She'd wonder, maybe even envision, what kind of women he'd go for next. She had no desire to sleep with Tom again, and that wouldn't improve the odds of him remaining faithful. Though that thought rankled her too, especially since she knew so many people—including her mother—who would deem it as 'human nature' for a man to look for sex elsewhere if his wife wasn't up for it.

None of these meanderings painted a future she wanted any part of. She didn't want to be suspicious of her partner. She didn't want to doubt him or question his words. Most of all, she didn't want to do these 'trust rebuilding exercises.' What would be the point? If Tom did it once, he'd be capable of doing it a second time. How could she ever trust him again? And to do all this work and still fail? No. She refused.

Thoughts of Tom once more led her back to Claudia, and that was also something she wished she could change. That she could separate this association as she felt she was doing Claudia an injustice by that, as Tom had betrayed them both.

There were even moments where Elizabeth felt almost grateful that Claudia had sought her out and told her about Tom. Yet that feeling also warred with a petulant resentment borne of an aspect of her that she didn't particularly like as it craved ignorance—that she'd never found out about Tom cheating on her. Change could be challenging.

She contemplated living such a lie if she'd never known, and that notion didn't appeal to her either. Maybe she wished Tom hadn't cheated, but that option had never been on the table. She supposed people could decide to put up with a lie, but to be involved unwittingly and unknowingly seemed harrowing—a fate that made her shudder. Her dissonant and conflicting feelings on the subject led to a sense of emotional whiplash. It had to be easier to work through all of this if only she could settle on one thing alone.

meeting in the middle

CLAUDIA HAD REFRAINED FROM telling Sammy about her recent incognito run-ins with Elizabeth. She'd enjoyed their brief interactions, and she feared Sammy, well-intentioned, would once more rain on her parade. Leaving food or bringing coffee was *not* unprofessional. Well, to be fair, Claudia had left more things for Elizabeth than vice versa (though the cherry tartlet had hit the spot), but again, penance. It had nothing to do with Claudia finding Elizabeth intriguing and wishing they could just... She didn't even know. So, she ignored such thoughts.

This week had overall seemed busier, or better, much more tiring. She'd tried to get more sleep, figuring her exhaustion stemmed from not getting enough hours most nights, but even now, after sleeping for almost eight hours, she felt drained.

She didn't understand why she was so tired. If she were still working at *Little Feet*, she'd assume she might be coming down with something given kids' tendency to moonlight as petri dishes for everything gross and infectious. Yet, no one at work had been sick.

On Thursday, she received a phone call from her mother who complained about *teta*, naturally about stuff that also drove Claudia insane when dealing with her mother. God, she hoped if she ever had children, she'd avoid moments where she realized she'd turned into her mother. Then again, if they weren't so close, that wouldn't be an issue, and Claudia couldn't imagine not having such a great relationship with her family, even if they drove her up the wall sometimes.

On Friday evening, she'd returned to her parents as *teta* had asked her to come by since she made Claudia's favorite dessert—figuring that given her granddaughter's sweet tooth, it would be the perfect plan to make sure she gained some weight. While Claudia would return on Sunday for lunch, there was no way she'd resist an opportunity to eat *meghli*, as she could only enjoy it rarely.

Afterwards, and after fielding many suggestions about her dating life—she didn't even want to *think* about dating for a long while—she left the house to return home. Before she could enter her car, though, a familiar voice called her name.

"Claudia! Hello."

She turned and saw Jane Grant cross the street.

"I haven't seen you in a while," Jane said.

"Oh, hi. How are you?"

"Good, good. Just out running an errand. How have you been?"

"Same old," Claudia said.

"Good. Tell your mom that I've finished a new batch of my quince jelly and she can pick it up any time."

Claudia smiled. "Will do."

"Take care of yourself," Jane said, patting Claudia's arm.

"You, too." Claudia watched Jane cross the street and head back to her home. She sighed.

Her mother had told Claudia about Jane's upcoming surgery, though she didn't know any additional details. Some information didn't lend itself to gossip, and her mother wouldn't share more than the basics.

In some ways, Jane reminded her of her own mother (in a less high-strung way), but she supposed that also hailed back to basically growing up in her house. Jane's husband, Lars, had passed away from a heart attack two years ago, and Claudia wondered if Jane would get remarried. She was only fifty-six, but for some people, life seemed over once you hit fifty. Would Elizabeth be like that? She was a decade younger, and she didn't appear to be the type to stay alone. Elizabeth seemed much more dynamic, full of energy, really. Claudia wondered how she was doing and if Tom would keep trying to change her mind. She shouldn't still be stuck on all this, especially since it wasn't her concern, but she couldn't help it, and her heart sank at the thought of them reuniting.

She didn't like the idea of Elizabeth taking him back. Just from their few interactions and all she'd learned about Elizabeth, Claudia felt she deserved better. And how could you trust a person again after they betrayed you? Wouldn't you always wait for the next treachery? Just sitting there, biding your time. Claudia would hate for Elizabeth to live such a life. But again, she reminded herself that this wasn't up to her. If only her mind would listen to her and act accordingly.

She'd been elated when she could support one of their patrons through filing a restraining order against her unstable ex-boyfriend. By now, she'd moved in with a friend and was looking for a new job. She'd even considered moving to another state, but she said she didn't wish to run, and that her life was here. Claudia had a follow-up appointment with her next week, and she hoped the situation had continued to improve.

On Monday, she once more spied the light on late in Elizabeth's office. Against her better judgment, she ended up knocking on her door.

"Hi," she greeted Elizabeth, who gazed at her with an almost resigned smile.

"Is it time for another drive-by coffee?"

"Or a salad?" Claudia stuffed her hands into her pants pockets. "I was just heading out to see what they have. I'm feeling peckish, and I wondered if you want something, too."

Elizabeth held her gaze. "The salad was acceptable."

Claudia stifled a snort. High praise indeed. "Enough to eat it again?"

"I suppose."

"Any beverage wishes?"

"No. I'm good. Thank you."

Claudia nodded. "I'll be right back."

When she returned fifteen minutes later with a bag full of food and a berry lemonade for herself, she knocked with her elbow and pushed the door open. Good thing she hadn't fully closed it before.

"You seem more than peckish," sounded Elizabeth's greeting.

"I felt tempted and as it turns out, I couldn't resist. They had too many choices, so I got a grilled cheese sandwich, an egg salad, and a chocolate chip muffin." Claudia frowned. "I should have gotten the PB&J sandwich instead."

"Peanut butter and jelly with an egg salad?" Elizabeth grimaced.

"Don't knock it till you try it."

"I believe I prefer to knock it."

Claudia chuckled. "Here's your Cobb salad." She lifted the container out of the bag and brought it to Elizabeth, along with the utensils. "Enjoy." She turned and grabbed her bag, ready to return to her office, when Elizabeth's voice stopped her.

"You might as well stay here and eat." The suggestion sounded bored, like an impulse for which the resulting answer would be of no consequence.

When Claudia shifted and caught Elizabeth's gaze, though, she noted a fissure of nerves that belied her guarded expression.

Elizabeth rolled her fountain pen between her fingers, and glanced away quickly.

"Are you sure this isn't breaking any professional boundaries?" Claudia asked.

Elizabeth narrowed her eyes. "It's not like you've been keen on observing them in the first place."

Claudia ducked her head. She had a point. "I told you, consider it a form of—"

"Penance, yes. And I told *you* I don't want that."

"You don't want me to do that or to direct it at you?"

Elizabeth flipped open the lid of her salad and tore into the dressing pouch. "Are you going to stay or return to your office?"

"I'm staying." Claudia brought her bag and drink to the coffee table and sat on the couch.

"Don't stain my couch," Elizabeth said.

"Wouldn't dream of it." Claudia bit into her sandwich.

When they were done eating, Claudia rose and put the trash away, shuffling on her feet, torn between saying something—anything—and just heading back to her office to finish up and go home. She was tired enough for the latter, but—

"Out with it," Elizabeth said. "If you think any harder, steam will leak out of your ears and set off the fire alarm, and the resulting mess would give Tilda a headache.

"We wouldn't want that." Claudia prevented herself from rocking back and forth on her heels.

"So?"

Claudia held Elizabeth's gaze, then straightened. "Could we keep doing this?"

"Eating? I fear that's a requirement if we wish to continue living."

Claudia smiled. "No, and... Look, if this is your way of preventing me from saying more, that's fine, and I can just leave, and—"

"Continue."

"I know you said we should try to be professional, and—"

"I don't recall saying 'try,' however, you've clearly understood the directive as a suggestion that you then failed at."

Claudia pouted. "I thought you asked me to talk?"

"Go ahead."

Claudia couldn't tell if Elizabeth was suppressing a smile or a grimace. She'd go with the former. "I don't want to talk about the past anymore, about the... issue of contention between us."

Elizabeth raised one eyebrow but refrained from interrupting Claudia again.

"That said, I find it unfair that an incident neither of us instigated should doom our chances to get to know each other."

"It's a pretty big *incident* to overcome."

"Yes, but perhaps that's the case because we're stuck in the past."

Elizabeth tilted her head. "And how do you propose to solve that?"

"I get the idea of us interacting only for work and keeping everything else shoved and locked into neat little packages is supposed to... destroy this association of what happened. I'm sure it's harder on you, especially, since this has cost you a lot more."

Elizabeth's gaze turned flinty.

"But remember when we first chatted via text, before we recognized who the other was, and then our little coffee meeting here? I had fun. I... I think I like you."

"I'm still your boss."

"And you can't be friendly with an employee?"

"It has never happened."

"What about Tilda?" Claudia asked.

Elizabeth only stared at her.

"Right. OK, but... I just don't see why we can't figure out if we could be... friendly. You seemed to enjoy our interactions, too."

"So, how would that work?"

Claudia shrugged. "We'd get to know each other, form a new association. A new connection. Wouldn't that be more effective than what we've been trying? Because let me tell you, I still want to get to know you."

Elizabeth's eyes widened.

an unnerving realization

Elizabeth didn't know what to say. Claudia unnerved her, and not just for the obvious reasons. She didn't hate her, and any resentment she may have felt had drained away. She should be thankful for that, as any other reality would make their work situation untenable. In the end, Tom had lied to them both, and Claudia had right away reached out to her once she'd found out he was married. That had to count for something.

And now this.

She wanted to get to know Elizabeth. The word 'why' immediately jumped to the tip of her tongue, and she once more wondered what was in it for Claudia. Yet, when she looked at her guileless, open face, she knew it was just this. A sincere interest in getting to know Elizabeth.

She supposed it must also be hard for Claudia to integrate this new reality, knowing she'd been involved in her boss's marriage falling apart. Could Elizabeth do this? And had Claudia's eyes always shone this softly? Always seemed so warm?

"How would we go about this? Remember, I'm your boss."

"We're here now, right? We shared a meal. In fact, we've been sharing meals, or treats, even if we didn't eat together before. How about we make this a regular event?"

"Meeting after work and eating in my office?"

"Why not?"

"Don't you have anything better to do?" Surely Claudia didn't wish to spend her free time stuck in the office with Elizabeth.

"Not really. I mean, I'm not suggesting we spend hours here, or do this every day. Maybe when we're both working late, anyway."

"So we can be in the office even longer?" Elizabeth threw Claudia an incredulous stare.

"On those days, our evenings are shot anyway, right?"

"I suppose that's one way of looking at it."

"We could order food. According to my grandma, I'm thin enough as it is, and I don't need to lose any more weight. I don't even want to contemplate what she'd have to say to snacks or sandwiches for dinner."

"She has a point."

Claudia groaned. "Not you, too!"

"Look at it that way, right now, you'll still get away with eating a lot while remaining relatively sedentary and not putting on a lot of weight, if any. Wait until you're my age. You'll start absorbing calories by *looking* at food."

Claudia laughed, and in that moment, Elizabeth almost smiled. Perhaps spending more time with Claudia, whose sunny disposition seemed to light up any room, would do her some good. After all, she had enough time now.

"So, are we on?"

"You really want to sit here with me after long workdays and eat takeout food?"

"Yes."

"All right." Heaven help her. What was she doing?

The next morning, Tilda strolled into her office and seemed... smug.

"It turned out to be such a fortunate circumstance that I forgot to send those documents to HR."

Elizabeth hummed.

"Claudia has been quite efficient at her job."

"She's all right," Elizabeth said while continuing her work, unsure if she wanted to hear Tilda's point.

"You don't often change your mind about something," Tilda said.

Elizabeth stopped working and glanced at Tilda. This statement rankled, reminding her too much of her mother. "I'm not unwilling to change."

Tilda laughed. "Goodness, no. Let's put it this way: you're rarely wrong in your assessments at work."

Elizabeth shifted in her seat. She supposed that correction was acceptable.

"I'm still surprised you'd let her go, but at least you came to your senses and rectified that error. She's a breath of fresh air in the office, especially after Martin." Tilda pursed her lips.

Tilda and Martin hadn't gotten along, and that was putting it mildly. Elizabeth could never figure out what had happened between them, and neither had ever outright complained about the other, so she had assumed it had been just a random disconnect.

"Well, Claudia shapes up nicely," Elizabeth tried to remain neutral. Had Tilda noticed anything she'd missed? She couldn't know about their recent agreement, and it didn't concern her, anyway.

"Yes, she does. You've been much more... present these days."

Elizabeth frowned. "I hadn't realized you found my work lacking."

"That's not at all what I said. Are you all right?"

"Yes, of course."

Tilda nodded, then seemed to drop that line of inquiry. "I know things are currently not that easy for you."

Elizabeth left hand fell into her lap as she balled it into a fist.

"I just wanted to say that I'm here to help, if you need it, and that I'm glad you rehired Claudia. I have a good feeling about her."

"Thank you," Elizabeth pressed out, still at a loss over this entire conversation.

"Of course. Well, I'll return to my office. The work won't finish itself." She rose and, without another word, left Elizabeth's office.

She stared after Tilda for a while, trying to understand what had happened. How did Tilda know about Tom and the divorce? And why was she so taken by Claudia? Not that Elizabeth could fault her, but still...

The rest of the week went by in a blur. She had to deal with lawyers, sent by Tom who'd apparently given up hopes Elizabeth would reunite, and now argued that their prenup was unenforceable because Elizabeth had tricked him into signing it. She'd choked on her water when she'd read that. She expected little from Tom, but this was a new low.

She'd been in communication with her lawyers and instructed them to handle this because if she became too involved in it, she'd book a permanent stay in migraine land, and consequently, might be liable to commit murder.

Things at *Helping Hands* ran fine, for the most part. She'd not seen much of Claudia, who'd headed home early each day this week. At first, Elizabeth wondered if she'd changed her mind about 'transforming their association'—Elizabeth still rolled her eyes at that one—but then she'd noticed the tired smiles and rings under Claudia's eyes when she passed her in the hallway, still offering that same, goofy wave. Elizabeth shouldn't find her this endearing.

She had tried (in vain) to keep the veneer of professionalism between them, despite Claudia's thoughtful efforts to topple that barrier. In fact, Elizabeth wasn't sure Claudia had even realized what she'd been doing, as in, she knew that this hadn't been a calculated plan to go against Elizabeth's directions from when she'd re-hired her. In the young woman's mind, she likely thought she'd been following this request to the letter.

When Claudia had suggested to form a new connection and to spend more time together, she'd wanted to shoot it down. At least, that had been her first impulse. But Claudia's eyes had contained such a hopeful glint, she didn't have the heart to disappoint her—another thing she didn't want to further investigate and chose to blame on Claudia's puppy dog eyes instead.

Her weekend started pleasant. She spent time with Raji, had a phone call with Kat in which her friend told her all about the newest blow-up with her co-star, then she exercised (running this time, which she hated but sometimes felt she needed to do more of), and ordered some food. She planned to finish a few contracts with new sponsors the next day and went to bed after indulging in a glass of red wine.

Sunday shaped up differently than intended (much like her entire life as of late). Elizabeth woke up at five in the morning and rushed to the bathroom to throw up. Her head seemed to have decided to host a party for a group of revved up sledgehammers intent on tearing down an entire skyscraper. Sweat poured down her back while her face and hands grew clammy, too.

God, she hated migraines, though she supposed no one liked them. Whenever she'd suffered one with Tom at home, he'd leave her be, darken the rooms and avoid making any noise. When Elizabeth schlepped herself back to the bed, out of breath, soaked in sweat—a trembling mass of misery—she realized that he'd never offered any comfort. Tom just stayed out of her way and did nothing to aggravate her situation, but now that she lay there, she realized nothing much was different with him gone. Dark, silent, and alone.

She'd once told him she couldn't interact when she had a migraine—even her own voice grated, and she'd asked for silence. But that hadn't meant that she'd have not appreciated his still company next to her in bed. She wouldn't have expected him to stay for hours upon hours, but he'd never showed up at all, and Elizabeth had just accepted this because it must have been what he wanted, or he'd have behaved differently.

Raji jumped on her bed, but instead of cuddling against her like he usually did, he stayed at the foot end of the bed and curled up, gazing at Elizabeth intently.

She smiled weakly. Elizabeth supposed she wasn't all alone after all.

mounting bridges

In the end, Claudia caved, unable to stop herself from calling Sammy and telling her about this new development with Elizabeth.

"You sound so excited about this prospect of getting to know her," Sammy said.

"I am. I told you I liked her from the start."

"You mean the bit of texting where she didn't know it was you."

"What's wrong with me?"

"Don't look at me like that. There's obviously nothing wrong with you."

Somewhat placated, Claudia grumbled, "Good. Is this all still because she's my—"

"She's your boss."

"I'm quite aware, but so far, we seem to be getting along."

Sammy sighed, her gaze finding the ceiling. "You can't be friends with your boss."

Claudia held back a laugh upon seeing Sammy's serious, pained expression. "Could this... attitude be a case of projection? Do you maybe have issues with another bill dying in committee or, worse, being vetoed?"

"Don't get me started. I'm still pissed she did that with the last bill we worked so hard on. But no, that's not the point."

Claudia rolled her eyes. "That's entirely your own fault. You went into politics in the state where your old mentor runs the show. In the end, what does that have to do with me getting to know Elizabeth?"

"Miriam isn't my mentor now, is she? She used to be my boss, and she still kinda is."

"Again, whose fault is that? You aren't innocent in your relationship falling apart."

Sammy's eyes widened. "Wow, whose side are you on?"

"Yours, Sammy. Always and forever. You know that, but it's the truth."

"That's true for me, too. I'm only looking out for you."

"I still don't see the connection. Despite everything, Elizabeth and I don't have your fraught history."

"I'd say yours is complicated enough. Either way, it's always a terrible idea to become too close to your boss. The power imbalance doesn't go away because you're friends. It was easier when you guys just tried to be professional."

"I'm not... It's just gonna be coffee and takeout."

"That's how it starts. You already sound smitten."

Claudia flushed. "I'm *not* smitten! That I like her doesn't mean more than that."

"Right now, sure. But what about down the road if you keep hanging out and get to know her? You already think she's hot."

Claudia frowned. "When did I say that?"

"I know you, and I'm fluent in 'Claudia's signs of infatuation.'"

She narrowed her eyes. "Once more, projection. Not every relationship like that is filled with sexual tension."

"What did I ever say to—"

"Oh, please." Claudia waved her off. "You realize you could just talk to Miriam? Call for a truce."

Sammy scoffed. "Please. As if. She'll eat me for breakfast at the mere suggestion."

"That would be one way to solve your issues. I can't believe you guys are still hung up over that little spat," Claudia said.

"You're not funny. It was a *major* conflict that changed everything. I can't just go there and talk to her. We're beyond that."

"I'm hilarious, more so when I'm not tired. Besides, you're never beyond talking."

"Keep telling yourself that. As for the rest, if you're right, then why do wars happen?" Sammy asked.

"Well, I can't account for whatever groups of people do, or nations, really. Worse, crazy politicians. Though are they any other kind?"

"Hey!"

Claudia grinned. "It's sweet of you to worry about me. I appreciate it, but I'm not concerned. We'll just create a... friendly association so that Tom is no longer so heavy between us. It'll be good for both of us."

"Famous last words."

Claudia frowned. "I don't think that's how they go."

"Oh, whatever. You're old enough to make your own mistakes."

"Sammy?"

"Yes?"

"I love you, dearly, but oh my God, talk to Miriam."

Sammy laughed, but it sounded hollow, resigned. "I sometimes wish I could have a smidgen of your optimism and hope."

"You fake it well enough in public. Maybe try to internalize some of that."

Sammy glared at her. "Again, you're not funny."

"Yes, yes."

"Anyway. I gotta go. Talk later."

"Will do."

"And Claud?"

"Hmm?'

"I love you, too."

Claudia smiled, waved at Sammy, and hung up.

The next time they both worked late again happened on Friday of the following week. She'd taken to check for light or activity in Elizabeth's office when she left late, which had only happened this Wednesday, since she'd been too tired before. Tonight, Elizabeth's light shone, and the door stood open. Drawing closer, Claudia saw Elizabeth sitting at her desk, typing on her keyboard.

Claudia hesitated for a moment. That Elizabeth was still here and actively working meant she'd interrupt her, and then she'd have more work left next week. Claudia didn't want to cause that. She worried her lower lip, contemplating her options, when Elizabeth's voice rang out.

"Are you planning on standing there all night, or did you change your mind about our little agreement?" She never even raised her head to look at Claudia, who still stood shrouded in shadows in the hallway.

She shook her head, then strode inside. "No. I was only worried about keeping you from work."

"I should be done in five minutes. How about you check who still delivers at this time? I'm actually hungry."

"Oh, of course." Claudia dropped her bag on the floor next to the couch and sat down, scrolling through her phone.

Silence fell over the room, aside from the clacking of Elizabeth's fingers flying over her keyboard.

Claudia looked up when Elizabeth stopped. "So there's Italian, Chinese, and Mexican. There are other options, but these are the closest."

"Any preference?"

"Italian. I'm in the mood for pizza."

"All right. Text me their menu."

Claudia nodded and busied herself with sending the text. "Right. You got it."

"Thank you."

After placing the order, Elizabeth rose and strode toward the spaceship masquerading as a coffee machine. "Same as the first time?"

"Yes, please."

Elizabeth set to make their coffees. "The next one will be on you."

"OK." Claudia didn't like this idea at all. Perhaps she could pick them up at the café across the street and come up with an excuse.

"I can see the terror in your eyes right now. Do you think you'll need further instructions?" Elizabeth drawled.

Claudia felt heat crawl up her neck as she shook her head. That voice and that subtle accent should be illegal.

"How has your week been?" Elizabeth asked, turning and stepping toward the couch with the two coffee mugs in her hands.

Claudia opened her mouth to reply but then started and fell mute as she took in Elizabeth for the first time. She wore a black pantsuit with a tight, pinstripe buttoned vest, a white blouse, and dark slacks. Her brown hair was once more coiffed in a tight bun, and her blue eyes had a more serious glint than the situation demanded.

"Are you all right?" Elizabeth placed the cups on the coasters on the coffee table.

"Uh, yes. Sorry. Lost in my head there for a second," Claudia rushed out.

"Forgive the extra formal attire. I had a meeting with a couple of important sponsors today to talk about the Christmas dinner."

"Oh, what's that about?"

"One of our annual charity events to drum up more support for *Helping Hands*. It's a dinner with celebrities in attendance. They donate various items and there's a raffle that people who buy plates to attend can win. It's pretty popular, and we'll have some exciting guests that should draw in more of those who have too much money and want to feel good by donating to the unfortunate masses while also schmoozing with celebrities as their reward."

"Do your sponsors know you talk like that?"

"Did I lie?"

"No, but I'm sure that's not something they'd want to hear."

"Well, I'm not talking to them right now." Elizabeth raised one eyebrow.

"Fair enough."

"I don't look down on them. A lot of the people who invest in *Helping Hands* worked hard for their fortune, though obviously, some are trust fund babies. Still, they're supporting a worthy cause, and I'm not just saying that because I head the charity. So, I am thankful for their backing."

"I wasn't criticizing you."

"I didn't take it as such, just an observation that I'm returning with one of my own."

"Good."

A moment later, Elizabeth's phone rang, and their food arrived. While Elizabeth dealt with the driver, Claudia remembered Sammy's words about the gulf that separated her and Elizabeth, and somehow, the words seemed especially apt tonight. She could feel this power differential, their difference in age, status, and everything, really. It stood out, and she wondered if this came from her talk with Sammy or if she saw things clearer tonight. Would this doom their attempt to get to know each other?

It shouldn't, though. You often learned more from people who were different. Claudia could only hope that Elizabeth wouldn't conclude that the divide between them spanned too wide to mount a bridge, or better, that doing so wouldn't be worth the effort.

expanding horizons

"Is this yours?" Claudia closed her pizza box, wiped her hands on a napkin, and pointed at a book on the table.

"Yes."

"May I?"

"Sure."

Claudia picked up the novel. "*Bury your Dead*. Hmm, I suppose that's generally good advice." She flipped it around and read the back. "Number six. How many are there in this series?"

"Sixteen or seventeen, I believe," Elizabeth said.

"Wow. That's a lot. I often get too intimidated to even pick up the first book in a series if there are more than four or five volumes."

"Understandable, but to me there's nothing like finding a series you love and then discovering that it comprises so many parts."

"You didn't know going in?"

Elizabeth shook her head. "I stumbled on the first one. I checked out the author afterward to see if she's written anything else. That's when I realized it's a series."

"Huh. I might research my reads too much. So, do you generally read crime or mystery fiction?"

"Most of my books fall into that genre, but I'll read anything if it sounds interesting enough. What about you?"

"I prefer true crime stories, and I've read a lot of those. For fiction... I don't know. I like fantasy."

Elizabeth shuddered.

Claudia laughed. "What?"

"How can you like true crime? It's horrifying!"

"It's fascinating."

"We'll have to agree to disagree here," Elizabeth said.

"How about we see how the other side lives?"

"Excuse me?"

"I'll read the first of the series, and you watch a few episodes of "See No Evil." That's my favorite true crime show."

"Why would we do that?" This woman must have lost her mind.

Claudia shrugged. "Why not? Consider it an extension of your horizons."

Elizabeth met Claudia's gaze. "And you believe they're in need of such an expansion?"

"Doesn't everyone's? How can it be wrong to learn more or to be exposed to new and different things? The same old gets boring."

"Indeed."

"Are you the type of person who brings books with them everywhere they go?" Claudia asked.

"Perhaps."

"What would you do if you ended up somewhere without your book, yet you'd have to wait and there's nothing else to distract you?"

Elizabeth stirred her cup. "I still have a phone."

"So you'd mindlessly surf the net or get lost on social media?"

Elizabeth suppressed a small smile. "You're mistaking me for someone from your generation, I'm afraid. Besides, there are reading apps, too."

Claudia pouted.

Elizabeth's gaze dropped to her lips before she straightened in her seat.

"You're not too old for any of that."

"No, but I'm still not in the habit of partaking in social media outside of *Helping Hands*, and even there I have other people in charge. Again, I'm never without something to read, even if I were to forget my book at home."

Claudia chuckled. “Naturally. So even without your book, you still have books to read.” She frowned. “That sentence makes little sense, but you know what I mean.”

“Yes. I love physical copies of books. To hold one in my hands and leaf through the pages. Still, eBooks are convenient, and how else can you carry around thousands of books wherever you go?”

Claudia frowned. “Why would I want to do that?”

“Why *wouldn’t* you, is the better question. Reading is comforting. It allows you to escape reality and submerge yourself in an easier, better world. It’s solace.”

“You read as escapism?”

Elizabeth held Claudia’s curious gaze, once more taken aback by how open she was. However, this conversation was steering into much deeper waters, and she hadn’t decided yet if she dared to tread there. “Isn’t most of life a form of escapism?”

Claudia’s eyes softened, almost like she’d noted and accepted what Elizabeth was doing here.

“Yeah. That’s true.”

One thing Elizabeth appreciated about Claudia was that so far she hadn't seen a hint of pity in her eyes, and she offered no platitudes of ‘time heals all wounds’ (It didn't.), or ‘he wasn't worth it’ (What did *that* say about her, since she had loved and married him?), or worse, ‘there are plenty of other fish in the sea’ (because rebound was fun for everyone). No, Claudia waited and seemed to follow Elizabeth’s lead in changing the topic.

Elizabeth had a busy week ahead of her, including a meeting with new potential benefactors who might participate in the December fundraiser for *Helping Hands*. To her consternation, she found herself looking forward to her little downtime moments with Claudia, which seemed like the ideal distraction from the stresses of her life.

How curious.

She should tell Kat that her master plan had failed, and that there was no way to keep Claudia at a professional distance. Lord knew she'd tried. Although, to be honest, a part of her hadn't wanted to succeed. Claudia and her beguiling openness intrigued her.

She received a text message on Saturday evening where Claudia apologized for potentially disturbing her, but that she wanted Elizabeth to know she'd read the first one hundred pages of the first *Inspector Gamache* novel, and she liked it so far.

Elizabeth felt touched. They sent a few more messages back and forth. She didn't tell Claudia that she'd started the first episode of "See No Evil," but struggled to continue. You could tell right away by the pain in the expressions of the young woman's parents that this would end terribly. She supposed it was also on par with the show itself.

Instead of continuing the episode, she'd plucked the name of the woman into a search engine and learned of her fate that way. She'd sighed, glad she'd stopped the show ten minutes in. She didn't understand the appeal of 'true crime-anything,' and she also felt this didn't fit Claudia at all. Then again, she didn't really know her. But they were set to change that, and at the thought, a long-forgotten excitement slithered through Elizabeth.

When she returned home on Tuesday, her mother called, immediately pushing her mood into a downward spiral. God, she was too old to still be this affected by her mother. With a sigh, Elizabeth answered the call.

"Hello, mother."

"Hello, Lizzie."

Elizabeth clenched her jaw. Her mother knew she hated that nickname.

"Tom has called me."

Elizabeth closed her eyes.

"When were you going to tell me that your marriage is over, or did you decide your own *mother* doesn't need to know that her only child is once more all *alone*?

"I was going to tell you, but—"

"You were afraid I'd say 'I told you so'?"

"Of course not, Mother."

"There'd have been no need to do that, as we knew from the start how this would play out."

Elizabeth bit her lower lip. Was that true? Had their relationship been doomed from the beginning?"

"There's just no way an older woman keeps a younger man. At least not for more than a few years."

"Perhaps. Either way, it's done."

"When will you return to England?"

Elizabeth refrained from groaning. Heading home seemed less appealing now than ever before. "Next year."

"That covers twelve months. Can you be more specific?"

Elizabeth pinched the bridge of her nose. "Summer?"

"That long! Your father and I aren't getting any younger," Mary sniffed.

"I see what I can do. It depends on what's going on at work."

Mary sighed. "How about I'll come visit you?"

Elizabeth's eyes widened, and she dropped onto the couch. *Please don't.* "Oh?"

"Yes. I think it's about time. I'll check with my travel agent and send you the itinerary. You'll pick me up at the airport."

"Of course." Elizabeth felt as if her heart attempted to escape through her throat. Her mother's visit was the last thing she needed.

"Good, good. Now, don't get lost in your head, dear. You're never going to fix what's broken that way."

"Nothing is broken, Mother."

"It's never a good idea to lie to yourself, Lizzie. Either way, I have to go. Expect an email from me within the next couple of days. Bye."

"OK. Bye." Elizabeth hung up. It took all her strength not to throw her phone against the wall. She couldn't believe she'd have to deal with her mother in her sanctuary.

Her phone beeped. Elizabeth's first impulse was to ignore it, fearing another message from her mother, but then again... She unlocked it, and at the sight of Claudia's name and a guess on who committed the murder in the *Inspector Gamache* novel, tears rushed to her eyes, and a sob spilled from her throat. What was she even doing, and how was she supposed to get through this?

Elizabeth took a deep breath, calmed her breathing, and then grabbed a tissue and wiped her eyes. Her life was fine, and things were moving upward again. She'd regained her footing, and overall, her life was good. She'd been on her path to being OK again, and she refused to let her mother topple her progress. Elizabeth refused to wallow in self-pity.

She opened her text thread with Claudia.

Do you really want me to tell you?

Of course not!!!

Elizabeth blinked furiously.

But then why would you tell me your guess?

So you can be impressed with my deductive skills.

Elizabeth snorted.

Don't expect me to call you Sherlock anytime soon.

So I'm wrong, huh?

What makes you say that?

Your comment...

Claudia may have left out the "Duh!" in writing, but Elizabeth still heard it.

Perhaps I'm misleading you?

Nah.

Elizabeth felt her curiosity rise.

How's that?

You're too kind for that.
And you don't mess with people.

Elizabeth swallowed hard as tears once more shot into her eyes.

You say that with such assurance.

Well, yeah. I'm a good judge of character.

Though Sammy always says
I like everyone. But that's not
true.

Personally, Elizabeth thought Sammy was spot on. Aside from seeming way too trusting, Claudia appeared to just love people. She wondered how she'd react to meeting her mother. "Good God," Elizabeth croaked.

Your Sammy might be on to something.

Hey! I resent that.

Elizabeth chuckled.

OK, name someone you don't like.

Dots appeared. Then paused. Once more they flickered across the screen, only to halt again.

Elizabeth chuckled.

Pol Pot

Elizabeth frowned. "What?"

You mean the former dictator of Cambodia?

Yes.

You weren't even born when he died!

A couple of minutes ticked by.

I was four!!

Elizabeth quickly typed his name into a search engine, groaning at the results. He had died in 1998. Lord, she was twenty-two, just coming to the United States after her grandmother's passing.

I'm not sure that helps
your argument.

Whatever. I'm an old soul.

Elizabeth laughed.

The most surprising thing of all, this brief exchange had done more to relax the dull throbbing in her head that had started during her phone call with the mother than anything she could have thought of doing. How very peculiar.

intentional savages

Claudia spent the rest of her Friday night reading before heading to the bathroom to get ready for bed. When she crawled into bed, she noticed her phone blinking with a notification. Expecting Sammy, she seized the device to check. She smiled when instead of Sammy, Elizabeth's name popped up. Once she opened the message, her grin only grew when a non-work related message greeted her.

I must confess I hate "See No Evil."

That's fair. True crime really isn't your thing.

It's so depressing. And scary. Fiction is better.

But that's not real.

Yes, that's the point...

Claudia laughed.

I suppose. But it still makes it a bit boring.

I thought you liked the book?

Claudia hurried to type.

I do!

She was about to expand further when Elizabeth's next message appeared.

I'm sorry. We'll have to continue this conversation another time.

I have to go.

OK, sure.

Claudia placed her phone back on the nightstand with a sigh. She hoped Elizabeth was all right. Then she chastised herself for worrying. What was there to worry about, anyway, and it wasn't her place to be concerned about Elizabeth.

They worked late again on the following Monday, and this time, Claudia just strolled through Elizabeth's open office door while knocking.

"Hey." She stuffed her hands into her pants pockets.

"Hello." Elizabeth seemed finished with her work and rose right away, walking toward Claudia. "What do you want to order tonight?"

Claudia shrugged, though she felt pleased that Elizabeth continued to be up for these little meetings. Weird, she'd never looked forward to staying late at work, yet here she hoped for it almost every day.

"No pizza and lava cake again?"

"Hey! That's a classic combo."

"To *you*, perhaps. People with a more... refined palate would disagree."

Claudia pouted.

"So?"

"Why don't you pick? I'm assuming you're one of those people with the sophisticated taste?"

"Naturally," Elizabeth drawled. "I'm in the mood for Mexican."

"Good with me."

They placed their order and after, Claudia dared to make coffee for the first time—the gadget neither exploded, came to life, nor flew away. She placed Elizabeth's mug on the table before sitting in her usual spot on the couch.

"You owe me an explanation," Elizabeth said after sipping her coffee.

Claudia straightened. "I do?" She wondered if she'd done something wrong. Everything had been going well with her patrons, and even Tilda had offered her a small smile this morning. Or perhaps it had been more of a grimace. It seemed Tilda was suffering from a bout of back pain.

Elizabeth nodded, and Claudia relaxed when she noticed the mirth playing in Elizabeth's bright eyes. "Yes, after Raji had so rudely interrupted our last conversation by throwing up all over my freshly laundered clothes."

"Oh, no."

Elizabeth shrugged. "So tell me, why are fictional crime stories inferior to true crime tales? Mind you, I don't agree with that statement."

"Of course not." Claudia suppressed a grin. "I suppose they aren't as enthralling as the real-life stuff. Because they're not, well, real."

"But isn't that what makes the '*real stuff*,' as you call it, so scary? To know what people have done? What they are capable of doing?"

"I suppose if that's your focus."

"Then what is *your* focus?"

"I'm more interested in the psychology behind it. Why do people do what they do?"

"Because they're insane?" Elizabeth said.

"Are they? I mean, yes, there have been killings by the clinically insane, but they're the vast minority, and the rest's a mixture of fear-mongering and self-placating."

"That's quite the statement. Care to elaborate?"

Claudia smiled. Did she ever. She loved this discussion, but sadly, most of her friends and family only groaned when she raised the topic. "OK, so it's much more comforting to believe that people who commit terrible crimes are insane because then you're not only relatively safe since you assume you'll notice someone like that and stay away from them, but also because you no longer have to contemplate the cause or reasoning behind the crime. You won't think about what we could do as a society to prevent such crimes."

"I never thought along those lines."

"But you know, by saying people are insane, you're also further stigmatizing a group that's already an outsider, and so there's no pushback. There's no lobbying arm that's interested in the well-treatment of the clinically insane. Even worse, many people lump all kinds of mental disorders into the mix. Mind you, those people aren't the ones committing these crimes."

"All right, then what *are* the true causes?"

"It depends. But the most interesting thing to me is that people who do such things don't believe that they're doing anything wrong."

"Then why do they cover their tracks?" Elizabeth asked.

"Well, they're aware that what they did is neither socially acceptable nor legal. They don't hide their crimes because they're ashamed or believe they did something wrong, but because they know they'll get arrested. And that means they can no longer do what they want to do. People rarely do things they believe are wrong."

"Hmm, I'm not so sure about that. People cheat, for example. And they know that's wrong."

Claudia exhaled roughly and ducked her head. "I'm sorry."

"You should stop apologizing. It's done. Besides, this wasn't a dig, just the first example that came to mind. I do want us to get on a different footing, and I thought we're heading that way. Don't you agree?"

"I do, and yes, it's understandable that this would be your first thought," Claudia said.

"Good. So, continue."

"With what?"

"What's your counter argument?" Elizabeth asked.

"Oh, well, they assume they'll get away with it, no?"

"For sure, but again, they know it's wrong."

"They know that *society* and their partner think it's wrong, but do they themselves believe that? If so, why do they do it? They seem to believe they have some kind of right to do as they wish. Most regret concerning cheating revolves around getting caught."

"He continued for months," Elizabeth said, her face turning stony.

Claudia hated that expression. She pressed her lips into a thin line to prevent another apology from spilling forth. "Yes."

"Do you think it would have continued? Were you serious about Tom?"

Claudia inhaled deeply. "We had fun. It was... not serious. To be honest, I thought of him more as my rebound guy. I'd come out of a nasty breakup not long before I met him, and he seemed... a good choice. At least that's how I saw it before..."

"Before you knew."

"Yes."

Stillness hung between them, but it was a contemplative silence, not uncomfortable or strained. Claudia still wondered if they'd ever manage to bury the topic of Tom between them.

Elizabeth seemed to grow tired of that discussion as well. "All right, off to greener pastures."

Claudia laughed. "I'm assuming that's your request for a topic change."

"You catch on quickly."

"I'm smart like that."

Elizabeth didn't reply, but Claudia would call her expression almost fond.

"All right, let's see. Do you have any siblings?"

Elizabeth shook her head.

"We have that in common. Do you sometimes wish you had one?"

Elizabeth hummed, her brows furrowing as if she were picturing how life with a sibling would have played out. "Yes, and no. I'd have loved a sibling, older or younger, but I wouldn't wish my parents on anyone else. Now, my nan, yes, but alas..."

Claudia frowned and on impulse, she reached out and squeezed Elizabeth's hand. "I'm sorry. Parents can suck." Her fingers were soft and warm.

Elizabeth chuckled. "Indeed." She held on to Claudia, then drew back.

"But hey, at least there's an ocean between you and them."

Elizabeth groaned. "Yes, but my mother will visit me soon, and that will be... Let's say I'm expecting another migraine attack either during or after her visit."

"Wow. That bad? I'm assuming she stays with you?"

"Yes, my house is big enough to where I couldn't justify her staying at a hotel."

"I'm not sure that would ever happen in our house, family visiting and then staying at a hotel, no matter the space."

"Yes, well, nothing to do either way."

"Do you suffer a lot of migraines?"

"It used to be worse, but I've changed my approach to work and... life, I suppose, in my mid-thirties. Since then, these incidents have reduced greatly, but recent events, well, let's say stress is something that can make them occur more often, and that's sadly been the case."

"Oh, I'm sorry."

"It's not your fault."

Claudia smiled, relieved that Elizabeth saw it this way, that there were no more hard feelings between them. Yet she also knew that in some way, the increase of stress in Elizabeth's life also rested on her. Perhaps she could find a way to lighten her load.

Elizabeth's phone rang. "Excuse me, I've got to take this."

"Of course, go ahead."

Elizabeth pressed answer. "Hi, Shani."

Hearing the lilt of a melodic voice, Claudia tuned out the sound to offer Elizabeth her privacy.

"What time?" Elizabeth asked, tapping her fingers on her leg.

A pause.

"That should work. Thank you, Shani. I'll see you then. You, too." Elizabeth hung up. "That was my friend, Shani. She owns Pat Stewarts Home. I'd called them after my latest migraine attack because I'd decided to redo the main bedroom."

"Oh, OK. That makes sense. I've heard of them, though I doubt they let people with my yearly income into the store."

"It's difficult to get an appointment. I only got on the schedule because I'm friends with the owner," Elizabeth said.

"Money and nepotism, I see how it goes."

Elizabeth laughed. "The way of the world, sadly."

"Hmm. But you're using your power for good."

Elizabeth frowned. "By redecorating my bedroom?"

Claudia laughed. "No, your charity. You're helping people in need, and you're using your money and your connections to do that."

"I don't put any of my money into *Helping Hands* anymore," Elizabeth said.

"That's fantastic because it means your charity is successful. But you did early on, and if the need were to arise, you'd do it again."

Elizabeth's eyes widened. "How can you be sure?"

"I dunno. Just am. You're the type. And I've seen you at work. I've seen what *Helping Hands* does. The way you talk about your charity, all the things you've done and continue to do for almost twenty years, it's—"

"A way to make me feel old."

Claudia chuckled. "No, it's impressive. Truly. You're so committed."

Elizabeth's cheeks turned crimson. "I never saw myself like that."

"Well, you're not an arrogant, self-involved jerk, so obviously."

Elizabeth shook her head. "What you just said? How money and nepotism, along with a good portion of bribery, rule the world. I'd noticed that as a child, though I didn't understand *what* caused all this inequality, all this pain and suffering. It just didn't seem fair that some people have everything, while others are left scratching in the dirt." She closed her eyes.

"Hey, are you all right? Did I say something to upset you?" Claudia's voice rang softly.

She took off her glasses and wiped her eyes. "No, you didn't." She cleared her throat. "I'm fine. It's just a long story."

"Will you tell it to me one day?"

"I just might." Elizabeth offered a small smile that warmed Claudia.

"I'd like that."

stranger things

ELIZABETH HAD MET NO one like Claudia, and while she'd encountered many more people than most due to her work with *Helping Hands*, she'd never faced someone who confounded her the way Claudia did regularly.

She'd come to look forward to these 'meetings,' and they offered a break from her self-imposed isolation at home. She'd experienced grief before, the worst when her grandmother had died, but the emotions that crashed over her now were different. In some way, Elizabeth was mourning the life she had, but more so, the future she'd taken for granted.

Leaving Tom meant giving up on that future, and worse, facing an unknown life ahead at forty-six. Perhaps she was being melodramatic. Life without a partner wasn't entirely new, and in fact, she'd spent more years single than as part of a couple. But she'd been set. Tom was supposed to be it. She was supposed to be done. And now she wasn't, and sometimes that realization threatened to knock her off her feet.

In all this, Claudia remained the unknown, undefinable, and most of all, unpredictable variable. Elizabeth loved to solve things, from puzzles to mysteries to equations. The only concern: she felt that the solution would hit her harder than she'd expect. And Elizabeth did not appreciate surprises. Much less did she enjoy the sensation of coffee gushing down her white blouse and cream-colored pants.

How had that accident happened? She didn't even know. They were chatting and eating when suddenly, Claudia shifted and her elbow jostled Elizabeth, who'd been in the process of drinking her freshly refilled coffee only to pour most of it over herself.

She grimaced at the pain of the burn shooting through her. They jumped off the couch at the same time.

"Oh my God, I'm so sorry," Claudia exclaimed. "Take off your clothes! You're burning."

By that time, Elizabeth had already been tearing off her soiled blouse while rushing to the bathroom, barely registering Claudia's shout of "I'll be right back."

Cursing, Elizabeth stripped down to her underpants in the bathroom, taking off her bra as well since it got hit, too. She ran cold water over a hand towel and used it to cool her stinging skin. Now she wished she'd installed a shower in her private bathroom as she longed to be submerged in ice.

She usually had a second outfit stashed in her office, but that currently rested with the dry cleaner as Amanda and her son Tobin (one of their patrons and her little four-year-old boy) had seen Elizabeth last week, and the boy had smeared sticky, melted residue of Swedish fish all over Elizabeth's pants and shirt. No one had realized the state of his fingers until it had been too late.

Now she had nothing to wear. She supposed she'd have to wait until her clothes dried some or, if not, she'd just have to wear them as they were—preferable to running around naked.

A while later, a knock startled Elizabeth out of her reverie.

She stepped behind the door and cracked it open. "Yes?"

The gap opened wider and one of Claudia's hands emerged, a pharmacy bag slung around her wrist while sweatpants and a hoodie lay on her outstretched palm.

Elizabeth's mouth opened, then closed again. When she didn't react right away, Claudia jostled her arm.

"Take it. I went to the drugstore and got you some petroleum jelly and aloe gel. The clothes are from my car. They're clean."

"Are you in the habit of carrying your wardrobe in your vehicle?" The question came out sharper than Elizabeth intended, and she tried to smile, but feared she'd offered a grimace instead.

"There's a fascinating story behind it that I'll gladly share once you've put on these clothes. You must be freezing. How are the burns? I'm so sorry. I told you I'm clumsy, but usually that means I hurt myself a lot, not others." She wiggled her arm.

"How reassuring," Elizabeth mumbled, then grasped the clothes and bag. "Thank you."

"Of course." Claudia's arm disappeared and Elizabeth shut the door behind her.

"I don't know if your bra fell victim, too, but I didn't have a spare, though mine would be too small for you, anyway."

Elizabeth flushed and ducked her head. Muttering to herself about the best of intentions, loss of control, and her exasperating employee, she slipped into the offered pants.

She trembled, just now realizing she'd indeed been quite cold. Elizabeth hurried to add the aloe cream on her burned skin before putting on the hoodie. The fabric of Claudia's clothes was soft and didn't aggravate her tender skin. Elizabeth gazed into the wall mirror over the sink and her eyes widened at her reflection—disheveled hair and flushed cheeks.

Claudia's clothing seemed to swallow her, making her feel small. Fragile, almost.

She shook her head in continued exasperation and took a deep breath before leaving the bathroom to join Claudia, who'd cleaned up the mess and returned the mugs to their proper place for washing.

Claudia still wore an expression that seemed to make her liable to rush close and inspect Elizabeth's burns. Heat, unrelated to her injuries, inched up Elizabeth's neck.

"Thank you." *You already said that.* At least her mind shared in her vexation. "I could have just put the clothes back on and headed home in a little bit."

"It was the least I could do, and no." Claudia grimaced. "Wearing wet clothes is just... ugh." She seemed to shudder in disgust.

A small chuckle left Elizabeth, which made Claudia break out in a grin before she sobered.

"Are you OK, though? I could take you to the hospital and—"

"No!"

Claudia flinched.

"I'm fine. Again, I appreciate your quick thinking and help, but I don't need to go to the hospital."

"OK."

The silence that overcame them made Elizabeth itch.

"It seems that you owe me another story." She pointed at the maroon-colored Texas A&M Law School hoodie.

"Oh, right. You want to sit down again?" Claudia asked.

"Sure."

They once more settled on the couch. A little closer this time, though Elizabeth could also be imaging that. She'd always been rotten at judging distances.

"Remember that terrible winter storm last February?"

Elizabeth winced. "God, yes. How could anyone forget?"

"Yes, well, anyway. On the day it started, I'd gotten stuck in my car on the interstate. Five miles took seven hours, though, to be fair, we stood still for most of that time."

"Oh, wow."

"It was awful. I was so cold and hungry. I had some water, thankfully, but I also worried it would freeze at some point." She released a wry sigh and rubbed her eyes.

"Are you tired? You look more drained than usual, if I may say so."

"I'm exhausted. Have been for the last few weeks. Don't know why."

"I've heard sleeping helps," Elizabeth quipped.

Claudia glared at her. "Ha ha."

"Go on then. How did the winter storm relate to your car housing your wardrobe?"

"Right. So, after I made it home, I was basically an icicle, and you know things didn't get any better for a while. When everything was said and done, I... prepared. I put a backpack into my car that carries snacks and water. I added several blankets to my trunk, along with a set of clothes."

"You know water isn't supposed to stay in a hot car. At least, water in plastic bottles."

Claudia smiled. "The water is in glass bottles."

"Smart thinking."

"High praise coming from you."

One of Elizabeth's eyebrows rose. "Indeed." She pulled the sleeve of her sweatshirt further up as it had slid over her hand. Elizabeth didn't share clothes with people—not that this was true sharing, but it came close. Kat and she had never had a reason to, and she'd not been close enough to anyone else where she'd have considered it.

She couldn't even tell if Claudia recognized the inherent intimacy of such an offer, or perhaps her generation saw this differently. Though she supposed it could also be a cultural thing. Then again, this wasn't a sharing for the sake of it, but a consequence of a sort of accident.

She'd worn shirts of her boyfriends before, and of Tom's, but even that had been rare and more relegated to their early days as a couple. The act of wearing someone else's clothes, to Elizabeth, seemed akin to allowing them inside your bubble. *Their* clothes were touching *your* skin, keeping you warm, and yes, the clothes were clean, but the other person had worn them before. And the clothes Claudia had given her felt worn and comfortable, to where Elizabeth assumed they were some of Claudia's favorites.

Wearing someone else's clothes also enveloped you in their scent. You didn't want too many people this close or could bear them that near. While Elizabeth smelled detergent, she could also detect a distinct scent she couldn't quite place, but it appealed to her. Worse, it distracted her.

"Hey, are you up for watching some TV before heading back home?" Claudia drew Elizabeth out of her contemplations.

"There's no TV in the office."

"Oh, sorry. Habit. I meant we could stream something and watch it on my tablet."

"I don't feel like watching true crime," Elizabeth said softly.

"Oh, no. I didn't mean that. I know you're not into it. I'd not... I wouldn't suggest that again."

Elizabeth once more thought about how she didn't know anyone like Claudia, and wondered where this was all supposed to lead.

"So, what do you say?"

Elizabeth blinked rapidly. She'd missed Claudia's suggestion. "Come again?"

Claudia's eyebrows rose, then a small smile formed on her lips. "I asked if you've heard of *Broken Time*? It's an almost campy science fiction show. It's not super popular, like, the crazy kids online don't lose their minds about it, but it has a committed following and it's quite good. Plus, most of the cast are pretty hot. So, eye candy, too."

"*Broken Time*? The show about that institute that tries to solve mysteries in the past by traveling through time. That one?"

"Yes! You know it! I knew you might like it, and—"

"That's Kat's show."

"Wait, what?"

"My friend Kat. I told you about her."

Claudia's eyes widened. "Are you serious?"

Elizabeth only stared at Claudia, squashing her rising exasperation—as if she'd make such jokes.

Claudia grabbed her phone and her fingers flitted over the screen.

"What are you doing?"

"Checking out the real names of the cast." Her gaze never left the screen. She shook her head. "Your best friend is Kathryn Johnson, who plays the lead role in *Broken Time*?"

"Yes. Who are your eye candies? The male lead, what's his name? Markus, something or other?"

Claudia narrowed her eyes, picked up a pillow and threw it at Elizabeth, who caught it, startled. "I'll never tell."

"No comment is most often an admission of guilt," Elizabeth argued.

"Uh uh, not true. It's a form of Glomarization and as such inherently neutral."

"But you're not a federal agency."

Claudia pouted. "You're telling me that now?"

"It never seemed relevant before." What on earth was going on?

"Do you even watch shows Kat plays in?"

"Why wouldn't I?"

Claudia shrugged. "I imagine it might be weird. You know her, and then you see her on there as this entirely different person. It seems strange."

Elizabeth waved her off. “I’ve known Kat forever, and it’s acting, so it’s not as if I have the expectation to see her like I know her. She’s playing a role, so…”

“I suppose. Is that a yes or no on watching an episode?”

“Sure. I’ve only seen the first season, though.”

“What kind of friend are you? They’re at the end of season four right now!”

“Hey! Look who’s rude now? First, you assumed I wouldn’t even watch it because Kat’s my friend, and then what… Now I’m a terrible friend if I’m not caught up? I live a busy life, and watching TV isn’t a priority.”

“What are your priorities?”

Elizabeth released a ragged breath but held Claudia’s inquisitive gaze, almost feeling like she could lose herself in the depth of her dark eyes. Why did Claudia always do that? She derailed their conversation, leaving Elizabeth breathless and in a state of strange tension that bordered on excitement.

“In what? Television?” She tried to defuse the situation as her heart thumped and she folded her arms to hide the tremble that had overcome her hands.

“I’m sorry for making you uncomfortable. I’m a bulldozer at times, and my head is always spinning. I jump from one topic to the next in there, and often that bleeds into my conversation. Especially when…” Claudia rolled her lips.

“Especially when?”

“I like you, and I find you quite interesting. So I have all these questions, and when they pop into my head, I just blurt them out. I too often only realize how inappropriate some of them are after I’ve said them.” Claudia flushed.

“You didn’t make me uncomfortable. I’m curious about you as well. Your mind is quite fascinating.”

Claudia maintained eye contact.

“Do you still want to know?” Elizabeth almost whispered.

“About your priorities?”

Elizabeth nodded.

"You can assume that my answer to anything relating to getting to know you will almost always be yes."

Elizabeth refrained from letting Claudia know how shocked and surprised she was by the developments of this night, more so by her own willingness to open up. "I'm not sure." She groaned. "That sounds quite pathetic. I'm sprinting toward fifty, and I don't know my priorities."

"That's not pathetic."

"You're obligated to say that."

Claudia laughed. "How's that?"

"I'm your boss."

"True, but I don't know. It feels like we're on the path to something more."

"And what would that be?"

"Friends?"

"Friends," Elizabeth intoned, making it sound like a foreign concept to her own ears.

"Yes. I'd like that. Maybe one day I'll even meet the famous Raji."

At times, Elizabeth thought Claudia seemed like one of the bravest souls she'd ever met. "He's a hard nut to crack. He never warmed to Tom."

"Ouch," Claudia said.

"All right, *Helping Hands* is a priority, but for my private life." She shrugged. "I don't know."

"Perhaps you can use this time now, this fresh start, so to speak, as an opportunity to figure it out."

"I've heard worse ideas."

Claudia smiled.

They watched two episodes of Kat's show—Elizabeth sometimes forgot what a talented actress her friend was. Claudia ended up telling her about the new cast member that had just joined the show for the latest season, and who added a lot of excitement and tension to the plot. Claudia's enthusiasm when talking about *Broken Time* had endeared her to Elizabeth, not that she'd pointed that out.

After feeling unmoored over her divorce, Elizabeth had managed to reestablish her equilibrium, focusing on work, and avoiding her mother's phone calls had helped. Most of all, her interactions with Claudia had aided in tethering her mood at a more sustainable level. While she still experienced pangs of wistfulness, she seemed to have cried out her sadness over this unexpected loss. It almost seemed like Claudia's mere presence acted as a buffer.

Elizabeth had wondered for a second if that meant she was taking advantage of Claudia and using her as an emotional band aid. But she'd dismissed this notion immediately as this budding affection for Claudia seemed genuine. Still, what was she supposed to do with all of that? Friends? She supposed stranger things had happened.

with hippies and gelato

Claudia was about to leave work shortly after five, when she ran into Elizabeth in the hallway. Before she could utter more than a greeting, a look of determination washed over Elizabeth's face.

"Claudia, I was wondering if you might join me at Pat Stewarts? You seemed curious about them, and I could use an unbiased opinion. My appointment is Wednesday afternoon. I can text you the details."

Claudia's eyebrows rose. "Really?" Excitement slithered through her, both at the thought of such an out-of-work outing with Elizabeth, but also that the woman would seek her opinion on something.

"Yes."

"Sure. Why not? I'm curious about how this all works." Claudia frowned. "Not that I need their services."

"Naturally. I'll be... anticipating your not-so-terrible ideas."

Claudia laughed. "Wow. What a vote of confidence."

"Well, we'll have to see, right? Our tastes might not align, and so it's possible I'll hate everything you like and vice versa, but it is still smart to have an unbiased observer with you."

"I'll have you know that I have impeccable taste, thank you very much."

"People always say that about themselves, given that we like what we like, so our preferences will always appeal to *us*. If they didn't, we'd have other preferences." She straightened, seeming way too pleased of her clever answer.

"True. That reminds me of my friend, Theo. Gosh, we were like fourteen or so at the time, and he'd come with us to my cousin's house. He looked at her music collection and then turned around, and..." She laughed.

"What?"

"He asked, 'Don't you prefer your cousin's music over your own?'"

Elizabeth frowned. "But if that were the case, then your taste in music would be identical."

"You don't say," Claudia drawled.

"Indeed, that fits along with what I said. Hence, my point that you believing you have impeccable taste means nothing because of course you'd like your taste."

"Point taken, but I have it on good authority that this isn't just a case of me being stuck in my own world."

"Huh. I suppose we'll find out on Wednesday."

"To quote a wise elder of mine, 'indeed.'"

Elizabeth's eyes widened. "You didn't!"

"What? Give props to my elder? Or recognize your tendency to overuse 'indeed?'"

"I do *not* overuse 'indeed.' I use it just enough. It's a great word and conveys a lot of meanings."

"Indeed."

"You're mocking me."

Claudia held up her hands. "I'm not! I swear. Though I might be teasing you."

Elizabeth's cheeks flushed. She dipped her head before finding Claudia's gaze again, and offering what almost amounted to a mischievous smile. "Oh."

"Now *you*'re mocking me."

"Of course not. But teasing can never be just one-sided, and you aren't the only observant one."

"Noted."

"Now, don't you have some work to finish?" And with that, Elizabeth had shooed her back into her office.

Claudia had an emergency at her parents' place on Tuesday—her mother and grandmother had gotten into an argument and acted as if that hadn't happened, yet her father had been at his wits end and called Claudia to come over and help (Translation: allow both women to fuss over *her* and thereby offer a common ground.). While rushing there after work, one of her first emotions had been relief over this occurring on Tuesday instead of Wednesday, so she'd still be able to accompany Elizabeth the next day, and thus, would disappoint neither.

Then, she'd immediately chastised herself over this foolishness. This infatuation would go nowhere. Not only was Elizabeth straight, but she also... well, she no longer seemed to perceive Claudia as a *child*, but work, their background and all the 'Tom business' remained. It was one thing to move from professional to friendly, but anything more would be preposterous.

Of course, the very first point made the rest moot, but Claudia preferred to remind herself of *all* the reasons why even so much as an infatuation would prove unwise. Yet, none of that stopped her urge to get to know Elizabeth more, better, to learn everything that the other woman would be willing to share.

She liked Elizabeth and enjoyed her company. So, even if nothing but a friendship would come out of this, she didn't see why she should deny herself that. Friends were great, and she could use a few more, especially with how busy Sammy had been since becoming a Texas state house representative. They got along well, and Elizabeth seemed as keen to continue their... association as Claudia.

On Wednesday afternoon, Claudia pulled into the parking lot of Pat Stewarts Home. She released a deep breath, turned off the engine, and exited her vehicle. She waved at Elizabeth as she approached with a small smile forming on her lips.

"Are you ready to impress me with your impeccable taste?"

"Yes," Claudia said, feeling a little breathless. Elizabeth smiled rarely, and each occurrence made Claudia's heart flutter. Ridiculous. "Be prepared to be amazed." She tried to act calm though she felt anything but that.

They wordlessly fell into step and strode toward the entrance.

Claudia wasn't sure what she'd expected—a stylish showroom with expensive, expressionist art hanging on the walls and modern furniture pieces without price tags, or an antebellum architectural hellscape. Instead, at least at first glance, this place resembled a homey bookstore, with comfy, worn leather sofas and quirky coffee tables alongside equally peculiar end tables harboring incense holders. Did they go to the wrong address? Was Elizabeth secretly a hippie? Was she even old enough for—

"Are you all right?" Elizabeth asked, interrupting Claudia's rambling train of thought.

"Yes. Sorry. Just taking it all in."

"Not what you'd expected, hmm?"

"What gave me away?"

Elizabeth put her index finger on her lips, drawing Claudia's gaze to them. "Let's see. Your wide eyes and gaping mouth?"

Claudia's mouth fell open before she snapped it shut and glared at Elizabeth, whose clear blue eyes sparkled. "You're not funny."

"And you make messing with you too easy."

"All of this is going on a list, and one day—"

"Yes, yes," Elizabeth said, patting Claudia's arm.

Claudia was about to say something when a scent distracted her. She sniffed. "Is that... Do I smell patchouli?" She lowered her voice and leaned closer to Elizabeth. "Is this a hippie place? I know you're quite advanced in your age, but you can't have been a hippie."

Elizabeth bumped into her. "Hush. I'm beginning to think I can't take you places."

Before Claudia could reply, a middle-aged woman with dark brown skin and long, black braids wearing a red and green dashiki strode toward them and immediately clasped Elizabeth's hands in hers.

"Elizabeth, dear, it's so good to see you again." She turned toward Claudia with a warm smile. "And who is your guest?"

"This is my friend, Claudia. Claudia, meet my good friend, Shani Mwangi, the owner of Pat Stewarts Home store."

Claudia blinked rapidly before shaking off her stupor at being introduced as such, and with a smile, grasped Shani's hand. "Hello. It's nice to meet you."

"Hello, Claudia. Are you here to convince Elizabeth not to turn her bedroom into a cold, modern, sterile, black and white landscape?"

Claudia's mouth opened, then closed. That indeed sounded awful. She straightened. "Yes, I hope so."

"It's pretty."

Claudia frowned. "For a show room, yes, for some HGTV show, sure, but for your bedroom? Shouldn't that be a cozy, warm, comfortable room? Like your sanctuary where you can recharge." Thank goodness Elizabeth had asked her to come along. Her subconscious must have known it would be a disaster otherwise.

"I like this one," Shani said.

"Because she agrees with you."

Shani shrugged. "I think Petra would be the best choice to help you with this. She should be here any moment. She called to say she's running late. Can I offer you a cup of coffee or tea while you wait? I just made a fresh pot of Earl Grey, and—"

"Yes, please." Claudia flushed. "Sorry. I'm just a big fan of Earl Grey."

"Say no more. You should keep her around, Liz. She's got good taste."

"So she claims," Elizabeth said, and when their gazes met, Claudia felt sure that the fondness she kept seeing in Elizabeth's expression wasn't just in her imagination.

They chatted for a couple more minutes before a tall woman with messy red curls and a face full of freckles dashed into the store. "So sorry I'm late, Shani. Today was nuts."

"No worries," Shani replied. "I'll leave you to it. Goodbye, Liz, Claudia." She nodded as they reciprocated her farewell before she turned and walked toward a door in the back.

The designer faced them. "Hi, I'm Petra. I'm assuming one of you is Elizabeth?"

"Hello. I'm Elizabeth, and this is Claudia."

"Hi," Claudia said.

They all shook hands.

"I'm excited to meet you. Come on, let's sit back down and discuss your vision for your bedroom. Shani forwarded me your floor plan, so we got the measurements down. We can first discuss general décor ideas, and then I'll show you some options. Any more tea?"

Elizabeth and Claudia declined and listened to Petra's ideas for the bedroom redecoration.

Claudia had never been that interested in interior design, and any knowledge she had came from HGTV shows she'd watched with her mother and grandmother—one of the few times when their bickering was hilarious. She herself more often agreed with *teta*, but she was wise enough not to say that out loud in front of her mother.

However, she enjoyed Petra's presentation and had some clear favorites, although she held back at first since this wasn't about her preferences. When Petra eventually turned to her and asked for her input, her gaze first shifted to Elizabeth, who eyed her expectantly.

"I think this look," she tapped the screen depicting a sleek, black modern bedroom set—angular and severe, "might be a bit too dark."

"There are lighter options," Patra said, and after a few keystrokes, the color changed to charcoal, then light gray, until she also showed a white version.

Claudia shuddered.

"It's very elegant," Elizabeth pointed out.

Claudia stifled a sigh. "It's not you." She flushed. Was that too presumptuous? But then again, Elizabeth had asked her to be here and offer her opinion. "This looks like Patrick Bateman's bedroom."

Petra tilted her head.

"The serial killer?" Elizabeth almost spluttered.

"Fictional?" Claudia said, her voice high and apologetic. It had to count for something that he wasn't real.

Elizabeth narrowed her eyes.

"It's always difficult when a couple has such divergent tastes, but I'm sure we'll figure something out that will appeal to you both," Petra interjected, a (failed) attempt to calm the situation.

"Oh, we're not. She's not..." Claudia stammered.

Elizabeth shot her a blank stare.

"My apologies." Petra quickly changed the screen to a different bedroom set. "What about this one?" she asked Elizabeth.

Claudia released a harsh breath. God, why on earth had Petra assumed they were a couple? As if Elizabeth would ever be interested in dating her. Annoyed by her own thought, she forced herself to refocus on the topic at hand, especially the absence of prices.

This lack of transparency made Claudia uneasy. How were you supposed to make an informed decision if you didn't know the price of the product or service in question? But she feared it would be rude to ask.

They left the store an hour later, Elizabeth having settled on a compromise, some modern features, but it wasn't black and white, nor did it look like a futuristic alien bar. It appeared quite cozy on the screen.

On their way back to their cars, Claudia halted and her hands found their way into her pockets. "Do you wanna get some ice cream?"

"What? Now?"

"Don't tell me you don't like ice cream?" Claudia asked.

Elizabeth released a small chuckle. "Don't sound so scandalized. I like it just fine, but it's October."

"Early October, and it's also sixty-two degrees."

"Exactly."

"That's not cold. Most definitely not too cold to eat ice cream, and we're close to my favorite ice cream shop. They make hand-churned gelato and house-made cannoli."

"Well, if *that's* the case," Elizabeth said.

Claudia froze for a moment, arrested by the playful yet intense glow in Elizabeth's eyes. She was lucky this woman was straight, or Claudia would be in deep trouble.

"Lead the way."

"What?"

"To your wondrous ice cream parlor."

"Oh, right, yes. But we still gotta drive." Claudia scrunched up her nose. "Drive together and leave one car here?"

"Sure. Let's take mine."

Claudia nodded and stepped to the passenger side of Elizabeth's car. She settled in the seat and closed her eyes when a mixture of bergamot and jasmine washed over her.

"What is it?" Elizabeth asked, fastening her seatbelt.

"Nothing. Just memories."

"Good ones?"

"The best."

"A random thought or did something provoke them?"

Claudia pressed her lips together. Saying, 'your scent,' might not be the best answer here. "The latter."

"Care to share?" Elizabeth pulled out of the parking lot.

"One day, yes."

"Good."

Claudia neither could nor wanted to quell the happiness that rose in her at Elizabeth's remark. She'd enjoyed this day a lot, and when they'd reached their cars, she had struggled to part from Elizabeth, and the ice cream parlor had sprung to her mind. She knew she shouldn't get this attached to Elizabeth, not just because of their history and the current work situation, but also because she didn't need a crush on a straight woman.

As such, she decided not to have one, and so far, she felt she mostly succeeded. It didn't count that Elizabeth's reserved and rare smiles made her heart tremble or that she felt at ease and content in her presence. The first one was a mere biological impulse and would pass with time. The second one, though? She loved it, and to her, it meant the beginnings of a great friendship. That was, until Elizabeth placed her order.

degrees of separation

"You cannot eat eggnog gelato," Claudia exclaimed with so much fervor that Elizabeth startled.

"Why? Is it gross?"

"What? How would I know? It's *eggnog*."

Elizabeth blinked rapidly, wondering if she'd missed something important. "And?"

"It's just... offensive."

"Excuse me? Are you the flavor police?"

"If you're committing a crime, yes," Claudia said.

"Well, I suppose you'll have to arrest me because I love eggnog. Since we're nearing the 'best time' of the year, and this lovely establishment has an 'eggnog fall special,' it seems like destiny, don't you think? Besides, I always pick that flavor whenever they offer it."

"But—"

"What? You can't be seen with someone who likes eggnog?"

"I sure haven't been before," Claudia grumbled.

"But your..." Elizabeth looked down at the listed flavors, "cookie butter gelato is better?"

"Yes."

"Why?"

Claudia shrugged. "It's cookie butter. And let me tell you, I may have had some weird cravings lately, but eggnog ice cream is on another level."

"Worse than the boiled eggs you had the other day with horseradish? Let's not forget, you wanted to eat a peanut butter and jelly sandwich with egg salad." Elizabeth grimaced.

"Still not as distasteful as eggnog *anything*."

Elizabeth shook her head. "Perhaps you should've asked what flavors I prefer *before* asking me out for ice cream."

"I didn't ask you out..." Claudia frowned. "I mean, I did, but not... as a date—"

"This is the second time today you freaked out over the idea of dating me. You're not homophobic, are you?" Elizabeth narrowed her eyes. "I have quite a few gay friends, and while I can accept you hating eggnog and judging those who love it—judging *me*—we have a real problem if you're a raging homophobe."

Claudia spluttered.

The staff handed them their gelatos, and both women strode to the corner to sit down at a table.

"I'm not a homophobe," Claudia rushed out. "I'm bisexual myself, so that would be kinda weird. Although I suppose internalized homophobia exists, but nope. That's not me."

Elizabeth's shoulders relaxed. "Oh, OK. That's a valid point."

Claudia stuffed a spoonful of gelato in her mouth. Her shoulders dropped, and she sighed, closing her eyes. "This is *so* good."

Elizabeth ate some of hers and released a low moan.

Claudia coughed.

"You're right. This is amazing." In fact, this alone might have made the entire ordeal with Tom worth it. She rolled her eyes. While not the biggest fan of exaggerations, sometimes they were indeed needed.

"Impeccable taste, remember." Claudia ate another bite.

"Not in ice cream, you don't," Elizabeth argued.

Claudia snorted. "Says the woman who likes the flavor of milk mixed with egg yolk." She scowled.

Elizabeth pointed her spoon at her. "You're very judgmental."

"Only when it's warranted."

"Like when you vetoed the modern look for *my* bedroom?" Elizabeth suppressed a smile at the furious blush that spread over Claudia's cheeks. Smiles seemed to be easier for her around Claudia. Another odd fact to contemplate.

"I did no such thing!"

Elizabeth bit her lower lip. "You do indignation so well."

Claudia folded her arms across her chest.

"Is that a family trait?"

"Perhaps. Either way, I vetoed nothing. What do I have to do with your bedroom, anyway?"

"Nothing, but you know, saying something looks cold and sterile and reminds you of the penthouse of the 'lead in American Psycho' is *not* a ringing endorsement."

Claudia ducked her head. "If you put it *that* way."

Elizabeth hadn't been this amused by anyone's company in a long time. Claudia shaped up to be a breath of fresh air, clichéd as it may sound, and annoyingly, also proving Tilda's assessment correct. And once more, the urge to remain in her presence overcame Elizabeth.

After leaving Pat Stewarts Home, she'd been tempted to suggest prolonging their time together, but hesitated, wondering if this wasn't out of bounds. Yes, they were trying to be friendly, but Elizabeth had already requested Claudia join her for this outing, so she couldn't suggest something else. Reciprocity had to be a thing. She'd been pleased when Claudia had proposed heading to the ice cream parlor, even if it was a bit too cold for ice cream.

"What about your family traits? Anything you need to forewarn me about?" Claudia asked.

Elizabeth looked perplexed.

"It seems relevant, no?"

"Any family traits I may have acquired are likely nothing to be proud of."

Claudia's face dropped. "I'm sorry. I didn't mean to bring down the mood. You'd mentioned your family being difficult."

Elizabeth waved her off. “It’s fine. And the mood isn’t ruined. It’s just the truth.” After a beat. “I suppose that’s another line on the list of circumstances that separate us.”

“I’m not a fan of you dividing us in this way.”

“But we’re separated by so many things,” Elizabeth pointed out, eating the last bit of her gelato.

“Do we have to be?”

Elizabeth wondered why this bothered Claudia so much. She’d been used to this growing up, to having enjoyed a more than privileged social position, and to interacting with people who were much like herself—at least while she was younger, before she could forge her own way. Well, except Raji, though that had also only happened because of her grandmother. Her mother, on the other hand, had always had very specific ideas about whom Elizabeth should interact with. It hadn’t just been Tom’s age and his handsome face that had bothered her.

“What do you mean?” Elizabeth asked.

“Do you think there’s a bridge to cross this divide? We could meet in the middle.”

Elizabeth leaned back in her chair, contemplating the intense expression on Claudia’s face. “What do you see that divides us?”

“Wait, you said we’re separated by so many things. Shouldn’t that be *your* question to answer?”

Elizabeth huffed.

“Well? You don’t like it when I throw your complaint back at you?”

“It’s not really a complaint, more a reality.”

“Enlighten me,” Claudia requested.

“All right. There’s the age difference, and—”

“I feel that is solely on you. You’re the one who saw me as a *child* when we first met.”

Elizabeth’s eyes widened, both at the notion itself and the vehemence in Claudia’s tone. “I did not! You’re quite a bit younger, but my focus with that was more on Tom, and the cliché of my husband, ex-husband, though I suppose we’re technically still married. Separated then? Anyway, your age stood out in relation to *that*, to Tom cheating on me with a significantly younger woman."

"Here it is again. *Significantly.*" Claudia raised her eyebrows.

"Is that your triumphant expression? If it is, it needs work."

Claudia pouted.

"The pout is good, though. You have an adorable puppy expression sometimes."

Claudia glared at her.

"Come on. Eighteen years *is* quite the difference."

"We're both grown-ups, and in the end, age becomes nothing but a number. It's not like there's an age range and you can only be friends with people who are plus/minus five years of your own age."

"Indeed." Elizabeth bit on her lip to avoid smiling.

"What other issue separates us?" Claudia asked.

"Finances. We grew up in quite different worlds," Elizabeth said.

"True, but I don't see how that matters. There isn't an income range you need to fall into in order to be friends with someone, either."

"That is correct, Still, people tend to move in their own circles."

"Yes, but we're not doing that."

Elizabeth raised one eyebrow.

"What?"

"Isn't it obvious?"

Claudia's eyelids flickered before she released a rough breath. "Tom."

"Tom."

Silence.

"I destroyed your marriage. You're right. That's hard to overcome."

"Tom's the one who ruined our marriage. But he's still a ghost that lingers. Now, if we'd been friends and you'd slept with my husband—"

"Hush!" Claudia's head swiveled around, taking in the other customers minding their own business.

"What?"

"Don't be so... *loud*. People can hear you."

Elizabeth leaned forward and placed her arms on the table. "Do you care what these people think about you?"

"Normally I don't, but this is something... I don't cheat. I don't..." She clenched her jaw.

"Oh, I didn't mean to—" Elizabeth said.

"It's fine. You did nothing wrong."

"Neither did you." Elizabeth raised one eyebrow.

Claudia sighed. "If you say so."

"I do. And I'm right."

"You're something, all right."

Elizabeth canted her head. "Is that a good thing?"

Claudia worried her lip and Elizabeth almost missed her answer. "Yes. Either way, this doesn't matter. Not to me. I don't have many friends, not close friends, at least. I get along with most people, and—"

Elizabeth snorted.

"Oh, hush."

She felt Claudia's earnest gaze it in her chest. "What is it?"

"I'm just glad we're doing this, and that we've even ventured out of the office. Please don't withdraw now because you think we're divided by all this nonsense. We can still be friends. None of your points would prevent that."

"And this is still something you want?" Elizabeth asked, suddenly breathless as her heart drummed wildly.

"Yes."

An awful thought resurfaced in Elizabeth's mind. "This entire friend-business, it's not about penance or because you think I'm lonely?"

"Of course not!" Claudia seemed indignant.

"Because I'm not lonely. Mind you, after five years of living with Tom, the house does seem too big for one person, but I'm all right. I'm..." She frowned. "I'm not sure at what stage of the grieving process I am, but it appears mostly fine. I'm not sure what that says about my marriage."

"Why does it have to say anything?" Claudia asked.

Elizabeth shrugged.

"I just enjoy spending time with you, and I'd like to continue doing that. I'm not saying that out of pity or a guilty conscience. And you already told me to quit the penance thing."

"I did, yes." Could this be true? She supposed Claudia hadn't lied to her yet. "That's good to know."

"So, can we?"

"What?"

Claudia flushed and sat straighter. "Continue this friends-business, as you call it."

Elizabeth's eyes widened, but before her brain could make her swallow the answer, a "Yes," spilled from her lips. When Claudia had first suggested that they could try to be friends, Elizabeth had been sure she'd tire of her quickly, and that this all related to a misguided attempt at penance. Yet, she'd been wrong.

Claudia's answering smile shone brightly, almost blinding Elizabeth.

"So, there's this detective movie coming out, and I've been meaning to see it. Since you enjoy crime fiction, maybe you could join me. This Sunday?" Claudia asked.

"What about your Sunday lunch with your family?"

Claudia smiled, looking pleased, as if she hadn't expected Elizabeth to recall any details or information about her. If she only knew how much space she occupied in Elizabeth's head, although that seemed ill-advised.

"The showing is at five. Plenty of time."

"All right. Text me the information."

"Great." Claudia's smile once more caused a lump to form in Elizabeth's throat.

Sometimes Elizabeth wondered if jinxing yourself was real or a self-fulfilling prophecy. Either way, she should've known better than to proclaim she was fine, as it was one thing to think it, but to say it out loud? Back home, she'd first settled on the couch with Raji and a glass of Merlot, sipping her wine while listening to the melodic voice of Ella Fitzgerald. She'd felt content and contemplated her day and future plans. Her lawyer had recently also delivered good news—the assurance that Tom had no leg to stand on.

She noted how much of this contentedness seemed to revolve around Claudia and their burgeoning friendship, and she didn't... hate this. Though Elizabeth also admitted that Claudia's quizzical reaction—twice—to the notion of being involved with her stung a little. She didn't assume a woman who loves women would be romantically interested in any woman she met, and tendrils of annoyance rose for even feeling like this, contemplating this. After all, she wasn't Blanche Devereaux and didn't bemoan the fact that a lesbian friend preferred Rose Nylund over her. No, this wasn't borne in ego.

It merely seemed like an odd, small ache. Not even akin to not getting picked for games during physical education or not being invited to the birthday party of the popular Elizabeth in her year in eighth grade. No. It just hurt. And she was being silly. She didn't even date women, not to mention, she was Claudia's boss.

Once she'd emptied the glass and Raji abandoned her to inspect the shadowy play of the last rays of sunshine dipping onto the carpet through the windows, she rose to pick up a book from the bedroom.

Her foot collided with something under the bed. Elizabeth frowned before checking.

"Oh, right." She pulled out an ornate wooden box and lifted it onto the bed. She stroked the lid before sitting down next to it. Elizabeth first eyed the box as if it were an explosive device, and in retrospect, she should have heeded her first instinct and hid it in the closet.

Instead, she opened the lid and sighed. Inside were mementos, sentimental items intermixed with letters, photos, and theater ticket stubs. How silly. She picked up the first photo, which pictured a teenage Elizabeth, grinning at the camera with her nan by her side. She supposed it wasn't uncommon for a mother to dislike her son's wife. Her nan surely had had plenty of reasons to criticize Mary, given all the things her mother tended to say about her husband's family (Parents so often think kids don't pay attention.), yet she'd never uttered a bad word about Elizabeth's mother, at least not in her granddaughter's vicinity.

It had been over twenty years since she'd lost her grandmother, and yet on some days it still felt like she'd gotten the news yesterday. She placed the image back and picked up a letter, frowning at first when she recognized Tom's handwriting. Then she recalled—how could she have forgotten the sweet notes and letters he used to write to her? She read half of the letter before she had to put it aside, her vision blurry and her chest constricted.

That bastard.

God, her marriage was over. He'd cheated on her, tried to screw her over financially after she'd financed his path to become a partner, then told her *mother* about their divorce, and here she sat mourning what they had. How incredibly pathetic, and she'd thought she was over it all.

She wondered if you could still appreciate what you had in the past even when the present had turned to shit and the future had all but evaporated? Because shouldn't she just be full of righteous anger instead of feeling this lump of sadness?

Elizabeth still felt utterly frozen at the prospect of spending the rest of her life alone.

She shook her head and then rifled through the rest of the contents of her little chest. More of Tom's letters, pictures of their wedding and honeymoon, a few candid shots of them laughing and enjoying life. Then she grasped a delicate golden bracelet, like interconnected tree branches, fragile, yet strong, and decorated with leaves. A gift from Tom she'd worn every day until Claudia had shown her those images, when she'd stuffed it unceremoniously into this box before stashing it under the bed.

It had been much easier to take off the ring than this band. She wanted to cram it into the chest and shove it right back beneath the bed so she'd not feel this heavy. Then she'd not have this pressure building in her chest and behind her eyes. Memories flooded her mind, and she fell back on the bed, crying, the bracelet clutched in her hand.

with a little pink help that lied

CLAUDIA COULDN'T ATTEND HER family's regular Sunday lunch because she'd spent all night vomiting. When she'd called her mother in the morning to let her know she couldn't make it, she naturally sent her father to bring her rice, plain yogurt, and 7up to tide her over. Claudia doubted she had a stomach bug as she didn't feel ill aside from a constant nausea that often led to her hugging her toilet.

She exchanged a few texts with Elizabeth, sadly canceling their movie outing. She was so sweet, asking if Claudia needed anything, but she declined. She would loath to infect Elizabeth with whatever ailed her. Later that night, she called Sammy.

"Hey," she croaked.

"Hi. Are you OK?" Sammy asked.

"Yeah. Well, I'm better. I was constantly throwing up last night and most of today. My stomach seems to have settled now."

"Did you eat something bad?"

"No clue. I have no other symptoms. Nothing I ate seemed off. Perhaps it was my exposure to eggnog gelato. That shit lingers."

"Wait what?"

Claudia chuckled. "Nothing. I'd been out with Elizabeth, and we ended up getting some gelato. She had the eggnog." She frowned.

"You went out with Elizabeth? I thought your efforts to be friendly took place at the office."

"Yes, well, she wants to redecorate her bedroom now that... They're getting a divorce, as you know, and—"

"Because you slept with her husband."

Claudia lips thinned. She still felt so terrible about this, especially now that they had embarked on a friendship. She wanted this relationship, but it still stood on such fragile ground, and she worried it would come crashing down one day. At least Elizabeth had no issue with her being bisexual. That would have sucked. A lot. "Yes, but that's beside the point."

"So you say."

"You know, you seem more stuck on that than even Elizabeth and I are, which is odd, given that it doesn't affect you at all."

"I'm stuck on it because it's a major conflict of interest, and it impacts me if you're hurt in the process."

"I won't be. I can take care of myself."

"All right. Why did she want you there to pick out a new bedroom set?"

"It's more than just a bedroom set. She went to this exclusive, insanely expensive designer, and I'd made a quip about them not allowing someone with my yearly income inside, and well, she thought I might like to come along and see. Be an unbiased second opinion and all."

"That's nice."

Claudia hummed.

"And then you had ice cream after because..."

"Why not? It's ice cream."

"Are you sure it wasn't a date?"

"Ugh, Sammy. No. It wasn't a date. I told you she's straight, and I'm... I won't go there."

"But you like her."

"That's irrelevant. I like her as a friend, and... I enjoy spending time with her."

"Mmhmm."

"Oh, shut up."

"Why did you call me if not for my amazing insights?"

Claudia snorted. "Please. I don't even know. All that vomiting must have addled my brain, too."

"Hey! Wait a sec."

"What?"

"When was the last time you slept with Tom?"

"Huh? What does that matter?"

"Well… the nausea."

Claudia waved her off. "No. That's impossible. We split… let's see… early August. So about nine weeks ago? And we always used protection."

"Did you get your period since then?"

Claudia scratched her head. She couldn't recall the last time she had her period. "Probably."

"You don't know?"

"I don't keep track. It's irregular anyway."

"Maybe you should get a test. Just to be sure."

"Sammy, come on. Be real. The chances for that are super low. The stress just messed with my period. It's not that unusual."

"Nine weeks is quite some time, and condoms aren't infallible."

Claudia groaned. That was the *last* thing she wanted to do, and as far as what she needed, being pregnant with Tom Pittin's baby didn't even make the list. Her eyes widened. "God, that would ruin things with Elizabeth."

"What things with Elizabeth?" Sammy asked, and Claudia felt like slapping her. Too bad she was too far away.

"Our nascent, fragile friendship, Sammy!"

"Right. OK, I mean, if she chose to be friends with you knowing you had an affair with her husband—"

"Ex-husband. And those are two entirely different things."

"They aren't divorced yet, and—"

"Separated. It's only a matter of time and legality," Claudia argued.

"Fine, but my point is, she seems fine with all of that. Why would this now be a problem?"

"You really don't see a difference between *knowing* that Tom slept with me for several months and me carrying *his* child? She wanted children, you know."

"Oh, shit. That would change things."

"I'd say. Thankfully, I'm not pregnant, so this is all moot."

"All right."

"Yes. Now, let's talk about you and your little drama."

"Politics is no little drama."

"I'll give you that."

She chatted with Sammy for almost an hour until nausea reared its head again. After once more emptying her stomach contents and drinking another cup of peppermint tea, she went to sleep, but first she'd replied to Elizabeth's message inquiring about how she felt—better but still too barfy—was likely not the most eloquent reply she'd ever typed, alas... She'd been overcome with a sudden bout of bone crushing exhaustion as well, and so she quickly succumbed to sleep after pressing send and turning off her phone.

The next morning, Claudia woke up and once more ran to the toilet to throw up. She hated vomiting bile with a passion. There should be a law against it. She'd suggest it to Sammy. Perhaps even Sammy's arch nemesis Miriam could get behind such a law.

Sweaty and frustrated, she called in sick from work, then spent the rest of the morning fretting about the bug Sammy had planted in her ear. What if she *was* pregnant?

One way to find out.

She drove to the closest store to buy the disgusting pink sludge that would hopefully kill her nausea (Could you take that when you were pregnant?). Claudia lumbered by the aisle with pregnancy tests, almost feeling her mere presence, worse, her purchasing such an item would jinx her. Not that she believed in such things. A lot. But why would this happen? Yes, yes, she'd had sex with a man, but protected sex!

She wanted kids, but not now, and most definitely not with Tom. Yet, the damage was done. She groaned. Claudia knew she'd feel horrible for having referred to her child as 'damage' if she were indeed pregnant. Because that was who they'd be, her child. She halted in front of the shelf containing both condoms and pregnancy tests. How quaint.

God, she didn't want to be pregnant for so many reasons, yet... She forced herself to grab two boxes (just in case) and darted to the registers. She hated everything about this and prayed to any God willing to listen that she wasn't pregnant, that the universe wouldn't mess with her like that.

Back home, she couldn't tell the origin of the nausea dancing through her stomach, but since it didn't make her throw up, she assumed it came down to nerves. She glared at the pregnancy test as if her will could speed it up *and* offer her the result she desired. Seconds seemed to turn into hours, and she raised her head and startled upon gazing at herself in the reflection. She needed a haircut, a shower, and sleep. Not in that order.

When she dipped her head, she faltered and grabbed onto the sink.

Two lines.

She couldn't be pregnant. Did the test expire? She grabbed the package and flipped it. Nope, good until next year. She tore open the second box and, with trembling fingers, pulled out another test. False positives happened, and she'd never hoped as fervently for anything before. God, she couldn't have a child now. Not Tom's child.

She left the bathroom and paced in her living room. Could you wait too long to look at the results and would that make them invalid? What would she do if she was pregnant? She'd have the baby—that wasn't a question. But God, her family. She closed her eyes and stilled. They'd be so disappointed. She most definitely would *not* share the circumstances surrounding this pregnancy.

With a sigh, Claudia returned to the bathroom and exhaling in a rush, she clutched the second pregnancy test—once more two red lines glared at her. They weren't even faint. She sagged down onto the toilet. God, what was she going to do?

Make a doctor's appointment because both pregnancy tests could be wrong. She had to be sure before she upended her life and... Damn it. If she indeed were pregnant, she'd also have to tell Tom, and she never wanted to see or hear from him again. What if he changed his mind and wanted to be a part of her child's life?

She marveled for a second that her first reaction about that notion had been: *I don't want him in my life, but I wish Elizabeth would stay.*

Fittingly, another stumble to embrace the toilet interrupted this thought.

When she fell back down on the couch later, she struggled to keep her mind from meandering down paths that only held suffering. You truly created most of your problems yourself, especially worrying. Her mind would come up with one horror scenario after the other—her family abandoning her, *teta* looking at her with eyes filled with utter disappointment, Elizabeth shouting at her, or worse, just shutting her out, refusing to answer her calls, blocking her even, Tom suddenly demanding shared custody, or worse, full custody, arguing that Claudia's financial situation would be harmful to their child. At least she had a better-paying job now at *Helping Hands.* Also, that worry was ridiculous, as Tom had stated more than once that he never wanted to be a father, and she doubted he'd ever change his mind.

Finally, losing the baby. Dying.

She supposed the last fear would rid her of all other worries. Claudia groaned. This wouldn't do. She couldn't just lie here and lose her mind in a swamp of useless fretting. There'd be answers to all her questions, but she'd not find them by sitting on the couch drowning in trepidation.

powder kegs and stones

EVEN THOUGH ELIZABETH LIVED a busy lifestyle and *Helping Hands* didn't lend itself to a stable routine, she remained a creature of habit. Some of them were old and founded in her youth, but plenty of new ones existed—some Tom had shattered—and the most recent one had snuck up on her over the last several weeks. She hadn't noticed it until the routine broke.

Claudia hadn't stopped by her office for anything all week. She'd seen her maybe once in the hallway, where she'd looked pale and tired. Elizabeth had attributed it to her recent illness. They hadn't been in the habit of talking daily—though they'd indulged in frequent short text exchanges, and now that she thought about it, these had stuttered to a halt as well.

At first, Elizabeth had been busy with work (A potential new sponsor had fallen into a bit of a scandal.), while at the same time, her lawyer had encountered a snag in the divorce proceedings. While Tom had tried to make Elizabeth's refusal to seek counseling despite his multiple attempts to 'save' their marriage an issue—from the destruction *he* had caused—no-fault divorce was still a thing, and that had gone nowhere. Well, aside from irking Elizabeth.

Yet, he argued that he shouldn't have to pay back the money Elizabeth had invested in his quest to make partner at his law firm, as it had been a gift. It hadn't. Elizabeth had no doubt this would fail as well, but the paperwork and back and forth communication still ate up a lot of her time and thoughts.

While Elizabeth didn't immediately realize it—the lack of communication between her and Claudia—she noticed that *something* kept bothering her, leading to her mood spiraling downward. She felt heavy, discontent and displeased, but she couldn't place it at first.

When she pinned its cause, she'd fallen speechless onto her sofa chair, having just risen to get a cup of eggnog out of the fridge when it hit her—Claudia. She'd fished her phone out of her purse and checked their message thread. Indeed, they hadn't really talked since Claudia had told her she'd been better after her bout with that stomach bug.

Elizabeth sent a quick message, hoping whatever was going on didn't relate to a serious health issue that Claudia had been trying to hide from her. She stared at the phone in her hand for a solid minute before rolling her eyes at herself and rose to get her eggnog. She'd just sat back down and was about to take her first sip when her phone beeped. Elizabeth smiled when she glanced at the screen. Leave it to Claudia to stop her from drinking eggnog even without realizing it.

The brief message rang wrong. With a frown, Elizabeth asked if she could call her, and did so once Claudia acquiesced.

"Hi." Claudia sounded breathless.

"Hey, stranger," Elizabeth said. "Don't tell me you're working out."

"Hmm? No, no. I was just... Never mind. How are you?"

Elizabeth clenched her hand. "I'm fine. What about you? You could have stayed home longer. You looked utterly exhausted, not that I've seen much of you over the last week." *Subtle, Liz. Real subtle.*

Silence.

"You are OK, right?"

"Oh, yes, yes."

"So, what's going on? We haven't talked in a while." Elizabeth froze when it occurred to her that perhaps Claudia intentionally hadn't contacted her. Had she upset her?

"I know," Claudia said, her tone stony as she seemed to avoid elaborating.

Elizabeth's eyebrows rose. "I'm sorry. I was insanely busy, both with Tom creating more trouble, and a sponsor who's giving us a run for our money." Her heart thrummed hard. What was going on here?

"I thought divorces are pretty easy if one partner cheats."

"They are, but Tom is... stubborn."

"What's still unclear to him? He needs to back off."

Elizabeth choked back a laugh at Claudia's incredulous tone and the sensation of tension finally ebbing. "That's a good question. I also thought that things were moving forward, but sometimes people surprise you."

"Doesn't sound like a pleasant surprise."

"It wasn't."

"I know this friendship business is new, and Tom is still a difficult topic between us, but I would listen if you want or need to vent. But you don't have to."

"That's sweet of you, thank you. But no worries. This will soon all be over."

"Good. That's good."

Elizabeth tilted her head. "Are you sure you're OK?"

"Why do you ask?"

"You seem off."

Claudia sighed. "It's fine."

"That sounds like fine spelled, 'on fire but I don't want to talk about it.'"

Claudia chuckled. "A lot of letters for such a short word."

"Well, what can I say, I have an extensive vocabulary."

"I see."

"So?"

"It's complicated."

"Does it relate to you being sick? You're not in the hospital right now, are you?"

"What? No. Why would I be? I was at work earlier, even if we didn't see each other, and—"

"Never mind. I'm sorry. I get... restless when routines are broken."

"What routine broke for you? Because Tom is gone?"

"What? No. I mean..." Elizabeth took off her glasses and pinched the bridge of her nose. "Us. We didn't talk. You didn't come by my office." *God, how pathetic can you get?*

"Oh." Claudia exhaled harshly, then fell silent.

"What's going on?"

"I... I gotta go. I... I promised my mom I'd run an errand for her and I'm running late."

Elizabeth checked her watch. "At seven in the evening? That's a late errand."

"Yeah, it's for..."

"Don't lie to me. You've been so honest with everything, and I... I appreciate that." *More than I can say*. She swallowed those words, but her mind still added them.

Silence.

"Claudia?"

"Hmm?"

"What's going on?"

"You don't want to know."

"You realize what people imagine in such situations is *always* worse than the truth?"

"What situation?"

"You being withdrawn, trying to avoid me, then lying, and now you're all cryptic." She tried to remain calm, but her heart once more drummed wildly in her ribcage, and she repressed the urge rush to her car and check on Claudia in person, though she'd first need to access her personnel file to get her address, and that would likely break all sorts of rules.

"I don't want to hurt you, and this—"

Elizabeth jumped out of her seat. "Are you back with Tom?"

"What? No! Of course not!"

Elizabeth released a stuttered breath, the relief making her sag back down almost bonelessly.

"I'd not do that to you. Besides, I don't *want* him back. I never did once I knew the truth."

"I know. It's just... Why are you like this?"

"Because I'm worried about your reaction, and it's just... It will change stuff."

"You being back with Tom is the only thing that would hurt me and change... I'm assuming you meant change our friendship?"

"Yes."

"I promise I won't get upset."

"You can't do that. You have no idea what it's about. What would you say if I told you I killed your mother?"

Elizabeth's eyes widened. "Good riddance?"

"Be serious. This isn't a joke."

"The thought of you killing my mother kind of is. The fact that you don't even know her name, nor her address, isn't even relevant for it to be impossible."

"How's that?"

"You're not capable of killing someone," Elizabeth said, almost surprised by the quiet conviction in her voice.

"Yes, yes, I'm not a killer, and I suppose it bodes well for our friendship that you think so, even if you do like eggnog, but that wasn't what I meant."

"You've interrupted me."

"How?"

"Not while talking. Drinking eggnog." She picked up her glass, and this time drank from it. She smacked her lips—not cold enough anymore.

"Ugh, stop it, please," Claudia sounded genuinely distressed.

"What? You can't be that offended. You can't even see or smell it."

"Stop! I'm a very visual person, and I just can't... I'm sorry."

Elizabeth's eyebrows furrowed, and she marched to the kitchen, dumping the eggnog into the sink before placing the cup in the dishwasher. "It's gone."

Claudia audibly gulped. "Thank you," she croaked.

"No problem." She decided not to say anything else on the topic as it seemed to stress Claudia out. But why? Aside from her general aversion to the beverage, this appeared to be over the top. Then all this talk about things changing between them, and how Elizabeth might be upset, yet Claudia wasn't back with Tom...

Elizabeth supposed she'd been sick, and a stomach virus could take a lot out of you. Though there were also her strange food cravings, and how tired Claudia said she'd been recently. She halted, stilling before she covered her mouth with one hand to muffle a gasp. Claudia was—

"I'm pregnant."

Elizabeth sat back down.

"Yes, I just caught on, too."

"I'm sorry."

Elizabeth frowned. "For what?"

"Come on! This is a lot, and I mean, it wasn't planned, and God, the last thing I need right now is a child, but I'm keeping the baby." She sounded defensive.

Did she think Elizabeth would ask her to... Surely not. "It never occurred to me you wouldn't."

"OK, good. I just... We talked about kids, and how... This never worked out for you, and here I am, pregnant with—"

"Tom's baby."

"Yes," Claudia murmured. "Which is why I'm sorry."

"Again, you apologize for mistakes that weren't your own. And I'm *not* calling your child a mistake."

"I know that," Claudia rasped, her voice rough.

"Are you crying?"

Claudia sniffed. "No."

"So you thought I'd be mad?"

"Obviously."

Elizabeth sighed. "I suppose I'm mad, in a way. But it's more abstract, and when it isn't, my anger is directed at Tom. Again, he was my husband. You and I were nothing to each other, so—"

"Yes, but neither is true anymore," Claudia whispered. "Right?"

"Correct, and that's also why I'm not upset with you. I'm assuming you just found out, or you did so recently, and that's why you slowed down our interactions?"

"Yes, but you could have come see me, too," her voice sounded petulant.

Elizabeth smiled ruefully. "True. Look, yes, it's... hard, that you're pregnant with Tom's child, but not..." She looked at the ceiling. "I'd made peace with never having children. Tom was clear he didn't want any kids, and I was fine with that."

"But?"

"It still sucks. Like a sick, cosmic joke. Although again, it would be worse if you were who I feared."

"The short, blonde bimbo with big tits and birthing hips."

"I'll never live that down, will I?"

"Nope."

Elizabeth chuckled.

"What now?"

"I have no experience with pregnancy, but I'd suggest you go see an OB/GYN, and—"

Claudia laughed. "No, no. I've already been. Yesterday. They did a blood test to confirm as I had clung to the hope that my home tests were false positives. But no. I was talking about us."

"Us? Why would anything change?"

"Because I'm pregnant with your soon-to-be ex-husband's child."

"Did you tell him yet?"

"No! I... I wanted to talk to you first."

"What if he wants you back? What if he wishes to raise the child with you? Your family would love that."

Claudia groaned. "Don't get me started. I'm in denial about my family, but as for Tom, I don't care what he wants. He's not an option, Elizabeth."

Elizabeth inhaled sharply as she once again found herself drowning in relief, while something else whizzed through her at Claudia saying her name like that. God, Tom's affair was putting her through some changes, but at least not all of them were terrible. Quite the opposite. Knowing she'd worry endlessly if they didn't clear the air, she blurted out, "How about you come by my place this Saturday?"

Silence.

"You can meet Raji and start your bribery."

Claudia chuckled. "Sounds like a plan."

They chatted for a bit longer, and after hanging up, Elizabeth felt like she'd waded through a powder keg, still wondering if it would blow up in her face. Sometimes she worried they were deluding themselves. Their history seemed to make conflict and strain a forgone conclusion, yet they'd decided to try to be friends—only for more drama to arise.

Now, Elizabeth was friends with the *pregnant* former mistress of her soon-to-be ex-husband, though she loathed to think of Claudia as such. Was this the universe throwing stones in their path or adding another reason why their endeavor would prove foolish?

But who decided all of this? Just because a situation usually played out a certain way didn't mean it always would. They both seemed to want this friendship, and they'd both been worried about their connection turning sour, so obviously neither wished for a change. The only issue, sometimes your desire or choice wasn't enough. Would that be the case here?

Elizabeth's heart fell at the thought. She didn't want to lose Claudia, but she also needed to be honest with herself and make sure she truly felt all right with all these recent developments, and what this would mean moving forward. If Claudia remained in her life, then their baby and potentially Tom, would as well.

a plan and lacking patience

CLAUDIA SHOULD HAVE KNOWN better. After all, her reluctance to tell Elizabeth about the pregnancy didn't stem from nothing. Obviously, she knew it wouldn't have been a long-term solution, and the truth would have come out eventually. From that perspective, her avoidance would have only been a postponed death—a delayed decay that would transpire regardless, but if she ignored that, she could fool herself into thinking they might have survived it.

Elizabeth's first reaction had been wonderful, more than Claudia could have ever hoped for or would have been able to imagine. And she didn't doubt Elizabeth, as in, she knew her words during that phone call had been genuine. But theory and reality at times clashed, and truly, Claudia should have expected this. Prepared for it.

She'd told no one else about the pregnancy, well, except Sammy, but she'd told her friend she didn't want to talk about it yet. Sammy had replied with a pouting emoji, but respected Claudia's wish. At least for now. Eventually, Sammy would have more questions, if only to make sure Claudia was OK. Her friend had a lot on her plate currently, and so Claudia hoped her call to finagle out the state of *everything* would take longer to arrive. Right now, she preferred not talking about this, especially since everything seemed to turn to cow manure.

First, Elizabeth had canceled their plans for Claudia to visit her and bribe Raji. Claudia had shrugged it off, given Elizabeth had promised a raincheck, but then she had been markedly absent at work. Tilda eventually informed her that Elizabeth was working from home. Three days later, she'd texted Elizabeth since she still hadn't heard from her.

It wasn't so much that Claudia expected them to communicate daily, but Elizabeth had been the one talking about routines being broken, and yet... The other day, when she'd witnessed two squirrels fight over a piece of ice cream cone next to a trashcan on her stroll through a nearby park, she'd sent Elizabeth a picture with the caption, "Raji would settle this fight fast." Yet, nothing. No reply. Not on that day, and not since then.

Elizabeth usually replied right away, and she supposed it was possible that she'd seen it, gotten distracted, and then forgot, but together with the rest, unlikely. Later, when she'd been about to write Elizabeth and ask her if she was OK, she noticed that at some point, Elizabeth had reacted with a "ha ha" emoji to her message. With a sigh, Claudia had closed their thread and gone to work.

Her patrons distracted her somewhat from the conundrum of being pregnant by Elizabeth's (ex)husband, though she questioned the value of said distraction, especially while dealing with a woman who micromanaged *everything* Claudia was doing.

"Are you sure this is the right form? What if the lawyer doesn't agree with this? I read online that..." And on and on Millie went, much to Claudia's utter consternation.

After lunch, which had been a nice break, but still not the same without Elizabeth in the office, she dropped the empty wrapper of her sandwich into the trash and rose. She needed answers, but the problem was, cornering someone who avoided you rarely had a happy ending. So, patience.

That meant waiting, and Claudia sucked at that.

Sammy sometimes said she had zero chill. She supposed Sammy had a point, but how on earth would Claudia even go about changing that? She felt she was being exceptionally patient, even if some of that came to life in a reservoir called fear. Beggars can't be choosers and all that.

God, she must have been deluding herself into believing she and Elizabeth could establish a friendship. How even?

The next day, still with no note from Elizabeth, Claudia texted her again, asking her how she was doing.

Fine. You?

Claudia released a shuddered breath. At least she got a quick reply.

All right. What have you been up to this week?

Busy with work. The usual.

"No, this is *not* the usual," Claudia muttered into the room.

When will you be back in the office?

Claudia typed after a moment of pause. What else could she say, especially since Elizabeth shaped up to be a total chatterbox right now. Claudia rolled her eyes.

Soon. Got to take care of something first.

That was it. Claudia had contemplated writing something else, but she got this 'shut up' vibe. Not that Elizabeth would say that to her—she didn't seem the type, but Claudia just got the feeling that Elizabeth would prefer to stop talking to her. So Claudia obliged. If she were wrong, Elizabeth would write again or say something.

On the other hand, Claudia said nothing herself. What if Elizabeth assumed she was the one who didn't want to interact and accommodated Claudia, also expecting her to say something if anything was wrong? Ugh, why were human interactions so difficult? Maybe she should get a cat, too. They had to be easier. Then again, the idea of cleaning a litter box or slipping on vomit while carrying a laundry basket and then promptly falling on her butt didn't appeal to her either (Sammy's tale of woe).

At first, she'd tried to distract herself with research into one of her patrons' issues, but everything relating to *Helping Hands* inevitably turned her thoughts to Elizabeth (as if the woman didn't already take up enough of her mental real estate), and so she shucked it all off and instead drowned herself in true crime mysteries. She'd been behind anyway, thanks to spending so much time with...

And there she went again, losing herself in memories of an easier time when they spent hours playing cards, before she'd taken that infernal pregnancy test and confessed to Elizabeth, causing everything to change once more.

"No, no, that's not how this goes," Elizabeth said with a laugh. "Look, everything under ten gives you five points per card, while ten, eleven, and twelve each add ten points, the skip fifteen, and the wild card twenty-five points."

Claudia scrunched up her face. "So there's no way to have sixty-seven points, huh?"

"No." Elizabeth's voice rang amused, while her eyes sparked with mirth. She'd almost cried tears when Claudia had told her she had sixty-seven points after losing the first round of Phase Ten.

Claudia pouted. "All right. Now I move on to the next phase? What is it? Three of a kind and a run of four?"

"No, I mean, yes, that is the second phase, but you never finished the first one, so you need to do the two sets of three again."

"Oh, OK. So I'm behind you now."

"Yes, but don't worry. Fortunes shift quickly in this game."

Fortunes hadn't shifted, and Elizabeth had thrashed Claudia both in points and in phases. She'd gotten stuck *forever* trying to complete her run of nine, always missing a card in the middle. An infuriating game, though she had enjoyed watching Elizabeth win—her eyes aglow, cheeks flushed, and a huge smile on her face. Claudia's heart had ached, and she'd longed for things she would never have, and that now seemed forever out of reach.

At this point, the fortunes had shifted—to a place Claudia hated with a passion. She wanted their easy-going, warm relationship back, and not feel trapped in this aggravating limbo where she seemed to hang in midair. Ugh, this sole focus on Elizabeth made her want to scream.

Communication, they said. Right? You just had to talk. Be an adult. Ask her what the fuck was going on. Not in those words, obviously. Too aggressive, which wouldn't help her case. What was her case, though? That she was pregnant? She couldn't change that, and she'd never blame her child. Not that she thought Elizabeth would expect that.

One of Claudia's biggest issues was a combination of hyper-focus and lack of patience. Together, they'd gotten her into more trouble than she cared to admit or contemplate. If something bothered her, really bothered her, it clung to her like tar. She could hardly think of anything else. No matter what she did, whether it was watching some show, reading a book, playing a game, or worse, mundane tasks like cleaning or doing laundry, her mind danced around this one issue. At times, it created the feeling she'd jump out of her skin if she didn't solve it right then and there.

So, when Wednesday rolled around and Elizabeth was still working from home, Claudia had enough. She called Elizabeth that same evening.

"Hi," Elizabeth answered the phone.

Claudia closed her eyes. "Hi."

Silence.

"Listen, I was wondering if we could talk?"

"Go ahead," Elizabeth said.

"I'd rather do it in person. Could we meet?" Claudia wanted to see Elizabeth when they were having this discussion, not just hear her.

"All right. I'm free on Saturday. Where do you want to meet?"

"Would you mind coming here, to my place, I mean?" Claudia flicked her fingers against her thumb.

"OK, sure. What time?"

"Maybe four?"

"Sounds good. Text me your address. I'll see you then. Have a good night. Bye."

"OK. Thanks, you do, too. Bye." Didn't Elizabeth have her address?

After she hung up, Claudia had wanted to shout, but instead texted Elizabeth her address, to which she received a thumbs-up emoji. She sighed.

Their interactions were worse and more stilted than they'd been when they first met. How was that even possible? Elizabeth had said she was fine with her pregnancy, but she must have lied as what else had changed?

Frying pans and fire

Elizabeth hadn't lied to Claudia, yet it felt like it. She had contemplated this bombshell revelation more than she'd intended and enjoyed, but her mind wouldn't stop going there, it refused to refrain from inundating her with images of the future—a time that should be free of Tom yet wasn't.

She also had spoken the truth when she'd told Claudia she was OK with not having children. Elizabeth was fine. Or she had been? It was a bit like how her granddad during the last several years of his life drove nowhere. Instead, their driver did, and if she wasn't available, then a family member would chauffeur him. He'd been perfectly fine with this arrangement and never even seemed to think about driving his own car until the doctor told him that because of his illness, he was no longer fit to drive. Suddenly, it was the end of the world, and he'd raged and complained. He'd been heartbroken.

Elizabeth finally understood, more than that, she *was* him. It was one thing to have resigned herself to a child-free life, also given that the man she'd fallen for and married hadn't wanted kids. But now, to deal with him cheating and impregnating his... God, and *that* made it all more complicated, and so much worse.

If she'd never hired Claudia, never gotten to know her, if she'd never befriended her, she'd now be able to just hate her guts. To resent her. To hate Tom even more. That way, she could work through this loss and let it go. But no, now, she found herself in a torrent of quicksand—torn between her affection for Claudia, the desire to continue their friendship, and the unexpected and still smarting loss of her marriage, combined with the fury, devastation, and resentment of facing a world where Claudia carried Tom's child.

She hadn't spoken to anyone about this dilemma, but seriously considered seeking a therapist. Kat, as much as she loved her and didn't mind her caustic tongue and cutting remarks to the crux of any issue, wouldn't help here. Elizabeth knew what she wanted—a continued exploration of this unforeseen and easy-going friendship with Claudia, and more importantly, Tom, out of her life forever. However, that was no longer possible.

Then she worried that Claudia's child would be a little boy who turned out to be the spitting image of Tom. In such a scenario, even if Tom was an absent (paying) father, which Elizabeth expected, if she stayed in Claudia's life, she'd still see Tom, the ghost of Tom, whenever she'd see that boy. Even if the child wasn't a boy, she'd know this was Tom's child. What if she ended up resenting the child? She felt terrible for even having these thoughts, and it seemed to make it plain that their friendship was doomed, yet she didn't want that. So, her solution? Going quiet.

How could she explain this to Claudia, especially after the reassurances she'd given her during their last phone call? She knew Claudia would be hurt by her sudden silence, and likely see through the canceled visit, not to mention the working from home spiel she currently employed because she couldn't face Claudia. She couldn't even make herself pick up the phone. What would she even say?

'Oh, I'm sorry. I realized I might not be able to continue our friendship because I fear that every time I'll later look at your child, I'll see my cheating ex-husband? And what do we do with work at this point?' She hated this. She hated not talking to Claudia, and she missed their interactions. But all she had to offer was hurt, so silence seemed the better option.

Naturally, right when she'd been at one of her lowest points, Claudia had called and asked to meet to talk. In the history of time, had such a request ever ended happily? Did cave men dread it when their women told them they 'needed to talk?' She'd obviously agreed, and they set up to meet at Claudia's place this Saturday.

Sadly, this wouldn't be like the relaxed after work meeting where they hung out eating takeout while watching Kat's show. No, this meeting would likely end it all. The very thought left Elizabeth with a painful emptiness in her chest. How had she grown attached to someone so quickly? Someone so ill-fated to remain in her life.

By Saturday, she'd spent the morning restless and out of sorts, halting her aimless pacing by doing yoga for an hour. It helped, and then, after a quick shower, it was time to head to Claudia's. Once there, she steeled herself before pressing the button next to Claudia's name.

The buzzer rang, and she went inside. Claudia, with her hands stuffed into her pants pockets, waited for her at the door when Elizabeth rounded up the stairs.

"Hey." Claudia rocked on her socked feet. "Come on in. I made us tea."

"Hello." Elizabeth followed her inside.

They made small talk and sipped their tea, seated on Claudia's couch until Elizabeth couldn't take it anymore. "What's this about?"

Claudia grimaced and placed her cup on the coffee table. She sighed. "I just... Since I told you I'm pregnant, things have been different."

Elizabeth remained silent, unsure of what to say to that. Claudia was right, but she didn't know how she could explain this without sounding like the horrible person she felt she was. It had been bad enough to admit her shortcoming to herself, but to share them with Claudia?

"I don't get it. I mean, I understand that it's different, me being pregnant with Tom's baby, compared to having had an affair with him. But just... What you said when we were talking first, and then... What changed?"

Elizabeth sighed. She knew she'd have to explain this, and a part of her wanted to, but the bigger part longed to run away and never even glance at this. If she could only be a bigger person here, if only she could change how she felt. "I thought about it some more, or better, it wouldn't leave me alone."

"My pregnancy?"

Elizabeth nodded. "Yes, but it's more than that. It's the future that this will bring along."

"Because you don't want kids." Claudia nodded.

Elizabeth frowned. "No. Yes, I mean." She clenched her jaw. "This child wouldn't be mine."

"Of course not. I didn't mean to—"

Elizabeth raised her hand, and Claudia fell silent. Why were they talking about it like *that*? "It will be Tom's child."

Claudia sat straighter. "It's *my* child. Tom doesn't matter."

Elizabeth smiled softly, wondering if this was their age difference showing or if it related more to Claudia's innate stubbornness. "It matters to me."

"Oh," Claudia said, her entire posture drooping. "I understand."

"I doubt that." Elizabeth shook her head. She reached out and grasped Claudia's hand.

Claudia's eyes widened as she stared at their intertwined fingers.

"I'm not mad at you, and I still want to see where this friendship business leads us, but I don't know how this can work when... when this will tie you to Tom forever. I want him out of my life." She squeezed Claudia's hand.

Claudia blinked furiously, catching Elizabeth's solemn gaze. "I want that, too."

"The child will make that impossible."

"How? I doubt he'll want to share custody, or let's be real, there's no way he'll want anything to do with my child." She scoffed. "Given how adamant he was about never wanting children, even though we were never serious."

Elizabeth bristled, wanting to protest before she slumped back against her seat. "Yes, you're right."

"Doesn't matter. I want nothing from him."

"Oh, he needs to pay."

"I'm not into revenge, and—"

"Child support, Claudia." Elizabeth's eyes twinkled with laughter.

"Oh, right. Yes. But back to us. You want the friendship, but you can't do it because this baby will remind you of Tom."

Elizabeth stilled, opening and closing her mouth, but no sound left her lips.

"At least I'm assuming that's what you really meant."

Elizabeth flushed. “I don’t… It’s just…”

“I get it.” Claudia worried her lower lip, drawing Elizabeth’s gaze. “I just don’t know how to fix that.”

“There’s no fixing it. That’s the problem.”

Claudia dropped her head, nodding slightly. She cleared her throat. “All right. I… I just… Do you want me to quit?”

Elizabeth sat frozen. This hadn’t been her plan. “No. We’ll just have to go back to being professional again.” Because that had worked out so well the first time. Yet, there was no way she’d allow Claudia to quit over this, or worse, fire her.

“Good. I’d have hated to lose my job.”

Elizabeth smiled, but it was brittle and didn’t reach her eyes.

“If this changes, like, if you feel you can or want to be around me again, don’t think you can’t let me know.”

Elizabeth canted her head.

“Don’t let pride stand in the way or assume I’d reject you. I’m here, and… I still want this friendship, too, and that won’t change. But this is much easier for me.”

Elizabeth blinked away moisture, nodding, as her voice seemed absent.

“OK, good.” Claudia offered Elizabeth one of the saddest smiles she’d ever witnessed, or perhaps it seemed that way because she felt just as gutted.

Elizabeth spent the week after the second end in their… relationship in a daze. Yes, she’d been a coward and did a lot of her work from home, though for the rest, she’d scheduled meetings and lunches with sponsors.

She couldn’t understand why this all upset her so much. They hadn’t even shared a long friendship, and yet her chest still felt hollow and constricted. It seemed odd, this change rattled her almost more than the divorce did. In a different way, but still. At least the divorce was supposed to be finalized by the end of January.

She’d distracted herself with work and had shot a few text messages back and forth with Kat, assuring her friend she was doing all right. She still hadn't mentioned Claudia's pregnancy or their falling out. Though she supposed you couldn't call it a falling out, more like Elizabeth's inability to separate Tom from Claudia.

On the other hand, it wasn't as if she could erase the years of her life with Tom. Even so, this seemed too much, and her head pounded at the mere thought. She knew this would come between them eventually, and it seemed the better, kinder choice to rip them out by the roots now.

Elizabeth groaned when her phone rang after arriving home Friday night from dinner with the most obnoxious (but ridiculously rich) sponsor, after a draining week and with her head still revolving way too much around Claudia. She didn't want to deal with anyone right now. All she wanted was to drink a cup of tea and curl up on the couch with Raji. Elizabeth reached for her phone and felt the urge to throw it against the wall when, out of all people, her *mother's* name appeared on the screen.

She pressed the green button. "Hello, Mother."

"Where are you?"

"At home?"

"I see. And why aren't you at the airport to pick me up?"

Elizabeth's eyes widened, and she gripped hold of the back of the couch because otherwise, she'd have crashed to the floor. Good Lord, she'd forgotten—repressed—that her mother would be visiting her for a week. A week from hell, after she'd just been through such a week, albeit with a different, self-induced cause. "I just got back from..."

"Work? You mean that charity of yours? I'd hardly call that work." Mary sighed. "I suppose I shall take a taxi, given it'll take you forever to get here. Do you think you'll manage to drive me to the airport next Saturday?"

"Yes, mother. Of course. I'm so sorry."

"Yes, yes. You always say that." She hung up without saying goodbye.

Elizabeth released a string of curses, startling Raji, who'd snug around her legs. "Sorry, boy," she mumbled and petted his head. "We're about to be invaded."

Raji meowed and rubbed his head against Elizabeth's palm.

"Guess I better get started." With that, she set out to prepare for her mother. Too bad she couldn't knock herself unconscious for a week as well.

with hope and surprises

For the first time, Claudia delighted in her exhaustion, as it meant she fell into bed earlier and didn't spend as much time feeling sorry for herself while also low-key cursing out Elizabeth for being... whatever she was being. Silly. Really. But no. She was hurt, and she had every right to be. Claudia couldn't imagine how she'd feel in Elizabeth's shoes or how she'd react. But she was hurt, too, and if she couldn't throw a pity party in her own head, then where could she?

She had no issues at work, though she missed the little after-hours meetings with Elizabeth, yet not only did they hardly see each other at the office (if Elizabeth came in at all), but neither worked late. Claudia waited, that was, she didn't leave at five on the dot on the days she'd noticed Elizabeth present, but by the time she ventured out into the hallway, Elizabeth's office stood dark.

Her family had also been relatively quiet and peaceful, which she almost resented as some drama there might have helped distract her from her current abysmal headspace.

On Thursday evening, she had just gotten out of the shower and wanted to curl up on the couch when her doorbell rang. Claudia frowned. While she was off work the next day, she'd made no plans to see anyone, nor had she ordered anything. She rose and padded to the door, looking through the door viewer and froze, then yanked open the door. "Sammy?"

"Surprise!" her best friend called, dropping her duffle to the floor and rushing forward to engulf Claudia in a crushing, long-lasting hug.

Claudia smiled while tears sprung to her eyes as she clutched Sammy closer. "What are you doing here?" she muffled into Sammy's neck.

Sammy pulled back and inspected Claudia's face. "Cheering you up, it seems."

A wry chuckle left Claudia's lips. "I need that, all right."

"Yeah, your blotchy face and red eyes, plus that wounded puppy dog expression leave no doubt."

"Hey! Not everyone can always be as... put together as you are." Claudia eyed Sammy, noting her curvy frame, tan skin, the brown, curly hair, and dark eyes. Claudia liked to describe Sammy's mouth as generous, though Sammy always said she had a big mouth, both literally and figuratively. What Claudia resented was Sammy's elegant, yet understated style.

She'd never understand (never mind replicate) Sammy's ability to carry herself with confidence and grace. She supposed her friendly, almost sunny public demeanor and approachability made her chosen profession in politics a perfect match. Claudia, on the other side, more often than not resembled a prickly, clumsy, unkept cactus. Most definitely when she was moping.

Sammy laughed. "Why, thank you! I learned that the hard way."

"Indeed," Claudia said, then bit her lip. *Damn it*. She'd been trying to banish that word from her vocabulary.

"All right, then, since we don't need to overcome any denials, how about we order some food and chat? I got a million questions, and some interesting tidbits to share."

Claudia's eyes lit up.

"Uh uh, first things first. You order takeout while I take a quick shower. Then we discuss your little conundrum, and as a reward, I spill my news. How does that sound?"

"Like a hard bargain."

Sammy grinned. "Perfect. I don't care what you order, but no pizza. I just had one earlier this week."

"And you can't have pizza twice a week?"

"Sure. But I don't want to." With that, and after pressing a quick kiss on Claudia's cheek, Sammy disappeared into Claudia's bathroom.

"You are staying the night, right?" Claudia called after her.

Sammy's head poked out of the bathroom door. "I'm staying the entire weekend." She waggled her eyebrows before vanishing once more behind the door.

"Nutter," Claudia mumbled and pulled out her phone to browse food delivery options.

An hour later, they sat on the couch eating Chinese takeout while an episode of "Snapped" played low in the background. At least Sammy didn't mind true crime. Claudia sighed.

"So, are you ready to talk now?"

"Is that why you came by? I thought you were insanely busy."

"I am, but I also desperately needed a break, and thought, why not? Two birds, one stone."

Claudia grimaced.

"What?"

"Nothing. I don't like that idiom."

Sammy's eyebrows rose. "All right. But seriously. How are you holding up? I know the pregnancy came as a shock, but—"

Claudia blurted out, "Elizabeth broke up with me."

Silence.

Sammy blinked furiously. "OK, you need to back up and explain. I didn't realize you guys were dating."

"No, no. We were just friends, but, well, the pregnancy kinda screwed us over."

"That sucks. I'm sorry. Why didn't you tell me?"

Claudia's shoulders slumped. "I don't know."

"I wouldn't have teased you or anything."

"Yeah. I was just... I wasn't ready for this discussion. It's a lot to process."

"I can imagine, especially when you want to date the wife of your baby daddy."

Claudia groaned. This was one reason she hadn't spoken to Sammy about this for real. Her humor, even when *not* teasing, didn't always work for her.

"I told you we were just friends."

"Right, that's why you started this conversation with, 'Elizabeth broke up with me.'"

Claudia waved her off. "Figure of speech, and you were the one who started this conversation."

"I don't think I've ever talked about any of my platonic friendships ending like that. Being dumped."

Claudia sighed heavily. "All right, so I may or may not have gotten a bit too emotionally attached to Elizabeth, and currently, even though we weren't dating, it still feels like I was dumped."

Sammy shuffled closer and pulled her into an embrace, kissing the crown of Claudia's hair. "I'm sorry, Claud. That must be awful." She squeezed her, then let go. "What are you going to do?"

"Nothing. Hoping she'll change her mind."

"About what, exactly? You never said why things ended."

"Isn't it obvious?"

"The pregnancy."

"Duh. She says she wants Tom out of her life, and with the baby... She'll always see Tom or be reminded of him."

Sammy snorted. "Good luck with that."

"What do you mean?"

"She was married to him for how long?"

"Five years, together for seven."

"Look, I get it. In the height of a break-up, a divorce, you usually hate your ex's guts and just want them to fall off the face of the earth. And for a while, maybe that is what you need. But they were still a part of your life, and to a degree, they shaped or influenced who you are."

"I'd say that depends on how long a relationship lasted, no?" Claudia pointed out.

"Of course, but I was talking about long-term relationships. You can't forget something because you don't want to remember it anymore."

"Ha! If only. You could make a lot of money if you ever figured out how that works."

"My point is, what she says now comes from a place of pain."

"She has every right to feel like this. She'd have wanted children if it ever worked out and it didn't. Tom never wanted kids. So for me to be pregnant by Tom is..."

"Harsh. Totally. Again, I'm not minimizing her feelings, and I'm not even saying her reaction is unreasonable or unfair. Considering everything that has happened between you, it's a wonder you were ever able to strike up some semblance of a friendship."

"It was more than that, Sam." Claudia grabbed a pillow and pulled it close to her chest. "We connected on a level that... I've not experienced, not so fast and so deep."

"Ow, thank you," Sammy deadpanned.

"You know what I mean. Present company excluded. But you're different, anyway. I've known you forever, and we have a very different foundation. Elizabeth and I should never have gotten this close given the circumstances, and yet it was so effortless." She pulled at a loose string on the pillowcase.

"Wow."

Claudia raised her head. "What?"

"You're really gone on this woman."

Claudia sighed. "It doesn't matter. Not only is she straight, but she also wants nothing to do with me anymore."

"Right now."

"What? How can you be straight right now?"

"One track mind, huh?"

Claudia ducked her head.

"I meant she doesn't want you around right now. I'm sure with some time, she'll change her tune. Once her reason catches up with her emotions."

"You think so?" Claudia hated how hopeful her voice sounded. But she'd had zero hope before Sammy, and now she latched on to this idea like Kate Winslet's character did on that piece of wood floating in the North Atlantic Ocean.

"Yeah. I'm sure. Based on what you said about her, she's not someone guided by emotions, well, aside from in extreme situation, which this is."

"She isn't."

"There you go."

"I hope you're right. I know we'll never be more than friends, and that's OK. I just want her in my life."

Sammy offered her a soft smile. "She's a lucky woman."

Claudia flushed. "Anyway, you wanted to tell me some news?"

"Oh, right," Sammy said, launching into a tale that resulted in Claudia listening with wide eyes before clutching her stomach laughing. God, she was so lucky to have Sammy.

brimstone and hellfire

ELIZABETH HATED HER LIFE. First, she'd lost her marriage, then Claudia, who funny enough (not really) she'd have met even without the dissolution of her marriage. Without that added weight, they could have had such an easy-going friendship. Though she didn't know if that would have even happened. How would they have gotten to know each other given the barrier Elizabeth erected between herself and her employees?

But now, not a week later, her mother showed up for the visit from hell. Since Pat Stewarts had finished their work the week before, she'd moved out of the guest room, although her mother's favorite guest room would have been vacant either way. Even if Tom wouldn't have told Mary about their divorce—she still didn't understand why he did that—her mother wouldn't have bought an excuse of, 'Oh, Tom's out on a business trip.' She was a bloodhound and would have sniffed out the truth and not hidden her disappointment. Now at least, it all laid bare between them.

Mary had sighed, a sound encompassing both her disappointment in her daughter and the smugness at having been right. Her mother had an extensive repertoire of sighs that all expressed different emotions, and Elizabeth knew them by heart.

"I'm assuming he left you for a younger woman? Tom hadn't been clear on the reasons behind your split." The 'I told you so' hung heavy and cloying between them.

"He didn't." That wasn't even a lie. "I filed for divorce."

Mary's eyes widened almost comically. "Why on *earth* would you do that? Do you really believe you'll find another man?"

Elizabeth bit her lower lip.

"Stop that. It's a terrible habit," Mary chided her.

Elizabeth contemplated that her mother and Lauren Daniels might get along splendidly. Perhaps she should take her mother to one of their canasta game nights. The most recent one had been quite peaceful, no snark from Lauren. Elizabeth had wondered for a moment if the other woman had been sick.

On the other hand, should you invite the Devil to team up with Baphomet? She chuckled.

"This isn't funny!"

It kind of is. Elizabeth schooled her features. "Of course not, Mother."

"You are forty-six years old! Now you've added divorced to the list." Her mother pursed her lips. "At least you have money. Although that is also a problem, as many men are intimidated by that or would only be interested in your money."

"How charming," Elizabeth drawled. "Has it ever occurred to you I may not want to be with another man?"

"What? Are you gay now?"

Elizabeth started. "People don't turn 'gay,' and that's not the only orientation that differs from heterosexuality." Claudia popped into her head, and of course she'd be smiling. Despite being somewhat exasperated about her mind's refusal to cede the mental space Claudia now seemed to occupy, the image of a grinning Claudia still offered a strange sort of solace.

Her mother waved her off. "That's hardly the point."

"I don't know, Mother. My focus isn't on sex or another relationship. Tom and I… The divorce isn't even finalized yet, and—"

"Then take him back!"

"What?"

"Call him! Right now. Hopefully, he will come back. You know how prideful men are. Or wait, I could call him, and we can all go out to dinner one evening this week."

"No! You won't call him, and I won't ask him to come back. I wanted this divorce. Why would I change my mind now?" A stabbing pain bloomed behind her temple. She had just wanted to relax. This confrontation wouldn't even make the bottom three on her list of things she wanted to do.

"Because you've seen the errors of your ways?"

"It's over, Mother. Just let it go."

"Let it go? Watching my only child ruin her life? If you at least had some kind of late in life sexual awakening and realized you're gay. But this? Why would you leave your husband?"

Elizabeth's mouth opened, then closed.

"What is it now?"

"I didn't realize you were this progressive."

Mary scoffed. "You live across the ocean from me. It's not as if you're likely to make a scene in front of my friends."

Elizabeth rolled her eyes.

"These days, they pronounce you all kinds of nasty names for not accepting whatever new lifestyle people want to live. Obviously, I'd prefer certain attributes in your potential partner, but in the end, I don't care."

"Obviously." Why did her mother still treat her like a wayward teenager?

"I'd have welcomed a rich man your age or a bit older, but I didn't cause a scene when you married Tom."

That was news to Elizabeth, though she supposed she didn't, at least not in public. Mary was too British for that. Still, she recalled her scathing and cutting remarks.

"If you were to find a suitable woman, who am I to judge?"

Who indeed. However, judgmental was her mother's middle name for a reason, so Elizabeth neither understood this newfound 'tolerance' nor could she fathom its origin. Or purpose, really.

"The point is, I don't want you to die alone."

"Are there any other ways?"

Mary glared at her. "Don't be so flippant. It doesn't suit you."

Elizabeth sighed. This would be a long, horrible week, and she had to watch that her mother didn't send Tom a message behind her back. The last thing she needed was Tom joining this week's festivities.

Wednesday saddled her with a terrible migraine attack, and to her utter bewilderment, her mother not only seemed concerned, but she brought her cold compresses and made her a peppermint tea with honey and brought it to her bedside. She stroked her hair.

"I worry about you, Lizzie," she whispered.

Elizabeth managed a weak smile and grasped her mother's hand. "I know," she croaked. And in some way, she did. Their relationship had always been fraught, but her mother loved her in her own way. They were just incredibly different, and Elizabeth had been her nan's girl, and perhaps that had also created a rift between them.

Still, you'd think a mother would stand above such petty jealousies and would want whatever was best for her child. She was sure Claudia would be like that. Tears welled in her eyes and her eyelids fluttered shut.

"Rest, darling. You'll feel better tomorrow." Mary stroked her cheek before rising and tiptoeing out of the room. She closed the door softly, almost silently.

Elizabeth buried her face in her pillow and cried. She hated what her life had become, and she hated that these moments where her mother cared, where she *showed* her love, left her with the desire for more, for repairing their relationship, and for a mother whose actions showed love over judgment more often. Then she got angry because at forty-six, she should be beyond this.

The rest of her mother's stay wasn't as awful as the start, but it wouldn't have been her mother without some final parting shots toward her age and her future as a lonely, old cat lady. She should be so lucky. Elizabeth had moments where she thought it not only a societal error to equate being alone with being lonely, but sometimes she thought it wouldn't be the worst in the world to remain by herself. Besides, being without a partner didn't mean you were alone. People had friends. There was Kat, even if she lived far away. And well, there had been Claudia.

Whenever Elizabeth thought of her—and she refused to count how often she did—a heaviness fell over her and she wished she could reach out. Oh, she knew she could. Claudia would welcome her, so she'd said at least, and given Claudia's earnest nature, Elizabeth had little doubt there. But then say what? That the week with her mother had fixed her issues?

And what if she went back, and they reestablished their friendship but once the baby was here, she realized she couldn't do it after all? How awful would that be? She refused to flip-flop— either she was in or out. Claudia deserved more than a fair-weather friend, and Elizabeth didn't trust herself to be more than that right now. That she missed Claudia seemed like a weak reason for reconnecting.

Sunday evening, Kat's phone call interrupted her moping.

"Turn on the camera," Kat said shortly into the conversation.

"What? Why?"

"I want to see your face."

Elizabeth chuckled but obliged and turned on the camera. Smiling at the sight of Kat with her red hair in a ponytail and her glasses hanging too low on her nose. "Hi."

"Hi." Kat shook her head.

"What is it?"

"You look dreadful."

Elizabeth's eyebrows rose. "Wow. That's what I needed to hear to round off this week. Thanks."

"No, no. You're still gorgeous, as always. But you look sad. Defeated."

Elizabeth flushed. "Well, I told you my mother was here until yesterday. For a week. So..."

"Yes, but I don't know. Your mother usually stresses you or makes you angry. She doesn't make you sad."

"Hmm, that depends." This time, there were some definite moments of sadness.

"Oh, what happened? Are you all right?"

Elizabeth cleared her throat. "Nothing major. Just moments where she showed more care than usual, and it messed with my head. It wouldn't have hit me so hard without…" Should she go there? Then again, they told each other everything.

"Claudia is pregnant with Tom's baby."

"What? Fucking hell. And now?"

Elizabeth shrugged. "I thought we could keep being friends, but then… It hit me how this will always tie me to Tom, and right now I can't. I can't deal with that."

Kat frowned. "Wait, your issue is that Claudia's pregnancy ties *you* to Tom? I'm not sure I follow."

"Well, if we keep hanging out, I will see the baby, and I'll always know who the father is. What if it's a boy and he looks just like Tom?"

"OK, but don't you already associate her with Tom? She will always be the reason your marriage ended."

"*Tom* is the reason my marriage ended," Elizabeth pointed out, a steely tone creeping into her voice.

"Right. And Tom is your ex, or soon-to-be ex-husband."

"Yes. And?"

"So why would you need Claudia or her child to be reminded of him? You spent seven years at his side, shared your life. Aren't you connected to him in some way forever? Sure, time will lessen this and make it easier. We don't have perfect recall and all. Hell, I usually don't remember what I had for breakfast the day before."

Elizabeth laughed. "You have a point."

"I'd have thought it was more about you wanting kids and Tom didn't, and now his mistress is pregnant."

"Don't call her that!"

Kat chuckled, shaking her head. "I swear, you're weirdly attached to this woman. If I didn't know any better…"

Elizabeth waved her off and sighed. "Well, not anymore."

"Right. Because no contact automatically also erases her from your thoughts."

Elizabeth ducked her head. She hated Kat's ability to cut to the chase and see right through her bullshit. "Indeed."

"So who are you punishing right now?"

"Huh?"

"Do you miss her?"

"Obviously. But didn't you say time will make all that easier?"

"Oh, yes. No contact is a good way to get someone out of your system. I'm a big advocate there, but I'm questioning your motivations. Don't rob yourself of a potentially great friendship because you're overly emotional."

Elizabeth released a soft laugh. "I'm not sure I've ever been called that."

"True, but you are that now. I get it. A lot has happened in a short amount of time. Life-changing stuff. Then your mother's visit, which didn't help."

Elizabeth scoffed. "That's one way of putting it."

"See? It's natural to feel overwhelmed, and perhaps you'd be better off without Claudia in your life, but... See!"

"What?"

"Your face when I said that. You grimaced at the idea of not having her in your life. You really like her."

Elizabeth straightened. "I didn't."

"You sure did."

"I just miss her, and of course I like her. This would all be so much easier if I didn't."

"I know, but I think your logic is flawed right now. Unless this all is about you never having kids..."

Elizabeth sighed. "It crossed my mind. I'm not thrilled about it all. It seems like a double punch, you know? But I also started to wonder if it was or is more..., I was fine with not having children, but when this now happened, I felt some kind of way. Like why her and not me, even though I had made peace with never having children. How crazy is that?"

Kat hummed.

"What now?"

"No, I'm just agreeing."

"So you think I overreacted?"

"Perhaps. I'd hate for you to lose out on an important... relationship because of an emotional overload."

Elizabeth hadn't considered that she might be suffering from an emotional overload, but Kat had a point. She had been under a lot of stress, and the easiest solution was to blame it all on Claudia and the pregnancy. It offered a clear-cut solution and didn't leave her with any confusion. Well, if you didn't count the vexation of *missing* Claudia, of longing to hear her voice. Her laughter. God, what was happening to her?

In the end, she didn't want to be pregnant, and since she didn't blame Claudia for the affair, why would she cut her out of her life because she was pregnant? Kat was right, she couldn't fully erase Tom from her life, and if she was honest, she rarely ever thought of Tom anymore when she interacted with Claudia. Perhaps she needed to reevaluate her stance, as she seemed to have acted rashly. Could she get Claudia back?

between trepidation and hope

Claudia still had moments when she struggled with how well Elizabeth seemed to have taken her confession at first. The contrast to the change, to her calling off their friendship—it rattled her. This still fresh memory left her with a mixture of pain and rage. Rage at herself and Tom. A little at Elizabeth, too, but then guilt rose about that part of her anger, which didn't improve her overall situation.

She wished none of this had ever happened. Perhaps then, she could have met Elizabeth through her job and they'd have forged a friendship from there, without all this drama between them. Though without Tom, she'd have never contacted his wife and so she'd have never interacted with Elizabeth in a non-work setting. Would she have ever realized how interesting the woman was?

Some said that it was better to have loved and lost than not to have loved at all. For Claudia, the jury was still out on that. Not that she loved Elizabeth like *that*, and she hadn't lost a lifelong friendship. Yet she'd lost a relationship she could have seen lasting a lifetime. Wouldn't you be better off not knowing that? Were fleeting moments of happiness enough to make up for the pain you felt when everything crashed down?

She also wondered if Tom would have cheated with someone else if they'd never met, and if that person would not have told Elizabeth, which meant she'd still be clueless and living her life at Tom's side. No. In the end, Claudia would never regret telling Elizabeth the truth about everything, even if it had cost her their friendship.

After Sammy had left, she continued to cling to the weak hope that things might still work out, but then she chided herself for that because hope so often proved to be a wicked mistress. At that thought, she gritted her teeth.

Mistress.

Tom had turned her into that, and whenever this word entered her mind, a familiar fury surged through her. Aside from there being no male equivalent (there should be), she'd never have put herself in such a situation, and she continued to resent Tom for doing that to her. In the future, she needed to be...

What? More thorough? Doubt her partner and hire an investigator to make sure they didn't lie and were secretly married or in a relationship? How ridiculous. Either way, she needed to make peace with all of this.

Claudia settled more during the week. She thankfully suffered no more nausea, and no drama arose at work. Elizabeth was back, too, and while she seemed more present, the distance between them persisted, and in some moments seemed to loom ever larger. Or perhaps that resulted from a culmination of... everything that had happened.

On Friday afternoon after returning from work, her phone rang, but she'd missed the call by the time she'd gotten out of the bathroom. When she picked it up, expecting a missed call from Sammy or her mother, she did a double take when instead Elizabeth's name showed up. She settled on a chair and stared at her phone log for a couple of minutes, then placed it screen down on the table.

She wondered what Elizabeth could want. Should she call her back? Would Elizabeth ring again? Would she seek her out on Monday at work if Claudia didn't call back? What if it was a butt dial? She knew how to obtain the answer to her first question, but she might hate the outcome. Then again, she doubted Elizabeth could tell her anything that would be worse than the conclusion of their last conversation.

Steeling herself, Claudia grasped her phone and returned Elizabeth's call. She picked up after two rings.

"Hi, Claudia," a breathless Elizabeth greeted her.

Claudia shuffled in her seat. "Hi. Are you OK?"

"I don't know."

Claudia frowned. "What's up? Your migraines again?" She closed her eyes. Why was it so easy to fall into this pattern with Elizabeth?

"No, not this week. Listen, I know how we left things last time, and it's... I don't like it."

"I don't either, but you said—"

"Yes, I know. I may have overreacted." The missing 'again' hung in the air, but neither touched it. Both instances were more than understandable, even if they sucked. And hurt.

Silence.

"Are you still there?"

"Yes." She'd wanted to hear this, and a part of her wanted to jump up and down for joy, but she also figured a certain amount of caution would do her some good. She didn't want to hope, only to lose again.

"Would you... If you're free tomorrow, would you come by my place so we can talk?" Elizabeth asked, and Claudia hated the hesitation, the wistful tone of her voice.

"About what?"

Silence.

Elizabeth sighed. "About how much my life sucks."

"I'm not sure how talking to me will help there."

Elizabeth released a wry chuckle. "What if I told you that your absence is one cause of this... suckage?"

Claudia's mouth opened, but no sound spilled forth while her heart sprinted as if she were being chased by a horde of zombie.

"Is that too much? I'm sorry. I thought... You value honesty, and it had been me who'd ended this, so it's on me to try to fix it."

"If it's what you truly want."

"I wouldn't lie to you, especially not about this," Elizabeth rasped.

Claudia closed her eyes. "When should I be there?" She thought she could hear Elizabeth's answering smile. Or perhaps her visual imagination was that great. Either way, Claudia felt about ten tons lighter.

"How about at one?"

"OK. See you tomorrow."

"Thank you."

Before heading to Elizabeth's the next day, she'd bought several cat treats. In fact, her purse mostly contained irresistible cat temptations. Raji better appreciate it, and she figured getting along with him might add some plus points to her column. She shouldn't assume Elizabeth's words would translate to a rekindling of their friendship.

When she arrived at Elizabeth's place, she rang the doorbell, a small container in her hand.

"Hi. Thanks for coming," Elizabeth said, seemingly unsure of how to greet Claudia, and instead pointed at the box in her hand. "Is that for me?"

"Yes." She held it up. "It's *madlouka*. That's sweet *knefeh* dough topped with fresh cream and crushed pistachios. It's one of my favorites." She flushed and dipped her head.

"That's sweet. Thank you. You didn't have to bring anything." Elizabeth accepted the package and motioned for Claudia to follow her inside. She placed the pastry on an entryway table and turned back toward Claudia. "Are you OK?"

"Yeah, of course." She stuffed her hand into her pants pockets.

"Still no morning sickness or anything, right?"

"No, the nausea has been a lot better."

"Good. Come on in. I made a chicken and vegetable stew. I hope you like it."

"Oh, I do, but I didn't expect you to go through so much trouble." What was going on here?

"I was in the mood, and it wasn't a hassle. I haven't felt like cooking in a while, though I usually quite like it."

"Huh. I can't say we have that in common. I live on too much fast food and processed, quick meals."

Elizabeth frowned, looking Claudia up and down. "I sometimes forget how young you are."

"Hey!" Not that again.

Elizabeth waved her off. "You need to eat healthier now. Are you taking any pre-natal vitamins?"

"Started them a while ago." Claudia worried she'd entered the twilight zone. Why was Elizabeth suddenly not just OK with the pregnancy that three weeks ago made her end their contact, but now she also acted all concerned and whatnot? This was giving her whiplash.

"Good," Elizabeth said with such evident satisfaction, Claudia blinked furiously.

They settled to eat shortly after she had arrived, and their conversation flowed easier than Claudia had expected, but then again, they always seemed to defy all odds.

"Too bad you can't partake in a glass of wine. The Pinot complements the stew perfectly."

"Oh, I rarely drink alcohol," Claudia said between bites.

"Any particular reason?"

Claudia chuckled. "It's funny. You're surprised that I'm not regularly consuming a cell toxin."

Elizabeth startled. "Come again?"

"It's just odd. Like if someone invented alcoholic drinks today and tried to get FDA approval or whatever safety certificate food and beverages need to be legally sold, they'd laugh and laugh and laugh before kicking them out."

"I suppose. I've never thought of it like that."

"Most people don't. Alcohol is such an integral part of our social structure, it's normal, even though it causes around three million deaths a year worldwide, not to mention all the social and economic losses society endures, or the hundreds of diseases and injuries it has a hand in."

"That's a condemning fact sheet."

Claudia hummed. "My relationship with alcohol is complicated. I drank more in my early twenties, but it never sat right with me. So now it's more like special occasions where everyone is drinking, and I don't want to look like the boring outsider of fun." She frowned. "That makes me sound incredibly pathetic."

"It doesn't. Peer pressure and societal expectations aren't easy to shrug off."

"But I'm old enough to... I don't know. Stand my ground? Especially when I feel strongly about something."

"I'm older and still succumb to those forces at times. You'll get there eventually, but don't be so hard on yourself on the way."

"We're our worst critics for a reason. We know all the stuff in our heads, and so we have the full picture when we fail," Claudia said.

"That doesn't mean you should never offer yourself grace."

Claudia held Elizabeth's gaze. Perhaps that was what they were doing here, too. Offering each other grace by returning to a more normal interaction. But would this work? Wouldn't they have to discuss the elephant in the room? Perhaps only Claudia felt like that, and Elizabeth had already moved on. But she had wanted them to talk, and Claudia didn't believe Elizabeth had a discussion about alcohol in mind when she'd suggested that. "I suppose not. Like I said, this is a complicated and heavy topic. I didn't mean to drag down our conversation."

Elizabeth canted her head. "You didn't. Is there a rule that we may only talk about happy or carefree issues?"

"Of course not."

"Besides, we already have one heavy conversation ahead of us. What's another one? That's if you want to talk about it."

Relief flooded Claudia that Elizabeth meant to discuss whatever was going on between them. But she also wanted to share this story with her. She had missed Elizabeth terribly, more so than she should.

At the same time, she rarely talked about her grandfather, and she also perceived the underlying tension that slowly rose between them, but oh, how she longed to be back on solid ground with Elizabeth. "My grandfather died when I was eighteen. Cirrhosis of the liver." She sighed. "The doctors told him he needed to stop drinking, or he'd die. He stopped. Or so we thought." She smiled, a reflex to ward off tears that rushed to her eyes. "We didn't know. He..." Claudia clenched her jaw. "After he died, we... we found bottles, small flasks filled with beer, and spirits everywhere in the house."

"I'm so sorry."

"Thank you. It was awful. He was... We were close. Whenever we flew back to Lebanon to see our family there, we'd always sit together and chat, and he'd tell me stories about growing up and take me places he loved." She shrugged. "We'd drink Earl Grey together, and so that scent is..."

"Bittersweet."

"Yes, but my memories are mostly sweet and fond, and they are much heavier than the loss in some ways. It's... A friend of mine once told me a metaphor about grief several years ago when I broke down sobbing as she offered me his favorite pastry."

"Care to share it?"

Claudia nodded. "Imagine an empty room, fully closed and contained, no windows, nothing. But there's this one green dot on the wall and there's a ball bouncing around. Forever. It never stops or pauses."

Elizabeth's intense gaze brimmed with compassion that it made Claudia's voice falter.

"That green spot is your loss, your pain and grief. When you first lose someone, that spot covers almost the entire room, so the ball bouncing through the room hits it again and again, all the time. But as time passes, the spot shrinks and while you still miss your loved one, you don't ache anymore. Yet, when it hits the green spot..." She shakes her head. "It's like you've just lost them."

"And what do Earl Grey and bergamot do? Do they make the ball hit that spot?"

"No. There's only a rush of warmth and fondness."

"It makes sense that your relationship with alcohol would be complicated. Aside from it being a cell toxin, as you've pointed out, it connects to a terrible loss."

"Yeah. Thank you."

"For what?"

Claudia shrugged. "Being you, and being back, I suppose." Elizabeth maintained her gaze, and Claudia couldn't decipher it, but it caused heat to spread through her body.

"Thank *you* for being willing to hear me out."

They finished their food and settled in the living room where Claudia encountered Raji lying curled up on the couch, fast asleep. Bribery would have to wait, especially as she'd been preoccupied with something else all day. "May I ask you a question?"

"Of course. You don't need my permission for that."

"It's just..." Claudia worried her lower lip. "It's hard to fathom that you're now OK with all of this again."

"It's complicated."

"I have time. Besides, that's what I'm here for, right?"

overload and regrets

A HUGE PART OF Elizabeth didn't want to have this discussion. It had been hard enough to allow herself to contact Claudia and ask for her to visit today. Doing so had devoured almost all of her courage. She wished they could just drop it, act like nothing had happened and continue as they did before. Wishful thinking galore, not to mention, things *were* already different. They were talking, yes, and sometimes their conversation flowed like it used to, but this high-pitched tension lay between them—even their greeting had been awkward.

After her mother's visit and her talk with Kat, Elizabeth had been examining the entire situation deeper, and she'd asked herself some uncomfortable questions. She couldn't erase Tom—the memory of their time together—from her life as if they had been nothing. And to be honest, she didn't want that. What she did want was no contact with him, at least for the foreseeable future. That Claudia was pregnant didn't mean Elizabeth would have to interact with Tom.

Moreover, she supposed the baby would be their own person. She didn't think of her uncle when she saw her cousin Hunter, though he had always been the carbon copy of his dad. Why would that be different here? Most of all, and here she'd been more honest with Claudia than might have been prudent, her life without Claudia did indeed suck. She missed her constantly—like a hollow ache in her chest.

"It was a bit like an overload, though I didn't realize it right away. There are moments when you feel like you'll explode if something doesn't change or give right this second. It's an immediate internal crisis and you feel you can't bear even a fraction of a second of whatever is going on."

Claudia nodded. "Yeah. I've had moments like that. It's funny because when I look back on them, I don't recall the exact emotion, and though I know how intense it was, in retrospect, I don't get it anymore."

"Yes, though I do still understand it. I haven't changed my mind on not wanting Tom to have any part in my life."

"I don't want that either, for myself, I mean."

"While that might not be as easy for you, given the pregnancy, we both know it's very unlikely he'll seek to be a part of your child's life. Still, you never know."

"I'll tell him, once I'm past the first trimester, or even later. There's no rush, but again, even if he wanted to be in the baby's life, it wouldn't have anything to do with you. I'd not ask you to be there for that."

"I know. But again, emotions aren't known for being rational, and in that moment, when I first thought about what this means and how it would affect me, my imagination ran away with me."

"That makes sense."

"I suppose it's a mixture. Me realizing that I've overreacted, and that Tom will always be a part of my past, though nothing can make me include him in my present and future."

"I'd never try that," Claudia said, once more wearing that sincere, earnest expression that tugged at Elizabeth's heart.

"I know. Again, I felt helpless. And even if Tom is responsible for us getting closer in a weird way, that doesn't mean he'll continue to play a role."

"I'm glad you changed your mind."

"Me, too."

"I missed you a lot," Claudia said, then froze as if bracing for an impact.

"That's... a relief to hear because I missed you, too."

Claudia's smile was blinding, causing a lump to form in Elizabeth's throat.

"I'll admit we've had an uncommon way to start a friendship, and it's perhaps not something you'd advertise in, 'and how did you two meet' questions, but it seems a shame to reject a connection because of how it has arisen, or because of fear for the future."

"Yeah. It's still... I don't know. A lot, isn't it?" Claudia groaned. "Sorry. Never mind me. I sometimes sabotage a good thing."

"Us being friends is a good thing?"

"Duh," Claudia deadpanned.

Elizabeth laughed, then sobered. "It is a lot. I won't lie. We might still encounter some bumps along the way. But it would be better to... take things easy and discuss whatever is bothering us rather than going nuclear like I did. I now feel OK, not... I'm still a bit gun shy, as they say, but I'll be OK. And I'm not saying this because it's what will allow our friendship to continue."

Claudia's eyes widened.

"The news of your pregnancy threw me for a loop, but in the end, it's a reality I can't change, nor would I want to as it's not my place. I realized, thankfully, that it has nothing to do with our relationship."

"You didn't wish it had been you?"

Elizabeth sighed. Of course Claudia would go there. "I had some moments of bitterness. As I said, it was a lot in a short amount of time, and my feelings were all over the place." She grimaced. "Truly unpleasant."

Claudia just looked at her.

"Ten years ago, perhaps I'd have wished it had been me. Maybe even right when we'd had gotten married, but now? No. I can't even fathom giving birth at forty-seven and chasing around a ten-year-old at almost sixty."

Claudia laughed. "You don't chase ten-year-olds anymore."

"Be that as it may, no. I don't wish for that."

"OK."

"What's really going on?" Elizabeth asked.

"I guess sometimes I struggle to believe a good thing can be real or that it's so easy in the end."

"I didn't say it was easy. It hit me hard, but in the end it doesn't matter."

Claudia frowned. "But 'doesn't matter' doesn't mean you're really at peace with it or that it won't... hurt us again," she said, clearing her throat.

"Perhaps, but it's a process, and if I felt uncertain, I wouldn't have asked you to come today. I don't enjoy endless back and forth, and I've already caused enough of that. I'd not put us through such an emotional rollercoaster again. I can't change what happened. It's done, but I can promise to try to find different solutions in the future."

"Together?"

"Yes. Together."

"That's good. I appreciate you being sure because I'd hate going through that again, too. And well, thank you for being so gracious about it all."

"Once more, I don't blame you for Tom's affair, even though you were a part of it. You didn't know, and as such you're without blame. More so, you contacted me right away and since then, you've been nothing but honest."

"Yes, but—"

"No, I don't think you understand how much that means to me. But it's also... I had two choices, right? I either let this go or I lose your friendship for good, and I chose the former."

"I'm glad," Claudia said. "But how do you *choose* to let go of an emotion?"

Elizabeth shrugged. "Because I decided to do it? I don't know. Maybe it depends on what is more important. Again, we'll likely encounter more moments where one of us gets their feelings hurt. But that's life, and it's something that happens in friendships regardless of the circumstances. I need you to remember that none of this is your fault. You're not causing this pain. It will dull and disappear with time."

"I still hate you suffered any pain because of something I had a part in."

Elizabeth reached out and clasped Claudia's hand. "That's because you have such a soft heart."

Claudia ducked her head. "I hope the decision to let go won't backfire on you."

"I doubt it. If an emotion were to destroy what you wish to maintain or prevent what you want from blossoming, you'd find a way to contain it and let it go. Or transform it into something else. I don't see that as an issue that keeps coming up once decided."

"If you're sure."

"I am." Elizabeth squeezed Claudia's hand. "This won't get in our way again."

"OK."

"But I have a question of my own, though it might be somewhat indiscreet."

Claudia snorted. "I'd say we're beyond that."

"Tom said he used condoms. He's always been quite diligent with that."

"Oh, we did. Every time." Claudia flushed and lowered her head.

"I suppose accidents do happen."

"That they do, for two women out of one hundred." She cringed. "I looked that up when I tested positive. But let's hope that all of this will be a blessing."

"I'm sure it will," Elizabeth said.

Raji stretched and rose, meandering toward Elizabeth and rubbing against her leg. She stroked his head.

Claudia eyed Elizabeth and Raji, before trying to hide a yawn.

"You're still so tired all the time?"

"Yes, but... I honestly don't want to go home yet."

Elizabeth's heart clenched at Claudia's words, delivered in such a soft, low tone. "Then stay."

"Do you think we could watch something?"

Elizabeth's eyes widened, once more surprised by Claudia's easy-going demeanor and candor. She knew most people wouldn't have been as forgiving as Claudia had been in their situation, nor would a connection have been this effortlessly reestablished. "Sure. What are you in the mood for?"

"Hmm, all my crime shows are out. How about *Broken Time* again? We could continue where we'd left of."

Elizabeth chuckled. "And you assume I own the show on DVD?"

"No, we can stream it again. I can log into my account if you don't have a subscription."

"You do that," Elizabeth said, still petting Raji who'd narrowed his eyes and hissed at Claudia when she reached out to take the remote control from Elizabeth. "So much for bribing my cat."

"Hey! I'm tired, and it's our first day together. To be fair, I was also a little distracted by Raji's owner. Besides, he'll learn to love me, don't worry."

"Is that so?" Elizabeth refrained from clearing her throat. Why did her voice sound so husky all of a sudden?

"Yes. I'm an acquired taste."

Elizabeth's eyes shone while Claudia blushed.

Claudia set up the show and pressed play, continuing where they'd previously left of ages ago, during another time. "That could be our thing." Claudia settled deeper into the couch.

"Hmm?"

"Watching your best friend's show together." Claudia yawned.

Elizabeth chuckled and got more comfortable as well. She felt so warm and content. They'd cleared the air, and she'd gotten Claudia back, her confidant who'd gotten close faster than anyone in a long time, and who had returned without punishing Elizabeth for overreacting, who demanded no groveling or penance.

Elizabeth gazed at Claudia, noting how her eyelids flickered closed as she drifted nearer, leaning against her shoulder, fast asleep.

Her future didn't look so bleak and alone after all.

with faltering infatuation

When Claudia had woken up in the middle of the night, mortified to find that she had not only fallen asleep but had cuddled up to Elizabeth, the other woman had just smiled that damn soft smile and ushered her to the guestroom, rejecting Claudia's suggestion of still going home.

"If you think I'll let you drive home at two in the morning, tired and exhausted like you are, you don't know me at all."

She'd given her a set of pajamas and left her with a bag of toiletries, saying she'd check on her again before heading to bed herself.

When Elizabeth had come back, Claudia had been once more about to fall asleep and apparently, had invited Elizabeth to go roller skating. They had talked about going before their... break. Claudia loved roller skating, and she hadn't been in ages because going alone was boring. When she'd mentioned it during one of their conversations, Elizabeth had confessed that while she hadn't been to a rink in decades, she used to love ice skating as a teenager. They'd talked about going one day, but then everything had ended.

She didn't know why this had been on her mind that night, but Elizabeth had agreed and come morning asked when they should go, and that they likely should do it soon as it might not be something Claudia could do later in her pregnancy. For various reasons, Claudia had been flummoxed because she had no memory of asking.

That was how they ended up at the local skating rink on a Wednesday after work because, "It'll be less crowded in case I make a fool of myself." Elizabeth shouldn't have worried about that.

She was utterly mesmerizing, almost floating across the track. Several times, Claudia almost collided with the few other skaters because she couldn't take her eyes off Elizabeth, who was smiling, her cheeks red and her eyes glowing.

"This was such a brilliant idea! I haven't had this much fun in ages," Elizabeth exclaimed when they stopped for a moment, leaning against the perimeter of the rink.

Claudia smiled, grinned goofily, more like it. She'd decided that since she couldn't seem to nip this infatuation in the bud, she might as well enjoy it, as it was harmless and would lead to nothing. Moreover, it came with no chance of once more picking a terrible significant other. Not that she thought Elizabeth would make an awful partner. That was likely *why* this would never happen. Besides, they had just reconnected, and she felt so, so happy about that. She sometimes had to stop herself from skipping instead of walking or whistling whatever song played in her head.

"Based on your grin, I'd say you're enjoying yourself, too. Although you've been living dangerously."

Claudia's eyebrows rose. "So you've noticed my close calls, huh?"

"Hard not to amidst the shouts and curses of your almost murderers. Or would they have been *your* victims?"

"Hey! There were no shouts or curses! A few yelps perhaps," Claudia grumbled.

"Hmm, then maybe I just have my eyes on you."

Claudia stared speechlessly after Elizabeth, who once more skated out into the open. If this had been anyone else, those words, that tone, and with that expression, Claudia would have sworn Elizabeth was flirting with her.

"You wish," she mumbled under her breath, and pushed off the border to chase after Elizabeth. Who knew sleepy, exhausted Claudia could come up with such a bittersweet proposal as roller skating with the woman who left her in a state of utter bewilderment while her heart vied for a reprieve.

They skated peacefully together, talking and joking for a while, but like most things, reality tended to interrupt quite rudely. Claudia was telling Elizabeth about a prank she and Sammy had come up with when they were ten (it had fallen completely flat), and she'd been so immersed in her tale that she missed a gaggle of teens—seeming to be just as oblivious to their surroundings—heading straight for her.

By the time she noticed the imminent collision, she froze.

Elizabeth called out her name and yanked at Claudia's arm, pulling her into her body. Elizabeth staggered under the weight and speed, dragging her toward the perimeter, where they collided against the border in a heap.

Claudia groaned, holding on to Elizabeth, struggling to keep them both up right.

"Are you all right?" Elizabeth asked, breathless, and her face a mask of concern.

She was so pretty. Claudia could only stare at her and bask in her nearness, in the subtle aroma of bergamot and jasmine, mixed with the uncanny scent of the outside.

"Did you hit your head?" Elizabeth reached out and touched Claudia's temple. "No. You couldn't have. Why can't you talk?"

"You're really beautiful." Claudia grimaced internally as a blush lit up her face.

Elizabeth laughed. "You must have hit your head after all."

"Don't do that."

"What?"

"Deflect compliments. Or minimize them, or somehow make it all seem... less."

Elizabeth only stared at Claudia.

They were so close. All Claudia had to do was lean forward and... No. She couldn't do that. But why did Elizabeth have to look at her like that? As if Claudia were a wonder.

"I wasn't aware I was doing that," Elizabeth rasped.

The sound of her voice shot heat through Claudia. "You do."

"I shall work on that."

Claudia could only nod, still trapped in Elizabeth's clear gaze.

"Are you all right?"

"Yeah. Just wasn't paying enough attention."

"You don't say."

Claudia flushed and ducked her head.

"Hey." Elizabeth placed a cold finger on Claudia's chin and lifted her head.

Claudia suppressed a shiver.

"I'm teasing you. But you do have to be more careful."

"Because I'm pregnant."

"That, but I generally don't want anything to happen to you."

Once more, Claudia only managed to nod.

Elizabeth pulled back and an odd mien Claudia couldn't place flickered across her face before she smoothed her expression. "Do you want to get something to eat? There's a great place nearby. They make excellent pizzas and desserts, and I seem to recall someone with an affinity for such... questionable combinations."

"Yes, and yes. And again, all that food still ends up together—"

"In your stomach, yes. But before it *reaches* your stomach, it *passes* your taste buds."

"What's wrong with pizza and desserts?"

"As long as you don't eat them together, nothing."

"I'm not eating them together," Claudia protested while following Elizabeth off the rink.

"You swallow a piece of pizza and then take a bite of that chocolate lava cake. What would *you* call that?"

"Eating one after the other?"

Elizabeth snorted. "You're so silly sometimes." They took off their skates and after returning Elizabeth's, they headed for the parking lot.

Claudia smiled as they strode to their cars. "Is that restaurant within walking distance?"

"It is, if you don't mind walking for about fifteen minutes."

"'That's fine. Let me put my skates in the trunk first."

"That's the plan."

At the restaurant, the conversation once more flowed easily and covered a varied range of topics. Claudia continued to marvel at their effortless connection and how even the pause, as she'd decided to call their little break, didn't seem to have much of an impact on their interactions. She'd truly never experienced such a friendship.

"Oh, you haven't seen my bedroom yet," Elizabeth said suddenly, placing her glass down on the table.

Claudia, having just swallowed a sip of soda, coughed, covering her mouth with her elbow. "Excuse me?" she pressed out.

"Petra and the crew from Pat Stewarts finished the renovations of my bedroom. You haven't seen the final results. I suppose I could send you pictures, but that's not the same. So, next time you're at my place, remind me to show you my bedroom."

"Oh, right. Yes, sure." Claudia struggled to stifle an eye roll at herself. She needed to get her mind out of the gutter. Infatuation was one thing, but she needed to keep this in check. "Hey, what are you doing tomorrow?"

"Nothing. We had plans to celebrate Thanksgiving with Tom's family, but that won't happen now. I'll spend some quality time with Raji."

"No, you won't," Claudia said with an assurance that seemed to startle Elizabeth.

"I won't?"

"No. There's no way I'll let you spend Thanksgiving alone. No offense to Raji, but you'll come to my place. Well, you'll come to my parents' place." She struggled to hold Elizabeth's gaze that shone, both with amusement and a challenge, leaving Claudia almost breathless.

"Is that so?"

"Yup."

"That's not how you'll get into Raji's good graces."

"That's fine. I'll set my devious plan to bribe him in motion the next time I'm at your place."

"He's peculiar, as you may have noticed."

Claudia laughed. "You don't say. With that human..."

Elizabeth narrowed her eyes. "Watch it."

"Besides, we gotta make up for lost time," Claudia said.

"What lost time?"

Claudia raised her eyebrows.

"You mean because of those three long weeks we didn't really talk?"

Claudia flushed. "It was almost four, and anyway, it seemed longer."

"That it did."

"I'm surprised I didn't get an 'indeed' for that." Claudia sought to lighten the mood once more to calm her pelting heart.

"So you knew I'd agree, or was that more of an assumption?"

"I told you before, I'm a big fan of hope."

"That you are. You hoped we'd fix things?" Elizabeth asked.

"Of course, but... hope is a fickle f'er sometimes."

Elizabeth snorted. "You don't curse?"

Claudia's gaze swept across their surroundings, noting a few couples sitting close by, lost in their own conversations. "I reserve such language for appropriate situations."

"Oh? And a semi-full Italian restaurant on a weeknight isn't one?"

"Not according to my parents, no."

Elizabeth shook her head. "You're too adorable for words sometimes."

Claudia blushed.

"Why is hope fickle?"

"Because whenever we hope, there's something we really want. So, if it doesn't work out, and let's be real, there's at least a fifty-fifty chance for an unhappy ending, we'll be disappointed. More so since, well, we wanted it badly."

"And other times we're not that attached to a specific outcome?"

Claudia shrugged. "I'm not saying people rarely have an overarching hope in life for stuff to work out. But I don't know, like when I'm actively hoping for something to turn out a certain way, then I'm more invested than in, let's say, the traffic lights all turning to green when I'm on my way somewhere."

"Unless you're in a rush," Elizabeth pointed out.

"Yeah. I suppose. But I'm still talking about more impactful stuff."

"That could be impactful if you're on your way to an important meeting. Could be life changing, even."

Claudia tilted her head. “Are you intentionally being contrarian?”

“A little. But those are good points, no?”

“I suppose.”

“I think I marvel at the fact that this friendship is so meaningful to you that you’ve extended that much energy and resources for it.”

Claudia didn’t know what to say to that, so she only stared at Elizabeth. She had been doing that a lot today. At least now there was no chance of a bunch of teenagers running into her and knocking her to the ground.

“Because I’ve rarely encountered a situation where such a connection and the desire for a friendship turned out mutual.”

Claudia’s eyes softened. “You’re not alone.”

midlife crisis and mud

IF SHE'D STILL BEEN with Tom, Elizabeth would have spent Thanksgiving at his family's home in the Dallas suburbs. She'd be lying if she said she missed attending that particular gathering this year. She liked Tom's family enough, but they had never fully accepted her, blaming her for their boy not giving them any grandchildren. Well, they should be happy to know that he'd managed to do so after all.

While sadness over her failed marriage lingered sometimes—memories were pesky little things—for the most part, she felt awash with relief, even more so since her relationship with Claudia was back on track, and not just that, but it seemed to continue seamlessly where they'd left off.

Even though she wanted Tom out of her life, Elizabeth didn't believe that love and affection just ended because you decided that someone wasn't worth it. She still loved Tom in some way, but she couldn't be with him anymore, and she had reached a point where that seemed all right. More than that, if she were being honest. At this point, this realization left her buoyant as it signaled—to her—that she'd come out on the other side.

She'd been surprised by Claudia's invitation to Thanksgiving, and then by her text message spam to make sure she was still coming, despite Elizabeth's assurances when they'd said goodbye after leaving the restaurant yesterday.

Elizabeth released her tight grip on the steering wheel after pulling up at the address Claudia had texted her. She seized the sweet potato pie she'd baked the night before and exited the car.

As she strode up the stairs to the Craftsman house, she recalled Claudia's last visit at her home, and how she had fallen asleep on her couch while watching *Broken Time*. She'd contemplated telling Kat that her show made people fall asleep, but then she'd have to unpack *everything* that had happened with Claudia and hear Kat tell her that she'd been correct in her assessment of Elizabeth's feelings on the matter.

Sometimes she worried that no one would understand their connection. And then, she would be swamped with questions she didn't want to hear and have to come up with answers she didn't have or even cared to seek, especially now that everything was so fresh and fragile again.

Elizabeth had been so touched that Claudia had drifted off like that, and yes, pregnancy fatigue likely played a role, but to Elizabeth it also signaled that she still held Claudia's trust. She had smiled and taken in Claudia's sleep-softened features, and she'd been startled by the wave of affection and protectiveness that had arisen within her at the sight. There'd been another emotion washing over her at Claudia's nearness, but she couldn't quite place it. It had been both warm and almost exhilarating, yet there'd also been a tension she toiled to understand.

Since Claudia hadn't told her family about the pregnancy yet, and given how busy her best friend was, she figured Claudia wouldn't have an easy time with any of this. Elizabeth's disappearance likely hadn't helped either. However, beating herself up over it wouldn't do them any good.

While looking at Claudia, and with Raji returning and head-butting her—she'd absentmindedly petted him—Elizabeth had felt inundated with warmth. A quiet contentment had spread while the determination rose to be there for Claudia through this journey and to help her in any way she could. It seemed odd, feeling so attached to someone who, a mere five months ago, had been nothing but an employee before turning into scammer-Claudia. God, how things had changed.

The door swung open, and Elizabeth couldn't suppress a smile when she came face to face with a practically glowing Claudia. "Hi."

"You made it," Claudia said, sounding almost breathless.

Elizabeth frowned. "Of course. Did you think I was going to stand you up last minute?"

Instead of an answer, Claudia surged forward and hugged Elizabeth, who barely managed to prevent the pie from slipping out of her fingers. Her face ended up pressed against Claudia's neck, and she inhaled deeply, her free hand tightening her hold on Claudia's back as the clean scent of lilies washed over her. God, when had she last hugged someone? And had it felt like this? She couldn't remember hugging Kat ever leaving her this buoyant and almost jittery.

"Careful," she whispered and withdrew, her hands trembling. She supposed she needed to add more exercise if carrying a pie exhausted her muscles.

"Oh, I'm sorry." Claudia drew back, dropping her head and stuffing her hands into her pants pockets—her bashful or uncomfortable pose, at least based on Elizabeth's observations.

"No, no, you're fine. I just meant the pie. Would be a shame to drop it on the floor."

"Right, OK. Come on in. I'll introduce you to my family." She leaned closer and murmured near Elizabeth's ear, "Just be prepared for a *lot* of questions."

Elizabeth shuddered, then blinked rapidly before following Claudia into the house.

There were more people present than Elizabeth had expected, including Claudia's aunt Sonia and her husband, Amin, along with their two daughters, and an old family friend of Claudia's mother. Thanks to Elizabeth's job, she adjusted quickly, and put on her charm as if this were a charity event. For some odd reason, she wanted Claudia's family to like her. Judging by the multitudes of questions that barreled her way—about her charity, how long she'd been living in the United States, what she missed the most about England, if she liked soccer, and oddly, a discussion about breakfast food—Claudia's warning hadn't been a joke.

Kareem turned out to be more than willing to share cute (embarrassing, according to Claudia) tales of his daughter's childhood—the time she had made a mud pie outside and her parents had played along and acted as if they ate their 'pieces,' resulting in Claudia shoving a handful of dirt into her mouth, only to spit it out and start crying. Or when Claudia had seen a woman with tattoos all over her body in the waiting room at the doctor's office, and then gave herself 'tattoos' of butterflies and rainbows with markers on her arms, legs, and belly, to where her bathwater had turned into a dark sludge.

Elizabeth had almost choked on her laughter when Kareem pulled out an old photo album. She'd 'awwed' at all those baby and child candid images of Claudia until present-day Claudia's face had turned as red as a tomato and she begged her father to stop torturing her. Elizabeth thought that if the baby came after her mother, they would be too cute for words.

Still, the evening went by with pleasant conversations, and with Elizabeth failing to suppress her urge to check on Claudia, though to be fair, she also remained on the lookout to empty Claudia's wine glass inconspicuously throughout the night. She had done more research on pregnancy than she cared to admit, and the notion of an embryo the size of a rice kernel or looking like a tadpole still blew her mind.

She'd known all that in theory, but she'd never been close to anyone going through a pregnancy. Apparently, she also seemed to want to make up for the time they'd lost. She remained in denial that 'lost time' here hardly meant four weeks.

Claudia's cousins, Talia and Aya, while nice and polite—the entire family had been incredibly gracious and welcoming and seemed to have decided Elizabeth needed to gain at least five pounds of weight—snickered and exchanged glances that confused her. She didn't sense that they were making fun of her, and most of those incidents occurred when she checked on Claudia or when they talked in subdued whispers as Claudia often played translator for Elizabeth—a thoughtfulness that had touched her greatly.

Later, Elizabeth walked into the kitchen to look for Claudia when she seemed to interrupt a somewhat heated moment between the cousins.

"I said drop it," Claudia hissed in a hard tone that made Elizabeth straighten.

"Is everything all right?" she asked.

"Of course." Talia smiled at Elizabeth. "We're just teasing Claudia a bit."

Elizabeth narrowed her eyes. "It doesn't seem like she appreciates it."

Talia chortled.

"It was all in good sport." Aya squeezed Claudia's upper arm and nodded to her sister, who followed her out of the kitchen.

Elizabeth took in Claudia's clenched fist and tight jaw. She drew closer. "Are you OK?"

"Yeah." She cleared her throat. "All good."

"Try that again."

"Hmm?"

"Your statement lacked feeling. I'm not convinced by this performance, but as you know, practice makes perfect. So, try again."

Claudia chuckled. "I really like you."

Heat crept up Elizabeth's neck. "I really like you, too."

Claudia sighed.

"You don't have to talk about what happened, but I'm here if you want to."

Claudia caught Elizabeth's gaze and for a second, Elizabeth felt the world halt.

Perhaps the wine had been spiked? That would certainly explain the sudden and frantic pounding of her heart.

"They kept asking how long we've been together and if I plan to tell the family, and to please do so when *teta* is not staying at their place," Claudia rushed out.

Elizabeth's eyes widened, and against expectation, her heartbeat only increased its wild jaunt. "And that upset you?"

"Well, yes!"

Elizabeth drew back, wondering for a moment why her heart had plunged into her stomach.

Claudia fidgeted. "I mean, not because... I'd... Oh, God." She covered her eyes with one hand, then dropped her arm back to her side and stepped closer to Elizabeth. "I'm sorry. I gave you the wrong impression. You know I'm bisexual, but you're straight, and it's always been my experience that straight women get uncomfortable about being thought to... well, if people think they're in a relationship with another woman."

"OK, but even if that has been your experience, and I'm not trying to discount that, but that doesn't mean this will always be the case or applies to all women."

Claudia released a shuddered breath. "No, but I did add, 'in my experi ence.'"

Elizabeth raised one eyebrow. "Indeed."

"You're OK then?"

"What? With your cousins thinking someone as beautiful and kind as you would give me the time of day?" She released a rough chuckle. "Yes. I'm fine with that." Elizabeth blinked rapidly when she realized she meant that.

Claudia's mouth opened, then closed. "You're not like anyone I've ever met."

"I hope that's a good thing."

"Most definitely."

"Are you ready to go back out and brave your family again?" Elizabeth asked.

"I wasn't hiding! I was in here to get another piece of your pie. It's delicious."

"Thank you." Elizabeth flushed. "Far be it from me to thwart your increased calorie intake."

"Ha ha," Claudia said. "Just for that, I'll cut a bigger piece. You want one too?"

"No, thank you. I'm not sure that point supports your argument."

"What? That your pie is delicious?" Claudia put a spoonful in her mouth and groaned. She closed her eyes.

Staring at Claudia as if mesmerized, Elizabeth concluded that the spiked wine was *not* to blame for her heart thrashing in Claudia's presence, nor for her stomach dropping at Claudia's words, facial expressions, and... sounds.

She had to admit that her previous realization that she enjoyed being in Claudia's presence, combined with everything she had felt over the past few weeks and the way Claudia's absence had hurt her physically, led to only one conclusion. This realization, however, propelled her into unfamiliar territory.

Could a midlife crisis make you gay?

a squishy impulse

THANKSGIVING HAD GONE SMOOTHER than Claudia had expected, and it had made her feel so full, like her chest might burst, to see her family and Elizabeth get along so well. Her father's picture show and her cousins' antics and delusions aside, the day had been wonderful. A small part of her also delighted that Elizabeth hadn't seemed freaked out by the idea of being in a relationship with a woman, well, with Claudia, really. Still, she needed to press pause (or stop) on this, not only because they had just recently reconnected.

She'd admit that she'd probably encouraged, or rather instigated, her cousins' suspicions, as she'd been completely enamored by Elizabeth charming her family. Claudia enjoyed Elizabeth's company, and she knew *Helping Hands* had been a success for many years, yet seeing her in action had been enthralling. She shouldn't blame Talia and Aya for jumping to such conclusions, especially given how attentive Elizabeth had remained throughout the day.

Claudia knew a part of this thoughtfulness stemmed from her pregnancy (maybe also from feeling needlessly guilty), but her heart didn't seem to differentiate, and like a lost wanderer set out to chase a dream that would turn into windmills down the road. Only unlike Don Quixote, she didn't even have a horse to console her over the heartbreak that awaited her on the horizon. Lost in her maudlin thoughts, she started when her phone beeped. Elizabeth.

Claudia smiled when she read the message, Elizabeth asking to call her when she had a moment. She pressed dial immediately. "Hey. What's up?"

"Hi. How are you?"

"All right. Just finished the newest episode of "See No Evil." Vegging on the couch."

"Isn't your first appointment to check on the baby coming up?"

Claudia rolled her eyes. She'd not be surprised if Elizabeth noted these things in her calendar. "This Tuesday. The first ultrasound, though there's not much to see yet. Just a growth check, I think. Wanna come along?"

Silence.

Claudia pulled at the edge of the pillow lying next to her on the couch. What was she doing? Although it couldn't be that unusual to ask a friend to come along to your ultrasound appointment. "You don't have to, I just thought—"

"I'd love to join you."

Claudia sagged deeper into the couch. "Yeah?"

"If you want me to, obviously, but you'd have not asked otherwise... and you just surprised me so..." Elizabeth seemed to run out of air after this unusual rambling comment.

If Claudia hadn't already been helplessly smitten, she'd have been so now—self-assured Elizabeth stumbling over her words. Realizing there'd be hell to pay if she called her adorable, Claudia swallowed those words. "I do. The appointment is at four. I tried to get it as close to the end of my workday as possible, but that was the latest appointment they had."

"OK. We could drive there together. In separate cars, though. I don't want to leave you stranded."

"Sure. That works."

"Great. Thank you."

Claudia laughed. "Shouldn't I be the one thanking you?"

"For what?"

Claudia's eyes widened. Elizabeth's question seemed genuine. "For being there for me." She cleared her throat against the lump that had formed. She knew she needed to be more careful and keep her distance emotionally, but she couldn't figure out how to do that when all she wanted was to spend more time with Elizabeth, to bask in her presence because that alone made her happy. God, she was pathetic.

"That's not something you need to thank me for."

Claudia grinned, a broad, goofy expression on her face, and she felt relief at living alone. "I still want to show my appreciation."

"All right. You may do that, then."

Claudia snorted. "You're so kind."

"I know. It's a tragic flaw."

"You're silly."

"You know, I don't think anyone has ever called me that. Perhaps it's your influence that brings out this side of me, as you know everything about being silly."

"I'll take that as a compliment."

Elizabeth chuckled. "You would."

"There's a lot of things I would." Claudia worried her lower lip. She needed to watch it.

"Such as?"

"Oh, you know…" She scrambled for an innocent, friendly idea.

"I don't."

Claudia suppressed a sigh. Leave it to Elizabeth to make this hard. "Like drink hot chocolate with pizza."

"Ew. I vividly recall."

"Hey! Those who drink eggnog may not cast the first stone!"

"That's not how that saying goes," Elizabeth drawled.

"Indeed."

"Watch it."

Claudia once more couldn't prevent a huge smile from forming.

They chatted a little while longer, and once she hung up, Claudia concluded that not only was she pathetic but also hopeless. Since she had admitted her infatuation to herself, her brain and heart seemed intent on marching ahead, heedless of what might be smart and logical to do, and instead just lived on hope. Claudia sighed. She didn't want to lose Elizabeth, so she would have to control these impulses. She'd just had a taste of such a reality and desired no repeat. Ever.

Then again, it didn't seem like Elizabeth minded. On the other hand, it was also possible that Elizabeth didn't register her sometimes flirty comments. Straight people could be so clueless when it came to flirting between people of the same sex.

Tuesday arrived in the blink of an eye, and work had become exceptionally busy again. They both stayed long the day before, though they only talked for a bit, as they both seemed drained.

Claudia continued to wonder if Elizabeth knew about her ridiculous infatuation and just chose to ignore it, or if this was her way of interacting with friends, oblivious to the undercurrent that sometimes swirled beneath their words.

She exited her car and Elizabeth joined her.

"I'm really glad you're here."

Elizabeth hummed. "Come on. It's almost four."

"I'm on time."

"Aren't you supposed to arrive early for doctor's appointments?"

"Aren't you always early for every appointment?"

"You say that like it's a bad thing."

"It's not bad. Just... prepared and responsible. Like you're a real adult." Claudia's eyes crinkled at the mock glare Elizabeth sent her way.

"I sometimes don't know what to do with you."

Claudia bit her lower lip to prevent herself from blurting, 'I can think of a few things,' but Elizabeth's gaze zeroing in on her mouth and both almost running into the glass doors of the office didn't seem like much of an improvement.

They only had to wait ten minutes and Claudia had just finished filling out a form the receptionist had handed her when they were called into the back.

Tammy, their tech, chatted a mile a minute, and Claudia felt almost dizzy from the information she'd thrown her way. Perhaps she should take a leaf out of Elizabeth's book and research this, given that Elizabeth nodded along with Tammy, completely at ease with it all. Then again, Claudia liked Elizabeth filling her in about the size and development stages of her child. God, she'd have a child.

Claudia swallowed hard and rubbed her clammy hands against her pants legs, settling on the chair.

"All good?" Elizabeth asked, stroking Claudia's shoulder.

Claudia nodded, not trusting her voice as nausea stepped-danced in her stomach.

"All righty, are we ready?" Tammy asked, holding the ultrasound probe in the air and squirting gel on the top.

Claudia pulled up her sweater.

"Brace yourself, this is going to be cold," she said as she placed the sensor on Claudia's belly.

She winced at the cold and the squishy wet feeling of the gel sliding over her stomach, then she turned her head toward the screen, nerves quickening along her skin as she tried to identify the swishy images.

Elizabeth's fingers intertwined with hers, and Claudia's heart swelled.

"Do you want to hear the heartbeat?" Tammy asked.

"Yes," Claudia and Elizabeth said at the same time.

Tammy pressed a button, and a staticky, rapid thumping sound filled the room.

"Isn't that too fast?" Claudia asked, reading the number of 153 with wide eyes.

"No, that's perfectly normal," Elizabeth answered before Tammy could reply.

Tammy smiled. "She's right. No need to worry."

"It doesn't look much like a baby," Claudia said after another moment, staring at the shifting white blob on the screen.

"No, but that will change soon. Will you guys want to know the sex of the baby during the anatomy scan at twenty weeks?"

"Oh, I don't know," Claudia replied.

"We could tell your spouse and she could tell you whenever you want to know. That's if you wanted to know," Tammy addressed Elizabeth, whose eyes widened.

"Oh, we're not—"

"Your partner, then." Tammy smiled.

"We'll see," Claudia said.

"Of course. There's still plenty of time. I just like to ask early on so you can think about it."

"That's a good idea." Claudia squeezed Elizabeth's hand as the woman still seemed completely shell-shocked.

When they exited the clinic, Claudia sighed. "I'm sorry. I didn't mean to make you uncomfortable in there."

"Huh?" Elizabeth looked at her as if she'd not heard a word in a while.

"Tammy and her assumption that we're married. Or a couple. I should've corrected her, but it seemed awkward, and I don't know..."

"Well, at least she didn't assume I'm your mother."

Claudia grimaced. "Gross."

"I agree."

"You're not mad then?"

"I think we've already established my attitude on this over Thanksgiving."

"Right." Claudia ducked her head.

"I was just surprised. That's all."

"OK. So, do you want me to send you the recording of the heartbeat?"

"I'd love that."

thoughtful consideration

THE DAY AFTER THE doctor's appointment, and after having listened too often to the heartbeat recording, Elizabeth still struggled to organize and understand her emotions. She'd made peace with the turmoil she'd first gone through after learning about Claudia's pregnancy. No matter what, their friendship was unusual, its origin at least, but it remained something she both desired and couldn't resist. To be honest, she didn't *want* to resist the pull between them, as being with Claudia made her happy and content, which sometimes appeared like a small miracle.

She often seemed so at ease around Claudia, yet this tension remained.

And that seemed to be the problem.

She didn't know what to do with this emotional upheaval, this pressure in her chest, this restlessness, and her inability to focus on anything but Claudia and the baby. This hyper-focus was both thrilling and exhausting. Elizabeth didn't consider it all that healthy to be so consumed by another, but she also had enough life experience to know this couldn't last. Tension wasn't sustainable for long periods of time. No matter how or where it would arise, it must snap eventually. If you took a paper cup and filled it with a bit of water, in fact, you wouldn't even need water—holding such a cup would be effortless, as it weighed next to nothing.

Yet, if you stretched your arm and held the cup there for a minute, two minutes. Three minutes. That cup would become heavy, and with each passing second, it would become harder to keep up the pose. At some point, you'd let go because the strain would become too much.

So no, tension couldn't be maintained indefinitely, neither physical nor emotional. The body will push for a return to equilibrium at some point. As such, this preoccupation didn't worry Elizabeth in the long run.

No, it came down to this ridiculous infatuation with Claudia. It had taken her too long to understand, but to be fair, she could've hardly seen that coming given her own life history and what lay between them. The issue didn't even rest in Claudia being a woman, nor in their different social standings. The age difference and the baby, however, were of significant concerns.

Age didn't matter with friendships, as the expectations were different. But in a romantic relationship—that also assumed Claudia would even be interested in Elizabeth like *that*—age seemed pretty damn important, at least with an age difference that put you into different generations.

All the things Claudia may still want out of life, and how she'd go about it, not to mention, the child. Elizabeth wasn't sure if she could fulfill such needs. Children changed everything, though Elizabeth didn't know that from personal experience, it was a mantra of all mothers she'd ever dealt with at her charity.

She was forty-six years old. It would be one thing being Claudia's best friend and play the fun auntie for the child, but if she were to enter into a romantic relationship with Claudia, she would be involved in their daily lives. Not necessarily as a second parent—once more assuming a lot—but how could she be involved with someone and share their life and say, 'Oh, yeah, but the kid is on you.' Aside from being selfish and inconsiderate and all kinds of awful, no relationship could ever work out like that.

Elizabeth didn't know. It simply came down to that, and so she felt immobilized. It was one thing to realize she might harbor romantic feelings for Claudia and to accept that and move forward or suffocate it in infancy—poor word choice aside—but knowing that pursuing Claudia would lead to an instant family gave her pause.

If she were to go there, she needed to be sure. Yes, yes, how arrogant to have those thoughts and worry without knowing for sure that Claudia wanted her too. But the problem was, if she *were* to find that out first, and Claudia *did* reciprocate her feelings, and Elizabeth belatedly realized she couldn't do it after all, that she didn't want a partner who had a small child (Baby. Newborn.), she'd hurt her friend. And that seemed unacceptable.

So, Elizabeth vowed to first figure out if she'd want the life she'd inevitably lead with Claudia. Only then would she contemplate what to do next—if anything. All other potential objections against such a relationship were moot as the first one would topple the rest.

They kept up their regular interactions—things had slowed down a bit at work—and come Friday, Elizabeth had invited Claudia over to continue watching *Broken Time*, and to show off her new bedroom. Although that notion suddenly seemed daunting as well. She had yet to update Kat on all these changes, and so far, she consoled herself with the assurance that she wasn't keeping this development from her friend. She was merely being considerate of Kat's busy life.

Elizabeth had been looking forward to spending this time with Claudia outside of the office—texting and chatting on the phone wasn't the same—but twenty minutes before Claudia was supposed to arrive, her vision blurred, and flashing lights appeared on the left side of her field of sight. She'd hoped her prodrome symptoms of a stiff neck and suddenly feeling parched were a false warning, or that she'd have more time before the migraine would be upon her. Naturally, it would start right now, not only ruining the evening she'd been anticipating all week, but also too late to cancel.

Claudia had started to arrive a bit early for their meetings, and so Elizabeth figured she'd be here within the next ten to fifteen minutes. She groaned. While knowing Claudia wouldn't be upset for needing to cancel or for having driven here in vain, she still felt awful, both for disappointing Claudia and for missing out on a night of togetherness.

The doorbell rang and Elizabeth cringed. She padded to the door and opened it. Before she could say more than "Hi," Claudia frowned.

"What's wrong? Are you OK?"

Elizabeth shook her head.

"What is it? How can I help you?"

Elizabeth's hand shot to her head.

"Oh, you have a migraine. All right, I've researched that the other day. May I come in?"

"You researched migraines?" Elizabeth's voice broke.

"Yes, do you have any ginger here?" Claudia walked into her house and, bewildered, Elizabeth closed the door behind her.

"I'm not that great at giving massages, so we'll skip that, but I'll make you some tea because you must drink enough. Have you tried sipping a caffeinated drink? I've read this can help, too. You should lie down in a dark, quiet room. Do you prefer hot or cold compresses?" Claudia placed her purse on the couch and strode into the kitchen.

Elizabeth remained rooted to the spot in the entry hall, still struggling to make sense of what was happening, while more dots sprang into her vision as her head pounded.

Claudia's head popped out from around the kitchen door. "Why are you not lying down?"

"You're staying?" Elizabeth rasped.

Claudia frowned. "Obviously. Go lie down."

Still dazed, Elizabeth could only nod and retreated to her bedroom to rest.

What seemed like a minute later, Claudia put a steaming cup of tea on the coaster she'd placed on Elizabeth's nightstand.

"I don't see all of your bedroom in the dim light, but what I can see looks nice," she spoke in a soft, low tone.

Elizabeth hummed.

"Do you want the cold or hot compress? You never answered."

"Cold," Elizabeth said, though she already felt cold. But cool compresses numbed the pain a little.

"All right." Claudia handed her an ice pack draped in a towel. "I hope that's OK. If not, I can also wrap ice cubes or get a wet towel."

"No. I usually use this," Elizabeth croaked, putting the ice pack around her neck. She hissed.

"What is it?"

"I'm so cold."

"Oh." Claudia looked around the bedroom before focusing again on Elizabeth. "How about you get under the covers?"

She grunted before shifting and with Claudia's help, who lifted the covers, she slid beneath the blanket. "Thank you," she whispered.

"No worries."

"You can leave anytime."

"I know. But I'd like to stay and make sure you're all right, if you don't mind."

"Sorry I've ruined tonight."

"Nonsense. I just want you to feel better."

"Thank you."

"I'll be right outside, OK?"

"Stay," Elizabeth mumbled after a moment of stillness.

"Yes. I'm staying."

"No, here. With me." Her eyelids drooped shut before she forced them open. "Please."

"As you wish." Claudia made to sit in the sofa chair standing against the wall when Elizabeth reached out and trailed her fingers down her arm.

"With me."

"Oh, all right. You mean on the bed, yes?"

"Mmhmm."

"Let me turn off the light fully first."

Elizabeth nodded and closed her eyes. She sighed in relief when the room went completely dark.

A moment later, the mattress dipped, and Claudia settled next to her.

"There are clothes in the drawer over there," she slurred.

Claudia's "Just go to sleep," was the last thing Elizabeth registered before drifting off.

When Elizabeth woke up, her migraine had receded to a dull throb she could easily manage. She stretched, then startled upon realizing she wasn't alone in her bed. She jerked upright and glanced at the person curled up on top of the blanket next to her. Claudia. She must be so cold.

Memories of the previous night rushed through Elizabeth's mind, and she once more felt touched by Claudia's care and affection.

She'd stayed with her.

Elizabeth rose and pulled out a blanket from her closet, covered Claudia with it before leaving the room to prepare breakfast. She hoped Claudia didn't have any plans today so they could spend more time together.

Half an hour later, the scents of freshly brewed coffee, bacon, eggs, and grits seemed to draw a sleepy Claudia out of the bedroom.

Elizabeth smiled at the sight—the tousled hair, squinty eyes, and the snug t-shirt that revealed a sliver of skin between the hem and the waistband of her sweatpants. "Good morning. I hope you're hungry."

"Starved, actually. You made coffee."

"It's decaf," Elizabeth said.

Claudia's eyes widened. "That's thoughtful. Thank you."

"I also have an assortment of herbal teas, if you prefer that." She'd recently purchased chamomile tea as Claudia had been drinking that lately.

"Oh, that's great. I'll go with a decaf for now, though."

"Help yourself. Will you have some of everything?" Elizabeth pointed at the stove.

"Yes. Thank you. The coffee same as always?"

"Just black this morning. The cups are over there." She pointed at a cupboard.

Claudia retrieved two mugs and filled them with coffee while Elizabeth plated their food and brought it to the table.

They ate mostly in silence, keeping any conversation light, and overall, Elizabeth enjoyed the quiet domestic atmosphere of their togetherness.

When they were done, Claudia set to clear the table.

"You don't have to do that. You're a guest."

"Well, you made breakfast and you've just had a migraine. So, yes, while I may not *have* to do this, I want to help."

"All right. What are your plans for the rest of the day?"

"I don't have any," Claudia replied, loading the dishwasher.

Elizabeth bit her lower lip. "Me neither. Want to stay here and do nothing?"

"Sounds like a perfect plan."

# of cats and bricks

After taking a quick shower and once more dressed in Elizabeth's clothes, Claudia joined her friend in the living room.

Raji had cuddled up next to Elizabeth, cleaning himself.

Claudia had almost tripped over the little beast last night in the kitchen as she prepared Elizabeth's tea. She'd given him a few treats, and he'd seemed receptive, even rubbing against her leg for a hot second.

"How did you come up with the name Raji?" Claudia asked, preening a little when the demon cat (No, she'd never call him that out loud around Elizabeth because she wanted to live.) not only allowed her to pet him, but even pushed his little head into her palm. A far cry from almost breaking her neck last night or the hissing distance he'd held the first time Claudia had visited Elizabeth. Bribery for the win. Would that work with Raji's owner, too? She refrained from pulling at the collar of her shirt.

"Oh," Elizabeth mumbled, frowning.

"Never mind. I didn't realize there's a story behind it that makes you sad."

"No, no. I don't believe anyone has ever asked me about that, and Kat knows the story, so there wasn't a need to..." She smiled. "He likes you now."

"Yeah, he tried to murder me last night, but we established a truce after some tuna treat bribery."

"Raji's affection can't be bought."

Claudia held back a smile. "Of course not."

Elizabeth glared at her. "Don't make fun of me."

"I'm not! I swear. It's... your devotion to Raji is adorable."

Elizabeth narrowed her eyes. “I’m almost twenty years older than you, and you’re calling *me* adorable?”

“As you like to say, ‘If the shoe fits.’”

Elizabeth chuckled before sobering. “I told you I grew up in England, and that my family weren’t or aren’t particularly loving people. Their idea of family revolves more around reputation and public perception.”

Claudia nodded, still entranced by being allowed to pet Raji without being nipped at or clawed.

“My nan was different, and I spent as much time with her as I could. Next door to her lived an Indian family that was... the opposite of mine. They were so warm and affectionate. They had a little boy who became my best friend. We’d play together for hours. He wanted to marry me.” Elizabet’s expression grew wistful.

“He sure started early.”

“I told him I would, but first we needed to finish school.”

“Very reasonable of you.”

Elizabeth swatted Claudia’s arm. “Hush.”

Raji’s gaze shifted between Elizabeth and Claudia before he rose and sashayed away, plopping down near the backdoor and stretching out in a sun beam.

“You made him leave!” Claudia pouted.

“Aww, who’d have thought you’d take to my *demon cat*?”

Claudia blanched, opening her mouth, but instead of words, only dissonant sounds spilled from her lips. She’d only muttered that when he’d almost made her trip. How had Elizabeth heard that?

Elizabeth pushed a strand of Claudia’s chestnut hair behind her ear. “You’re lucky I like you.”

“I’m sorry. He’s not really a demon cat, but you know—”

“It’s fine. Raji is an acquired taste, and an excellent judge of character.”

Claudia’s shoulders sagged, and she sighed. Crisis averted.

“It’s sweet that you try to get along with him. It... it means a lot to me, and not because I love cats.”

Claudia nodded, wondering how wise it would be to meander farther down this road.

"Anyway. We had spent three blissful years together, playing and living the way only kids enjoy life. Then Raji..." She shook her head. "He got sick. They didn't know what it was for the longest, and by the time they found out, it was too late. It ravaged him. I didn't understand what was going on, but... They let me say goodbye. I'll forever be grateful for that."

"I'm so sorry."

"It's not your fault.

"I know. I'm not... I'm sorry you went through that, and that Raji... passed."

"Thank you. The last time I talked to him, he told me that our marriage won't work out but that... if I came across the tiny gray cat with black spots on his belly, to name him Raji." She wiped her eyes.

Claudia's eyes widened. "But that's..." She pointed at Raji who'd by now rolled on his back, sleeping, and showcasing the black spots littering his belly.

"I know. I found him one night after I came home from an event. He was so tiny, stumbling across the street toward my house. He could barely walk. I picked him up and brought him inside."

"Wow. That's crazy."

"It was dark, so I didn't get a good look at him at first, and I wasn't thinking of his coloring or anything. I needed to get him warm and fed."

"I'm surprised you didn't have a cat already."

"Oh, Domino had passed a month before I found baby Raji. He'd been with me for six years. I'd adopted him at the shelter when he was already nine. His previous owner had abandoned him, and I... I used to volunteer at animal shelters, and so..."

Claudia suppressed the urge to reach out and hug Elizabeth. She looked so small sitting next to her.

"I brought Raji to the vet the next day, and he's been with me ever since. Once I saw the black spots on his stomach..." She shrugged.

"How long ago was all this?"

"About eight years," Elizabeth said, her gaze resting fondly on the by now snoring Raji.

"I'm glad he found you."

"You're sweet."

Claudia averted her gaze.

Doing nothing turned into relaxing on the couch, each lost in a book. Then they ordered food, and while eating, they watched a cooking show—one of those competition types *teta* liked to watch.

"My grandma makes a lot of snide remarks during these shows," Claudia said.

"She seems quite the cook, if Thanksgiving is anything to go by," Elizabeth said.

"That she is."

"It's always harder to watch something like that if you're good at it yourself, or if it's your profession. Kat hates shows about actors and her remarks are often quite scathing."

"I can see that. But I like cooking shows."

Elizabeth's brows rose. "Really? Because there are knives?"

"Ha ha. Something doesn't have to involve true crime for me to enjoy it. May I remind you of my affinity for *Broken Time*?"

"I thought this was a rare exception because of eye candy."

"I'm not that shallow," Claudia said, suppressing a pout.

"Have you seen the Halloween specials of some of these cooking shows? Their displays are quite... bloody."

"Will you let that go?"

"I'm serious! They are good. It's fascinating what they can do. I enjoy cooking and find it relaxing. But all this timed, high stakes business on these shows would give me hives." Elizabeth shuddered.

"You crack under pressure, huh?"

"Shouldn't I still enjoy a reprieve from insults, given the debilitating headache that almost killed me last night?" Elizabeth sniffed.

"Wow. Yes, of course. I was teasing, mind you, not insulting you. I'd never. Raji would be liable to murder me if I dared to insult his human."

Elizabeth seemed to suppress a small smile. "I'm glad you realize that."

"Did you know cats have eaten their owners' eyeballs after they're dead?"

Elizabeth's eyes widened. "What?"

"Like if you die at home alone with your cat and no one finds you for a while. There've been cases of cats starting to... snack on their owners."

Elizabeth groaned. "I'm starting to regret this. We're watching something as harmless as a cooking show, and yet you brought it back to murder, death, and this time, you even involved cats!"

Claudia shot Elizabeth an abashed smile. "I'm sorry. It just entered my mind, and I mentioned before that I tend to... say stuff then, well, when I'm comfortable enough in the presence of... whomever I'm around." Claudia cringed. Why was she like this sometimes?

"I'm glad you're comfortable in my home and around me, and I don't mind your random thoughts, but I'd prefer less knowledge of cats and murder, especially as a combination."

"You know, I never said that you were murdered in such a scenario."

"Claudia?"

"Yes?"

"Don't make me throw this pillow at you."

Claudia smiled. Elizabeth wasn't truly upset, but she still made a note to keep facts about gruesome incidents involving cats to herself. Pillows could be filled with bricks, after all.

stunning and tongue-tied

Elizabeth had been insanely busy with preparations for the Christmas dinner that would take place this Friday evening. She'd invited Claudia to attend, as she wanted her to meet Kat and their friend, Andrea. Claudia had been reluctant, pointing out that she'd be taking up space another sponsor would pay for, and had outright refused Elizabeth's offer to pay for her plate if that would ease her worries.

People were so sensitive about money, and Elizabeth knew she could be a bit of a bulldozer there. Not to say she believed you could solve all problems with money, but she never gave it much thought. As in, if money helped get what she wanted or needed, why wouldn't she spend it?

Aware that this originated from a privileged position, she still fell into that habit quite often. After Elizabeth had argued that as an employee of *Helping Hands,* she'd be representing the company, Claudia had agreed, and admitted that her curiosity had gotten the better of her. Elizabeth had been pleased.

In the week leading to the event, she and Claudia only saw each other in passing, no after hour meetings, as by the time they were done with work, it was already quite late. Elizabeth loathed the idea of adding to the increased exhaustion Claudia still experienced. Still, the reduced contact between them annoyed Elizabeth.

She didn't blame Claudia or anything. Those were the times, but she still missed their interactions, which once more brought her conundrum to the forefront of her mind. She'd been thinking about this almost non-stop, how to move forward (if there even was a forward), and how she could best figure out if Claudia would be interested in her without making things awkward and weird between them. Elizabeth supposed if she ever figured *that* out, she'd add to her already substantial wealth.

She had even contemplated asking Kat for advice, but they'd only talked once shortly as Kat's show was finishing up the latest season. Elizabeth did mention that she had been watching her show with Claudia, which seemed to have pleased Kat quite a bit.

Wednesday evening, Claudia called her frantically. "I just realized I have nothing to wear! What do you even wear for this event? How fancy does it have to be? Where am I supposed to get such a dress from now? Or should I wear a suit? I'd likely be more comfortable in a suit, but would that be inappropriate? What about shoes!! I should stay home."

"Breathe! I'm surprised you didn't pass out after that stream of words."

"This is serious!"

"Indeed. Give me a few minutes. I'll call you right back."

"OK?"

Elizabeth chuckled and hung up. Then, she called Susana, owner of a fashion boutique downtown, and after a few pleasantries, asked if they could stop by tomorrow late afternoon. Once she received a yes, she called Claudia back.

"Hi. So what happened over the last... ten minutes?" Claudia asked as a greeting.

"We have an appointment with my friend Susana tomorrow at her store."

"And this Susana has a solution for my problems?"

"I don't know all your problems, dear, but we'll get you an outfit there."

"Ha ha, you're not funny."

"I suppose the truth can't be amusing to everyone," Elizabeth said.

"I'm glaring at you, so you're aware."

"Noted."

"I have one problem left," Claudia said.

"What's that?"

"If your friend Susana is anything like your friend Shani, then I'm assuming said outfit will be way out of my price range."

"We get a discount."

"That likely won't change much."

"You didn't let me buy you a plate at the dinner, so I should be allowed to pay for your outfit."

"Elizabeth!"

"Oh, hush. It won't hurt me, and just look at it this way, I'm dragging you into this mess, so at least I can cover your costs."

"I'm not sure most people would consider it a hardship to attend a celebrity studded affair."

"Good thing you're not most people."

"There's that," Claudia said.

By the time they made it to Susana's boutique, it was all but closing time, so Susana ushered them inside and locked up behind them.

"Liz, it's so good to see you." She hugged Elizabeth, who returned the embrace.

"Good to see you, too. Susana, this is my friend Claudia, who is in need of an outfit for tomorrow.

Susana shook Claudia's hand. "Nice to meet you."

"Hi. Thank you for seeing me on such short notice."

"No worries. So, let's see. You're quite tall."

Elizabeth suppressed a smile while Claudia seemed to stifle an eyeroll.

"So I've been told."

"Dress or suit?"

"Either. I'm open to suggestions," Claudia replied.

"All right, we can try different outfits and see what you like better. Liz, lead the way. I'll select a few choices and bring them to you."

Elizabeth nodded and put her hand against the small of Claudia's back to guide her toward the back room.

"Wait. Don't you need my size?" Claudia called after Susana, who turned and smiled.

"No need. I've seen you. That's enough."

Claudia's eyes widened, focusing on Elizabeth again. "I'd ask where you meet those people, but then again..."

"Indeed. Come along."

They settled in the dressing room and waited for Susana who reappeared less than five minutes later.

"Here we go. Let's try this one first." She handed Claudia a dress made of burgundy velvet. "You can change right in there. Come outside when you're ready. There's a bigger mirror back there." Susana pointed behind her.

"Thank you." And with that, Claudia disappeared into the dressing room.

Susana sat next to Elizabeth.

"Isn't red a bit cliché for Christmas?" Elizabeth asked.

"Perhaps, but her complexion will make the color look stunning."

"You're the expert."

When Claudia exited the dressing room a little later, Elizabeth inhaled sharply. Claudia looked gorgeous. The dress's fabric shimmered in the light, making Claudia look like she was glowing. "That's..."

"It's a good look, but something's missing." Susana rose and stepped closer to Claudia. "Turn around."

Claudia spun until she once more faced them.

"What do you think?" Susana asked.

Claudia strode toward the mirror. "It's more comfortable than I expected, but..."

"Yes. I agree."

Elizabeth wondered what they agreed on as her brain still searched for the reboot button.

"Elizabeth?" Claudia turned to her.

"It's nice." She refrained from closing her eyes. *What is wrong with you?*

"Try the blue one." Susana held out an azure silk dress.

"OK." Once more, Claudia headed to the dressing room.

"You're awfully quiet," Susana voiced as she sat next to Elizabeth.

"It's her choice, isn't it?"

"Of course. That has never stopped you from offering an opinion before."

"Perhaps I don't want to influence her."

Susana smiled, seemingly accepting Elizabeth's argument. For now, at least.

The blue dress, while beautiful, appealed to none of them. Its form didn't do Claudia's figure any justice.

"All right. Let's try the suit."

Once more, Claudia disappeared to change. When she returned, Elizabeth gasped, her fingers tightening in the leather arm rest of her chair.

Claudia wore an exquisite black suit with a subtle sheen of burgundy, making it both sophisticated and elegant. The carefully tailored suit fit her lanky figure, giving her an effortlessly chic look. The overall effect was one of timeless elegance. She paired the suit with a crisp white shirt and Elizabeth assumed black heels would complement her outfit.

"That's it, don't you agree, Liz?"

Elizabeth could only nod.

"Now, about the hair. We could go with a neat bun to further emphasize her classic style. I'm picturing her carrying a small black clutch, and a delicate silver necklace hung around her neck. That will add a touch of refinement to the ensemble. I might have a purse that would fit. Liz, I recall you owning such a necklace."

"Uh..." Claudia stammered.

"You don't like the bun idea?" Susana canted her head. "Your hair seems glossy and smooth. We could also have it cascading down your back in a lustrous curtain, with the ends lightly curled, giving it all a polished look."

Elizabeth blinked furiously as both images only reinforced her stupor.

"What do you ladies think?" Susana's gaze drifted between Elizabeth and Claudia.

That I wish I was here with her alone. Elizabeth shook her head.

"You don't like it?" Claudia asked, sounding almost dejected.

"No, no. It's... striking. Uh, both hairstyles would suit you. So, go with what you're more comfortable with.

"I want to wear my hair down. I like the curls idea."

Elizabeth swallowed hard.

"Good. Now, about that necklace, Liz?"

Against her better judgment, Elizabeth had suggested that Claudia join her for an early nightcap (She'd rolled her eyes at herself when she'd asked *that* question.). She'd told herself it would be easier to give Claudia the necklace Susana mentioned tonight than to do it in a hurry tomorrow, given how busy they'd both be.

Raji greeted them with a pitiful meow before running toward his food bowl that had the audacity to stand half empty.

"Let me feed him quickly, and then I'll get the necklace. Do you mind waiting in the living room?"

"Sure. That's fine." Claudia strode toward the living room with an assurance that made Elizabeth falter and stare after her.

She shouldn't have asked Claudia to join her tonight. Elizabeth already felt overwhelmed by the dress fitting. She'd been cognizant of Claudia's beauty when she met her, but she'd never been this distracted by it. Elizabeth decided she would avoid looking at Claudia during her speech tomorrow.

Elizabeth stared at the silver necklace in her hands, rubbing her thumb over the links before she dragged herself back to the living room. She wanted to spend more time with Claudia, to her complete exasperation, but right now she felt untethered and... strangely weak, which made her dawdle.

"Hey. I thought for a moment you'd gotten lost," Claudia said when Elizabeth joined her in the living room, pausing at seeing Raji cuddled up next to her on the couch.

"In my own home?"

Claudia shrugged. "Stranger things. It's a big house."

Elizabeth sat down next to her. "He seems quite taken by you."

Claudia petted Raji's head. "As I've said, I tend to grow on people..."

"Raji is people now?"

Claudia chuckled. "Aren't cats like... not babies, but companions to people who love them?"

"I'm not sure I can speak for all cat lovers." Elizabeth dipped her head, afraid of getting lost in Claudia's warm, dark gaze.

"So modest. You've been quiet tonight."

At that, Elizabeth raised her head and caught Claudia's gaze after all. "I'm sorry. I suppose there's a lot going on."

Claudia smiled. "I get it. But please don't apologize. You're fine however you are."

Elizabeth pressed her lips together, not daring to reply—too afraid of the words she might utter. Instead, she held up the necklace. "Here."

"Oh, it's beautiful." Claudia reached out and traced the line of it resting in Elizabeth's hand.

Elizabeth stilled as an odd tension overtook her.

"Should I try it on?"

"Sure."

Claudia directed another, almost blinding smile at Elizabeth before turning around. "Will you put it on?" She moved her hair to the side, baring her neck.

Elizabeth clenched her jaw. Yes, inviting Claudia over tonight had been a spectacularly bad idea. Her hands trembled while her heart pelted in her chest. *Ridiculous. How old are you?*

"Yes, of course," she husked, closing her eyes. She had *not* meant to sound like that. God, help her.

with rude candor

CLAUDIA HAD MADE THE mistake of telling her parents that she'd attend the Christmas charity dinner with Elizabeth. Her mother was bursting with excitement, while *teta* also acted like this had to be *the* event of Claudia's life. She wasn't sure if they were rooting for additional professional or romantic networking. Probably both. Not together, though. And good God, at this point, Claudia had accepted the reality that she wanted the latter too—with Elizabeth.

Elizabeth had told her to be ready by six-thirty as she'd pick her up. What she'd neglected to tell Claudia was that she'd do so in a limousine. At least her parents didn't see that. When she entered the car (after getting her hair and make-up done by another one of Elizabeth's friends), she almost choked on her greeting as she dropped into the seat.

Fortunately, she first encountered Elizabeth's outfit while sitting. She'd donned what seemed to be a floor-length charcoal grey evening gown with a thin burgundy belt cinched around her waist. The dress had a low neckline and long sleeves with intricate beading along the edges. She accessorized with a diamond necklace and earrings. Elizabeth wore her brown hair pulled up in a tight bun and she added a pair of matching diamond bangles on her wrists.

Elizabeth's soft, silver eyeshadow complemented her dress, and her deep red painted lips made her eyes pop. Her contoured cheeks gave her face a natural glow, and her mascara added a sense of depth to her lashes. Claudia was mesmerized and could only stare at Elizabeth.

"Hi," she finally managed to say, flushing at how breathless she sounded. "You look amazing."

"Thank you. You're quite stunning yourself. How are you feeling? Ready to mingle and have fun?"

Claudia chuckled. "Thanks. Not really. I'm good, though. Feeling very expensive. My hair has never looked this nice. Marla is a true artist."

"She is that. Still, an artist can only work with the canvas they have in front of them."

Claudia ducked her head. She sometimes didn't know what to say to some of Elizabeth's comments. She *had* to be aware of how this all sounded. Could you keep flirting like this and not realize it?

When they arrived at the venue, Claudia was excited and overwhelmed at walking the red carpet next to Elizabeth. They met up with Kat, who embraced Elizabeth with a huge smile on her face. Kat, with her pale skin, dark auburn hair, and classical features, looked even more attractive in person than on the screen. Not that Claudia would comment on that.

Elizabeth introduced them, and for a second, Claudia felt distracted by Kat's rich voice that her own reply of "Nice to meet you," came a bit late.

Kat and Elizabeth stood for several pictures, soon joined by tennis player Andrea Krieger. Claudia managed not to make a fool of herself, as she'd first worried she'd not be able to string two words together around her favorite tennis player. After another round of introductions, they headed inside.

Claudia's steps faltered a bit as she first spied the decorations. She gazed at tables decorated with festive centerpieces and poinsettias before her eyes were drawn to the twinkling lights and evergreen garlands that hung along the walls. She noted a grand Christmas tree standing in the corner, adorned with sparkling ornaments and fairy lights, as they strode along a red carpet that lined the entrance where servers welcomed the guests with a warm Christmas drink.

A mix of traditional Christmas songs and more modern renditions played in low notes in the background, boosting the overall festive and relaxed atmosphere. Claudia couldn't have said what she'd expected inside, but it wasn't this warm or comfortable. She should have known better, though, given all she'd learned about Elizabeth over the last months.

As the night progressed, the guests settled for dinner. Elizabeth had told her she had hired a team of professional chefs who would prepare traditional Christmas food and a few gourmet dishes. So far, Claudia had spotted roasted turkey and steamed vegetables, potatoes in different variations, risotto, and tamales, as well as lobster bisque and filet mignon. She couldn't decide what she wanted to eat as everything looked delicious, and she had to leave room for desserts, too.

As they walked along the tables, Claudia realized with a smile that Elizabeth had also ordered dishes for her vegetarian guests: vegetable tartlets, squash risotto, roasted portobello mushrooms, and sautéed spinach.

Personally, Claudia was more interested in the dessert table as she'd spied chocolate truffle and berry tarts. There were also more festive treats, such as spiced gingerbread and peppermint cheesecake, but chocolate would hit the spot tonight.

Claudia mostly observed her surroundings. She didn't feel shy, though a part of her remained quite dazed. Claudia couldn't tell if being surrounded by this mixture of rich people and celebrities was to blame, or the fact that she couldn't take her eyes off Elizabeth. She was a vision tonight. Still, Claudia realized she preferred her in casual homewear like when they'd lounged at Elizabeth's all day.

After dinner, Elizabeth gave a quick speech, thanking all their generous supporters and highlighting recent successes and new avenues for *Helping Hands*. Claudia loved hearing Elizabeth speak, not only could she listen to her voice all day, but like this, in her element, Elizabeth glowed.

When they started the raffle, they introduced the items several attending celebrities had donated. Claudia couldn't blame the woman who did a little cheerful dance when she won a tennis racket signed by Andrea Krieger. The silver necklace donated by Kat also seemed beautiful and appeared to delight the older woman who rushed up to accept her prize.

Claudia hadn't heard of Patrick Sterne, but the man who won the signed copy of his latest book seemed quite pleased, though not as happy as the woman who won the guitar Alina Ciane had donated. She feared the woman was a second away from passing out from sheer excitement.

Claudia had spent most of the evening so far, not on the outskirts, but still somewhat away from the main action, and instead, she watched her surroundings—the meet and greet of rich people with various celebrities—picturing her mom and *teta's* reaction to all this, and how cool and collected Sammy would be in such a setting.

After the raffle, wine and champagne kept flowing as the guests mingled again, and Claudia's attempt to once more draw back was foiled.

"Claudia Khouri. Elizabeth has told me a lot about you," Kat's voice graveled as she stepped up next to Claudia, a glass of champagne in her hand.

Claudia smiled sheepishly. "She's told me about you, too."

Kat chuckled. "Are you enjoying yourself?"

"It's not too bad, but to be honest, I'd rather be home."

"Most people pay a lot of money to be here."

"True. I'd prefer donating without having to attend something so..."

"Showy?" Kat asked.

"Yeah. I suppose. No offense. I'm assuming, given your profession, this is your normal, but it's not my thing."

"Why are you here then?"

"Elizabeth invited me."

"I suppose we're here for the same reason," Kat said.

"You don't enjoy such events either?"

"I don't hate them. But this is my free time, and if it had been anyone else's event but Liz's, I'd have told them to go kick rocks, not flown halfway across the country on one of my rare weekends off."

Claudia nodded. "She seems to have that effect on people."

"That she does."

Claudia continued to chat with Kat, but Elizabeth kept drawing her gaze. She seemed glued to the way Elizabeth's charcoal gown hugged her curves.

At one point, Elizabeth noticed Claudia staring and she seemed to smile knowingly.

Claudia dropped her gaze to the floor, her cheeks growing warm.

"You seem quite taken by Liz, if I may be so bold," Kat said, her gray eyes twinkling.

Claudia wanted to distract, to deny, to make a joke, but a wave of determination rushed over her, and she straightened, catching Kat's gaze. "Yes. Can you blame me?"

Kat laughed. "Look at you. Not so much the shy, intimidated girl I thought you were."

Claudia's eyes narrowed. "I'm not a girl."

Kat raised her glass. "I believe it." She chanced a glance in Elizabeth's direction before returning her focus to Claudia. "Our Liz might not know what hit her."

In that moment, Elizabeth turned and her eyes found Claudia's. A blinding smile spread over her face before she nodded and turned back to continue her conversation with Andrea.

"Wow. Or perhaps she will," Kat mumbled, chuckling before sipping from her flute again.

Claudia's pulse hammered in her neck as she gazed at Elizabeth in her element, full of energy and life, and so breathtakingly beautiful it almost hurt. Claudia wished she could move, but her feet felt like lead. All she could do was stand there and take in the vision of Elizabeth, her heart trembling in her chest.

She didn't know for how much longer she could suppress her feelings. She wanted to run to Elizabeth, to tell her how she felt, and while this wasn't possible right now, she knew something would have to give. For the first time she thought this infatuation might not be as one-sided as she'd assumed, and if that was the case, well, then all bets were off.

With the evening dwindling towards its end, Claudia had lost sight of Elizabeth and distractedly gazed around.

"She left," Andrea Krieger, who'd joined Kat and Claudia at the table they'd commandeered earlier, pointed out.

Claudia sighed. Was she that obvious? But wait... "She left her own event? Without me?"

Andrea smiled. "No. She just went out on a balcony to get a little breather. She does that sometimes. These parties are quite taxing on her."

"I can see that."

"Someone should check on her." Kat seemed to hide a smile behind her glass.

"She'll be fine," Andrea said before turning to chat with another guest.

"Go little grasshopper. Make sure our friend is all right. I can see you're itching to ditch us."

Claudia glowered at her. "Are you ever *not* blunt?"

Kat shrugged. "I don't believe in coddling anyone's delicate feelings. I rather get to the point."

"I suppose people will overlook rudeness when it comes from such a beautiful countenance."

Kat's eyebrows rose before she laughed, a low, throaty rumble. "Get going."

Claudia rose and once more looked around.

"Just around the corner." Kat picked up her glass once more.

"Thank you." Claudia stepped away.

As she strode up the stairs to the balcony, Claudia felt Elizabeth's gaze on her before she fully saw her.

"I see you found me." Elizabeth's intense stare unnerved Claudia for a moment before she shook it off.

Taking a deep breath, Claudia kept walking until she reached the balustrade, her heart pounding. "I didn't realize you wanted to be found."

"And yet you did."

Claudia smiled. "A little rude bird told me how to get here."

Elizabeth's brows furrowed before she chuckled. "I'm assuming you mean Kat?"

"She called me a grasshopper!"

Elizabeth snorted. "That means she likes you."

"So she's only rude to people she likes?"

"Oh, no. She's rude to everyone if the mood strikes her. Although she can also be incredibly charming and diplomatic when needed."

"I can see that." Nerves once more skittered through Claudia. Was this the time and place? They'd never approached this topic, but then again, how or when? But what if Claudia was wrong and misinterpreted all the signs, only seeing what she wished to see? Would this damage their friendship?

"What are you worried about? Was anyone here rude to you?" Elizabeth drew closer.

"What? Oh, no. I mean, aside from your best friend."

Elizabeth waved her off. "Kat doesn't count. She reads people well enough and doesn't dish out more than they can handle."

"Good to know."

"So?"

Claudia tilted her head and held Elizabeth's inquisitive yet focused gaze.

"What has you so worried?" Elizabeth raised her hand and pushed a strand of Claudia's hair behind her ear.

Shivering at the barely-there touch, Claudia leaned into the gesture.

They stared at each other, drifting imperceptibly closer.

Elizabeth's gaze dipped to Claudia's lips.

Before Claudia could lean in, Elizabeth surged forward and claimed her lips, seeming to savor the contact before pressing closer and wrapping her arms around Claudia.

Claudia gasped; her eyelids fluttered shut as she felt the softness of Elizabeth's lips against hers. Warmth spread through her body, and she eagerly reciprocated as Elizabeth deepened the kiss. She raised her hands and cupped Elizabeth's cheeks, her fingers tingling at the contact, at finally being this close to Elizabeth.

Elizabeth's breathing sped up, and her fingers dug into Claudia's back.

Claudia tasted the sweet flavor of Elizabeth's lipstick before she lost herself in her heady taste as their kiss continued to grow in intensity. She pushed Elizabeth back until the banister of the balcony anchored them in place.

Elizabeth's grip tightened.

Claudia's hands roamed over Elizabeth's body as she sucked at her tongue. A tremble raced through Elizabeth's frame and Claudia felt light-headed.

Elizabeth broke their kiss with a groan and pressed her hands against Claudia's chest, putting some space between them.

"I'm sorry. I didn't mean to—"

"Hush." Elizabeth pressed her index finger against Claudia's lips. "I'm only stopping us from getting carried away."

"Oh, right." Claudia flushed.

"Perhaps we can continue this... *conversation* later tonight?"

"I'd like that," Claudia said, not even embarrassed about the eagerness of her tone or her rapid nodding that made Elizabeth smile.

"Your eyes make it very hard to leave and return to my guests," Elizabeth whispered, once more drawing closer, almost freezing Claudia to the spot with her fierce gaze.

"My eyes?"

"Your pupils are blown. And your lips...Then there's a flush trailing down from your neck to your chest." She traced a finger from Claudia's cheek to her collarbone, ghosting over bare skin.

Claudia's breath grew shallow while goosebumps unrelated to the weather formed. "If you plan on seeing your guests again tonight, you need to leave. *Now.*"

Elizabeth held Claudia's hard gaze, nodding as she bit her lower lip.

Claudia groaned. "Go," she croaked.

And at that, Elizabeth left with quick strides.

Claudia closed her eyes, releasing a heavy sigh. She couldn't wait to get away from here. Did the limousine count as later tonight?

temptation Foiled

Elizabeth shouldn't be this hot in December, but for most of the evening and night she'd felt too warm, almost like burning. While today had been a relatively warm day, it was still early December. Then this moment with Claudia on the balcony—a harbor of solitude she always sought on such occasions—had left her feeling like an inferno.

She'd been distracted during her final conversations and almost missed Kat asking her when they'd be leaving. In that moment, she recalled. Her suggestion to Claudia had been hasty.

"Soon. I just have to take care of something first," Elizabeth replied before rushing off to search for Claudia. She spotted her near an alcove and hurried over, grasping her arm to drag her out of sight.

"What the—"

"Shh," Elizabeth whisper-shouted. "Kat is riding in the limo with us."

"OK? Did you think I'd jump you as soon as the door closes? I might have, mind you, but I can read a room, or a car, and I'd not—"

"No, no. She's staying with me for the weekend. I can't..."

"Oh, all right. That's... fine."

It *wasn't* fine. She had looked forward to spending time with Kat, yet this moment on the balcony... But there was no way she could either bring Claudia home, too, or go to her place now.

"We can just text, or talk on Monday, and see when we can... hang out next."

"Shouldn't we talk first?"

"No!" Claudia looked like she was ready to stomp her foot. "You'll just try to talk us out of this."

"That you're against talking shows you also think there might be an issue."

Claudia rolled her eyes and leaned closer. "It only means that I know you enough, and given the chance, you'll come up with all these nonsense reasons why this is a terrible idea."

"They aren't—"

"Look, I know you have a mile-long list of why we won't work, and I'll disagree, better, counter your every argument."

Elizabeth raised one eyebrow, awash with both amusement and surprise, along with something physical she felt in the pit of her stomach.

"Let's just see, OK? That moment on the balcony..." Claudia trailed off, her gaze drifting to Elizabeth's mouth, making it hard to resist connecting their lips once more. Arousal still coiled in her stomach at the memory of the taste and feel—of Claudia in her arms.

"I liked it a lot."

"I did, too," Elizabeth admitted.

"Good. So go have fun with Kat, and we'll talk."

"I thought you said we wouldn't?"

"You're not funny."

"I beg to differ. Go say your goodbyes. We're heading out in ten minutes," Elizabeth said.

"Yes, ma'am."

"That is *not* helping your case." She shot Claudia a glare and left her standing alone in the alcove.

The car ride home—first dropping off Claudia and saying goodbye in an awkward mixture of a hug and kiss on the cheek—went without a hitch, and Kat held her tongue until they were in Elizabeth's home.

"Claudia, huh?" She joined Elizabeth in the kitchen after placing her carry-on and purse in the guestroom.

"What about her?"

"She's nice." Kat traced her fingers along the counter of the kitchen isle.

Elizabeth sighed. "Indeed. Do you want a cup of mint tea before heading to sleep?"

"Yes, please. You'd make such a great wife."

Elizabeth snorted. "Tell that to Tom." She set up water to boil.

Kat sobered. "I'm sorry. That was insensitive. I'm just touched you remember."

"It's fine. I'm over it. It hasn't been easy but I'm happy with my current life, and while there might still be moments that'll make me wistful..., It feels good. This feels right."

"I'm glad."

"And why wouldn't I remember or make note of your habits? We've been friends for how long?"

"Too long."

"Hey!"

Kat waved her off. "In relation to our ages. Saying the number only makes us sound old."

Elizabeth laughed.

"So, what happened on that balcony tonight? I hope I wasn't too forward in sending Claudia after you, but you both had been just ridiculous, and I thought a... *helping hand* might be needed."

Elizabeth rolled her eyes, contemplating denial or evasion, but this was Kat, not only her best friend, but also someone who'd understand her more than anyone else she could talk to. "We kissed."

"Yes!"

Elizabeth frowned. "You weren't all that keen on Claudia when we were talking on the phone." She poured the water into the cup after placing a tea egg full of mint tea inside.

"That was before I met that earnest, little grasshopper and saw how gone she is on you! I already knew you were into her, and so..." Kat pulled the mug closer and shrugged.

"What are you talking about?"

"She could hardly take her eyes off you all night. Mind you, you do look amazing. And come on, you should've heard yourself during all our phone calls. Who is *that* preoccupied with a friend? It was always, 'Claudia this, and Claudia that.'"

Elizabeth flushed. "It's still a terrible idea."

"Why?"

Elizabeth's eyes widened. "I'm not even fully divorced yet."

"I thought it would be finalized by the end of January?"

"Well, yes."

Kat stared at Elizabeth. "So, you're worried she's a rebound? She's young. She'll bounce back if it were, besides, I doubt she wants to move in with you tomorrow." Kat took a sip of her tea.

"I'm not that callous. I wouldn't want to hurt her, and if that were the case, I'd lose her friendship, too. Not to mention, I'm still her boss. So there are ethical concerns as well."

"That didn't stop you on the balcony. Besides, you never answered my question."

"What question?"

"Is she a rebound?"

Elizabeth worried her lower lip. "No," she croaked, pausing to stare contemplatively at Kat. "Do you want to hear something crazy?

"Sure."

"Compared to Claudia, Tom seems like a rebound."

"Well, shit."

"Indeed. And that is the problem."

"Because you think she's not serious?"

"I don't know. Again, she's so young, and the work aspect..."

"You're really hung up on the age thing. Maybe I'm just too used to being around age gap relationships. They seem to happen so often in my business. Though usually it's older men with younger women."

"Yes, and how do you look at them? Don't you think those guys are pathetic for chasing after such young women?"

"Are they chasing when they are together?"

"You know what I mean."

Kat sighed. "It depends. Some couples are ridiculous. There was this one guy, old school director, he was eighty-two when he married a twenty-three-year-old up and coming actress."

Elizabeth cringed.

"True love comes in all shapes and sizes, and I don't think we can always assume that if an age gap is wide that something untoward is going on, or worse, that it's predatory."

"She could be his grandchild!"

"Yes, and in that one case, it wasn't a marriage of love, but both got what they wanted, and so, is that wrong?" Kat asked.

"I don't know. But again, that's not the case here."

"No, it's not. Now, if Claudia were nineteen or twenty, I'd be more skeptical. But she's twenty-eight, and you're—"

"Forty-six," Elizabeth blurted out, her mind stuck on the years between them.

"Right. That's still manageable."

"But don't we want different things out of life and are automatically doomed?"

"I don't know. Do you? Shouldn't that be a conversation you have with her?"

"I suppose."

"As for the work thing, there has to be some kind of a solution that makes it less... terrible. Like some way that you aren't her direct supervisor anymore."

"I'm still in charge of the charity, so no matter what, she'll always be under me." Elizabeth pointed out.

Kat grinned and wiggled her eyebrows.

"Not like that!" Her cheeks flushed.

"You guys would have to trust each other there. If she wouldn't believe that you'd not retaliate, then you can forget moving forward."

"True."

"Anyway, isn't the pregnancy a bigger issue?" Kat asked.

She closed her eyes. "Yes and no."

Kat leaned back against the backrest of the barstool. "Explain that some more."

"Isn't it late? We should get some sleep. We both still need to shower, and I know how cranky you get when you don't get enough sleep."

"Now you're evading *and* projecting. Wow. I rarely ever get enough sleep, and if anyone is turning into a grouch at not getting enough sleep, it's you."

Elizabeth grumbled. "It's... I needed to be sure that if I went there with Claudia, which again assumes she's into me too—"

"Oh, she is."

"Anyway. I wanted to be sure that I'd be OK with it, with the pregnancy, with her having the baby, and—"

"Tom's baby. I imagine that makes it even more complicated."

"At first, yes. It was all too much. And for a while I withdrew as you know. But I missed her more than I'd expected, and it seemed worse to not have her in my life. I saw her still at work, whenever I did go into the office. Besides, the child is Claudia's baby in the end. I doubt Tom will want anything to do with them."

"True. But you can't have a relationship with someone just because you miss them when everything else is wrong."

"I didn't say that. I wanted clarity, and I was heading that way. But then she had to wear that damn suit and look just so... Ugh."

Kat laughed. "She looked quite appealing tonight."

Elizabeth covered her face with her hands. "Don't I know it."

"So, what will you do?"

"Well, she wants to see where it goes. I suggested we talk."

"Oh, Liz. It's too early to have such a conversation. Don't scare her away."

"You're making my head spin. Sometimes you're for this, and then against it, only to revert to supporting our... whatever is growing between us."

Kat grasped one of Elizabeth's hands. "Liz, listen. I'll always support you. No matter what. I'm on your side, and I think you're quite smitten with Claudia, and you've been strangely obsessed with her since that weird catfish text message exchange." Her brows furrowed.

"It wasn't about catfish, but—"

"Yes, yes. You like her."

"I do."

"And you're attracted to her."

"Apparently."

"And you kissed a girl, and you liked it."

"Oh my God, Kat. How old are you?"

Kat grinned. "Just see where it goes."

"But so much is at stake! What if I'm wrong and I can't handle a baby or things don't fit after all, and we realize we make good friends but nothing more? What about work?"

Kat shrugged. "Then you split. Again, no one is proposing. You aren't making a lifelong commitment by exploring what's between you. You're both grown-ups, so you'd also figure the work thing out after a break-up."

"What if the sex is awful? What if I may have liked kissing her but I won't like sex with a woman?"

"I wouldn't worry about that."

"Don't look so smug! It's not... What if we don't—"

"Again, you're not—"

"Moving in together, yes. That's your solution to everything."

"It's true. But let me ask you this: If I hadn't been here, and you guys would have been alone on the way back home in the limo, with the privacy screen up. Would you have sat there talking?"

Elizabeth flushed as heat rushed through her and her stomach clenched. No. She'd had very distinct and detailed plans for Claudia.

"Yeah. That's what I'm thinking, too. I wouldn't worry about sex." Kat emptied her tea.

Elizabeth narrowed her eyes. No. She likely didn't have to worry about sex, but she'd worry about everything else.

with gall and nerves

SUNDAY MORNING, CLAUDIA SCROLLED through the blocked contacts on her phone, staring at Tom's number, and wondering why she still recalled most of these digits. Her fingers hovered over the screen, but after a moment, and with a sigh, she unblocked his number and sent him a text.

We need to talk

Who is this? He wrote two minutes later.

Claudia scoffed. "The nerve." She sent her name.

I don't think that's wise.

"Too bad, asshole."

It's important. I don't want to discuss this over the phone.

We're done.

"No shit." Claudia hated having to deal with this, but he had a right to know, and this was something she wanted to take care of before Elizabeth and she had their talk. One more obstacle removed.

Indeed. I don't want you back.

Fine. I'm out at a bar later tonight.

Come by before, say at 6?

Claudia rolled her eyes. It would be helpful to know *which* bar. She agreed and asked for the name of the place, which he sent back without further comment. Yay. She'd see Tom later at O'Malley's.

She spent the rest of her Sunday morning cleaning before she headed to her parents' house for lunch. Beyond asking questions about Elizabeth and the gala, Mona inquired about Claudia's plans for Christmas. Apart from dinner with her family on Christmas Eve and the next morning's present exchange, she had none. To be fair, what was left of Christmas after that?

This conversation once more turned her mind to Elizabeth—as if she needed outside input to linger on her. She could only hope Elizabeth wouldn't talk herself out of whatever might be between them. Claudia also hoped that Kat hadn't ended up secretly hating her, and, as a result, spent the weekend discouraging Elizabeth. Though that assumed Elizabeth would bring up the kiss.

And when her mind went *there*, she lost track of everything around her, to where *teta* suggested Claudia should make an appointment with their ENT. This also led to thoughts of her upcoming conversation with Tom. At a bar. How funny. They'd kissed for the first time at a bar after meeting at that ill-fated alumni conference, and now she'd tell him she was pregnant at one. Could you call that the circle of life?

When she entered O'Malley's a couple minutes after six, a wave of nausea scrambled through her and she swallowed hard, trying to focus on why she was doing this. Claudia straightened and headed for the counter, spotting Tom at the far end.

"Hello." Claudia sat down on the barstool next to him.

He nodded, then took a sip of his beer.

Claudia declined the bartender's question to order anything.

"So?" Tom said after a moment of silence ticked by.

She hated doing this in public. Then again, she hadn't wanted Tom in her apartment either. "I'm pregnant."

Tom's eyes widened. "Congratulations? Who's the lucky guy?"

Claudia glared at him. "You."

He coughed, slamming his bottle back on the counter. "I doubt that."

"I've not been with anyone since you."

"All I have is your word. And if you recall...," he leaned closer, "we always used protection."

"Yes, but it's not foolproof."

"It's not mine. Funny how you've waited months to tell me."

Claudia sighed. She knew he'd react like this. "I won't argue the truth just because you refuse to believe me."

"What do you want? Money? My ex is already cleaning me out."

Claudia suppressed a smile while internally cheering for Elizabeth. "Good for her."

He grimaced.

"I just wanted you to know since it's your baby, too."

"Consider me informed. You can leave now."

"We could do a paternity test once the baby is born."

Tom shrugged. "I don't care. Even if it's mine, which I still doubt, I want nothing to do with the kid."

"I figured that. Don't worry. I don't want you in my child's life either."

"Then why are you here, if it's not for money or leeching off my time and energy?"

"Wow. I don't get what I ever saw in you." Claudia rose. "Have a good life, Tom."

He reached out and grabbed her arm. "Hey! You don't get to complain about me having an attitude when you come here trying to make me pay for a child that can't be mine."

Claudia snatched her arm back and inhaled deeply. "I don't want your money. I suggested the paternity test as a courtesy so you can be sure the baby is yours. I already know that's the case."

"You're up to something." His self-assured smile looked ugly now when she'd considered it charming before.

"I only came here to tell you that you'll have a child. That's it."

He grunted. "I never wanted children. Can't stand them."

"Why didn't you get a vasectomy? Or, you know, quit having sex with women." She turned and left, not waiting for his reply. She'd done what she came for, and now she could tell Elizabeth that Tom wouldn't be in their lives, although that assumed Elizabeth *wanted* to be a part of Claudia's life as more than her friend.

On Monday, Claudia prepared and honed her arguments to combat Elizabeth's list of reasons why they'd not work and therefore should settle for a friendship. Not that a friendship with Elizabeth would be considered settling. She'd love to be Elizabeth's friend, but if more could be on the table, Claudia wanted that. Badly.

They were reserved at work all day, with the understanding that the professional setting caused this, not any negative attitude by either woman. When Claudia left her office shortly after five and saw Elizabeth's light still on, she rushed over. She had wanted to be patient and allow Elizabeth to determine when and where they'd talk, but the need to tell her about meeting Tom urged her forward.

After entering Elizabeth's office, almost storming in there with a single-minded purpose, she halted, suddenly tongue-tied and unsure.

"What is it? Are you all right? Did something happen?" Elizabeth asked, jumping out of her chair and rushing toward Claudia, who still could only stare at her with wide eyes.

"Claudia!"

She shook her head. "Sorry, I just... I'm OK, but..."

"What?"

"I saw Tom."

Elizabeth's eyebrows rose. "I don't..."

"I told him I'm pregnant," Claudia continued, taking Elizabeth's stunned silence as a request to keep talking.

Elizabeth remained silent.

Claudia sighed. "Much like you said, he doesn't believe he's the father, and even if he is, he wants nothing to do with the child."

Elizabeth swallowed hard. "And... that disappoints you?"

"Yes!"

Elizabeth's face fell.

"No! I mean, I'm disappointed or... more like insulted he didn't believe it's his child, but no. I've told you I don't want him as a part of the baby's life. And that's likely super selfish, isn't it? But all I felt was relief because... because him out of the way meant you'd be more likely to agree to be with me."

Elizabeth's brows furrowed. "I'm not sure what—"

"You said you'd wanted him out of your life, right? That's why you'd ended things. Back then."

"Yes, but I thought we'd cleared that up. It's not feasible and well, I'm in a much better place now. I don't want him in my present or future, no, but I also understand that he's the father of your child, and if I want to be with you, it's likely not possible to never run into him at all."

"And that's OK?"

Elizabeth sighed. "I made peace with the Tom situation, and so that's not an issue. I'm glad you told him, to be honest. That was another unknown hanging over... us."

"That's why I did it. Well, it's why I did it now. I'd been pushing it off because it doesn't matter to me, but that doesn't mean it won't matter to the kid, you know? But with us, I felt this needed to be out there."

"You told him about us?" Elizabeth hated how shrill her voice sounded.

"No! Of course not. There isn't an us yet officially, and besides, I'd never... This isn't something I'd unilaterally do. We'd have to discuss that."

"OK, good. It's none of Tom's business, but I agree. It's something we should discuss first. Still, I'm sorry he acted like this. He's a total arsehole for not believing you."

Claudia smiled. "So now that's cleared up, can there be a continuation of what we started on the balcony?" she asked with a grin. She loved the look of a flustered Elizabeth, when her cheeks flushed, and she became all shy. Claudia hadn't realized before that she had the power to affect her in this way, but now that she'd caught on, she struggled to resist temptation.

Elizabeth cleared her throat. "Right, that. Uh, I still think we should continue this conversation first."

Claudia sighed. She'd been afraid of that, and even though she had her arguments set up, she still worried. "Here?"

"I'd planned to invite you to my place this weekend and thought we could talk there."

"A whole week? You wanted to wait an *entire* week?"

Elizabeth chuckled. "You really are impatient."

"Well, yes. So? The office is pretty much deserted now, so I doubt we'll have any interruptions. Or we could head to my place and talk there?"

"I'm not sure it's smart for us to be alone in a private setting right now," Elizabeth said. "At least not until we've had this conversation."

"Oh, I'd behave."

"Yes, but who says I'm worried about you?"

Heat slushed through Claudia, and she had to close her eyes for a split second. "Wow. OK. So, let's talk. Here. Now."

"All right." Elizabeth looked around her office. "Coffee?"

"No, thanks. I'm good." The last thing Claudia needed was caffeine. Her body seemed liable to go on strike and knock her unconscious given her nerves were already acting like she was about to go down a rollercoaster without a seatbelt.

"OK, let's sit then."

They settled on the couch, and at first, they only stared at each other, both seemingly unsure of what to say.

Claudia started at the same time Elizabeth did.

"OK, so I..."

"You might..."

They smiled at each other, then Claudia said, "You should start."

the age of insecurity

ELIZABETH HAD HAD THIS all planned out, how she'd cook for them, they'd sit together, eat, then talk everything over. They'd decide how to move forward and how to handle everything, how to overcome the issues still standing between them, even if most of them were in Elizabeth's head. Naturally, and as had been the story of her life recently, Claudia upended all of this. While the age difference still worried her, the first thing she'd wanted to say related to something else.

"You might have gotten the wrong impression of me on that balcony," Elizabeth said.

"Oh?"

"I'm not usually that… forward." Elizabeth refrained from cringing. Was she going to talk to Claudia about *that* now? Just because it had been her first impulse, didn't mean she had to follow up on it.

Claudia smiled. "You're not in the habit of *snogging* your employees in dark corners during Christmas parties?"

Elizabeth frowned. "No. And on that note, I'm your boss."

"Yes. You are."

"Don't you think that will complicate things?" Yes, a much safer topic.

"Perhaps, but there's a simple solution," Claudia said.

"Will you enlighten me about that?"

"I told you I'm prepared to shoot down your every argument. You can delegate. Put… Tilda in charge of me. That way, you won't be my direct supervisor."

Elizabeth tilted her head. How odd that Kat and Claudia ended up with the same idea. "It could work. However, this is my charity, and even with Tilda in charge of you, I'd still oversee her. Wouldn't you always have to assume that she'd do what I wish in the end?"

"I suppose. But I'm not worried about that."

"How so?"

"I can't picture you retaliating. Just consider… Tom. You had the means to ruin him, but you didn't do a thing."

Elizabeth leaned back against the cushion. "I'm making him pay back the money I invested in his partnership, even though I don't need it."

"Rightfully so. He cheated. Would you have demanded the money back if you guys had split because your relationship no longer worked?"

"Of course not."

Claudia smiled. "Again, not worried."

Elizabeth shook her head. "So you'd… trust me not to abuse my position?"

"Yes. But again, we could have HR draw something up. That way, you'd feel more secure, I guess."

"What about you? Wouldn't that make you also feel better?"

"No. Either I trust you or I don't. And if I don't trust you, then why would I even be your friend, or want more than that?"

Elizabeth swallowed hard. "And you do?"

"Trust you, yes."

"No, I meant…"

"Oh, yes. I want you."

Elizabeth ducked her head, biting her lip. God, how could Claudia just sit here and say such things like it was nothing? Meanwhile, Elizabeth didn't know what to say or do, and her body… *Let's not go there.*

"OK," Elizabeth finally managed to say.

"So, what's your next issue?"

"I'm not sure the work situation is resolved. There's still—"

"I have no doubt that you'll investigate this further and all, but this can work, well, if we *want* it to work. And that's the crucial question in the end, isn't it? Do you want me?"

Elizabeth flushed. "The balcony incident speaks volumes, doesn't it?"

"Being physically attracted isn't the same as wanting to be with someone long term. I'm not up for games or short-term flings. It's no longer just me."

"Physical attraction isn't… that easy for me." Of course, she'd find herself back there.

Claudia canted her head.

"I…" She ground her jaw. "It's hard to explain and quite embarrassing."

"Then we don't have to discuss it. Or at least, not now. You can tell me in your own time, or not. I don't need you to bare your soul to me."

Elizabeth smiled. "You're annoyingly sweet and understanding sometimes."

Claudia chuckled. "Isn't that a good thing?"

"It's disarming."

"Again…"

Elizabeth sighed. "Yes, and I'll take that raincheck."

"OK, good."

"I'm serious about you, about us, if we manage to establish a relationship that works. And I know that includes your baby."

"But you said you couldn't imagine running after a ten-year-old when you're, as you said, 'nearing sixty."

"Well, you informed me you don't run after ten-year-old children anymore."

"True. But what does that mean?"

"That I know you're a package deal, and I wouldn't have kissed you if I wasn't aware of that."

Claudia smiled one of those smiles where Elizabeth's body seemed to believe someone sat on her chest and had taken her heart in a vise-grip.

"That was the biggest issue, or my greatest fear. That you want me, but you can't see a life with me because of my child."

"I understand."

"What is your biggest worry? Or was it work?"

"Work is a major one, but your idea, which incidentally is also something along the lines of what Kat suggested, might work."

"I could look for another job," Claudia said. "Though for the record, I might like your rude friend after all."

"I'll be sure to tell her that." She held Claudia's gaze. Then, after a beat, "I thought you like this job. Would it be so easy to leave?" She hated the idea of Claudia not working at *Helping Hands*. Not just because she was fantastic at her job and replacing her would be a headache, but she enjoyed seeing Claudia every day, working with her.

"I love my job," Claudia said.

"But then why—"

"Because I won't let it stand in the way of a potential future with you. There are other jobs out there that I'm sure I could enjoy as well. I don't want to quit, but if it comes down to this job or you, well, that's not a contest."

Elizabeth's eyes widened. She wondered if this had ever happened before—that anyone had chosen her in a moment where there hadn't even been a choice yet. A preemptive decision, unprompted.

"You seem surprised."

"I am." Surprised was an understatement of epic proportions. Elizabeth's professional life had always flourished, but her personal life had been a different tale.

"I'm sorry if this is too much too soon. We've been through a lot, and in a way, honesty is the only thing that saved us. I want to keep it that way. And I'm... all in, if you are, but I understand if you need more time or if you want to think about this some more, and—"

"I'll be fifty in four years."

Claudia's mouth opened, then closed. "Yes. Math has never been my favorite subject, but—"

"Be serious!"

"I am! I take it this is your biggest concern?"

"Rationally, yes, and don't you dare try to wash it away with, 'age is just a number,' again."

"First of all, that's not what I meant," Claudia said. "Second, I swear I wasn't joking. I take you seriously, and that includes your worries, even when I don't share them. That said, you surprised me, and my go-to reaction when feeling unsettled is often humor."

"All right."

"Let's start from the beginning. What exactly about our age difference is bothering you?"

Elizabeth's brows furrowed. "The age difference."

Claudia chuckled. "All right. What's an acceptable age difference to you?"

"I never contemplated this much before... you, but I'd say five to ten years in either direction."

"If we met when I was eighteen and you were twenty-eight, would that have been all right?"

"I was thirty-six when you were eighteen." Elizabeth flinched. "God, that makes it sound even worse."

"Humor me. Let's imagine we were only ten years apart, and we got together when I was eighteen. Would that have been fine?"

"Of course not."

"But you said a difference of five to ten in either direction is fine."

Elizabeth pinched the bridge of her nose. "There's still a difference between what ages we're looking at. I'm not sure I'd have dated you if you were eighteen when I was twenty-two, but I'd have dated someone who is thirty when I was forty."

"Right. I agree. But I'm almost thirty, and you're not that far from forty, so shouldn't that be fine then?"

Elizabeth laughed. "I'm not sure I've ever heard a twenty-eight-year-old refer to forty-six as close to forty."

"Well, I'll be twenty-nine next month, and you turned forty-six this summer, so for a while, we'll be only seventeen years apart."

"And that'll make all the difference?"

"Mmhmm, definitely."

"Again, you're silly." She didn't understand the lightness that Claudia brought to her life, even in serious situations like this one. Yet Elizabeth felt she'd never tire of it.

"Yes, but not childish. Look, I get it. And if I were twenty and you thirty-eight, I might say you have a point. So much changes in your early twenties. Sure, you're more settled than I am, especially professionally, but we're not worlds apart."

"No. We're not." She never thought they were. Sometimes she wondered if her objections were more an aspect of socialized expectations, instead of an inherent problem.

"Do you think of my age when we're together?"

"No. We've always seemed the same, I mean, once we started to interact."

Claudia smiled. "I feel the same way."

"But I'll be in my sixties when you'll be in your forties."

"And?"

"Doesn't that bother you?"

"All I hear is that you believe our relationship has a future, and to be honest, I only feel happy when I think of that."

"I suppose that's one way to look at it."

"I mean, I also have struggled with how different we are socially and financially, but that never seemed to matter in our interactions, and—"

"It doesn't."

"Just like the age difference doesn't matter."

Elizabeth sighed. "I guess I mostly worried that our age difference dooms us because we want different things out of life."

"From what I can tell, we want the same. The child is obviously the biggest change and they'll affect everything, but I love the idea of a quiet life with you."

"Yes. Though stillness might not be realistic once the little one arrives."

Claudia chuckled. "True, but that's not what I was talking about. Peaceful. A settled life of... I don't know, contented togetherness?"

"I'd like that." Elizabeth's heart felt warm and full. Could they truly have this?

"Now, you said rationally the age difference was your biggest issue. What's the other one?"

Elizabeth drew her hand over the seam of a pillow. "That's just... I don't think I've ever... This sounds so stupid."

"Is it the woman thing?"

Elizabeth waved her off. "No, I don't care about that. Although I'm sure my mother will have a field day with it, given that she'll once more get not to say 'I told you so', while making clear she told me so."

"Then what is it?"

Elizabeth lowered her head. "I've never found myself so preoccupied by another." Elizabeth's heart picked up its beat, but if Claudia could be this brave, so could she.

"Oh," Claudia breathed. "Me neither."

"You don't have to say that."

Claudia frowned and shuffled closer, grasping Elizabeth's hand. "Hey. I mean it, OK?"

Elizabeth caught Claudia's gaze.

"I wouldn't lie about this or try to sweet-talk you, or however you call that."

Elizabeth snorted.

"I'm serious. I've been in love before, so I'm not saying this is completely new or whatever. But it differed from the start. We connected so effortlessly, and I've had the urge to be close to you from the beginning, despite everything that stood between us."

"I've never failed at keeping my distance before."

"That's a good thing, isn't it?"

"I suppose," Elizabeth grumbled. She'd have picked exasperating, but...

"Then why are you upset about it?"

"It's not... I'm not upset, just a tad worried. This has so much potential to be devastating, and—"

"Why are you already worrying about the end of a relationship that's just starting?"

"It's not an active disquiet. I don't agonize over this. It's more an awareness that what we have... is already strong enough to hurt. When we stopped speaking, it hurt."

"Yeah."

"And we were friends then. So it goes to reason that it would be much worse if things were to fall apart after we've been more."

"Isn't that life, though? Besides, you never know what'll happen, so wouldn't it make sense to just make the most of every day and enjoy a good thing for as long as life allows you to do so?"

"You're pretty wise for your age," Elizabeth said, her eyes full of mirth.

"What can I say? An old, wise lady must have rubbed off on me. Or better, will be rubbing me off. Wait. Isn't that British slang? No, you guys use wank, right? But that's just for men, isn't it?"

Elizabeth dropped her face in her hands and groaned. "You're killing me."

# of hunger and clothing

They exchanged text messages during the remainder of the week, where Elizabeth asked Claudia if she was truly OK with coming to her place this Saturday, or if she'd prefer to meet at her apartment. Claudia hadn't been surprised Elizabeth favored the comfort of her home after their emotional discussion the other night, and she didn't mind. Whatever made Elizabeth feel more secure was a plus in Claudia's book. None of them suggested a phone call, as they both felt all-talked-out (Claudia assumed), and it was much easier to just type a message.

At first, their interactions had been benign and even a bit awkward. How did you act when you made out and wanted more, would have had more that night if not for Elizabeth's overnight guest, and then had an "all cards on the table" discussion about your fears and worries? Especially since Claudia figured this wasn't something Elizabeth made a habit out of.

Then, sleepy and overcome with the desire to be close to Elizabeth, one of Claudia's texts changed in tone and content.

I miss your taste.

When Claudia realized she'd not just thought that but wrote it, all tiredness vanished and in its stead rushed a reckless mixture of alarm and excitement. It seemed like her heart spasmed in her chest when the three dots of Elizabeth typing appeared. Should she send an apology? But she wasn't sorry. Though she also didn't want to push Elizabeth out of her comfort zone. Then again, Elizabeth had initiated their first kiss, and after their talk, they seemed to be on the same page.

Perhaps you can refresh
your memory on Saturday.

Claudia groaned and fell back on the bed. God, she hoped she'd survive Saturday. Hell, she hoped she'd make it through the rest of the week.

She did, in fact, make it through, although along the way, she found herself in an almost perpetual state of low-key arousal. Their messages never crossed any lines into sexting, however, they were innuendo-laden enough to keep Claudia on her toes.

Saturday arrived, and with it, Claudia rang Elizabeth's doorbell, rocking up and down in her sneakers. She'd packed an overnight bag but since they hadn't talked about her staying the night, she left it in her trunk. She didn't want to seem presumptuous, but well, she had hope.

"Hello." Elizabeth opened the door, sounding as breathless as Claudia felt.

"Hi." Claudia did that stupid little wave thing, but before she could roll her eyes at herself, Elizabeth reached out and pulled her into a tight hug.

Claudia smiled and squeezed Elizabeth before stepping back. "How are you?"

"I'm fine. How about you?" Elizabeth was dressed in a pair of black leggings and a crème-colored blouse. Her hair fell in loose curls over her shoulders and her face was devoid of make-up. Her eyes crinkled with warmth when she smiled.

Claudia had to refrain from pulling Elizabeth back into her again, so she stuffed her hands into the pockets of her blue jeans. "Good, good."

"Are you hungry? Do you want to talk, or..." Elizabeth trailed off, and she seemed so aimless and almost fragile, Claudia couldn't help but step closer, filled with the urge to reassure her.

"I'm not hungry and kinda done talking." She raised her hand and trailed a finger from Elizabeth's temple down her cheek. "I missed you."

Elizabeth sighed softly. "I missed you, too."

Claudia's heart sped up. "You're so beautiful."

Elizabeth released a puff of air and leaned into Claudia's hand. "You're ridiculous," she whispered.

"Why?"

"I'm neither dressed up nor am I wearing a lick of make-up."

"I know." Claudia tilted her head, holding Elizabeth's gaze. "My favorite look on you were my clothes after the coffee spill, or your lounging wear at home. Besides, you look absolutely lovely in the morning."

Elizabeth closed her eyes and groaned. "Not the outfit for the Christmas dinner?"

"That dress was something else, but no. I prefer you... dressed down, I suppose."

"I don't think I've ever been with anyone who felt that way."

"Their loss."

"You sometimes make everything seem so easy."

Claudia released a chuckle. "Now, no one has ever said *that* about me."

"Their fault."

"May I kiss you?" Claudia asked, and when Elizabeth nodded, she ducked her head and connected their lips in an achingly soft kiss that swiftly deepened with Elizabeth tugging Claudia closer.

After a breathless moment, Claudia remembered they were still standing in the entrance hall. At the same time, Raji made an appearance and snuck around their legs, purring. Claudia pulled back. "Can we take this someplace else?" she asked, her voice sounding almost hoarse.

Elizabeth bit her lower lip. "Are you sure?"

"Yes. Unless you don't want to. We can wait. I want you, and you know it's not just physical, so—"

Elizabeth silenced her with a kiss and led Claudia to her bedroom.

Anticipation coiled in Claudia's stomach while nerves scurried down her frame when Elizabeth drew her close to the bed and settled on the mattress.

"You know, I made dinner for tonight."

"Is it going to burn?"

"No. I'd turned the oven off right before you arrived."

"Perfect timing."

"Mmhmm."

Claudia held Elizabeth's gaze as she kicked off her shoes, grasped the hem of her shirt and pulled it over her head. She dropped it onto the floor before reaching behind her back to unfasten her bra.

Elizabeth's gaze remained glued on Claudia's every move.

Claudia peeled the bra off her body and let it fall to join the shirt on the floor. Her hands dropped to the buttons on her jeans, opening one after the other. Heat rose and flushed her skin as Elizabeth's gaze seemed to burn her.

Elizabeth's avid eyes watched unblinkingly as Claudia slid her pants down her legs, shimmying out of them.

Claudia rose, now standing only dressed in her black panties in front of Elizabeth. "I feel underdressed." She noted Elizabeth's raised breathing and parted lips.

"I… Yes. Right."

Confidence rose in Claudia at seeing Elizabeth this affected and she stepped closer, right between Elizabeth's legs. "May I?" She reached for Elizabeth's blouse.

"Yes." Her gaze refocused on Claudia who carefully undid the buttons and slid the garment off her shoulders.

Elizabeth shivered; a flush of pink blossomed on her cheeks as she licked her lower lip.

Claudia halted, entranced by the sight of Elizabeth's tongue, yearning to taste her again. She leaned in, her lips a mere breath away from Elizabeth who'd closed her eyes as her hands clutched the sheets. She worried Elizabeth's lower lip, pulled at the soft flesh with her teeth before drawing back. "I want you naked," Claudia pressed out.

Elizabeth pushed Claudia back and rose to shed her clothes in quick succession. She watched how Claudia's gaze traced the curves of her body once she stood completely bare in front of her. She sat back down on the bed. "I'd say now you're overdressed."

Claudia scrambled to shrug off her panties and rushed closer.

When Elizabeth scooted farther back, Claudia followed, placing her hands on either side of Elizabeth's head to hold herself up and keep their nude bodies separate.

"I don't think you understand how much I ache to taste you," Claudia breathed, hovering over Elizabeth whose eyes fluttered shut. She was entranced by the fine contours of Elizabeth's face and her long lashes.

"Don't say stuff like that," she rasped, trembling.

Claudia watched goosebumps rise across Elizabeth's skin. "Why?"

Elizabeth cupped Claudia's cheek, stroking her thumb over her lips. "It leaves me breathless."

Claudia smiled, kissing Elizabeth's digit. "That's good."

"Kiss me."

Claudia did, claiming Elizabeth's lips in an ardent kiss. She loved Elizabeth's taste, and she hadn't lied. She'd dreamed about being with Elizabeth like this, and even though for the longest she didn't believe her chances high or even existent, that hadn't stopped her mind from picturing them like this, of her lying on top of a nude Elizabeth, just like they were now, and from hurrying down, spreading her legs and—

Claudia broke the kiss and groaned when Elizabeth's fingernails dug into her lower back. She pushed forward, pressing her groin against the juncture between Elizabeth's legs.

Elizabeth pressed her head deeper into the pillow, exposing the straining sinews of her neck.

Claudia bent her head and once more licked into Elizabeth's mouth.

Elizabeth scratched her nails up Claudia's back.

She arched into the touch and once again broke the kiss. "Spread your legs for me," Claudia croaked, her voice rougher and deeper than she'd ever heard it.

Elizabeth clenched her jaw and while holding Claudia's gaze—her bright eyes intense, and almost timid—she widened her legs.

Claudia shifted down, nibbling at Elizabeth's breasts before licking down her stomach. She trailed her tongue along Elizabeth's groin, her hands anchoring her hips.

Elizabeth panted. Her chest heaved as her hands tightened their grip on the sheets.

Claudia ghosted a finger along Elizabeth's labia.

Elizabeth trembled.

Claudia smiled, then parted her folds. "You're so wet and swollen."

Elizabeth groaned and flung one arm over her face.

"You're beautiful here, too."

"Claudia, I swear—" Elizabeth's words halted, and a broken sob poured from her lips when Claudia lowered her head and sucked Elizabeth into her mouth.

Claudia dug her fingers into Elizabeth's hips, pressing her deeper into the mattress as her tongue painted fast and hard circles over Elizabeth's clit.

Elizabeth's body grew taut, her knuckles paling as she moaned amidst the onslaught of Claudia's tongue.

Claudia sucked harder before releasing the aching bundle of nerves and trailed her tongue down, licking along the labia and pulling one into her mouth.

Elizabeth groaned, her hips rocking against Claudia, who'd now also added her fingers in the mix to massage Elizabeth's entrance.

Claudia felt lost in touching Elizabeth so intimately, and her own arousal that had grown steadily now seemed like a contained ball of need, far away yet still at the back of her mind as she shifted and once more sucked Elizabeth's clit into her mouth, flicking her tongue against the hardened nub.

Elizabeth gasped. "Go inside."

Claudia closed her eyes for a moment, feeling utterly overwhelmed. She pushed two fingers into Elizabeth's sodden heat, overcome by the snug, velvet sensation of being inside her.

Elizabeth's back bowed and a sheen of sweat glistened on her skin.

Claudia increased the speed of her tongue lashing Elizabeth's clit while picking up the tempo and depth of her thrusts. Heat coursed through her, and she felt almost blinded by the need to see Elizabeth fall apart.

Elizabeth writhed beneath Claudia; her eyelids closed as she moved along the rhythm Claudia set. A low moan spilled from her lips.

As Elizabeth arched up, Claudia tightened her grip and continued her ministrations.

Elizabeth's body stiffened, then trembled when a hard shudder rushed through her frame. She balled the fabric of the sheet between her fingers, "Claudia," she called, her walls fluttering around Claudia's fingers as a hard climax seemed to ripple through her body.

She continued lapping at Elizabeth's heat, while her fingers slowed, her movements growing shallow.

Elizabeth panted, then laughed. "Come up here."

Claudia smiled, and releasing Elizabeth, she climbed up and sunk onto her hot, slick body.

Elizabeth pulled Claudia's head down and kissed her deeply.

Claudia groaned into the kiss, the arousal she'd been able to contain broke free and threatened to consume her.

bashful bewilderment

Elizabeth had a complicated relationship with sex. For most of her adult life, she felt somewhat inhibited. She enjoyed sex, and she'd experienced good sex before, but there always seemed to be a certain shyness involved she never fully understood nor could vanquish. It seemed odd to her as she generally wasn't a shy or inhibited person, yet concerning sex, it had lingered. Elizabeth had eventually just accepted this as a facet of her personality, and it had caused no problems, so she'd figured there were bigger issues to tackle than that.

Claudia's single-minded focus to bring her pleasure, and her sincere adoration seemed to ease something within Elizabeth. She still felt remnants of bashfulness course through her, especially at first when Claudia had asked her to spread her legs only to comment on her... Yes. That moment would likely make most people feel overwhelmed.

After her weekend with Kat and some more thinking, after endless replays of kissing Claudia on the balcony, recalling how it felt to be so close to her, Elizabeth had decided that if Claudia would still be interested in her, they could talk about trying to be together.

And when Claudia had pushed this talk forward—at work, which Elizabeth wouldn't have thought in a million years would ever happen—she'd felt assured that this was something they could have. Still, she had *not* planned on falling into bed right away. She'd cooked a mushroom risotto and placed a chicken and vegetable casserole into the oven, ready to sit down, eat, and enjoy the anticipation of what was to come, much like they'd done over the course of the week with their text messaging.

Yet, seeing Claudia standing there had derailed all her plans. One step and they were too close again. She had struggled to release her from the hug before, but when Claudia had drawn close again and they'd kissed, all ideas of anticipation vanished, and instead, Elizabeth found herself swallowed by want.

Instead of reveling in her post-orgasm bliss, Elizabeth needed to bring Claudia to similar heights she'd just returned from. She kissed her hard, sucking her tongue into her mouth and scraping her teeth over the muscle.

Claudia clutched her closer.

Elizabeth considered flipping them around but found herself too impatient to touch the waiting well-spring of liquid heat between Claudia's legs. When she slid her fingers through Claudia's slick flesh, she moaned into the kiss.

Claudia shuddered, shifting as if seeking to sink onto her fingers.

A gasp left Elizabeth's lips at the conjured image, and she surged up, kissing Claudia harder while pressing two fingers inside.

Claudia shuddered. She broke the kiss with a groan and sunk her face into the crook of Elizabeth's neck, nuzzling at her skin while rocking her hips to match the rhythm of Elizabeth's thrusts.

She tangled her other hand in Claudia's hair, and after a few more strokes, she pulled out and her fingers danced higher, circling Claudia's clit in fast circles.

Claudia moaned, her hands gripping the sheets as her hips followed Elizabeth's fingers. "God." She panted.

Elizabeth suppressed the urge to cant her hips up, too, and instead sped up her movements, adding pressure while changing the direction of her motions.

"Liz," Claudia breathed.

She shuddered at Claudia's hot breath against her neck. "Look at me," Elizabeth whispered, turning scarlet at her request—in complete disbelief she'd uttered it at all.

Claudia lifted her head, and her gaze burned.

Elizabeth felt frozen in place, yet somehow, she managed to continue stroking Claudia higher. She was mesmerized by Claudia's parted lips, the color high in her cheeks and her blown pupils.

Claudia's eyelids fluttered.

"Stay with me," Elizabeth pressed out, watching as Claudia struggled to fulfill her request.

The long moan that left Claudia's lips shot directly to Elizabeth's core, and she felt her own arousal coil. God, she needed more of this woman.

Claudia worried her lower lip, then she halted, seemingly frozen in place before a hard tremor rushed through her.

Elizabeth watched with wide eyes and a surge of need how Claudia tumbled over the edge before collapsing bonelessly on top of her. She caressed Claudia's back, painting idle patterns on damp skin.

"I can't believe I ever thought you were straight," Claudia mumbled after a while.

Elizabeth chuckled. "I've never slept with a woman before."

Claudia raised her head, her mouth opened, before she snapped it shut. "Are you serious?"

"Why would I lie to you?"

"No, no. I didn't mean that." Claudia rolled off Elizabeth but stayed snuggled close to her side. She rested her head on her palm.

"Oh, I know. No need to worry."

"So, is this a recent development, then?"

"Being attracted to another woman?"

Claudia nodded.

"Perhaps. I'm not sure."

Claudia frowned. "How's that?"

"I've noticed attractive women before. And in retrospect, there may have been some... infatuations in the past, but I've spent no time contemplating sex with another woman or desiring it."

"Until me, right?"

Elizabeth snorted. "Isn't that obvious?"

"Just checking."

"You're silly." Elizabeth shifted and pressed a lingering kiss on Claudia's lips.

"So you keep saying."

"Hmm. Yes, but I still don't feel like talking."

"You don't, huh?"

"No, but I wouldn't mind hearing some more sounds from you." Elizabeth drew closer to where only a fraction of an inch separated their lips.

"By all means," Claudia whispered.

Elizabeth smiled as she once more pulled Claudia into a kiss. This time she flipped them and straddled Claudia who groaned, her hands shooting to Elizabeth's breasts.

Later that day, when they sat down to eat the meal Elizabeth had prepared, Claudia seemed ravenous.

Elizabeth chuckled. "I'm glad you like the food. Do you have room for dessert?"

"That's not a real question, is it?"

"Perish the thought." Elizabeth rose to get the lava cake she'd prepared last night.

"Oh, my God, you didn't!"

Claudia's speechless expression when she placed the dessert on the table filled Elizabeth with joy and a slight sense of wonder. She'd never met someone with no guile.

"You appear to have worked up quite the appetite, and this seemed... appropriate."

"So it had been your plan all along to jump me the moment I got here?" Claudia grinned.

Elizabeth's eyes widened. "What? No. I just meant—"

"I'm messing with you. This week of anticipation had me on edge, too. I doubt I could have enjoyed this delicious food right when I got here."

"Indeed."

Claudia took the first bite of the cake, the ganache leaking out onto the plate. “Oh my God. I’d marry you for this alone.” She moaned.

Elizabeth flushed and lowered her head.

“Hey. I’m sorry. I’ve noticed you seem a bit... shy at times? Is that the right word? I don’t know. I’d never before have used that to describe you, but earlier, and now...”

Elizabeth sighed. No one had ever commented on this, and she thought she’d been good at hiding it. Once more, leave it to Claudia.

“I’m sorry. I didn’t mean to upset you.”

“No, no. You didn’t. This relates to the raincheck you gave me on Monday.”

Claudia nodded. “I thought it might. But it’s really nothing we need to talk about.”

“I agree. It’s not going to be an issue, but I would like to talk about it. If that’s OK.”

“Yes, of course.” Claudia put her fork down, half of the lave cake still resting on her plate, yet her entire focus rested on Elizabeth.

“You’re right. I’m not shy in my life. I’m not sure if I used to be and then my job changed that, or if I just never was, and this just relates to... physical intimacy.”

“OK, there’s nothing wrong with it, though. Being shy, no matter how or in what situation.”

Elizabeth frowned. “Of course not. That didn’t even cross my mind.”

“All right, then I don’t understand what—

“I’d like to change it, not because there’s anything wrong with it but because it exasperates me as it just doesn’t fit. But more than that, there’s... stuff I’d like to do, or try, but I’ve never felt comfortable enough to voice any of this.”

“Oh?”

Elizabeth chuckled at Claudia’s rapt attention.

“I’m all ears.”

“That you are,” Elizabeth drawled. “I might need some time to sort this out in my head and to talk to you about it. But I want that, the conversation and the... more practical side of things.”

"I'm very interested in both. So, take your time. I'm not going anywhere."

Elizabeth smiled. "I like that."

After dinner, they retreated to the living room, Claudia once more having bribed Raji who head-butted her before sprawling on the floor in front of the couch.

"Cats are so weird." Claudia sat down next to Elizabeth.

"That's not how you get on my good side."

Claudia waved her off. "I'd say I already am, given that you let me lie between your legs and—"

"Claudia!"

"What?"

"You have a one-track mind."

"Have you looked at yourself lately? Who could blame me?"

Elizabeth flushed. Claudia truly would be the death of her.

a crowning hope

Claudia would never tire of flustering Elizabeth. Perhaps she felt this appeal so keenly because it occurred seldom and was a new facet, as their friendship before didn't lend itself to such moments. Now, though, everything had changed.

On Sunday, they went for a walk along a nearby trail after their lunch. Claudia loved running, but she rarely went walking just for the sake of it. A new scent seemed to waft around them, and the cool air sang on her skin.

"Do you do this often?"

"Go for a walk?" Elizabeth asked.

"Yes."

"I used to do it more before the pandemic. I should get back to it." She raised her head and gazed at the tree crowns above them, swaying in the wind.

"We could make a habit out of this," Claudia suggested.

"You mean like watching *Broken Time*?"

"Yeah. Why not? At least until this little one makes an appearance and all I want to do is sleep."

Elizabeth hummed. "There's that, yes."

"I want to tell my parents. I mean, I have to soon. Right now, I'm not really showing, but I'm eighteen weeks in, and according to my research, my belly is gonna blow up soon."

"What's holding you back?"

"Disappointment. *Teta's* especially. I'm not married, yet I'm pregnant. Even worse, the father was... married."

Elizabeth squeezed her hand. "I can see that."

"The thing is, I'm overall not scared about the pregnancy, the baby, or anything. But telling my family?" She released a harsh breath. "We've always been close, and I love that. I don't think they'll reject me or anything, but I'd still see it, the disappointment in their eyes, and I just can't. Or I couldn't. Not while we were still hanging up in the air."

"That's cleared up now."

"Yes."

"Do you think that will also be an issue?"

"Hmm, I don't know. Like, I want to say no, but you never know. Still, I'm less nervous about sharing that news than the pregnancy."

"Will you combine the two? Or better, will you tell them everything?"

"Oh, hell no. I mean, I'll likely say that the father was married, and I didn't know, but I won't connect that to you. That's just... weird."

"Is this a secret you generally want to keep?"

Claudia shrugged. "I don't see why this is anyone else's business. People won't assume anything like that. I mean, Kat and Sammy know, and it's not that I'm ashamed or want to keep it a secret. It's just... How will that even come up?"

"Good point." Elizabeth pulled Claudia closer. "I haven't thought much about that, but you're right. This is a part of our history than can remain dormant."

"Until the little one asks," Claudia said.

Elizabeth chuckled. "I somehow doubt that'll be on their mind."

"You never know. I'm a very curious person, and if the baby takes after me..."

"Yes, there's that. Have you decided if you want to know the sex?"

"I think so. The ultrasound is on the twenty-sixth. You want to join me?"

"Do you have to ask?" Elizabeth shot a mock glare at Claudia, but an expression of fondness and affection remained on her features, and Claudia wished she could bathe in it.

"No. I don't."

Her answer seemed to mollify Elizabeth, and they continued their walk, chatting about lighter topics. All the while, a previously unknown contentedness settled over Claudia.

After dinner, Claudia suggested relaxing on the couch, clearly with an ulterior motive, as she right away pulled at Elizabeth.

Elizabeth followed Claudia's tug and stretched out on top of her.

"How the tables have turned," Claudia said.

"Did your plans include lying beneath me?"

"My plans included another visit of your talented tongue between my legs."

Elizabeth tightened her jaw. "I see."

"It's been a while."

Elizabeth chuckled. "Last night constitutes 'a while' now?"

"Yes."

"In what world?" Elizabeth asked; her lips so close, Claudia could almost taste them.

"Ours." Claudia lifted her head and kissed her. She nibbled at Elizabeth's lower lip before deepening the kiss.

Elizabeth's hands disappeared in Claudia's hair as she sunk into a kiss that escalated quickly and left them both panting. Elizabeth broke the kiss to suck and lick at Claudia's neck.

Claudia's hands grabbed Elizabeth's butt and pulled her closer. She needed pressure, already in utter disbelief at how fast her arousal skyrocketed in Elizabeth's vicinity, under her touch.

Elizabeth shifted lower and pulled up Claudia's shirt. "No bra," she mumbled.

"Seemed wise." Claudia's reply morphed into a moan when Elizabeth's searing mouth engulfed one of her nipples.

Elizabeth sucked the pebbled flesh into her mouth, scraping her teeth before swirling her tongue around it.

Claudia's hands shot to Elizabeth's head, torn between pulling her closer and pushing her lower.

Before Claudia could decide, Elizabeth meandered south—kissing along Claudia's torso—her fingers tracing the barely there bump of her stomach. She dipped her tongue playfully into her bellybutton before she reached the waistband of Claudia's pants. "Lift your hips," Elizabeth rasped.

Claudia stifled the urge to press her thighs together and instead followed suit, allowing Elizabeth to pull down her pants and panties.

Elizabeth rose and, without seeming to give the clothes in her hand a second thought, shoved them off the couch.

"Someone's impatient."

Elizabeth narrowed her eyes at Claudia as she settled between her legs, spreading them wider. She dipped her head and blew hot air against Claudia's wetness.

Claudia gritted her teeth, pressing her hips deeper into the couch as anticipation twisted in her lower stomach.

Elizabeth's hands clasped Claudia's hips, anchoring her while she dipped her head and licked along her length.

Claudia panted, her fingers digging into Elizabeth's scalp.

Elizabeth ran her tongue along her entrance in swirls before pressing inside.

Claudia groaned, her eyes falling shut. She forced herself to keep them open as watching Elizabeth between her legs left her lightheaded.

Elizabeth trailed her tongue up, licking along her labia before sucking her clit into her mouth.

She released Elizabeth's head and instead gripped the couch, bowing her head back.

Elizabeth sucked harder before withdrawing.

A soft whimper broke from Claudia's lips, and she rocked her hips up.

Elizabeth added her fingers, running them through Claudia's heat before she once more lowered her head and drew the hardened nub into her mouth.

Claudia groaned, then sighed when Elizabeth entered her with two fingers.

Elizabeth kept up a fast rhythm while also speeding up her tongue.

Claudia arched her back as Elizabeth's ministrations pushed her ever higher. "Liz," she gasped.

Elizabeth moaned into Claudia's flesh, and the sensation of that, coupled with the overall onslaught on her senses, soon proved to be too much.

Claudia's body trembled, then arrested before she quivered when hard quakes rushed through her as Elizabeth pushed her over the edge.

Elizabeth continued, though she slowed down her motions and fully stopped when Claudia tugged at her upper arms.

Elizabeth shuffled up and kissed Claudia, who placed her hands on Elizabeth's lower back. "Did that go according to plan?" she asked after ending the kiss.

"The first part, yes, but now I got to fulfill the rest."

"Oh? And what's that?"

"Making you come even harder."

Elizabeth flushed.

"Where were we?" Claudia grinned. "How about we take this to the shower?"

Later that night, when they made their way to bed, Claudia sighed happily and pulled Elizabeth closer, placing a kiss on her hair. "What do you think about spending Christmas with us? My parents would love for you to join us."

"You mean as your..."

"Friend. I know I said I'm not nervous about telling them, and that's true. But I'm not ready yet... Is that OK?"

"Of course. This is all incredibly new. I like the idea of it just being between the two of us for now."

"Me, too. But..."

"What?"

"I want to tell them. For the first time, I want to introduce them to my... girlfriend? Partner? Significant other? Do you have a preference?"

Elizabeth sighed. "Why did you have to bring logic and consideration to such a heartfelt statement?"

"Huh?"

"Never mind. I'll get used to it."

"You're one to talk. As if you don't jump topics! That's how it all started, you complaining about catfish and talking about cats."

"Well, the result seems worth it," Elizabeth sniffed.

"That it is."

Silence.

"So?"

"What?"

"Which one do you prefer?"

"You may introduce me however you wish once you tell your parents that we're together."

"How gracious."

"Thank you."

Claudia groaned.

"What?"

"I'll have to tell *teta*, too."

"Come to think of it, I feel like this might be a conversation you should have on your own with your family."

"Oh, no. Don't you take that tone with me!"

"What are you talking about?"

"You went all diplomatic and appeasing. You need to make use of that when *we* talk to my family."

Elizabeth groaned.

changes and irreverence

After sharing her life with Claudia for the last eighteen months, Elizabeth realized she'd never had a genuine relationship before. Or perhaps she should say she'd never experienced a relationship that worked like this. Their friendship had been effortless, and while that was much easier for a friendship to achieve, she'd say their romantic relationship, so far, had also been easier than Elizabeth had ever imagined. She sometimes struggled to believe how happy she was, and how full of life and joy her existence had become.

They had signed additional documents for *Helping Hands* to ensure that Elizabeth had no supervisory position over Claudia, and as such, Tilda handled everything work related. Nothing else much changed there. They now also often had lunches together, and while they had had to endure some knowing and smug smirks from Tilda, it had all been worth it. Claudia had shaped up to be the best legal advisor they could have hoped for.

Claudia's parents (and *teta*) had been more taken aback by the age gap between them than by the fact that Elizabeth was a woman. By the time they told them, they'd been together for almost three months, and they'd all spent quite some time together beforehand. Kareem and Mona liked Elizabeth and only grumbled about having been kept in the dark. *Teta* proclaimed that at least Claudia would no longer have to worry about returning to her stick figure after the baby, and since she now had to 'eat for two,' she continued to add more food to Claudia's plate during their

Sunday lunches. Since their announcement, Elizabeth was always welcome to attend these gatherings.

Elizabeth sometimes wondered if Mona and Kareem had still been reeling from the pregnancy announcement and the explanation of why the father was not and would not be in the picture, so that the shock of them being romantically involved seemed lighter in comparison. Then again, they also could still have been numb to it. At the same time, Mona and Claudia's grandmother had been over the moon about the prospect of the new family addition.

Alice. Claudia had given birth to a little girl, Alice, who, based on all the baby pictures Elizabeth had seen, looked just like her mother. Life with a baby who was about to turn one and would soon start walking (bringing even more chaos to their lives), had been an adjustment, to say the least.

As promised, Tom wanted nothing to do with Alice, and after Elizabeth had convinced Claudia to petition for child support (Why shouldn't he contribute?) he'd demanded a paternity test. Claudia had been reluctant to press the issue, but Elizabeth had argued that he should have to finance part of the cost of having a child, since Claudia hadn't created Alice on her own. As neither wanted a single cent of his money, they had opened a savings account for Alice and deposited each of his checks in there.

Tom was also still making monthly payments based on their divorce settlement. Since he'd cheated, he owed Elizabeth the money she had paid for him to join his firm as a partner. Consequently, they both received quite a bit of Tom's monthly paycheck. She'd also never seen someone flush such a deep shade of crimson before turning deathly pale as when he'd learned of their relationship. Elizabeth wished she had a recording.

Claudia had moved in with Elizabeth when Alice was a few weeks old, realizing that they'd not see each other at all otherwise, not to mention it was much easier for Elizabeth to help Claudia with Alice and everything else. They had talked about moving in together before, but Claudia had hesitated as she felt she'd be living off Elizabeth that way. They'd had a few arguments, but then Elizabeth had let it go, until one day, when Alice had been asleep and Elizabeth had stayed over, Claudia had fallen into her arms and cried.

"What's wrong? Are you all right?"

"I'm so tired."

Elizabeth pulled her close. "Go to sleep. I'll handle Alice when she wakes up."

Claudia shook her head.

"You know I don't mind. I want to help you and be there for you. For both of you."

Claudia wiped her eyes. "It's not that, or just that. I… I miss you, and…" More tears fell.

Elizabeth wiped them away. "What?"

"I don't know how to balance everything, and I feel like a total loser. I just… I'm still hurting from the birth. Who knew it hurts to cough or sneeze, or even laugh after giving birth? And for so long!"

Elizabeth grimaced in sympathy.

"And I'm so tired all the time, and she… I love Alice, and it's not her. It's me."

"This is hard, and you're by yourself when you don't have to be. You don't need to shoulder this alone."

"But I can't ask you to—"

Elizabeth pressed a finger against Claudia's lips. "You're not asking. I'm offering, and I've been doing that for a while now. I understand your independence is important to you, and I'd loath to make you feel beholden or kept or whatever. But this is a partnership, right? We're together, aren't we?"

"Yes, but—"

"There are no buts. Things are never equal in a relationship, but that doesn't imply inequality. Everyone is doing their bit to keep things working, and sometimes one does more than the other. In the end, we both need to be happy with however we choose to live. Are you happy right now?"

"No. Yes. I'm both because I got you and Alice, and my parents accept us, and I love my job, even though I'm on maternity leave right now. But I'm also completely overwhelmed, and I don't know how to do this."

"How can I help you?"

"I don't know." Claudia once more wiped her eyes.

"All right, how about I take care of Alice for tonight while you take a long shower or a bath, then eat something and go to sleep? I'll place an order in a bit, comfort food, I'd say, so—"

"Pizza and lava cake?"

Elizabeth groaned. "Sure, you lunatic."

Claudia smiled weakly.

"After you get some sleep, we'll discuss this some more and find a solution."

"You always do that," Claudia said, her voice soft and almost full of wonder.

"Do what?"

"Solve problems you didn't even create."

Elizabeth cupped Claudia's cheek. "Those are easier to solve than your own."

Claudia hummed.

"There's just one thing I'd like for you to keep in mind. I love you. I love Alice. I'd love for us to be together more often, and again, I want to be there for you. That's not me trying to pressure you or saying you can't handle things on your own."

"I know," Claudia whispered, leaning in to press a soft kiss against Elizabeth's lips. "I love you, too. I'm just scared of losing this. Of losing us because I can't be there for you like before. What if you grow tired of me always having to prioritize Alice, and—"

"You need to prioritize a newborn? What a novel concept."

"Come on!"

"You seem to labor under the delusion that I went into this relationship blind or with rose-colored glasses. I knew how this would go. And yes, I miss you and our quiet time together, but these moments will return. Right now, all that matters is that you and Alice are all right."

"What about you?"

"I've been taking care of myself for a long time. I can handle it."

"But I want the same, to be there for you, too."

"You are, Claudia." Elizabeth kissed her before shooing her to the bathroom. She ordered the food and tidied up Claudia's apartment.

After Claudia had gotten some sleep, they'd talked some more and decided life would be easier if Claudia and Alice moved in with Elizabeth, and so they had. Elizabeth had once more hired Pat Stewarts Home to create and decorate a beautiful nursery for Alice, which she'd revealed to Claudia and her family when they'd visited them one Friday afternoon. Claudia had cried, while *teta* had patted Elizabeth's arm and called her a "Good egg," causing a lump to form in Elizabeth's throat.

Currently, they were prepping for Alice's first birthday party, where Elizabeth had had to promise that she would not go overboard, both with the party and the presents. She wouldn't. At least not a lot. She reminded Claudia of her recent work trip out of town, where she'd networked at a conference with a lot of people in attendance who could turn out to be quite lucrative new sponsors for *Helping Hands*, when *Claudia* had overdone it.

That reminder had made Claudia flush, though Elizabeth knew it wasn't embarrassment that colored her cheeks. She grew hot at the memory as well. Claudia's earlier worries that they'd not reconnect after Alice had turned out to be quite unfounded.

Elizabeth had never had phone sex before, but then again, she had never done so many things until she'd met Claudia. The nerve of this woman! At the same time, Elizabeth wondered if she could complain as this had been one of the fantasies she'd mentioned to Claudia in bed one night—both overheated but still intertwined.

Elizabeth was staying at a hotel during this important business trip, and she had to get up early in the morning, yet she lay here panting, covered in a sheen of sweat, throbbing, but not able to do a damn thing about it.

"Are you wet?" Claudia rasped in a tone that by itself would have made Elizabeth clench her legs together.

"You know I am," she ground out.

"But you've still not touched your clit, like I asked, right?"

Elizabeth clenched her jaw. "No."

"Good. I'm surprised by your willingness to drag this out."

Willingness? Claudia had said she'd hang up if she were to...

"Are you still there?"

"Yes," she breathed, barely stopping herself from pressing her thighs together. She needed friction, but she feared it would undo her. She'd not known arousal until she met Claudia, and now that infernal woman had her drowning in it, craving it, ricocheting it through her veins like the lava from Mount Vesuvius when it buried Pompeii.

Yes, she was being dramatic, but they'd been at this for over an hour, and she'd been dancing on the edge for most of this time—thanks to Claudia sending her several risqué text messages earlier, while she'd been in a conference. Elizabeth had wanted to murder her or sink her face between her legs, and neither had been an option since they were so many miles apart.

"I love how you sound when you're so turned on that you want to climb the walls."

Elizabeth's eyes screwed shut, and she bit her lower lip.

"Where are your fingers?"

"Where you asked me to put them," Elizabeth croaked. She had her index and middle finger splayed on top of her outer folds, opening herself up to... nothing.

"Good. Now, trace them down toward your entrance and coat them."

Elizabeth shuddered and followed Claudia's request. She felt swollen, sticky, and so hot that—

"Don't go inside."

Elizabeth groaned, but instead of pushing in like she wanted to, she twirled her fingers around her entrance, massaging the sensitive flesh.

"God, I wish I was there."

Elizabeth grunted.

"I'd spread your legs wider to lie between them and I'd kiss your thighs, lick up and down that place where your leg meets your hip, right next to where you want me the most, and I'd keep licking and sucking until you shiver with need."

Elizabeth rolled her lips, stifling the moan that wanted to spill forth. She trembled.

"I love how you taste, but I treasure the anticipation, waiting until you can't bear it anymore and are a second away from grabbing my head and—"

"Claudia," she ground out.

"Go inside," she rumbled.

Elizabeth sighed and shuddered when she pushed two fingers inside.

"Two or three?"

"Two," Elizabeth said breathlessly.

"I wish I could see this. We should have video chatted instead."

Elizabeth choked out a laugh. As if she could have handled *seeing* Claudia while they were doing this—her intense and intoxicating focus. She could feel heat crawl up her neck and suffuse her cheeks at the mere thought.

"Next time?" Claudia asked, and the hopeful lilt in her voice almost crumbled Elizabeth's resolve. But she couldn't.

"You wish."

"I do. Much like I wish I could suck your clit into my mouth right now."

"Oh, God," Elizabeth said, her eyelids fluttering. She pressed in and out, faster, but she craved pressure on her straining clit. "Please," Elizabeth breathed.

Claudia sighed. "All right. We've drawn this out long enough. Touch yourself."

Elizabeth hissed when she pulled out and her hand shot higher, rubbing her clit in fast, hard circles. She shook, arousal coiling low in her stomach—a tension that refused to ebb. Her body tightened and the fingers of her other hand clenched around the cotton bedsheets.

Elizabeth's chest heaved, and she released the fabric to palm her breast. She moaned as she pulled at a stiff nipple.

Claudia panted.

The sound tore through Elizabeth like lightning, and she arched her back, wishing Claudia were here with her, so that she could feel her warm weight on top of her as she pressed her into the mattress.

Her fingers sped up. "Claudia," she whispered.

"Are you close?"

Elizabeth could only whimper.

Claudia sighed. "I long to see you," she said in a tone so wistful it filled Elizabeth with warmth, a sensation unlike the blinding arousal rippling through her, more like a glow of contentment. Happiness.

"I wish you were here," Elizabeth managed to say before her frame tightened and her body stretched, her toes curled as she stilled. Then a stuttered breath left her, followed by a low groan as she quaked in a long climax—her nerves on fire until she sunk into a languid relaxation.

"I love the way you come," Claudia said with a little sigh. "I could listen to that all day. I should record it."

A sound of discontent left Elizabeth's lips. "You will do no such thing."

"Not a video. Just the sound."

Elizabeth rolled her eyes, trying to cling to her bliss. "No," she said.

"As you wish."

Elizabeth smiled.

"Can you do me a favor?"

"What?"

"Where are your fingers now?"

Elizabeth swallowed hard, almost pouting when she felt her body stir. Really? "On my stomach."

"Put them back."

"Claudia, I have to get up early, and—"

"Please."

Elizabeth closed her eyes, and against her better judgment, she dragged her fingers once more through her wetness. Her body twitched in response, and she held her breath, both excited and apprehensive about what Claudia would say next.

"You're still wet, right?"

"Yes." Obscenely so.

"All right, just coat your fingers liberally."

Elizabeth did.

"Now taste yourself."

Elizabeth froze, and her eyes widened.

"Put your fingers in your mouth and tell me what you taste like."

Elizabeth feared her heart readied itself to crack open her chest and speed away.

"Elizabeth, are you there?"

"Yes," she croaked, unmoving and with her hand still between her legs.

"You know I'd have my mouth all over you if I were there now. So at least tell me what you taste like."

Elizabeth's eyes fell shut. Claudia continued to be the death of her. She swallowed hard before raising her hand and sliding her arm upward. Gazing in wonder at her glistening fingers, she wiggled them and watched as a gossamer thread stretched between her index and middle fingers. "OK," she said, before tentatively placing a fingertip on her tongue.

"And?"

Not bad, she supposed, though she much preferred Claudia's flavor. "Tangy?"

Claudia groaned. "Why didn't we turn on the camera? I can't believe I'm missing this."

Elizabeth chuckled. "Next time, dear."

"Yes!"

with laughter and family

LIFE WITH ELIZABETH HAD turned out better than she'd hoped. To be fair, Claudia had mostly prayed it wouldn't end in disaster. All these changes. She sometimes felt overwhelmed, especially when she'd been so scared of her family's reaction to her pregnancy. In the end, she shouldn't have worried. They'd all been more upset with Tom for having betrayed his wife, and for misleading Claudia. According to *teta*, he wasn't a good man, and he'd taken advantage of her granddaughter.

Being overwhelmed and her desire to remain independent had created some trouble. Although it wasn't about a need to be independent, as it related more to hating the idea that Elizabeth could ever have an errant thought Claudia was taking advantage of her financially. This all had been the root cause of most of their early arguments, but thankfully, they'd overcome that, too.

Claudia still marveled at the patience and care Elizabeth had shown before Claudia had finally come to her senses and moved in with her. This reluctance had also stemmed from insecurity given that their financial and social statuses were worlds apart, so even if Elizabeth didn't think Claudia was with her for her money, what if others saw their relationship that way? However, Claudia had concluded that she didn't care in the end, and the only opinion that mattered there was Elizabeth's.

Much to Elizabeth's utter frustration, Claudia still insisted on participating financially in their cost of living. Since Elizabeth owned the house, there was no mortgage or rent to share. So, Claudia had opted to pay for half of the groceries, all streaming services, and the internet. She'd wanted to pay for some utilities, too, but Elizabeth had glared at her, then opened her laptop, typed furiously for a while before she pushed it in front of Claudia, saying that what she saw on the screen was her bank account with the lowest balance.

Claudia had blanched and shut the laptop. "OK. You have a point."

"Thank you," had been Elizabeth's only reply. Money hadn't been an issue between them again, and Elizabeth never made it seem like Claudia owed her nor reminded her that she covered most of their living expenses.

Alice. Claudia tried to push the memory of her birth out of her mind, and had vowed, out loud, "Never again," to which Elizabeth had only replied with "Amen." Claudia wasn't sure how to take that, but she supposed one child was more than enough for Elizabeth, and Claudia wholeheartedly agreed. She probably could handle another once Alice reached the age of three or four, and while the pregnancy itself had been fine, she'd never *ever* give birth again.

She supposed they could adopt, but Elizabeth would likely remain in the 'no way,' column since she already complained at being "Too old to race after a toddler." Never mind that Elizabeth often seemed way more energetic than Claudia, and she did a lot of the work with Alice.

Alice. She'd picked the name because she loved how it sounded, but to be honest, it also reminded her of Elizabeth, though she herself rarely called her Liz. Not that Claudia had mentioned that association, but Elizabeth was clever enough, and Claudia vividly recalled her stunned expression when she'd told her the name she'd picked for her daughter.

In the end, Claudia's family was complete, and she sometimes stared at them in wonder, overcome with both joy and disbelief, the latter especially pertinent when she recalled the circumstances of their beginning. If someone would have told her where she'd be not even two years after discovering Tom's secret, she'd have asked them what they were smoking.

Her family's acceptance of them had been a bit of a surprise, not that she hadn't known they'd eventually come around—she'd been sure of that—but how fast and complete the acceptance had been. Alice had completely bewitched both her parents and *teta*, and she couldn't blame them.

Elizabeth's mother had been... another adventure. Claudia still couldn't believe Elizabeth had told Mary about their relationship via *email*. Why she'd been surprised to receive a call from her mother in the middle of the night (early morning in England) where she'd raved and ranted about Elizabeth being inconsiderate and rude, Claudia didn't know. It wasn't as if Elizabeth didn't know her mother. After that headache inducing (for Elizabeth) call ended, Elizabeth had dryly informed her that, "Mother says hello. She wants us to join them next Christmas. Not this one, as too many of her friends will be in attendance."

Claudia had blinked rapidly, nodded, and then contemplated the likelihood of the world ending before next Christmas, and how much she should root for such a catastrophe.

Elizabeth had planned Alice's first birthday party, and the only thing Claudia knew about it was the guest list. To be honest, she'd been a little scared of this event. Elizabeth organized lavish celebrity studded events for *Helping Hands*, and she excelled at organizing anything. Yet, this was a birthday party for a one-year-old, and Claudia didn't know what to expect.

The day arrived and started with Claudia and Alice being ushered into the bedroom after lunch and not being allowed to leave until Elizabeth had finalized the party prep. She'd brought them snacks, along with Claudia's laptop and tablet, as well as a box of toys for Alice.

"I hope she's not going completely nuts, little one." Claudia tickled Alice's belly.

Alice giggled, then stuffed two fingers into her mouth, which immediately resulted in drool seeping out and dribbling down her chin.

Claudia sighed and picked up a cloth to wipe her face and neck. "Poor baby." Teething truly was a bitch.

The party, to which Elizabeth led them after two hours of confinement, turned out to be... not what Claudia had expected. Elizabeth tended to go over the top sometimes, and she'd apparently had made it her mission to spoil them rotten, but this set up was perfect.

Elizabeth had decorated the living room and kitchen with purple and blue balloons and streamers. A banner reading, "Happy 1st Birthday Alice!" hung on the wall, and she'd filled one table with snacks and treats. The kitchen island held food, some of their favorites for their guests. There were two birthday cakes, one smaller with lots of icing that included another birthday message for Alice, and then a bigger one with fresh fruits on top of layers of biscuits and icing—Claudia's favorite.

"Do you like it?" Elizabeth asked.

"Yes. It's exactly what I wanted."

"Really?" Elizabeth asked dryly. "I'm shocked."

Claudia bumped into her, making Alice squirm in her arms and reach out to seize a strand of Elizabeth's hair.

"Oh, no, sweetie. I know it's your birthday, but that hurts." Elizabeth grasped Alice's hand and freed her hair.

The doorbell rang.

"Right on time." Elizabeth strode to the door and invited their first guests, Claudia's family. Even her cousins and her aunt and uncle attended. A little later, Sammy arrived, followed by Elizabeth's canasta friends, Catherine and Sandra.

The party, the small gathering of family and friends Claudia had wished for, turned out to be a fun time for all. Alice ended up with half the cake on her face and the other half on the floor (there were some tears), and Elizabeth took endless pictures and videos of Alice and their guests.

After everyone said their goodbyes, Claudia gave Alice a quick bath (or not that quick as washing cake out of all nooks and crannies took longer than expected) and then laid her sleepy baby into her bed. She stood there, with her hands on the frame, watching Alice's chest rise and fall. Claudia couldn't believe Alice was already one. Her life had changed so much and left her with a contentment that sometimes made her feel like crying.

"Hey." Elizabeth startled Claudia out of her thoughts. She leaned against the doorframe, gazing at Claudia with a fond smile.

"Hey, yourself."

"I put away everything that needed to go into the fridge, but I'm exhausted, and the cleaners come tomorrow to do the rest. I was wondering if you'd like to join me on the couch. We could watch the newest episode of *Broken Time*."

Claudia frowned. "The new season doesn't start until September."

"Mmhmm, but Kat gave me a copy as her apology for missing Alice's birthday party."

"Really? Tell her she's forgiven."

"I'll go set it up."

"Be right out. I just want to take a quick shower."

After her shower, the two of them cuddled up on the couch and watched the season opener of the sixth season of *Broken Time*.

Claudia groaned after the credits rolled. "I'm gonna kill Kat."

"I thought she was forgiven."

"I take it back! This ends in a cliffhanger and now we gotta wait until September or early October to see the next episode! Who starts a season with a cliffhanger?"

Elizabeth chuckled. "Good thing Kat is far away from your wrath right now."

Claudia pouted.

"Did you have a good day?"

"It was perfect. Thank you." She leaned close and kissed Elizabeth. "And Alice had a blast."

"She did. To be fair, she has a blast when she can play with empty boxes. I swear this child is like a human cat."

"Hey!"

"Please. You've turned into a regular cat person, too. I saw you coo to Raji and give him treats."

"You saw nothing."

"Right." Elizabeth pulled Claudia close and kissed her forehead.

Claudia snuggled into her and pressed her hand against Elizabeth chest, feeling the thudding of her heart against her palm.

They stayed like this for a while as silence filled their home. A rare stillness that lulled Claudia into a relaxed drowsiness, heightened by Elizabeth's fingers trailing lightly over her back. She felt herself getting heavy and released a small, contented sigh. Sleep would befall her any second and she wondered if she should suggest retiring to the bedroom as Elizabeth didn't like to sleep on the couch, when she blinked rapidly, unsure if she'd heard right.

"What did you say?" Claudia asked, suddenly feeling more alert than a mere second ago.

"I asked if you'd consider marrying me," Elizabeth said, not looking at Claudia, her voice mostly controlled, but Claudia had heard a slight wobble in intonation. She also noted the tension that suddenly filled Elizabeth.

"Are you *asking* me to marry you?" Claudia said, her eyes wide as she shifted to fully look at Elizabeth, whose eyes shone solemnly.

"Yes."

Claudia broke out in a blinding smile. "Yes."

mailing list

The last chapter of this extended epilogue sees a continuation of the hotel scene.

Join my mailing list to access it, and receive a free copy of *The Fall*, a fantasy romance wherein Death falls in love with a grief counselor.

https://sabrinablaum.com/#mailing-list

coming next

Coming in late fall of 2023, the final installment of the *Constellation* series. Get ready to read Tempe's tale.

also by sabrina blaum

Fantasy

The Well of Shadows

Romance

The Chase

The Deal

The Truce

A Question of Sincerity

acknowledgements

W.B. Gerard, my late friend and mentor who remains an inspiration to me—in writing as in life.

Leo, das Bedauern ist was schmerzt und nachklingt.

Tatiana, thank you for saving this one. I was truly lost and had no clue what had gone wrong. I truly appreciate your patience and willingness to help with my writing projects.

Cecilia, thank you for reading this. Your feedback is always incredibly valuable to me. Also, thank you for allowing me to ask you a million questions during my final edits.

Mark Paxson, thank you for your continued support and insights. You offer a unique perspective.

Rebecca Taylor, thank you for giving this a read and offering your feedback.

Juanita Barrett, I treasure our friendship, and you'll forever be my grammar guru.

Kim, thank you for enduring my hatred for prepositions, and for not murdering me during *that* Uno game.

Flo, Willow, Silas, and Rodna, thank you for allowing me to share your lives. I am blessed with the most loving and supportive family, and you mean the world to me.

Flo, thank you, as always, seems quite inadequate to express my gratitude and love for your role in my life. I hope my actions speak louder.

about the author

Sabrina has always written and used to tell her grandmother bedtime stories. She is a German native, and currently resides with her family in east Alabama.

For more information and updates on future releases, check out her website: sabrinablaum.com, or follow her on Twitter: @BlaumSabrina, or Instagram @blaumsabrina

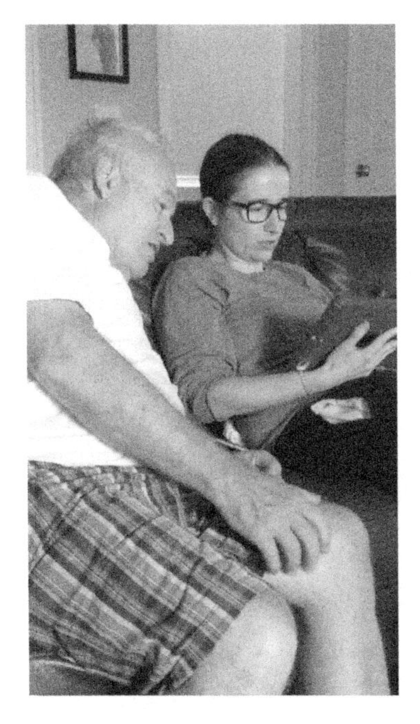

UNSER LEBEN IST DAS
WOZU UNSERE GEDANKEN ES MACHEN. LEO.

publisher

Babette B.

Publishing

300 Opelika Rd

P.O. Box 581

Auburn, AL 36830

Printed in Great Britain
by Amazon

46747036R00179